Deadly

The truth

Gordon Bickerstaff

Lambeth Group Thriller
Deadly Secrets
The truth will out …

Gavin's life will be turned upside down when he joins a
company to work on a product that will revolutionise the food
industry. His initial gut instinct is to walk away until he
discovers one of the company directors is the former love of
his teenage life.

The financial implications are global and incredible. Powerful
individuals and countries are prepared to kill as they compete
to seize control of the company. Corruption at high levels, a
deadly flaw in the product, and the stakes jump higher and
higher.

Against overwhelming odds, Gavin must rescue his former
love from the hands of an evil cult as they prepare her for a
living nightmare.

Also in the Lambeth Group Thriller series:
Everything To Lose
The chase is on
The Black Fox
Run for your life
Toxic Minds
The damage is done
Tabula Rasa
The end is nigh
Tears of Fire
The clock is ticking

First published in eBook format in Great Britain Aug 2013 by Endeavour Press Ltd.
This revised edition published September 2018 by Gordon Bickerstaff. © Gordon Bickerstaff 2013

*

Acknowledgements

Emily, for her patience, inspiration, and support.
I am very grateful to Alex, Helen, Clarissa and Harmony for their work on the production of this book.

*

The Lambeth Group

During the early 1990s, rapid progress in science brought increased public fears that science was galloping out of control. UK politicians became concerned that science and technology could damage business and endanger human life.

The Lambeth Group came into being when a group of twenty-six, university vice-chancellors, from elite universities met secretly with Home Office mandarins at the Imperial War Museum, Lambeth Road, London, to formulate a covert doomwatch policing strategy for protection of the country from criminal, unethical, unprincipled scientists and technologists.

Sir Christopher Aden-Brown, Group Leader, is based in the Peel Building at the Home Office in Marsham Street, London. He provides expert liaison and counsel between the Home Office and university vice-chancellors in the UK and Commonwealth.

Alan Cairn, civil servant, from the Centre for Protection of National Infrastructure (CPNI), represents government interests.

Gavin Shawlens, bioscience investigator, joined the Lambeth Group six years ago. As a natural cover agent, Gavin uses his genuine profession as cover for clandestine work. In return for his expertise on investigations, he receives funding for his enzyme technology research team. A loner, reluctant, sceptical and lacking confidence in spy business; Gavin is a weak link in the team.

One
East Kilbride, Scotland

When his death throes fired crescendos of searing pain into his body, every nerve screamed pain and he didn't understand. Instinct told him death loomed close. His brave heart craved for the love and safety he knew from his brother.

Exhausted from searching, and too petrified to stand, he lay on his side and shook uncontrollably. Traumatised by relentless pain, his brain finally abandoned his body.

Suffering subsided and calm descended with a false sense of well-being.

He wanted to jump up, run to his brother, and kill more rats for him. His brother hated rats and screamed at them madly. Together, they'd killed many rats and he loved killing them.

A vision appeared. Rats scurrying through a hole in the wall, close to the bed they shared. His brother lay helpless; calling for help. Terror filled his mind as hordes of rats attacked his brother.

His brother fought them off, but they swarmed over him, biting, tearing and squealing. The vision drained his heart. He squealed but his muscles refused to move. While he panted long puffs of moist air into the cold night air, he stared ahead.

The woman stepped out of her warm office and rubbed her arms on her jacket. His razor-sharp senses had dulled, so he didn't hear her footsteps crunch the fine gravel as she approached his cage.

The woman knelt down beside him. Their eyes met and she flinched with concern. His fragile spirit reached out, *help me,* his dark eyes pleaded.

A few strands of her chestnut-brown hair worked loose and she pushed them back behind her ear. Concern twisted new lines around her mouth. She sighed loudly. Slowly, she shook her head from side to side as she stood up.

The woman closed the cage door quietly to avoid disturbing the others. She went back into her office and flicked the light switch, which brought cold darkness back to the yard.

Fluid filled his stomach, his gullet and lungs. Then, crushing feelings brought panic and helplessness. Painful coughing expelled a thick fluid, and each cough became a hurdle that strangled his will to live.

He gasped and gurgled while pockets of gas escaped from his lungs. White fluid from his mouth spilled onto the ground, where it formed a pool beside his head.

*

Colin Blunt glanced up at the sky and then climbed into his Land Rover Discovery. The first week of March had arrived, and remnants of a cold and blustery winter had faded. Spring lurked just around the corner and west-of-Scotland flora prepared for a new year.

Overnight, the temperature had dropped to single figures. Normal, for early March in Glasgow. The dull morning sky appeared miserable but rain had held off. If asked, Colin would have said the morning was 'right dreich'.

Reginald C. Blunt, a senior partner at Fairfells Pet Centre, hated his first name and insisted people call him Colin. Annabel called him 'Reg-ann-old', and he hated her for it.

Tall brick walls surrounded the back yard of the Pet Centre. More to keep wild animals out than keep boarders inside.

The concrete cubicles and wire mesh kennels had few comforts other than a large plastic tub bed in one corner, and a stainless-steel water bowl in the opposite one. Some boarders had toys and blankets provided by thoughtful owners.

The night duty veterinary nurse, Carol Donginger, had finished her paperwork in the small office attached to the kennels. An attractive and well-spoken woman in her mid-twenties, she wore her chestnut-brown hair tied in a ponytail. A few strands worked loose and she pushed them back behind her ear.

Carol knelt down in the centre of a ring of twelve metal bowls laid out in a circle. Wielding a wooden spoon, she dispensed dog food into each bowl.

Colin stormed into the yard and searched side-to-side for a clue. The self-closing door slammed shut.

The noise startled Carol, and the dogs began pounding against their kennel doors, barking and squealing.

The familiar strong odour braced Colin's nose. He cleared his throat. 'Where is it?'

Carol regarded his grumpy morning face. 'Morning, Colin, he's over here.'

She led him to an isolation kennel set against the back wall.

On the floor, lay an adult black-and-white mongrel dog with long matted hair, speckled white ears, and two white front paws. It lay on its side opposite the cage door.

Carol tucked her wooden spoon under her armpit and moved over to the door. 'This poor soul arrived last night in a police van. I've called him Lonely. Apparently, he attacked a man in the street but didn't bite. The police dog handler brought him to me.'

Colin glanced at the dog. Annoyed, he prepared to tear a strip off her for giving sedation without permission. 'Why did you sedate it?'

'I didn't. He's dead.'

'Dead.'

Puzzled at his surprise, she said, 'Yes. I told your wife what happened.'

He grunted loudly, lifted his case and turned to walk away. Not for the first time, his wife hadn't told him the full story.

Carol raised her voice. 'He barked for ages and wouldn't settle.'

He turned back. 'Look, Carol, I'm not angry with you but you mustn't make an emergency call to my home unless it's essential. Have you got that?'

He stormed off and made his way to the door that led to the surgeries.

'Something you should see before I clean up,' Carol called out.

He stopped in his tracks, hunched his shoulders and rolled his eyes skyward.

She slipped the bolt on the cage door and edged, hesitantly, inside the kennel.

His eyes narrowed. *You little witch*. He retraced his steps, crashed his case down and followed her inside.

She pointed at the dog. 'I've never seen rabies but—'

'*Rabies*. Don't be silly, girl.'

Two

Colin examined the scene inside the kennel. White fluid had seeped from its anus and spread out in a small pool on the ground. Similar material formed a larger pool around its mouth.

'Look at this damp patch under his body. As if he's been sweating, I can't understand it.' Carol looked to him for an answer. Dogs only have sweat glands on their paws.

He shrugged. 'Probably vomited.'

Colin moved around to the back of the dog for another view. Something crushed under his shoe.

He knelt down on one knee, and shifted a sheet of newspaper for a closer look. He raised a concerned voice. 'What the hell's this—teeth?'

Carol sprang to her feet and turned her back on the dog. She covered her mouth with the palm of her hand. 'Oh, that poor baby must have been in … terrible pain.'

Colin leant over the dog, and with his right hand, he pressed on the body.

He shook his head. 'This isn't right. Its abdomen has collapsed.'

The dog gave out a loud burp.

'*Christ,*' Colin shouted.

His prodding had disturbed the lay of the chest, which collapsed and forced trapped air to expel like a deflating balloon. Carol composed herself and squatted down beside him.

Colin snapped with his fingers for her to pass the wooden spoon. Then, he poked the handle end into the dog's mouth. He pressed hard to prise open its mouth but its gums had stuck together.

'The jaws are … aargh!'

His stick slipped off its gum and brushed the dog's eye, causing fluid to spurt out of its eyeball.

Splashes of vitreous fluid landed on the back of his hand. He stared at the dog's head while fluid oozed out of its eyeball, rolled down and dropped onto a sheet of newspaper.

Carol's voice trembled. 'How could he decompose so quickly?'

Gently, Colin drew the stick across the back of its body. Clumps of dark hair stuck to the end. The stick rippled and tore the dog's skin, exposing a white gel-like tissue underneath. They glanced at each other with concern.

Colin's anxiety peaked when a surge of adrenaline flushed through his blood and made his heart thump.

Beads of perspiration formed on his hairline. His thoughts became turbulent. *What the bloody hell happened here?*

Ready to burst into tears, Carol sounded like a worried pet owner. 'What happened to him? Why did his teeth fall out?'

Colin searched and analysed but he didn't reply. Carol broke the silence. 'His body can't be rotting. Haven't you noticed it?'

A pang of irritation sprang in his mind. He gave her a sharp sideways look.

Carol pointed to the pool of material expelled from the dog's mouth. 'There's no smell. He doesn't smell of anything.'

Colin remained silent. He retrieved a handkerchief from his trouser pocket, dabbed perspiration from his forehead, and wiped his hands. When he saw the splash of vitreous fluid on the back of his hand, he jumped to attention, and wiped it vigorously.

Perplexed, he tried to recall events immediately following the death of an animal. Then, he thought back to his student days at vet school.

They'd taught him little about death but he remembered something from the biochemistry class. Post mortem, resident bacteria consume simple molecules to grow and produce more bacteria.

When simple biochemicals are exhausted, bacteria would secrete suites of digestive enzymes to demolish organs and tissues and reduce them to simple building blocks.

The characteristic smell of death would develop slowly as a complex cocktail of small odour-bearing biochemicals accumulate beside rapidly-growing numbers of bacteria.

Confidence returned to his voice. 'Okay, what we have is a massive bacterial infection.'

'Bacteria.'

He ushered Carol out of the cage. 'I don't know how, but bacteria decomposed the dog without producing the usual smell.'

'Shall I clean up now?'

He shook his head. 'No, fetch protective clothing and wait. I'll come back in a few minutes. I need to make a call.'

Colin headed to the door that led from the kennels to the main building. In the foyer, a receptionist sorted the morning mail.

'Morning,' Colin announced as he hurried into his surgery.

As usual, staff had his surgery open, brightly lit, sparkling clean and ready for business.

Tall and thin-faced, Colin spoke with a confident voice much appreciated by worried pet owners. The receptionist followed Colin to his surgery.

'Morning, Colin. It's a bit miserable again today. At least the rain is holding off.'

Colin didn't reply.

She noted his distraction. It wasn't unusual for him. With an eye-roll, she turned to walk back to the reception desk.

Colin slipped his suit jacket onto a coat hanger and put on his white coat. Smartly, he moved around the examination table in the centre of his surgery and followed her to the reception desk.

'Coffee?' she asked.

He took hold of her arm, and pulled her into the office behind the reception desk before he closed the door behind them. Concern crinkled her face as she stared at his hand on her arm.

Colin lowered his voice. 'I want you to dig out the hotline number for the Health and Safety Executive. We have a RIDDOR.'

'A RIDDOR. Are you sure?' she replied, although she knew it meant reporting injuries, diseases and dangerous occurrences regulations.

'Quickly.'

Alarm grabbed her face as she rubbed her arm where his fingers had pressed. She found and copied the number for him.

With a piece of paper bearing the number, he retreated into his surgery, and closed the door behind him.

When he got through to the HSE, he spoke confidently. 'Good morning. My name is Colin Blunt. I'm a senior vet at Fairfells Pet Centre near Glasgow. I have a dead animal here. I think it's been infected with a super bug.

'No, it's not natural death. I think it may have escaped from a research lab. I want you to send someone over here now. It is urgent. Yes, now, good. Yes, I will, thanks. Yes, of course, bye.'

Colin felt rattled but relieved as he stepped back into the foyer. The receptionist stared at him with concern and waited for an explanation.

He half-smiled. 'Someone will be over from the HSE. Let me know when he arrives. I'll be down at the kennels.'

Alarmed and flustered, she replied, 'What happened? Should I close the surgery?'

'No, absolutely not. Carry on as normal. I have everything under control.'

He strode back to the kennels.

Three

At his flat in Clarkston, on the south side of Glasgow, Dr Gavin Shawlens had prepared his breakfast when he received a call from the head of the Lambeth Group, Sir Christopher Aden-Brown.

'Dr Shawlens, good morning. I hope I didn't wake you?'

'No, sir, I'm having breakfast.'

'I've just taken a call from the HSE. A vet in your area has reported a RIDDOR incident. Apparently, an animal with a super-bug infection. The vet believes the animal may have escaped from a research facility. I'm sending details to your phone.

'Can you pop over there and make a preliminary assessment? If he *is* on to something, let me know. I'll make this an official investigation.'

Gavin checked the time. 'Now?'

'Yes, now.' Aden-Brown sounded annoyed. 'If the vet is correct, we need a lid on this as soon as possible.'

'Fine, sir, I'm on my way.'

'By the way, I read the final report on your last investigation. A fine piece of work. Congratulations.'

'Thank you, sir. I'll be in touch after I've visited the vet.'

In his sitting room, Gavin peered out from behind the curtains on the bay window. A busy stream of traffic on the Busby Road headed through the Clarkston Toll toward Glasgow. He would head in the opposite direction, toward East Kilbride.

His apartment occupied the top floor of a traditional four-storey, yellow sandstone tenement building. A comfortable living space, it had two bedrooms, kitchen, dining room, bathroom and sitting room.

He checked the weather app on his phone. The changeable Scottish weather meant he'd still need his winter jacket. Roll on warmer days and less heavy clothes.

Gavin lived in a prosperous Glasgow suburb, and the communal entrance to the flats and stairwell were well maintained and clean. Brown resin covered the stone floor and steps, and dark terracotta-red resin decorated the walls to dado height then magnolia paint coated the remainder, including the ceiling.

Each landing boasted a pair of long rectangular sash windows, and the banister had the original hard wooden top with authentic black-painted wrought iron railings.

Gavin worked part-time for the Lambeth Group, and had gained a great deal of experience over the past six years.

In fact, he had a government security clearance of Top Secret Level D, which meant he had knowledge of the highest category of Official State Secrets. He knew where some of the nastiest skeletons lay buried. He'd been present at the burial of one of them.

A thirty-six-year-old academic, Gavin stood at five-eight in his socks and occupied a lean and muscular frame. Occasional visits to the university judo club kept him fit. Regularly, he jogged up the three flights of stairs to his top-floor flat. His neighbours pegged him as an oddball.

Fifty-two minutes after taking the call, he stood with Colin Blunt and Carol Donginger as they faced the dead dog. Colin hadn't disturbed the body.

The three of them wore protective head visors, disposable coats, over-trousers, latex gloves, and disposable plastic bootees.

It didn't occur to any of them that their strange attire had set most of the boarders into a frenzy of barking and jumping.

'It's been dead for less than six hours, yet it has massive decomposition.' Colin pointed while Gavin examined the body.

'The cold last night should have slowed any decomposition. Something sped it up even against the cold. Interesting,' Gavin said.

Colin gesticulated nervously. 'This white matter has seeped from both ends. All its teeth are out and its hair is loose. Tissue and skin are … well … white jelly.'

Gavin circled the dog and took photographs with his Lambeth Group secure encrypted mobile (SEM) phone. He didn't tell them the photos were simultaneously transmitted to the Lambeth Group office or that his phone also transmitted their conversation.

Gavin asked, 'How did the dog come into your possession?'

'Police rounded him up and brought him to me,' Carol replied.

Colin agitated his hand while he spoke. 'Obviously—this isn't a typical infection. I think it escaped by accident or design from a university research laboratory.'

'Really!' Gavin raised his eyebrows.

'Animal rights people or students—probably set this dog loose,' Colin replied.

Gavin nodded but sounded unconvinced. 'It wouldn't be the first time that happened.'

Research laboratories didn't use mongrel dogs because they didn't have the defined genetic profile needed for provenance. *You're a vet, you know this*, Gavin thought.

Colin raised his voice. 'I want full microbiological and viral screens done on this animal. I want to know what I'm dealing with here.'

Gavin stepped back and frowned at the dog. 'Full screens are a lot of work. What do you think you have?'

Impatient, Colin pointed anxiously. 'Looks to me like strep. The flesh-eating one.'

Gavin replied, 'Streptococcus pyogenes.'

'That's the nasty one, isn't it?' Carol asked Gavin.

Gavin had to rummage through a corner of his memory for a moment. 'Yes, it can be. It occurs naturally in humans. Occasionally, it causes sore throats. Rarely, it causes necrotising fasciitis or flesh-eating.'

'How does the flesh-eating business work?' Colin asked.

'… Erm. Strep bacteria secrete enzymes to digest tissues. Blood vessels in skin are so thin they're digested quickly. Exposed skin tissue is destroyed.'

Colin's eyes widened. 'Killer enzymes.'

Gavin said, 'Not intentionally. Imagine if I gave you a giant loaf of bread the size of Edinburgh Castle. Before you could eat it, you would need to break it down to mouth-sized chunks.

'Bacteria are too small to consume our organs directly. They need to use enzymes to demolish huge structures down to small building blocks, which they can use to make new bacteria.'

Colin pointed at the body. 'The bloody dog is dead—is it not?'

Gavin walked out of the kennel to join Carol. He'd had enough of Blunt's aggression. Carol's expression appealed more and they exchanged smiles.

Gavin shook his head. 'This type of infection is rare. Probably less than ten people in the country each year.'

Carol turned to face Gavin. 'They say large doses of antibiotics are useless.'

Gavin engaged her eyes. 'That's almost true. Antibiotics do kill the bacteria but not its enzymes. If the bugs secrete large quantities of enzymes into the blood, then antibiotics won't stop the ensuing tissue destruction. Death can follow rapidly.'

Through their visors, Gavin and Carol examined the fine detail on each other's faces. Colin paced around the kennel, evaluating his options.

Carol pointed at Gavin. 'You're not convinced it's strep— are you?'

She had read Gavin's facial tell correctly.

Gavin cocked his head. 'Strep doesn't occur naturally in dogs. They have immunity.'

Colin raised his voice. 'What? Are you certain?'

'A strep infection is unlikely in a dog,' Gavin replied.

Colin thought for a moment. 'It must be a genetically modified strain.'

Gavin nodded half-heartedly. 'That's … one possibility.'

'Get the screens done,' Colin demanded as he pressed his hands downward against his thighs, causing the latex gloves to tighten around his fingers. Perspiration beaded on his forehead, and a mist of condensation formed on the top of his visor.

Gavin shrugged a reluctant agreement. 'Okay, I'll collect samples and send them off. We'll find out soon enough.'

Without another word, Colin went to the kennel office, changed out of his protective clothes, marched back to the main building and into his surgery.

Carol fetched a sample transit box and helped Gavin collect a dozen specimens. He helped her to move the dog into a body bag.

In the small office that faced the kennels, they removed their protective clothing. Gavin put his SEM phone back on standby.

'I'm sorry we had to haul you out of your bed to come here.'

'I was having breakfast. I'm an early morning man.'

She smiled. 'I like the morning.'

He returned a smile. 'Best time of the day for me. No distractions—well, not usually.'

'Sorry about Colin. He's quite upset about this thing.'

'I got that message loud and clear but why?'

Her voice dropped a notch. 'We've never seen anything like this before. It must be bad.'

'There's nothing to worry about.' He pointed to the protective clothing. 'This is good quality.'

She didn't respond. Light tremors made her head shake. Silent, she sat with her head bowed.

He sensed he didn't have the full picture. 'Okay, now I feel like I've missed something.' He leant forward to look at her face, now pale and drawn.

When she turned to face him, her expression revealed fear. 'I touched the dog without protection. Colin got a splash of fluids on his hand.'

'*Shit.*'

Gavin wanted to point out their stupidity but he knew it wouldn't do any good. She searched his eyes for support and then turned her gaze to the floor.

His heart thumped. If she'd been exposed to something, he shouldn't be sitting so close to her. Or breathing the same air.

He thought hard. Streptococcus wasn't responsible, and no official research laboratory would experiment on a mongrel dog with an unknown genetic profile. However, he couldn't rule out a rogue company experimenting with genetically modified strains.

17

His mind swung back and forth, trying to decide whether he should advise Carol to seek a course of antibiotics.

Hospital treatment would draw attention and create a problem for the Lambeth Group if a secret research project had backfired.

Hairs on the back of his neck pricked his skin while he checked Carol's fearful face.

Her left hand fidgeted with the seam of her trousers. She placed her trembling, damp, sweaty right hand on the back of his. He wanted to—but didn't pull his hand away.

'Dr Shawlens, please, tell me what to do. I don't want to die like that poor dog.' Tears ran down her cheeks as she squeezed his hand.

Four
University of Kinmalcolm, Scotland

With the deftness of a Persian cat, a last-minute student snuck through the upper rear door of the Watt Lecture Theatre. She scanned the rows of heads and spotted her friend near the end of a middle row. Two minutes later, she slipped onto the seat beside him.

'What's Shawlens on about today?' she whispered.

'Collagen diseases,' he whispered back.

The student eased back in her seat and listened to the last few minutes of Gavin's lecture. She would ask her friend for a copy of his lecture notes.

Gavin's thick mop of hair had a light straw-colour in summer that darkened in winter. A tousled fringe covered his forehead.

His voice resounded with a strong Scottish accent, although years of lectures and public speaking had smoothed out his Glaswegian tones.

'… and patients with this syndrome can bend their hands backward to touch their arm. Their skin is loose and translucent, which is particularly noticeable in the skin between the fingers. Also, the fingers tend to be long and spidery.'

He held his left hand high with the fingers spread open. A sea of hands floated into the air for self and near neighbour examination. None of the students found translucent skin in their friends. One girl received close examination for spidery fingers but it turned out to be long false nails.

'Last one I need to mention, briefly, is scurvy. It's characterised by skin sores, spongy gums, loose teeth, and painful joints.'

His next slide showed a list of scurvy symptoms. 'These symptoms are caused by another fault in the foundation matrix of tissues. This time, the fault lies within the collagen structure itself.'

He paused for them to catch up. 'Collagen synthesis requires an enzyme to make the bonds that hold collagen proteins together in a fibre. This enzyme is prolyl hydroxylase, and it requires vitamin C as an agent or cofactor.

'Lack of vitamin C produces poor prolyl hydroxylase activity. Just like a pop group without an agent doesn't make chart-topping hits; this enzyme without vitamin C doesn't make good collagen. The fibres unwind like split ends in your hair.'

He showed a slide with a diagram of a collagen fibre unwound at the ends. 'This weakens the foundation matrix and causes symptoms we associate with scurvy. Now, you know why your mum wants you to eat your greens and drink your OJ.'

A rapid succession of beeb-beebs from Gavin's phone announced the end of his lecture. He concluded quickly. 'All of the diseases I've talked about today arise because of faulty or missing enzymes, causing defective collagen and poor tissue foundation. Make sure you understand the link between disease, collagen structure and enzymes.'

He paused to gather his notes and look around at the faces. 'Any questions?' he shouted above the rising noise level.

From the back of the room, an unknown voice called out, 'Will collagen be in the exam?'

'Everything is examinable. Any problems, you'll find me in the enzyme technology lab.'

Gavin powered down the lecture hall computer and projector. One student and her friend hung back to ask about possible research projects.

He nodded. 'Yes, I have a project on protease enzymes.'

The student exchanged eye contact with her friend. 'Protease enzymes. I don't think we've done them yet.'

'They break protein down to its amino acid building blocks. A bit like demolition of a house to a large pile of bricks,' Gavin replied.

'What makes them interesting?'

'The ones I'm looking at have the potential to destroy blood clots. Think about eradicating heart attacks and strokes with a simple self-medicated protease.'

'Thanks, Dr Shawlens—I'll think about it.'

Gavin didn't say that his interest in clot-busting proteases was personal, or that his father had died suddenly of a heart attack caused by a massive blood clot. A death that could have been prevented if a clot-busting drug had been more widely available.

As a student, Gavin had studied biochemistry and developed a passion for enzymes while completing postgraduate research for his PhD.

He enjoyed teaching but research dominated his life, and he had built up an international reputation for research on protease enzymes.

He spent most of his time with his laboratory with his enzyme technology research group; comprised of two postdoctoral biochemists, one research technician, and three research students.

Naturally, he worked in the best space in the lab. A corner site beside a large picture window, which looked out onto a green field with three large oak trees.

Along the far wall, he had a glass-partitioned office, which he used as a repository for papers, box files, piles of reports, exam scripts, essays and stacks of lab notebooks.

His two postdocs were best described as an odd bunch working on odd projects. Dr Sharon Bonny, a large girl, came from Buffalo, New York. She collaborated with a brewery on the use of protease enzymes to eliminate chill-haze in beer.

Every month, the brewery sent a barrel of beer for her 'research' studies. Not surprisingly, she became popular with staff and students.

Dr Brian Herding, a cocky Londoner with a roving eye; collaborated with medics from a local hospital on an artificial pancreas project. This gave him access to impressionable nurses, and together they generated much heat but very little light.

Christine Willsening provided technical support for the three researchers. She prepared their reagents and maintained fresh stocks of chemicals and consumables. She kept their laboratory equipment operational, calibrated and accurate.

Christine's dependable work kept the research projects moving along simultaneously. The least qualified academically, she had by far the most important qualifications—keen observation and sharp common sense.

*

Strong sunlight streamed into the laboratory and danced a dance of many reflections on assorted glass beakers and bottles on benches and shelves.

Gavin strode into the lab, wearing a big smile. He dumped his lecture notes on Christine Willsening's bench.

'All done?' she asked, and greeted him with a smile.

Christine had a wonderfully broad smile. It sprang into place with such precision that it seemed to be pinned to each ear with an elastic band. In photographs, she always revealed a happy face.

'Yep. And it feels good.'

Gavin resumed his experiments on pineapple protease enzymes while Christine ran tests on protease inhibitors she'd extracted from raw pineapple juice.

She asked, 'What are we doing for our anniversary? Next Tuesday.'

Gavin and Christine had worked together for six years and become a close-knit team. He enjoyed working with her and she enjoyed his company. They'd agreed at the start that his work and their friendship were too special to spoil by having an affair.

It didn't stop them tantalising and flirting with each other like two sixteen-year-olds. Like Gavin, she was a dark horse. The person people saw on the outside wasn't the person hiding inside.

'Dinner, on me. How does that sound?'

'Great. I'll book a table for two. Glasgow?' she replied.

'Okay.'

She lived in Paisley, and he lived in Clarkston, so Glasgow made for a good compromise for both of them to have a few drinks and return home by train.

Christine mothered him like a protective sister. At times, she contrived to fracture relationships with women she thought would hurt him. Sometimes, she forgot to pass messages on time, or a little incorrectly.

She knew someone in his past had left him in a lot of pain, and she believed she had to stand guard until he found the right person.

Brian Herding propped the door open with his foot, and announced, 'Right, I'm off down to the pub. See you all later.'

'What if someone wants you?' Christine called over.

'If it's important, I'm in a meeting. If she's gorgeous, tell her I'm down the pub panting like mad. Otherwise, tell them to bugger off and get a life.'

'Will do.'

Gavin thought to remind Brian he'd fallen behind with his targets but, too late, he'd gone.

Christine retrieved a piece of notepaper from her pocket. She'd taken a call from Carol Donginger at Fairfells Pet Centre.

She handed it to Gavin. 'She sounded worried. She'd like you to call her back.'

Gavin retreated to his office and closed the door. He kept the Lambeth Group and his government work secret from his university colleagues.

From a cabinet, he fetched a report on the results from the Fairfells' dog. Three weeks had passed since he'd collected the samples.

He called Carol. 'How are you?'

'Fine. It's almost a month. If I had an infection, I'd know by now. I'm just wondering what happened to the dog.'

'I sent a report to Colin Blunt.'

Sounding deflated. 'He hasn't told me anything.'

'I see. Well, good news. The tests were all negative. No bacteria or viruses of any kind.'

'I don't understand. What killed the dog?'

'I have no idea. Certainly not a bacterial or viral infection.'

Carol raised her voice. 'I don't understand.'

'Sorry, I meant no viable bacteria and no functional viruses. Everything in the samples was dead and destroyed. No living material.'

She pressed for more detail. He fobbed her off with a suggestion that it might have been a type of super-aggressive cancer.

He lied because not only had they found no viable viruses or living bacteria in the samples but no functional cells from the dog either.

The samples of white fluid should have contained millions of cells from the dog as well as bacteria and viruses. They were there, or rather, the remains showed that they had been there but they had all been destroyed.

He replaced the receiver and before he closed the report, he examined a photograph of the black-and-white mongrel dog with its speckled white ears and two white front paws.

He tapped his finger of the photo. 'What happened to you?'

Whatever had decimated the dog had not passed to Blunt or Carol, and for that mercy he felt a great relief as he returned the report to the cabinet.

Lambeth Group technicians assumed the samples had been wrongly collected or damaged in transit. The dog had been cremated, so no further samples were possible.

They had searched widely for unusual animal reports, and for unexplained or unnatural deaths. They found nothing and closed the case as an unknown, unsolved, nil-threat.

Five

Gavin came out of his office when he heard raised voices. The atmosphere in the laboratory had become supercharged. Sharon Bonny argued face-to-face with Christine.

Sharon had produced a set of erroneous results in recent experiments and cast doubt on the accuracy of the lab equipment.

With determination, Christine defended the equipment.

Just as Gavin moved to intervene, the Head of Department's elderly secretary popped her head around the door and interrupted them.

Sharon appreciated the intervention and walked away. Although a forceful and strong-minded woman, Sharon had been losing the argument. She'd hoped Christine would side with her to help another female under pressure.

The secretary stood at the open door. 'Gavin, the boss would like you in his office.'

Gavin shared an alarmed look with Christine. 'Shit.'

The secretary spied his concern. All the academics were on edge because the Department needed to make space reductions.

She smiled to suggest good news rather than bad. 'He has visitors looking for help with enzymes. That's all.'

'Thanks, I'll be along in two minutes.'

On his way to the door, Gavin stopped at Sharon's space and returned her notebook. 'You need to repeat these. I won't accept them.'

Her expression reflected her discontent. 'No way, Jose. They're good.'

Christine shook her head. 'Your duplicates are all over the place.'

Sharon turned to Christine. 'Your damn machine is all over the place!'

Gavin shook his head. 'Sharon, just do them or—'

'Or *what*?' She glared back at him.

'Just do them.'

Sharon turned away and mumbled curses under her breath as she hurried out of the laboratory.

Gavin shook his head. 'Her work is worse than a first-year biologist. I don't understand what she's playing at because her references said her lab work was brilliant.'

Christine flicked her hair off her face. 'I think she's having man trouble.'

Gavin nodded and then headed for the Head of Department's office.

*

Professor Crawford's office occupied a substantial corner position in the building. A warm room with a dark-red carpet, royal-blue leather chairs and a long mahogany desk. Academic books and journals filled matching floor-to-ceiling glass-fronted bookcases.

When Gavin arrived, Crawford introduced two businessmen who swapped business cards with Gavin. He glanced at their cards. James Patersun and Walter MacDougill.

Crawford explained that his visitors ran a small biotechnology business in the town of Greenock. He handed over to Jim Patersun, who explained that he wanted an enzymologist to help with a new process.

Crawford shepherded the three to his door and urged Gavin to show the visitors around the enzyme technology lab.

In the lab, Gavin introduced Christine. She showed them around the range of equipment the team had for their research. Walter MacDougill paid scant attention to Christine or Gavin.

Instead, he wandered around with his hands behind his back like an inspector. He paused to peer over Sharon Bonny's shoulder while she worked. Postcards from home, a US flag and other personal items from New York adorned Sharon's bench.

Jim Patersun listened to Christine. He stood a little taller than her. Apart from patches of grey hair behind his ears, he'd gone bald, which made his jug ears more prominent.

Distinctive high cheekbones dominated his face and he wore a smart, dark-brown, three-piece suit.

'What can I do for you?' Gavin asked.

'I'm developing a new food ingredient,' Patersun replied.

Out of the corner of his eye, Gavin watched MacDougill as he picked up and inspected bottles of chemicals on a shelf. A pessimistic cloud settled in Gavin's mind.

Patersun smiled proudly. 'My wife and I created this project. Walter built our pilot plant and I have financial backing to see us through a pilot stage.'

Gavin nodded. 'Sounds good.'

'Emma, my wife, is our business brain. I make all the important decisions and she makes all the routine ones. So, she negotiates contracts and I buy coffee machines.' He guffawed.

Patersun spoke with a pleasant Lancastrian accent, mostly unchanged, although he mentioned during the walk to the lab that he'd lived in Scotland for over thirty years.

Walter MacDougill called from the opposite end of the lab. 'We need an enzyme man. How well do you know your stuff?'

MacDougill wore his hair in a crew-cut style, and a grubby six o'clock shadow defined his face. He reminded Gavin of Humphrey Bogart in *The African Queen*.

He wore a badly fitted, un-pressed, off-the-peg, dark-blue suit, which appeared the worse for wear. His scuffed shoes hadn't seen polish for many months. He spoke with a distinct Aberdeen accent, which became difficult to follow when he spoke quickly.

Gavin turned to face him. 'I've worked with enzymes for sixteen years and—'

MacDougill walked toward Gavin. 'We know all the CV stuff.'

Patersun showed the palm of his hand to MacDougal in a 'shut up' gesture.

Christine engaged Jim Patersun. 'Have you been in the biotech business long?'

'No. My business is spices and condiments, wholesale and distribution. This is my first venture into biotech.'

Gavin frowned. 'Who developed the science?'

Jim replied, 'Walter is an engineer. He worked on great shipbuilding projects on the Clyde. Redundancy forced a career rethink. Their loss is my gain.'

MacDougill chimed in and sounded aggressive. 'I know all I need to know about enzymes. I need some practical work done for our patent. Nothing else.'

Gavin recoiled with a worried expression on his face. *Spare me, please, a shipbuilder who thinks he'll dabble in biotech.* He imagined that working with MacDougill would entail a series of unpleasant confrontations.

Patersun tried to set Gavin at ease and spoke to Walter. 'Dr Shawlens will provide technical support. He won't change the methods.' Then, turning to Gavin. 'We have a successful process. Your job will be to characterise our system and generate data for the patent. Completely separate from Walter's process development.'

'What sort of process?' Gavin asked.

No one replied. Christine watched them all carefully. Patersun cleared his throat. MacDougill stared straight through Gavin.

Then, Patersun spoke. 'If I take you on, and you sign our confidentiality contract, I'll be able to say more.'

Gavin nodded. 'Of course.'

'Good. I suggest you visit our pilot plant in Greenock. We're having a board meeting at lunchtime tomorrow. It would be useful if you met our financial backers.'

Gavin agreed and they shook hands. Then, he escorted them to their car and returned to his lab.

'What do you think?' he asked Christine.

She'd watched while they jostled Gavin between them. 'The old guy, MacDougill, will be a serious pain. He doesn't want you to interfere. If you do, you'll lose your legs.'

Gavin sniggered. 'Yes. I'm not sure if MacDougill plays with a full pack. They were too vague about their process.'

'I don't like either of them. I feel something odd about their behaviour. And, well, I don't think all the cards are on the table. By the way, I've put your mail on your desk. This came from the health clinic.'

Christine handed him a small, plain brown envelope with 'University of Kinmalcolm Health Clinic' printed on the top and addressed to Dr G F Shawlens (Strictly Private & Confidential).

'Thanks.'

She smiled. 'I hope you've got the all clear.'

He frowned. 'I've not got an STI—cheeky. It's my donor card. Stick it in the drawer for me, please.'

Like a plastic credit card with a black strip on the back, it contained details of his tissue types so precious time could be saved when harvesting his donated organs.

She inspected the card. 'You have to put this in your wallet.'

'There's no room. Stick it in the drawer.'

She extended her arm and opened her hand. 'Give me your wallet.'

Christine replaced an old Biochemical Society membership card with the donor card. She extracted Jim Patersun's business card and read it aloud. 'SeaPro Limited.'

Gavin nodded. 'That explains it.'

'What?'

'The fish smell from MacDougill's clothes—almost choked me.'

Christine smiled awkwardly when she remembered a recurring bad dream she'd had over the past few months. A sudden nervousness gripped her while elements of the dream fused to show more of the picture.

A feeling of déjà vu intensified. She stared at the back of Gavin's head, and felt sheer panic like a mother who'd lost her child on a busy street.

'That's why old Crawford hustled us out of his office. He was scared the fish smell would take root in his good chairs,' Gavin said, then he saw her face. 'Christine. Are you okay? You're white as a sheet.'

Concern edged her voice. 'I'll … help you … with this SeaPro work.'

'That would be great, thanks.'

Christine turned away, folded her arms and gripped them with her fingers as she gazed at the trees outside. She sensed Gavin in trouble, surrounded by darkness and danger. The word SeaPro echoed in her mind. Her eyes narrowed. *Those two creeps are up to something. I can feel it.*

Six
Doncaster City University, England

In his red and gold ceremonial robes, black mortar and gold tassel, the Chancellor of Doncaster City University, rose from his chair to address the audience of invited guests assembled in the foyer of the new Barscadden Library.

The Chancellor raised his voice to overcome background chatter. 'Vice-chancellor, chairman of Court, members of Court and Senate, Lord Provost, distinguished guests, ladies, and gentlemen.

Please show your appreciation as I ask Sir James Barscadden of the Barscadden Foundation to join me for the opening dedication.'

Applause followed Sir James Barscadden when he joined the Chancellor at the lectern. They gave each other a salutary nod and smile.

Barscadden waited, and with an air of superiority, he scanned the audience. Although a confident and articulate speaker, he felt apprehensive like an accused waiting for a verdict. It made him anxious but he hid it well.

The Chancellor nodded to Barscadden. 'Sir James Barscadden is a world-renowned businessman. He is the driving force of the Barscadden Corporation, known to all of us as BARSCO. A hugely successful company that provides employment for over eight thousand people throughout Britain.'

The Chancellor heaped loads of praise on the Barscadden Foundation programmes for disadvantaged people, underprivileged children, and women returners. He outlined other special initiatives designed to help people without formal qualifications to receive a university education.

Finally, the Chancellor praised the Barscadden Foundation for supporting the construction of the new high-tech library. He didn't say that the computer system had been custom designed and installed by BARSCO engineers.

As guests fidgeted (probably wishing he would sit down), he turned to face Barscadden.

'It is with great pleasure that I ask the chairman of the Barscadden Foundation, Sir James Barscadden, to say a few words.'

He smiled, stood to attention and nodded to Barscadden. The two men exchanged places. Barscadden surveyed his audience while he switched on a Samsung tablet, which he placed on the lectern. He adjusted his stance from stiff-backed to relaxed and leaning forward. The background chatter subsided and he launched into his speech.

'Chancellor, Vice-chancellor, Chairman of Court, members of Court and Senate, Lord Provost, distinguished guests, ladies, and gentlemen. The library is the heart and soul of a university.

'A place where students study and researchers keep up with new developments. As we move through this new century, we find libraries are undergoing vast changes.

'No longer is a library a simple repository for dusty journals and books. Computer-based information technology is reshaping library services.

'Academic libraries must adapt to ensure future students and researchers have access to all available information. A sea change is underway from traditional book holdings to electronic storage and retrieval.

'At the Barscadden Foundation, we are delighted that Doncaster City University seeks to be at the forefront of this information superhighway, and we are keen to help you.

'Already, the joint academic networks JANET and superJANET enable electronic transfer of documents and articles all over the country, and indeed, worldwide.

'I've seen research papers containing video clips, sound, 3D digital images and animation sequences, which conveyed a thousand times more understanding than a traditional written research paper. The future is digital.'

To emphasise his point, he waved his tablet in the air.

'No doubt, some will mourn the passing of dimly-lit storage rooms and endless rows of shelf stacks.

'I understand that a few of our eminent academics are addicted to the smell of accumulated dust on old books. Or is

31

it the glue used in bookbinding?' He paused for the audience to appreciate his humour.

'This magnificent library has been designed for the future, and I am confident it will take full advantage of new technology.

'So, without further ado, it is with the greatest pleasure that I declare this library open. I wish success and prosperity to all who pass through these doors.'

To applause, Barscadden stepped away from the lectern and over to a nearby wall where he paused. He took hold of a golden cord while cameras clicked and flashed.

When he pulled the cord, two royal-blue curtains parted to reveal a golden metal plate mounted on a dark-mahogany board.

The lettering, engraved and coloured with dark-blue wax, revealed that Sir James Barscadden had opened The Barscadden Library on that date.

While all eyes focused on the plate, a young woman with short black hair, scampered away from a group of students. She wore a short denim jacket and faded tight-fitting jeans that had frayed at the knees.

Distressed, she threw a handful of tomatoes up toward the golden plate. They splashed hard on the floor two metres away from where Barscadden and the Chancellor stood.

She turned to face the onlookers, and shouted, 'Murderers! Bloody evil murderers!'

Then, she pointed to Barscadden. 'He kills sweet innocents for blood money. You fucking carnivores keep him and his evil meat trade in business.'

As the woman raised her arms in an accusing manner, three police officers pounced on her.

In stunned silence, the audience watched the spectacle. She didn't attempt to run but as they bundled her away, she struggled until they locked her arms.

While they marched her out of the foyer, a loud bustle of background chatter filled the hall when people asked each other what had happened.

*

For someone in his mid-fifties, Barscadden could pass for a man ten years younger. At five foot six, he appeared sturdy and powerful. His lightly-tanned face was rugged and his grey hair had started to recede.

Originally a child of Peckham, London, records revealed that both his parents died during his young teens. An aunt on his mother's side had raised him and he spoke with a pronounced 'BBC London' accent.

A young and determined entrepreneur, he had set himself up in business selling goods from an old brown suitcase in London's street markets. He learned business skills the hard way and just after his nineteenth birthday, he started Barscadden Traders.

His company supplied fine quality meat to hotels and restaurants, and he made his first million before his twenty-third birthday.

From then onward, he expanded with precision and resolve to establish a massive food manufacturing company, and he remained sole owner.

Cheerfully, all of Barscadden's employees referred to him as 'King James'. He had involved himself in every single appointment of his eight thousand employees over the past thirty years.

One of his most important management secrets lay hidden in the personal tablet computer that he always had with him.

On a database, he stored ID photographs of all his employees, and associated with each person, he kept pages of essential personal and professional details.

Before visiting a part of his business, he examined relevant files to study faces and information. A ritual he'd developed when travelling around the country, which he did in his Rolls Royce, Lear jet, or Bell helicopter. He remembered faces and linked them with details.

Nothing proved more potent for creating loyalty in BARSCO than Barscadden addressing an employee by their first name and knowing exactly what job that person did in his company.

The Chancellor approached Barscadden. 'Excellent speech, Sir James.'

Barscadden forced a false smile onto his face. 'I'm impressed with your new library.'

A round of verbal back-clapping took place for twenty minutes or more as the Chancellor introduced Barscadden to various VIPs. The University Secretary walked with Barscadden to a nearby table to deposit their empty glasses.

The Secretary was no more than one or two years away from retirement. He wanted to apologise for the disturbance. 'Sorry about the commotion. She was probably drunk.'

Barscadden smiled. 'It's nothing. Animal liberation people attack my farms and slaughterhouses regularly. If the country becomes vegetarian, I'll be happy to adapt my business. At the moment, people want meat, and my companies supply the people.'

The Secretary mused. 'I don't know what she hoped to achieve. A world full of vegans will surely spawn plant liberation people. I'm told the plants don't believe they were put here to provide food for animals.'

'Truth be told. I believe they have a point.'

The Secretary frowned. 'Surely not?'

'On my pig farm in Yorkshire, we used to have a pet sow, a large beauty called Alice. She had one ear much bigger than the other and she had a gigantic snout. The silliest looking pig I ever saw. My cook kept her as a pet.'

Barscadden smiled as pictured Alice in his mind. 'Alice had a straw bed in an outhouse off the kitchen, and she sat in a corner every day. Anyway, cook retired, and my slaughterhouse men came for Alice.

'For the first time ever, she ran off into the fields, and it took five farmhands a whole day to deliver Alice to the slaughterhouse. Until that day, I assumed animals were dumb.'

The Secretary nodded. 'I guess it's convenient for us humans to believe animals have no feelings and no emotions.'

Barscadden caught sight of someone he wanted. 'Yes. I … sorry, excuse me. I must speak to this man.'

When Barscadden walked away from the Secretary, a senior academic stepped directly into his path. Professor

Henry Steadman, Head of the Business School, glared at Barscadden with venom in his eyes.

'You've been exceedingly generous to this pothole,' Steadman said, accusingly.

Barscadden narrowed his eyebrows and glanced disapprovingly at Steadman's nicotine-stained fingers, which wrapped around his wine glass.

'And, your point is *what*, Mr Steadman?'

Steadman pointed an accusing finger. 'What's your payback on this deal? I'll find out. With God as my witness, I'll bloody well find out.'

The Chancellor made a timely interruption and ushered Barscadden away. He knew Steadman disliked Barscadden and criticised BARSCO. At Senate meetings, Steadman had questioned Barscadden's motives.

Steadman retreated to a clique of like-minded cronies.

Barscadden glanced back at him with cold, infuriated, eyes.

Outwardly, Barscadden smiled at other academics fussing around him, but inwardly, he sneered at them. He despised academics, their ivory towers, and their pointless traditions.

He thought only of the great benefits the library would give to him. Secretly, he imagined academics as pigs milling around in a field, fattening up, waiting to go to the slaughterhouse, his slaughterhouse. Food for his business to grow.

Seven

With his hand, Barscadden beckoned Andrew Portcairn to join him. Together, they walked away from the main throng of people.

Andrew Portcairn worked for BARSCO as Deputy Head of Computing. A tall, thin, man, he had a gaunt face, dark-brown hair and he wore loose fitting clothes.

He wore John Lennon style round-rim spectacles, and a well-trimmed, beatnik-style, goatee beard. Like his idol, he spoke with a Liverpool accent.

Barscadden rubbernecked Andrew, and whispered, 'Are we done here?'

Portcairn appeared animated and excited. 'Yes, Sir James, everything is good. I have everything fully operational.'

Barscadden placed his hand on Portcairn's arm, partly to subdue him, and partly to turn him away from being observed.

'Any critical issues?'

Portcairn shook his head. 'No, sir, none. Their IT people nose around of course but their head of IT is ten bits short of a megabyte. The only trouble I'm having is that pest, Steadman. Why is he such a nuisance?'

Slowly, Barscadden turned his head to sneak a quick look at Steadman, still in a huddle with his cronies. 'How serious is it?'

'He doesn't know system RAM from strawberry jam but he's running around with a badger in his bonnet. If he asked their IT staff the right questions then I suppose they might find out what I've done.'

Barscadden acknowledged Portcairn's concern with a glance and nod. 'I'm sick of this highbrow shit, and these three-faced hypocrites. Mind you, if they had half a brain between them, we wouldn't be here.'

'No, sir. Way too risky with a top-notch IT department.'

Barscadden winked as he cocked his head. 'Good work. By the way, there will be a meeting of Gyge's Ring quite soon. It is time for you to join and brief them on your work here.'

'May I speak personally?'

'Of course. What is it?'

Portcairn's voice sounded fragile. 'On behalf of the people in my department, probably everyone in the company, I'd like to thank you for what the company has done for Jenny Doyle.

'Jenny cleans our offices and mothers all of us to bits. We love her, we are heartbroken for her, and I know she is deeply grateful.'

Barscadden nodded. 'No way were those murdering thieves going to walk after what they did to our Jenny's husband.'

Portcairn agreed. 'It's a small comfort that they're in jail but it's important for Jenny to have this kind of closure.'

All the head office staff in BARSCO knew larger-than-life, Jenny Doyle. She had lost her husband on an overseas holiday when thieves stabbed and killed him.

Barscadden sent two people from personnel to accompany Jenny's eldest son and take care of arrangements. They supported Jenny, dealt with authorities and arranged to bring the body home for burial. Other Barscadden people tracked down the killers, and handed them over to police.

Barscadden learned early in his career that success depended on people who were committed, loyal, and trustworthy. His high-profile attention to welfare generated a solid bond between him and his people.

Often, Barscadden said hearts and minds were more valuable than stocks and shares. BARSCO provided good employment, and when required, a refuge from the occasional vulgarity thrown up by normal life.

In return, his loyal people gave him absolute power. In a ring-fenced sanctuary, he addressed his secret agenda. A quest for absolution for his deeply damaged soul.

When Barscadden created BARSCO, he'd embedded in its core, a secret organisation called Gyge's Ring. With himself as Ring Master, he recruited a group of handpicked Ring Leaders to do his bidding.

His oldest and trusted friend, Peter Bromlee, joined him as the first Ring Leader and commander of WRATH. A team of ruthless ex-military men and women.

With WRATH on hand to remove anything or anyone from his path, Barscadden took what he wanted, when he wanted it, from whoever was unfortunate enough to have it.

Peter Bromlee received a sleeve-tug from Barscadden's driver, Duncan. Barscadden wanted to leave. By the time Peter Bromlee reached Barscadden's side, he had finished speaking to Portcairn. Barscadden gave his apologies to the Chancellor.

Duncan brought the midnight-blue Rolls Royce Phantom to the entrance. He opened the car door just as Barscadden left the building.

Barscadden closed his eyes and welcomed a feeling of tranquillity. His body sank into the deeply-couched, cream-coloured hide seat.

As if to remove the scum from numerous handshakes, he rubbed the palm of his right hand on the armrest.

Peter handed him some wet-wipes and a small towel. The magnificent V12 engine purred while they glided away from the building.

Barscadden let out a sigh of relief as he shifted in his seat. Air conditioning and environmental control kept the cabin interior in perfect comfort while he released his stress by playing with the silky-smooth gold, wonderfully tactile, clunk and clack of his air vent control knobs.

He glanced back for a full view of the library. 'A whisky, please.'

Peter opened the drinks cabinet and poured a large glass of Glenmorangie fifty-year-old malt.

Barscadden took a sip, allowed the whisky to roll down his throat and then watched the light reflecting sparkles on the crystal glass.

He sighed and then with disappointment in his voice, he said, 'I rather hoped Julie would be here to keep that academic dirt out of my hair.'

Professor Julie Blackhest, his director of R&D, had given her apologies at the last minute.

Peter raised his eyebrows to indicate he would reveal a confidence.

Barscadden acknowledged with his eyes.

'Julie is attending to an urgent development on a major new project.'

'What new project?'

'You know her. She keeps her cards well-hidden but she's planning to discuss new business at the next meeting of Gyge's Ring. A new process with mega potential is all that I know.'

Barscadden patted Peter on the wrist. His expression conveyed his thanks. 'But WRATH is covering her back?'

Peter shook his head. 'Erm ... actually, not yet.'

Barscadden shook his head. He disapproved of her operating in the field without backup.

'Ah. That woman. Brilliant she is, but Lara Croft—she's not.'

Barscadden's expression informed Peter he'd done well to reveal this information.

'Shall I organise backup for her?'

'Yes, please. Get eyeballs on her backside.'

'Done.' Peter opened his laptop and typed a communication.

'Make a note. Andrew Portcairn is ready to join Gyge's Ring.'

Peter examined his calendar. 'The next meeting of the Ring is scheduled to follow the Board meeting of the seventeenth.'

Barscadden took a large swallow of whisky. 'That's fine.' He furrowed his brow. 'That horrible man, Steadman. I don't think he's a happy hobbit.'

Peter nodded. 'I did notice.'

Barscadden handed over his empty glass. 'He's blowing soapy bubbles at me. My eyes are beginning to sting.'

Duncan caught Barscadden's eye in the rear-view mirror. 'Give me the nod. I'll stuff him down the toilet like any other lump of shit.'

Barscadden glared back at the mirror. 'No! Duncan. There's enough pollution loitering on the beaches.'

'How much of a problem is he?' Peter asked.

'Portcairn believes he's a serious risk to my new business at Doncaster.'

Duncan chimed in. 'Maybe he moonlights as a bus inspector.'

Peter raised his voice a notch. 'He's an academic. He'll look out of place under a bus.'

Sounding like a harassed referee, Barscadden raised his voice. 'Gentlemen, please. I want a less violent solution.'

Peter thought for a moment. 'Maybe, drink driver meets his match when he tries to run down an oak tree.'

Barscadden recalled Steadman's nicotine-stained fingers. 'Hmm, he pollutes the air with his carcinogenic smoke. I think he should have lung cancer.'

'Lung cancer is doable. Would you prefer that in the short or medium term?' Peter asked.

Barscadden jerked his head back with surprise. 'Is that an option?'

'Simply a question of amount and location. Professor Blackhest has done all the calculations.'

Barscadden smiled. 'So be it. The sooner the better. We can all benefit from less pollution.'

Duncan sounded confused. 'I thought WRATH had decided that the radioactive stuff was too risky.'

Barscadden turned to Peter for an answer. 'We stopped using plutonium six months ago. The new stuff is called iodine-131. It has a short half-life.'

'Half-life?'

'Radioactive iodine has a half-life of just one week. It will degrade and disappear completely after a couple of months.'

'Excellent. Clean, environmentally friendly. Just the job.'

'Okay, I'll instruct WRATH to put Professor Steadman on the critical list for go away therapy.'

*

Henry Steadman didn't notice anything different or unusual in his home. Two WRATH agents had entered his house covertly during the day. They examined personal effects on bedside cabinets and discovered his side of the bed.

They exposed his side of the mattress, and sprinkled a small volume of water containing radioactive iodine.

Within a week, Steadman experienced persistent nausea. By the end of two weeks, he suffered incapacitating flu symptoms as body fluids leaked into his radiation-damaged lungs.

By the end of three weeks, he coughed up blood at night as he lay in bed.

His doctors found transformed cells in his blood. As far as they were concerned, another heavy smoker had developed lung cancer.

The secret that Barscadden had embedded in the library would remain hidden.

Eight
Victoria Harbour, Greenock

When shipbuilding dominated its people, Greenock played a major part in Scottish life. With strong engineering traditions, the town gave birth to James Watt and his steam engine.

Times move on, and with the demise of heavy engineering, Greenock town fathers encouraged new light industry to fill the gap.

Greenock SeaPro Ltd had emerged from the ashes of past factories. One of many fledgling companies the town fathers hoped would build success in a former warehouse near Greenock harbour

In SeaPro's boardroom, Jim and Emma Patersun welcomed board members as they arrived. Loudly, they debated Government plans to increase indirect tax, and they all pontificated on how the additional tax would affect their respective businesses.

Emma served coffee and biscuits and then retired to her office at the end of a narrow corridor. She brushed her silky, straw-blonde hair as she rallied her thoughts for what she expected would be an awkward meeting.

Her hair lay on her shoulders with the ends curled into her neck. Parted in the middle, long whispers covered her forehead to form a fringe on her eyebrows.

When she walked, airflow lifted her hair away from her face to reveal a firm and slender neck. As always, she dressed in expensive designer clothes. She wore a dark-blue jacket and skirt suit with a pearl-white silk blouse.

Around her neck, she wore a thick diamond cut gold rope chain with the distinct softness and deep colour of solid gold.

Normally, Emma chatted with other board members. On this occasion, she preferred to be alone with her thoughts. Excitement gripped her mind, and she tried to temper her anticipation with thoughts of possible sharp disappointment.

A bell above the front door tinkled loudly. Emma's pulse raced when she heard the sound of shoes walking on the gritty linoleum floor in the corridor.

'Hello, Dr Shawlens—in you come.' Jim Paterson beckoned.

Jim escorted him back along the corridor and into the main processing hall. Gavin surveyed SeaPro's impressive and expensive-looking pilot plant equipment, and smiled. It reminded him of a brewery he'd visited as a student.

In the centre of the hall, six gleaming stainless-steel storage tanks dominated the space. Like small grain silos with conical bottoms.

'Very impressive kit you have here.'

Jim Patersun strutted like a proud father. 'All designed and installed by Walter with help from a business enterprise grant.'

'What are you using it for?' Gavin asked.

'We're producing a high-quality food ingredient.'

Jim grinned, pleased that his pilot plant had impressed Gavin Shawlens.

A sharp seawater and fish smell pervaded the whole hall. Not obnoxious but dominant.

'From fish?'

'Yes, Dr Shawlens—good guess.'

'Please, call me Gavin.'

Jim led Gavin back to the office corridor and into an old storage room. 'I want our analytical work to be done on site. I want to equip a small laboratory in here. That's why we're having a board meeting today. I want to agree finance for your work and equipment.'

Gavin smiled. 'That's good. I already have complaints from my boss about a waste fat project we are running.'

'Our product is high quality with no smell or taste.'

'From by-catch?'

Gavin assumed they wouldn't use white fish. Already overfished and subject to government and EU quotas.

'Not quite,' Jim replied with a knowing smile. 'Have you ever heard of the black fiddle fish?'

'Sounds like something I should have in my tropical fish tank.'

'Not this one. It's a deep-water fish. It's not fished at all, so stocks are plentiful.'

43

'What's wrong with it?'

'It's an ugly brute with dark fillets, which no-one will buy.'

Jim opened a fridge and picked up a bottle containing white fluid for Gavin to inspect. He unscrewed the top and sniffed. It glistened in the light, thick, like syrup.

Gavin agreed that it had no odour but declined to taste the product. Jim called the product GSP36. He explained the pigment had changed from dark-grey to white.

'What market are you aiming for?'

'As you know, the food industry adds ingredients to manufactured foodstuff to provide special functional properties. Like gelling agents to make gels, foaming agents to add foam, and so on. What do you think of a single ingredient with multi-functional properties?'

Gavin didn't appear impressed. 'The industry has single ingredients that do both gelling and foaming.'

'Correct, but what price for one ingredient that can emulsify, form a gel, produce a foam, bind a food dye, retain water and is also a damn good preservative?'

Gavin shook his head with disbelief. 'You're joking, right?'

Jim clapped his hands. 'Absolutely not. Because I've got it.'

'That would be the ultimate food ingredient. Every food manufacturer in the world could replace three or four ingredients with just one. They would save an absolute fortune.'

'Do you have a dog?' Jim asked.

'Yes.'

Jim placed the bottle of white fluid on a table for Gavin to collect later. 'Customer trial. Let me know if your dog likes it. I'm also looking at the pet food market.'

Walter joined Jim. They discussed the whereabouts of their young helper, Davy.

Jim pointed to the tanks. 'They need to be cleaned out. Where is he now?'

'He's still searching for Boggin.'

Jim frowned. 'Still searching? I thought he'd given that up by now.'

'He won't give up until he finds his dog dead or alive. Don't worry. He knows he still has these tanks to clean out.'

Jim shook his head. 'It's a pity. I liked that mongrel. But I understand. Davy and his dog are like two brothers.'

Gavin asked Jim, 'Is Davy your technician?'

Jim sniggered. 'He was thrown out of school at fourteen. Reputation as a troublemaker. He's unskilled but hard working.'

Walter pointed to the tanks. 'Davy does the dirty work around the pilot plant. He named his dog Boggin because he found him abandoned on a council rubbish tip.'

Gavin raised surprised eyebrows. 'He took in an abandoned mongrel pup?'

Jim replied, 'Yes, Davy heard a squeal as he rummaged through the rubbish tip. From that day on, like brothers, they've been inseparable.'

Walter raised his voice a notch. 'Boggin also works for us as rat-catcher general.'

Alarm sprang onto Gavin's face. 'Have you got a *rat* problem?'

Jim backtracked. 'Had! When we first moved in. Not any longer. Boggin killed them all. Probably learned how to kill them in the rubbish tip.'

Jim guided Gavin back into the corridor leading to the office. He called on Emma to put a kettle on for coffee then directed Gavin to walk down the corridor to the office.

A feeling of disappointment flushed through Gavin's mind while he thought about what Jim told him. *An ill-conceived project, unskilled support and a mongrel dog in control of a vermin problem.*

Another crackpot idea destined to fail. He didn't want to waste his time trying to make it work. Only last month, he'd had to explain to another crazy inventor why a vacuum fridge wouldn't work.

Before the vacuum fridge, he spent time with a woman who had an insect repellent formula that protected her but no-one else. Gavin wondered if Crawford deliberately channelled all the crackpots to him.

As he walked along the corridor with Jim following, he considered his exit strategy. He decided he would make his fees unaffordable. Force them to find someone else to do the work.

Gavin turned into the office and stopped hard. Stunned like a deer caught in headlights. Emma Baxster stood in front of him.

His first serious teenage girlfriend. She radiated the beautiful smile that had captured his heart once before when she'd become the one and only love of his life.

Nine

Twenty years ago, sixteen-year-old Gavin became the envy of all his school friends when he dated Emma Baxster for all of twenty-four glorious months. Four years older, Emma worked in a bank near his school.

Their relationship flourished until a bank training course at head office resulted in a more mature man in Emma's life. His bliss ended abruptly and they hadn't met since.

He absorbed every detail on her face while his choked voice uttered, 'Emma.'

She stared past him to the corridor. 'Tea or coffee, Dr Shawlens?'

His heart leapt into his mouth. He fought a stomach-churning tumult to force out a reply. 'Coffee.'

Jim breezed into the office. 'Coffee for me, too.'

Jim extended his hand. 'I'd like to introduce my wife. Emma, this is Dr Gavin Shawlens.'

'Hello, nice to meet you,' she said as they shook hands.

Her hand cool and soft, slipped into his; warm and trembling. Their hands together for a few seconds longer than necessary. Their eyes locked while Jim Patersun searched his desk for his papers.

Colour drained from Gavin's face. Many times, he'd wondered if he would ever meet her again. He imagined he would notice her browsing in a shop, he would approach her casually, and she would be startled.

He'd rehearsed exactly what he would say. As it happened, he stood rooted to the ground in shock.

Jim gathered his documents. 'Did you have time to go along to the grave?'

Emma's eyes flicked between the two of them. 'Yes. No-one seems to know anything.'

Gavin's face remained puzzled as he accepted his cup of coffee from Emma.

Jim noticed his bewilderment. 'Someone has started leaving bunches of flowers at the grave of Emma's dad.'

Emma saw Gavin needed time to pull himself together. 'I've asked everybody I can think of. It's no-one we know.'

Jim tucked his papers under his arm, picked up his mug of coffee, and said teasingly, 'I think your old man had a secret admirer.'

Emma frowned. 'My father? You must be joking. I don't know anyone with a kind word for him, let alone visit his grave and leave flowers.'

Gavin hung onto every word to refresh his memory with the sound of her voice.

Jim asked, 'Is that scruffy drug addict still hanging around the cemetery?'

'Yes, she's always there watching to see if I'm watching her. I've told the caretaker she's obviously dealing drugs. He won't do anything.'

Jim turned to Gavin. 'What do you think of our set-up?'

Gavin forced his expression back to normal. 'Excellent.'

Time had worked in her favour and she appeared more attractive than he remembered. Like a battery re-charging, his mind filled with new visions of Emma.

'Milk and sugar?' Emma asked Gavin.

'Milk … thanks.'

Jim strode out of the office. 'Bring your coffee to the boardroom.'

Gavin hesitated to follow. He glanced at Emma for guidance. She shifted her head slightly from side to side, pressed her index finger against her closed lips and narrowed her eyes. He understood and nodded.

In the small boardroom, two large tables were surrounded by ten chairs of various design and size. Everyone stood while Jim Patersun introduced Gavin to them, one-by-one.

Jim pointed. 'Walter, you already know.'

Six local businessmen had joined the SeaPro board. Gavin gave each one his business card but received only one in return, from accountant, Tony Mascarri.

Gold embossed lettering adorned the card of Mr Tony E Mascarri B.A. F.C.C.A.

Emma didn't attend the meeting. With eight astute businessmen skilled in reading faces, they would have noticed Gavin's reaction. She expected him to rake through their past. She agonised over his response following the initial shock.

Discussions centred on how many hours per week Gavin could work on their project. They discussed the cost of specific equipment required for laboratory work.

While Gavin listened to the others, he thought about Emma, past and present. He had loved her completely, and it had taken him a long time to displace the pain of losing her.

He quickly established new feelings for her. He didn't hate her and his melancholy had long since gone. He had strong residual feelings but didn't know what he wanted.

Feelings of something misplaced—love, friendship, infatuation, or retribution? He couldn't decide. His mind battled with the emotional puzzle.

He put up no resistance to their financial proposals and they concluded he had no head for business.

Ten

Jim asked Gavin to leave the boardroom while the partners discussed their financial arrangements. He peeked into Emma's office but she'd gone. He wandered back along the corridor and into the processing hall.

A young man painted a section of concrete floor with grey paint. Davy? Gavin approached, smiled and prepared to nod a hello but the boy seemed upset.

His eyes appeared bloodshot, his face glistened with sweat and he wiped his nose on his sleeve repeatedly. Gavin thought of asking him if he'd found his dog, so he could find out more about the rat problem.

'Dr Shawlens,' Emma called out, and beckoned with her arm.

Gavin followed Emma outside to an open yard where large plastic containers on wheels bulged with black fish mixed with salted ice.

Emma walked past them and over to the harbour edge. She watched a car ferry pass.

The sun sat high in a light-blue cloudless sky. A gentle breeze from the river cooled the air. Gavin joined her as she shifted her gaze over the estuary to Dumbarton Rock.

A group of seagulls caught Gavin's attention. They squealed, paced and bobbed up and down on the roof of an adjacent building. He guessed they were calculating the risk in stealing fish from the containers. Emma turned around to face him.

He wondered what he should do. Show affection, or not, a hug and a kiss. Shake hands—definitely not.

Emma broke the awkward silence. When they were youngsters, she always led. It may have been her extra years or her strong personality but she always led the way.

'No longer the baby. I expect you need to shave every day now.'

'What?'

Emma smiled. 'The girls in the bank used to call me a baby snatcher for going out with you.'

'You never told me,' he said, and it sounded like a rebuke.

She shifted her gaze back to Dumbarton Rock, and changed the subject. 'Will you help us with our enzyme?'

She folded her lips inside her mouth.

He moved his head to look at her face. 'I've said yes.'

He wanted to see her reaction but the wind blew her hair over her face. He missed the opportunity.

'Good.' She turned to faced him with a cool and business-like expression. 'Walter has built this pilot plant but he doesn't understand enzymes. We need an enzymologist on board.'

As he listened, their eyes locked and he re-experienced the elation he felt when they were together.

'I'm amazed at meeting you again after all this time.'

She nodded. 'Yes, it feels strange. Tell me, are you married with children and a mortgage?'

'Mortgage, unfortunately. I have a flatmate, Kim. I pay the mortgage and the bills but she owns the place.' He laughed.

Emma hid her surprise. She didn't know anything about Kim. With a tinge of disappointment, she said, 'Seems like a very modern arrangement.'

'Well, she looks after the flat and I'm never lonely with her about.'

'I'm pleased you have someone to come home to after a hard day's work. Where are you living now?' she asked, although she already knew. Emma had done her homework.

'Clarkston, near the Toll.'

'Clarkston? My goodness, we're practically neighbours. We live in Newton Mearns.'

Kim, she thought, *I wonder what you're like.* Others described Gavin as a workaholic, and Emma tried to work out how Kim fitted into his busy working life. She felt a little jealous and dismissed the feeling straight away.

Gavin didn't want more scrutiny of his private life. 'When did your dad die?'

Emma sucked in a deep breath and spat it out. 'Six months ago. Prostate cancer. I don't know if you remember but he was a first-class bastard. I still haven't shed a single tear for him.'

'What's the mystery?'

A cynical tone defined her voice. 'Weird. He must have had one friend. Someone started leaving bunches of flowers on his grave. Not proper flowers from a florist shop with a card. Just wildflowers, cheap, hand-made posies. The sort of thing my sister and I used to make when we were little.'

'Obviously, it's someone not willing to spend money on him.'

'It must be a woman, yet he hated women. He drove my mother and my sister into early graves. I would have followed them if I'd stayed in that house.'

Sadness shaped his face. 'Oh dear, I didn't know about Donna. I remember she always had a big smile for me. She was lovely.'

'Well, you helped her with her school homework, didn't you?' Emma offered him a smile.

'Donna hated homework and was good at getting me to do it for her.'

'She died almost a year after I left home, just before her thirteenth birthday. Dad refused to contact me because I was out of the house. I didn't know until two years later when my mother died. Can you believe that?'

Anger clipped her words. 'I found out about my little sister when I went to my mother's funeral. I'll never forgive him for that … never.'

'Maybe an old aunt visits the grave. You should leave a note for her.'

'I'm not interested. I only go because my mother and sister are buried there, and I have to walk past his to reach their grave.'

Emma had thought it through. If her father had found someone else after her mother died, she didn't want to know and certainly didn't want to speak to her.

'Anyway, you've done well. Dr Shawlens, no less. I envied you back then. Now, I'm pure pea-green.'

'Me?'

'There you were in school, talking exams, universities, and careers. When I got home on my last day of school, my mother's eyes were dark-red from crying. My dad told me I was starting in the bank on the following Monday—office junior. No discussion. No choice. I was just sixteen.'

'What would you have done if you'd had the choice?'

'I dreamt of becoming a pharmacist. I wanted independence with my own shop and a couple of girls working for me. I read pharmacy books in the library. Chemicals that fight disease and pain have always fascinated me.'

Bad times in her youth re-surfaced. Fierce battles over her pay packet every Friday night. Her father took her wages and gave her back a pittance for pocket money.

Not enough for a teenager with cosmetics, hygiene, clothes and music on her mind.

His blank refusal to say what he did with her money only magnified her anger. As head janitor in a large school, he had a good pay and he never drank or smoked. He couldn't bet on a horse even if he knew the name of the winner.

For a long time, she thought he'd been blackmailed but she found no evidence. Eventually, she decided he must have kept another woman. Whatever her father did with her wages, she never found out and all of his money vanished.

Life insurance, endowments, bank accounts, all cashed out and gone. He left no provisions for his funeral, and she paid to have him buried in the same cemetery but not beside her mother and sister.

Sharp reality slapped her back into focus. She needed to clear the air if they were to work together on this important project.

'Look, I'm sorry about the way I dropped you cold.'

His eyes pleaded. 'Did I do something wrong?'

'We were both too young and you were still at school. Something better came along,' she replied, and sounded more callous than she intended.

'Jeffrey?'

She grimaced. 'A chance for me to get out of that damn house.'

Emma had married Christopher Jeffrey, a bank clerk and part-time judo instructor. Their marriage lasted six years.

'What happened to him?'

Emma shrugged. 'Chris is good-hearted. He always wanted children, and when we discovered I can't have them, things became difficult between us.'

'That must have been tough.'

'That's life. I had to get on with it. He started to drink heavily. One night, he snapped and punched me in the face. I divorced him. Now, he's remarried with two lovely daughters. He's devoted to them and much happier now.'

'Jim Patersun seems a nice guy?'

Emma smiled and realised that he hadn't changed much. 'So, it's just as well—really.'

'What is?'

'That we didn't stay together. I couldn't give you children.'

They were difficult words for her to say and her voice reflected deep sorrow. She felt incomplete and her eyes reflected a fragile heart.

Gavin raised his hands, and for a moment, he wanted to pull her to him for a hug, but instead, he blinked, lowered his hands and cleared his throat.

'Is there nothing they can do for you?'

Typical, she thought. *He's a scientist—analytical, investigative, tactless and thoughtless at times.* As teenage lovers, they read and discussed the physiology of sex exhaustively to help her understand how the contraceptive pill worked on her body. At least, he would be able to understand her problem.

'If I were a normal woman, my hormones would change the fluid that bathes my womb from watery liquid to a thick tacky gel when I got pregnant.'

He nodded to confirm he understood. 'It's a natural barrier to keep bacteria away from the baby.'

'My hormones are unbalanced. It seems they produce a thick barrier continuously. An ideal contraceptive. I suppose some women would be delighted.'

'I'm sorry.'

'Don't be. Jim is very happy with what we have.'

Emma had directed their conversation to the point she wanted to make. Her eyes grabbed his attention. 'Look, I'm sure Jim wouldn't mind knowing we were teenage lovers. We've both had marriages that didn't work.'

Gavin gave her a flat-lipped smile. 'Of course. I understand.'

'Please, don't say anything. We have fond memories and I treasured the time we had. Let's leave it at that. Okay?'

Her words, varied tone in her voice, and her body language contained guidance but Gavin couldn't be sure where it led. As they walked through the door to the processing hall, they saw an angry-looking Jim Patersun speaking to young Davy.

The boy seemed upset as he scurried up a metal staircase. He scampered along a metal gangway, which allowed access to the tops of the large stainless-steel tanks.

'Is Davy all right?' Emma asked.

'He's behind with his chores. Hasn't started to clean out the tanks.' Jim spoke loudly as he glanced back at the boy.

Emma sounded sympathetic. 'Did he find his dog?'

Jim shook his head. 'That dog is long gone. I wish he would accept it and move on.'

Then, Jim addressed Gavin. 'Okay, we have finance for you and equipment. Are you in?'

'Yes,' he replied without hesitation.

Gavin and Jim shook hands enthusiastically.

'Let's sign that bit of paper and get some fish smell into your clothes.'

*

A short while later, Gavin opened the sunroof in his car. Retained heat escaped, and he stared out through the windscreen while he reflected on his meeting with Emma.

He re-played fresh images of her, seeking clues as he evaluated his feelings and tried to read between the lines.

For twenty-four months, she'd filled his every waking moment and he'd walked on cloud nine. She'd featured in all of his dreams and fantasies.

He'd luxuriated in an overwhelming feeling of satisfaction. He'd loved the girl that every older boy in his school wanted to go to bed with but only he could.

He'd had a resolute and powerful image of them sharing a wonderful home and richly satisfying life together. It became an obsessive love and he couldn't bear to be without her. Then, without warning, she had walked out.

For months, he'd spent each night alone in pain, convinced he couldn't live without her. His older sister, Siobhan, managed to keep him from falling apart.

Slowly, she re-started his life, but for years after, he still saw Emma's face in every crowd. The intense concentration and determination required for his university studies served to pull him back together.

Now, Emma had dropped back into his life, and be believed he'd found a new light at the end of the tunnel. Either a beginning or an end. As he started his car, his heart raced with new excitement. An urgency to reach the end of that tunnel.

Then, it occurred to him that tunnels are dark and dangerous places with hidden secrets and horrible monsters; waiting to terrify children of all ages. He stalled the car.

Eleven
Schiphol Airport, Amsterdam

With plenty to see and experience, Amsterdam is easy on the visitor. It's a sociable and friendly city where people can relax with alternative forms of living. Amsterdam offers two very different experiences.

On the one hand, there is an opportunity to fumble around in the red-light district. On the other hand, there is beautiful art and profound history to be found in sophisticated museums and galleries.

Tony Mascarri flowed with an arrivals crowd at Schiphol airport. His mind filled with stories he'd read about the famous 'shop-window' prostitutes.

Eagerly, he anticipated his first trip to Amsterdam as he pushed forward to the front of the queue, excited by the prospects of a lucrative business deal.

It grieved him that he would have no time to sample the delights. He made a mental commitment to return for a long weekend and experience raw pleasure. After all, he would soon be able to afford it.

Mascarri followed instructions given by his business contact and took a cab from Schiphol Airport direct to the Anne Frank museum in Amsterdam centre.

Not having read the book or taken an interest in Second World War history, he had assumed the house would be a coffee shop or bar.

The cab driver unfolded Anne's story, the secret hiding place of the Frank family and the diary of Anne Frank.

Mascarri voiced his disappointment when he arrived outside the museum, and the cab driver felt equally disappointed, no tip for his trouble.

If he'd known his passenger's occupation, he would have understood that an accountant like Tony Mascarri only ever offered one tip—*you need an accountant.*

He had arrived an hour early for his meeting. A long queue of people waited at the entrance to the Anne Frank museum, so he went for a walk.

While he browsed in nearby shops, he wondered if the red-light district was nearby. A woman dressed in 17th century traditional Dutch costume passed him. He sniggered then tried to estimate how much wear a pair of wooden shoes would provide.

Her clogs blended nicely with the tinkling tunes from the street clock towers and the wooden bridges of the old city.

At one o'clock, Mascarri made his way back to the house. As expected, a canal boat had moored next to the building. In the sunshine, the varnish on the dark wood and polished brass plates shone brilliantly.

He spotted a woman sitting in the first seat of the glass-covered boat, reading a broadsheet newspaper. His business contact, according to the instructions he'd received.

The boat had two rows of twin seats and a central passageway down its length. The seating, arranged back to front, meant that four people sat in pairs and could face each across a wooden table between them.

He loitered beside the boat for a minute. He surveyed all around before he stepped inside. Once on board, he eased into the wooden seat opposite the woman then placed his thin briefcase on the table between them.

With a sheepish look, he asked, 'What's the headline today?'

She moved her fingers and allowed the top half of her newspaper to fall down on the fold. She regarded him and made a comment about Dam Square in Amsterdam. He recited the precise response he'd been given to verify his identity.

All very cloak and dagger for an accountant but he was there to sell SeaPro technology to a secret buyer. He expected there would be some subterfuge to deal with.

In a noticeable Dutch-German accent, she asked, 'How was your flight from Glasgow?'

His eyes scoured the top half of her body. 'Fine, I return on the five-fifteen tonight.'

'This canal boat will return close to Dam Square. You can pick up a taxi there to take you to Schiphol. You will have time to spare.' She noticed him undressing her with his eyes.

The woman lifted his briefcase and placed it on the seat beside her. She twisted her body to inspect the papers inside. She glanced at his passport and dropped it back into his case.

Next, she picked out a report. In large bold lettering, it had SeaPro Ltd on the front cover. She read the executive summary. A glowing statement and by the look on her face, it exceeded her wildest expectations.

In his groin, feelings stirred while he continued to examine the woman's curves.

She wore her short platinum-blonde hair brushed back to one side. Large dark sunglasses protected her eyes from his. Her lips appeared attractively shaped and her fingers well-manicured.

Her tailored clothes were expensive, and she wore a double-breasted jacket buttoned to protect her from the cool breeze on the canals.

He had trouble keeping his eyeballs in his head.

The woman couldn't avoid his ravenous stare.

'Do you have authority to negotiate?' he asked.

'Yes, of course.'

He glanced out of the boat window to pluck up courage. 'Then, I have one condition.'

'Go on.'

'A little personal business, you need to perform for me to seal the deal.'

Unconcerned, the woman peered at him over the top of her sunglasses then she pushed them back onto the bridge of her nose. 'I am not a prostitute.'

He fidgeted as he stared at the table between them. Then, he extended his hand to take back the report. 'There are other parties interested in SeaPro. They'll be happy to provide me with a personal bonus.'

A frown settled onto her face and she held onto the briefcase. 'Very well, I agree to one half-hour for you on my body. My offer for the exclusive report is fifty thousand in cash. Do you accept this offer?'

'Yes, that's good for me.' He beamed with pleasure.

With clinical coldness, she said, 'I give you fifty percent now and the rest after you have been serviced back at my hotel room.'

The woman slipped a brown envelope into the fold of her newspaper. Casually, she passed the newspaper to Mascarri.

He held the envelope open and ran his thumb over the wad of notes. Then, he slipped the envelope into his inside pocket. Satisfied, he flashed a wicked smile at her.

In silence, they watched a group of tourists gather outside the museum. He visualised having sex with her.

She took out a silver hip flask and two silver cups from her shoulder bag. Then, she separated the cups and returned one to her bag.

The remaining cup, she placed on the table and filled it to near the top. Carefully, she replaced the top on her flask, picked up the cup and sipped her drink.

An erotic hum of pleasure came from her. Half of the cup disappeared into her mouth when she drank. A distinct ring of lipstick marked the point where her lips caressed the vessel.

She pushed her tongue inside the cup and rolled it around to scoop up the last drop. He watched every movement. She smiled a sexy smile at him.

'This will help me to relax. Just for you. What is your attention span?' she asked.

'What?'

She pointed a finger down toward his groin. 'Your attention span.'

Tony ignored her question. He performed like a dog and had an attention span of less than forty seconds on a good day with a full bladder.

Mascarri scowled at her. 'Selfish bitch, are you going to share that flask?'

'If you wish.'

Tony pointed to her bag. 'I'll have the spare cup.'

The woman rummaged through her bag.

An arrogant smirk defined his face. 'I don't want to catch herpes from you.'

She refilled her cup and filled the second cup before handing it to Mascarri.

He drained it in one swallow and recognised a sweet Sauternes white wine.

'*Zum wohl!*' She said then smiled when she saw he didn't understand.

'It's not bad. A bit too sweet for my taste.' He grinned, relieved that their transaction hadn't been as dire as he'd feared.

She ignored him and wondered whether he was funny or stupid. While she ruminated, she collected the empty cups, pushed them together and replaced the cap on her flask.

Done, she returned her attention to her newspaper, and her expression signalled she would not speak again.

She had prepared thoroughly for the meeting. Background information on Mascarri suggested how he might conduct his business.

He had played his cards exactly as expected, and she had played her cards exactly as she wanted except for one forced change to her original plan. She'd regrouped her thoughts and ran through the worst possible scenario.

The possibility of a disaster had set off a swarm of butterflies in her stomach. Panic surfaced while she worried she'd taken on more than she could handle.

Maybe she should have had someone covering her back in case Mascarri became violent. *It is not going to happen. I will walk away and I will have SeaPro*, she thought.

Twelve
Prinsengracht, Amsterdam

The bonus of a quickie before his journey home gave Tony Mascarri plenty to consider. He felt more relaxed when a stream of tourists boarded the canal boat.

The Captain untied the mooring ropes and made ready to leave. The engine drummed a steady tune and the Captain rotated a large brass wheel to steer away from the berth.

A petite, bouncy, smiling, red-headed girl with a heavy German accent introduced herself and the Captain before she began her guide talk with parting comments about the Anne Frank museum.

She spoke fluently in English and French. In position on the bulwark, she perched her backside on the edge of the craft.

To steady herself, she held onto the back of the Captain's chair. In her free hand, she held a small microphone.

She talked about the closely packed houses that lined the canals. Tall, narrow houses, characterised by various shades of brown brick, steeply pitched roofs with red tiles, and (typically) nine large windows for maximum daylight.

Enthusiastic, she explained that canal houses had been busy storehouses and workshops that buzzed with commercial activities.

Each house had its own distinctive roof style, and many boasted detailed and ornate facades on their roofline to advertise prosperity.

The boat passed moored houseboats varying from grand to dilapidated. She gave the tourists anecdotes about some unscrupulous houseboat people, their avoidance of local taxes, and their inclination to 'borrow' electricity from streetlights.

When the boat approached an old wooden drawbridge, called the Skinny Bridge, people pushed up toward the front of the boat.

They jostled with each other to photograph the bridge as the boat sailed toward it. People bustled, leaned over each other, squeezed and pushed forward for a special photo.

The journey from the museum to a berth near to Dam Square took just over twenty minutes. After the boat had moored, the guide thanked the tourists for taking the trip and wished them a good day.

The crowd queued to alight and thanked her as they filed past. Many dropped Euro coins on a plate placed on a wooden shelf near the exit.

The platinum-blonde eased out of her seat and walked around to stand behind Tony Mascarri. She smiled, placed her hands on his shoulders, leaned forward and brought her lips close to his head. Then, she blew sharply into his ear before she checked that his body was securely wedged in his seat.

She had already left when a man at the end of the queue patted Mascarri's shoulder and then placed two fingers on Mascarri's carotid artery while he waited for the queue to move on.

He wore a beige baseball cap, black bomber jacket, and had a long-lens camera hanging from his neck.

The boat had disgorged all of its tourists, except for Mascarri. He sat stiff and erect, staring at the back of the boat and leaning against the seat window.

The Captain found no signs of life and assumed the poor man had suffered a stroke or heart attack. His face, cooled by a crisp wind on the canals, had turned pale as snow and his lips a deep purple.

The silver cup the woman handed to Mascarri contained fifty milligrams of enhanced neurotoxin from the blue-ringed octopus.

The toxin had spread rapidly in his blood, blocking nerve transmissions and had progressively shut down his organs. Groups of muscles locked in place when his neuromuscular nerves froze.

A blue-ringed octopus isn't much bigger than a golf ball. It isn't designed for fast pursuit. It can't go swimming after its prey so its toxin is fast-acting. One octopus carries sufficient venom to kill twenty adult humans in a few minutes. Or one man in a matter of seconds.

*

When sensations of pins and needles surged down his legs, Mascarri didn't suspect anything. In fact, with cool air blowing through the boat, he didn't notice the onset of paralysis.

When he realised that he couldn't move his arms, he also discovered he couldn't move any muscles in his face. He felt rage when the woman glanced at her watch, reached over and jabbed a sharp pencil into the back of his hand.

She had peered into his eyes, winked, and smirked at him. His brain and eyesight remained functional when she retrieved her envelope from his jacket pocket.

He watched her transfer the contents of his briefcase to her bag and saw her place bottles of an orange liquid and a handful of wraps in his briefcase.

Then, she wedged his briefcase between his waist and the edge of the table to prevent his body slipping to one side.

The hustle of tourists jostling for position to take snaps of the Skinny Bridge had given her a perfect distraction for her activities.

When he realised he'd been drugged, he wondered how long it would take for the drug to wear off. He thought of excuses he would have to make to police and paramedics when the boat reached its berth. Each time he blinked, his eyesight deteriorated further.

Despair followed when his vision became speckled, like looking through black metal mesh. Seconds later, a myriad of fragile stars in a night sky extinguished in waves of blue-white death flashes as the rod cells in his eyes progressively stopped working.

In darkness, he pleaded for his life. Many times, he confessed and apologised profusely. He pledged his money, his time for church work and his love.

He promised no more thieving, no more prostitutes and no more beatings for his wife, Theresa. The same guilt-driven pleadings for forgiveness he'd made many times before.

He promised to return the money stolen from Alzheimer patients he'd targeted, even though he knew most of them had since died penniless.

He pledged to help the family of a client who committed suicide when his business failed because Mascarri had stolen too much from the accounts. He begged and begged for another chance to make things right.

Mascarri's final seconds were dark and silent while paralysis swept relentlessly through his body. In the black void, he waited anxiously for the forgiveness he believed would come, and for the white lights to guide him into heaven.

The woman had sentenced him to forty seconds and now his time was up. The toxin had reached the pacemaker deep in his heart muscle. His heart stopped beating and Theresa became a widow.

*

The woman walked confidently through Dam Square with a spring in her step. Mascarri would still be alive if he'd been more careful with his words. He would have received the bonus he craved, not with her but with a prostitute.

He made one fatal error. A stupid threat, which she took seriously. She believed he would double-sell the SeaPro report, and she couldn't allow him to do that.

The SeaPro report, which Mascarri should have handed to Jim Patersun was now in the hands of Gyge's Ring. Ruthless people, desperate to take control of SeaPro's new process, no matter the cost. Mascarri's greed put an end to his life and now everyone associated with SeaPro faced imminent danger.

While she waited at a taxi rank, her head and shoulders filled the viewfinder of a long-range camera as it clicked through a dozen frames.

The photographer tugged his baseball cap, and allowed his camera to hang on his neck while he spoke into his mobile phone. He watched the woman's taxi drive away and reported what he'd seen to his Ring Leader.

*

The Dutch police had little to work with. They believed his clothes were British but couldn't decide if he resided in Amsterdam or not. His fingerprints weren't on record.

In his briefcase, they found six one-gram wraps of amnesia haze (strong cannabis), and two bottles of orange-coloured krokodil.

The scene had all the hallmarks of a drug deal gone bad. The police concluded he'd been poisoned by krokodil, which is a concoction designed to convert codeine pills into desomorphine.

On the street, crude conversion of codeine is done in the bottle with a cocktail containing petrol, iodine, hydrochloric acid, phosphorus and paint thinner.

Thirteen
Square Mile, Central London

BARSCO head office has a large and intimidating presence on the edge of the London's business square mile. An imposing architectural design with dark-blue marble and smoked-glass windows.

Proudly, it boasts confidence and success. In common with all large buildings in the district, security has a high profile.

Every person entering the building must pass through airport-style arch scanners. They must surrender personal mobile phones and use an issued company mobile for all communications at work.

The busy lobby has three general lifts to all floors and one express lift to an exec suite on the twenty-sixth floor. On this level, executive and secretarial offices complement a large boardroom.

Two impressively carved oak doors guard the entrance to the boardroom. Triple-glazed, metalized windows, block electronic surveillance, and the west wall offers a spectacular view over central London.

In a black leather executive chair at the head of the table, Barscadden presided like a king holding court.

The board meeting had lasted three hours, and many areas of BARSCO business had been the subject of a progress report, discussion or proposal. Barscadden ended the meeting and people checked their company mobiles for new messages.

Five board members remained. They lifted their papers and moved closer to Barscadden at the end of the long table.

When the last person closed the oak doors, Barscadden removed his jacket and placed it over a nearby chair. Then, he pressed the intercom key on his phone and spoke to his office secretary.

'Yes, Sir James?'
'Is Andrew waiting?'
'Yes, Sir James.'
'Show him in, please.'

Andrew Portcairn followed the secretary into the boardroom and joined the group at the end of the table. The secretary veered left and approached a panel in the wall.

'If I may, I'll collect the minutes.'

'Yes, of course,' Barscadden replied.

Underneath Barscadden's papers lay a darkened touch screen built into the table. He moved the papers to one side and pressed the top right-hand corner of the screen.

It flickered into life, revealing touch-screen buttons and icons. He tapped a computer icon.

A panel on the wall slid to one side to reveal a cabinet containing a computer server, keyboard, and screen. Software and hidden microphones used voice pattern signatures to convert verbal discussions to electronic transcripts.

When the secretary had finished, Barscadden ended the programme.

She pulled the oak doors closed behind her.

Barscadden raised his voice. 'Ladies and gentlemen, welcome to the two hundred and thirty-seventh meeting of Gyge's Ring. It is my pleasure to welcome Andrew Portcairn from IT. Andrew joins us today for his inauguration into our Ring.'

They smiled and greeted him by rapping the table with their knuckles. Barscadden surveyed the faces around him. 'Andrew will be promoted to head of IT and will support the computer needs of our Ring. He has a briefing, which will set your silk socks on fire.'

Barscadden stood beside Andrew Portcairn who rose from his seat. They faced each other. Barscadden opened a small black box and removed a gold band, which had Andrew's initials A.K.P. and the word Gyge engraved on the inside. He held the ring between his thumb and forefinger for all to see.

'With this symbol, you join Gyge's Ring. Accept the responsibilities of a Ring Leader. Commit your life to the work of Gyge's Ring.' As he handed the ring to Andrew Portcairn, Barscadden's tone sounded solemn.

Intimidated, Andrew's heart raced past 130. The most senior people in BARSCO stared at him, and he felt a wall of pressure bearing down on him.

People he considered his superiors would now welcome him as an equal—it seemed surreal.

His voice weakened but he managed to make his pledge. 'I, Andrew Portcairn, pledge myself to the philosophy and aspirations of Gyge's Ring. I accept responsibility for development of my Ring. I pledge support for my fellow Ring Leaders in all their endeavours. I pledge my life to the Ring Master.'

He placed his ring on the middle finger of his left hand. The other Ring Leaders acknowledged him by standing and clapping. Barscadden shook Andrew's hand.

Barscadden tapped his pen on the table. 'Andrew knows what each of you do for BARSCO but not what you do for Gyge's Ring. Peter, would you like to kick off.'

'Good to have you on board, Andrew. My Ring handles intervention and security. To that end, I have a dedicated team known to us as WRATH, which means waste removal and tactical help.

'It was WRATH who explained our no-whistle-blower policy to your former boss, Mr Habeema,' Peter Bromlee said.

Leejay Habeema had been BARSCO's head of computing and a close friend of Andrew Portcairn until he died in an unfortunate car accident.

The inquisitive Habeema had found out too much about Portcairn's work at Doncaster City University. His conscience troubled him and his predicament subsequently proved fatal.

Barscadden turned his gaze to Portcairn. 'Habeema was a good man but his lapse does serve to highlight our need to be ever vigilant about absolute security.'

Bromlee continued, 'WRATH has twelve full Ring members. Most are ex-police and ex-special forces. Supporting them are twenty-eight associate Ring members that we call ARMs. They provide muscle when required.

'We have a training camp at Cape Wrath on the northwest tip of Scotland, and we have an operational base in a small factory on the south side of Glasgow, near Govan. WRATH will handle all of your waste removal and tactical help.'

Barscadden turned his head to Julie Blackhest. 'Julie's nickname in the Ring is "Brains". I believe you already know why.'

Professor Julie Blackhest exchanged eye greetings with Portcairn. They had worked together on his project at Doncaster City University.

Julie spoke confidently. 'Like all of us around this table, my BARSCO role and my Gyge's Ring role are similar. My Ring handles research and development.

'I have a Ring of twenty academics in this country, and soon, my Ring will extend to France and Germany. Academics are valuable assets with access to key resources.

'With Andrew's help, my Ring will identify those high-flyers with a golden egg up their sleeve. Later, Andrew's briefing will explain how we will harvest those golden eggs.'

During his pledge, Andrew had kept an eye on Julie. His mentor, she had the friendliest face around the table. He kept his feelings hidden but he still felt upset by Habeema's death.

If he'd been more careful to keep his work secret, his friend would still be alive. He'd witnessed, first-hand, the uncompromising mercilessness of Gyge's Ring.

The three other Ring Leaders explained the functions of their respective Rings in finance, personnel, and procurement.

Barscadden turned his attention to Andrew. 'It goes without saying, we work as a team. Use the expertise of your fellow Ring Leaders when you require it and they will call on you when they require computing support.'

The Ring Master and his Ring Leaders adjourned to a small bar, near the west wall of the boardroom. Barscadden served drinks as they chatted beside a huge, plate glass, window that offered a spectacular view.

As he listened to their conversations, Andrew felt unnerved by harrowing stories of past activities recounted by his fellow Ring Leaders.

Earlier, he'd asked Julie about Gyge. 'Was he a Greek God or something?'

Julie told him, 'No, Gyge was a poor, downtrodden, shepherd but honest. He sheltered in a cave one day and found a gleaming gold ring. When he put it on, he became invisible. Cut a long story short, he turned bad, deceived, swindled, betrayed and stole from others.'

Andrew's doubts escalated as he realised it was far too late for second thoughts about joining Gyge's Ring.

Fourteen

With the induction of Andrew Portcairn done, Barscadden returned to his seat and called on the others to follow. 'Colleagues, there are no apologies and nothing to report from our last meeting. We move on to consider progress reports. Peter, can you update us on the Rehab programme?'

'Certainly, Sir James.'

Peter tabled a detailed summary of quarterly finances for the Rehab AVC programme. He allowed a minute for them to scan the paper then gave his report. 'Our Rehab programme has operated now for eight years, and to date, we have welcomed over four hundred and seventy former violent and dangerous criminals onto our programme.'

'Excellent news.' Barscadden enthused.

Peter read from the paper. 'Sales of goods from our Rehab AVCs are progressing well. In the past quarter, they have made thirty sales and generated almost fourteen million. Profit levels are strong and looking positive for the future.'

'Is the new technology working out?' Julie asked.

'Yes, our customers are well pleased. Julie's new technology has made a dramatic impact on the range of goods that our Rehab AVCs can produce. UK sales are still few, of course, slightly more in Europe. The best markets for our products are the Middle East, Far East, North and South America.' Peter read from his papers.

Julie looked up from the paper. 'Payments to caseworkers have increased significantly.'

Silence as they scanned the paper to find the details, then Peter spoke. 'Yes, that's correct. Recruitment of violent criminals onto our Rehab programme is dangerous work. When we started, WRATH handled the casework until I trained the specialist caseworkers. I reviewed their performance and I decided on a new fee of twenty thousand for each successfully recruited violent criminal.'

Julie shook her head. 'An extra five grand is a hefty increase for each one.'

'Agreed, and reflects the fact that caseworkers often accept a Rehab case at short notice, and therefore, at much greater risk,' Peter replied.

An uneasy silence descended over the table while Julie considered the figures. Andrew watched the opposing body languages and kept quiet.

He liked Julie and wanted to take her side but didn't know about the Rehab programme or what they were talking about, and didn't want to show his ignorance.

The finance Ring Leader raised a hand before he spoke. 'The new price will have little impact on overall profit. I'm happy to support the fee increase.'

Peter said, 'Thus far, all criminals contracted onto our Rehab programme have joined in good health, and have been fully integrated back into the community. That's not a trivial achievement.'

Barscadden ended the impasse when he said, 'I suggest we agree these finances so long as their work continues at this high level of success. Let's move on. Julie, can we have your report on new business?'

Julie gave a hand gesture to show she agreed. 'And now for something completely different, as they say. I'm working on a new food process. It has potential for massive financial gain and immense political advantage.'

Julie handed out copies of a twenty-nine-page report entitled SeaPro Ltd. 'May I have the projector?' She rose from her seat.

On the table screen, a BARSCO screen saver moved around the screen until Barscadden tapped a slide projector icon.

A large piece of the wall behind him floated upward and disappeared into the ceiling. A large silver-grey screen appeared.

The lighting adjusted automatically to dim the light above and beside the screen. Curtains glided from recessed panels in the wall to cover the windows.

Julie walked to the screen and an infrared beam detected her presence. She accessed the presentation slides on her PA mobile. It connected wirelessly with the projector.

She turned to address the table. 'The process is simple. Fish fillets are converted by an enzyme process to produce a high-quality ingredient for the food industry.'

Then, she turned her attention to the screen. 'Slide one.' Her first slide showed a range of BARSCO products stacked on a table.

'These products all have one thing in common. They need food ingredients to add functional properties for product improvement.'

'Slide two,' she called out.

A second slide replaced the first, showing familiar fish laid out side by side on a large stone slab.

Peter Bromlee threw his copy of the report to the centre of the table.

'This isn't viable. Fish extracts aren't—'

She turned and rounded on him. 'Hold that thought right there, Peter.'

'*Julie.*' Barscadden's voice carried a reprimand.

'May I be allowed to continue?' she asked.

Barscadden exchanged eye contact with Peter, and replied, 'Please.'

'Here, we have endangered fish: haddock, cod, herring and whiting. Stocks are low and fishing quotas are tough.

'My new process will use vast reserves of other fish that the average house person would never buy because they're ugly or odd-coloured. In particular, a cheeky rogue called the black fiddle fish.'

'I've known a few of them.' Barscadden sniggered.

'Slide three,' she called. The screen changed to show the stone slab, bearing a long black fish with a large gaping mouth. It had the overall shape of a fiddle, with peculiar line markings, which extended from the middle to the end of the tail like the strings of a fiddle.

'Slide four,' she called. It showed a trawler making its way through heavy seas.

'The British fleet is tied up with EU quotas. Fighting has broken out over fishing rights. There have been cod battles and herring skirmishes.

'This new process will send the UK fleet to fish vast stocks of black fiddle fish. When fully operational, this process will provide enormous support for the UK economy, and it will attract significant political leverage.'

'Why this particular fish?' Peter asked.

'It's a deep-sea fish and as you can see, it's not a pretty sight. Stocks of black fiddle are high. Its reproductive capacity can accommodate extensive fishing. This fact is well documented in the report.'

'Why now?' Peter asked.

'The fiddle fish fillets are grey and dirty-looking,' Julie replied.

The finance Ring Leader shrugged. 'So, there's no market for them?'

'Correct, but the new process eliminates colour and reduces the fillets to an acceptable off-white, odourless and tasteless liquid.'

'Useful, but fish soup is hardly new.' Peter sounded disappointed.

Another Ring Leader chimed in. 'It does not sell well.'

Julie smiled. 'Fish soup is a fair description. I'm not selling fish soup. My product will sell as a premier food ingredient with unique functional properties.'

'Functional properties?' Another asked.

Julie spoke slowly. 'Food manufacturers use single function food ingredients to add gelling, or foaming, or water retention to their food products.

'The new product is multifunctional. That means, one ingredient with several properties will replace several ingredients with one property.'

'Do you have any figures?' Barscadden asked.

'In BARSCO products, we use four separate food ingredients. Annually, we buy four hundred tonnes at a cost to us of two grand per tonne. I calculate we can reduce the volume to around sixty tonnes of one multi-functional ingredient.

'Plus, we will sell the multi to the food industry for a premium price. Food manufacturers would still make significant savings on reduced volumes,' Julie said.

Peter clapped his hands. 'Impressive. I apologise for my earlier comments.'

Barscadden tapped the table. 'Does the process work?'

Julie pointed to the tabled document. 'This report details analysis and tests by an independent food research institute. A comparison has been made against a range of traditional food ingredients. It seems that a multifunctional food ingredient works better than a cocktail of single function ingredients.'

Julie turned to the end of the report and read aloud. 'It has functional properties near-perfect in foaming, gelling, emulsification, binding of colours, and binding of water.

'The raw material is economical, renewable and has unlimited commercial potential. It will greatly reduce the environmental impact of food manufacture around the world.'

Barscadden beamed his delight with an open mouth smile. His mind latched onto the prospects of a global prize with magnificent potential. Then, one thought grabbed him like a vice. He wanted this jewel. Only he could turn this product into a world phenomenon, worth tens of billions.

Fifteen

Barscadden joined Julie at the screen to examine the trawler. He turned back, beaming an ear-to-ear smile. Then, he returned to his seat, unable to conceal his delight.

'This is excellent. Of course, it makes sense to have one ingredient replace a basket of others. Globally, such a product would have a great impact on the environment.'

Julie basked in the smiling admiration of the other Ring Leaders. 'If we put the British fishing fleet back in business—the political kudos will be substantial. Not to mention spin-offs in shipbuilding, finance and production.'

Barscadden stared at the slide as his mind switched to hyperdrive. Others showed their recognition by rattling and tapping on the table. For some, admiration turned to envy.

'Did you have any difficulty obtaining this report?' Peter asked, although he knew the answer.

She smiled. 'I had a rather pleasant trip to Amsterdam.'

Barscadden waved his copy of the report in the air. 'Tell me you have an asset in this company.'

'Unfortunately, the asset was prepared to double deal. I had to put him out of business.'

'Maybe that should have been a job for WRATH.' Peter sounded concerned and chastised her with eye contact.

Julie frowned. 'I always had the situation under control. Early indications suggested negotiations would be amicable. However, it became clear the asset had other ideas.'

Peter nodded supportively. 'Situations do change. I would prefer you to have someone watching your back.'

Julie glanced back to the slides. 'I hear you. In fact, Amsterdam afforded me an opportunity to make a conclusive field test on BRO.'

Barscadden raised his eyebrows. 'Yet more good news. I'm overwhelmed.'

Rather than continue to slide five, Julie jumped to slide seven. The screen displayed a close-up picture of a blue-ringed octopus.

'As you know, the Barscadden Foundation supports academic research in anti-venom sera for combating snakebite.

77

I have adapted their research to produce the BRO product for WRATH.'

Peter asked, 'Are you saying you've overcome the delivery problem?'

Julie addressed the other Ring Leaders. 'For those not familiar with BRO, the blue-ringed octopus, its venom blocks nerve endings to produce paralysis. An octopus bite can inject venom directly into the bloodstream of its prey. We need an oral delivery but stomach acid destroys the venom.'

'What's your improvement?'

'Recently, my researchers discovered that high levels of sugar protect the BRO venom against stomach acid. I have now confirmed their finding with a field trial.'

Barscadden rapped the table. 'Well done.'

'I can report the asset achieved total body paralysis in less than a minute.'

The finance Ring Leader tapped a finger on the table. 'Good work on BRO. But who owns the IPR on the food ingredient?'

Julie returned to her original sequence. 'Slide five.'

The screen showed the entrance to a modern industrial building. 'A company in Greenock hold the intellectual property rights. They have a small factory financed by the inventor and a group of local businessmen.' After a short pause, she called out, 'Slide six.'

The screen showed a picture of two men and a woman standing in a car park. 'The inventor on the left is a wholesaler of spices and condiments. The woman is his wife. The other man is an engineer. Insignificant people with no notable contacts.'

Julie signalled to Barscadden that she'd finished.

Barscadden shuffled his meeting papers together and now appeared anxious to leave. 'Let's move on now. Andrew. Is ALICE getting her snout dirty?'

Andrew jerked his head excitedly. 'Absolutely.'

'Then, please, brief the others on all of ALICE's beguiling charms. I have another meeting to attend. Peter, will you chair the remainder?'

Barscadden left the room, his mind on fire with new business ideas. He summoned his secretary and ordered her to line up four successive phone calls.

*

As Andrew tabled a small booklet, Peter asked, 'What's this about?'

'I've successfully raped Janet,' he replied.

'What?' Peter and the others drew concerned expressions.

Julie shook her head. 'He *means*, the joint academic network, JANET.'

Andrew agitated apologetic hands. His attempt at humour fell flat. 'Sorry.'

Julie said, 'As you know, the Foundation built a new library at Doncaster. We installed a supercomputer for their library services. It's linked to JANET and Andrew has configured it so we can hack into almost any academic computer in the country.'

Several Ring Leaders whistled through their teeth. 'I knew there would be something for us,' one Ring Leader said to another.

Andrew explained, 'Most academic computers are linked to a central computer via a server in their university, so they can access e-mail, libraries, databases and the net. A joint academic network system, called superJANET, links all UK university libraries.

'I've piggy-backed a powerful hardware processor on Doncaster's supercomputer. Our processor is called ALICE, and through ALICE, we can access almost all PCs on the entire superJANET network.'

'How does it work?' Peter asked.

'Choose an academic target and we send them a loaded email. When it's opened, our hack installs and we access the target computer by remote through our processor. Full details of what, when and how are in the booklet.'

Peter shook his head. 'People will ignore spam email.'

'Yes, they will. Our email will be sent from the academic's local library. A query about possible fines for overdue books. An academic will open that email,' Andrew replied.

'What does ALICE stand for?'

'It's not an acronym. The Ring Master chose the name. Draw up your shopping list of academics. Professor Blackhest will co-ordinate the targets.'

Julie lifted the booklet. 'Read through the instructions and select your targets. We'll find out what they're doing. If you have any questions—contact me or Andrew.'

Peter browsed the booklet. 'Thanks, Andrew. It sounds promising.'

No-one intimated further business, so Peter closed the meeting.

As they left the boardroom in pairs, Andrew kept step with Julie.

She scanned her messages while she walked.

She side-glanced him. 'We need to work on your presentation skills.'

'Yes, sorry about that. This Rehab AVC programme sounds fantastic.'

'Yes, it is.'

'We're actually involved in rehabilitation of violent criminals? Does it work? I mean, don't they re-offend when they return to the community?'

With a wry smile, she toyed with his ignorance. 'It works exceptionally well, and yes, they are successfully re-integrated back into the community. There are no guarantees, of course, but thus far—we've had no re-offenders.'

'How does it work?' he asked as they stepped into the busy executive office.

She stopped, faced him and leaned closer to his ear. 'With simple lateral thinking, you can achieve absolutely anything.'

Then, she raised her eyebrows and cocked her head to one side. After a momentary pause, she turned and moved along the corridor with a broad smile on her face. When one of the secretarial staff passed her, she returned a smile.

Julie stopped and turned around to speak to him. 'Oh, Andrew, I'm sorry, I almost forgot to ask. How is your mother?'

'She's good. Running around like a ten-year-old.'

Julie nodded positively. 'Glad to hear it.'

'I can't thank you enough. When her heart surgeon told me her heart was failing, and she only had a few weeks to live, I felt so helpless. I thought I'd lose her. I don't know how you convinced Sir James to admit her to the clinic for a heart transplant. I will always be grateful.'

'We own the clinic. It provides senior staff with the best health care. You are now a senior, so your mum became a priority for us,' Julie said.

'Her surgeon said she would need to wait years for a donor heart. How did the clinic find one within ten days?'

'Our surgeons are the best in the world.'

Andrew felt guilty and emotional.

Julie asked, 'What is it?'

'BARSCO has given me back my mother, and it's like someone has taken out an old battery and put in a new one. I have my mum back. I feel I should be paying into a health fund or doing something to show my gratitude. What should I do?'

'Serve the Gyge's Ring to the utmost of your ability and that will be payment enough.'

Sixteen
Victoria Harbour, Greenock

During the first week of April, Gavin had installed everything he needed to run a small laboratory for SeaPro. As he parked his car, he thought of how to arrange the laboratory to suit his style of working, especially since he didn't have Christine Willsening to help him with basic lab work.

He did his SeaPro work in the evenings and weekends, and didn't want Christine making complications while he talked to Emma.

'Hello, Gavin,' Emma called as she stood at the entrance to the building.

Gavin noticed her checking the time on her wristwatch. 'Hi, Emma, sorry I'm late. I was walking with Kim and the time slipped.'

'It's all right.'

Gavin felt a need to explain. 'She's in a foul mood. I thought a walk might cool her temper but I'm glad to be here.'

Emma walked on ahead. Inside the building, she stopped and turned. 'Jim and Walter are scouring the city for a new valve.'

'No problem. I've plenty to do in the lab.' He stepped past her in the corridor.

She followed him into the laboratory and asked, 'How is Siobhan getting on?'

While he opened his briefcase and retrieved his papers. 'Fine. She's married to a physics teacher called Allan. They have a daughter, Kirsty, and they live in Renfrew.'

'I'm pleased for her. I liked Siobhan. Are you still close to her?'

'She's my rock. University was tough. I'm not that bright and she pulled me through it.'

Emma smiled. 'I remember the first night I met her in your house. You went to the bathroom and Siobhan waved a clenched fist in my face.'

'Why?'

'She told me she would punch my lights out if I hurt you.'

'Did she, really?'

'Yes. I thought it wonderful how she cared so much for you. I expect she would like to thump me now.'

Gavin smiled. 'Not now. I've told her I'm working for you.'

Gavin had been born at home, on the living-room carpet, in Govan, on the south side of Glasgow. He grew up in a two-bedroom tenement flat and shared a bedroom with his eight years older sister.

When he reached his teens, they devised a makeshift partition with curtains for their privacy. They shared the bedroom for much of his teenage years, and while sharing had no effect on his sister, it left him with a natural shyness.

Siobhan had taken him under her wing, and her group of school friends adopted him as one of their own. For eight years, he hung out with Siobhan and her friends, and almost by a process of osmosis, he became their pet boy.

Emma walked around Gavin to cast her eye over the new laboratory, which had begun to take shape then turned to face him. 'Do you have everything you need?'

'Yes, thanks. I'm curious, though. Why six of everything? Six beakers. Six flasks. It's like a grand tea set.'

'We got a job lot and six was the minimum.' They laughed.

Gavin switched on several machines. 'All the equipment is up and running.'

'Thank goodness. The supplier is dropping in later to check you're satisfied. Everything else okay?'

'What safety procedures does Jim use with his enzyme?'

'You'll need to ask him. Is it important?' Emma raised her eyes.

Gavin inspected a bottle of the enzyme solution Jim had provided for the SeaPro process. They stored the dark-brown solution in an old clear plastic water bottle, which he rotated in his hand. 'This has no product label or safety advice.'

Emma glanced over. 'What do you need?'

'Fresh pineapples until I can order inhibitors.'

'Why?'

'In case of accidents.'

Her voice deepened with concern. 'What kind of accident?'

'The enzyme is used to digest protein. Even a small splash on the skin or the eyes could cause scarring.'

Emma frowned with concern. 'Oh, goodness—that does sound risky.'

Gavin smiled. 'The pineapple plant has natural protection. A set of inhibitor molecules that block protease enzymes. Fresh pineapple will do fine until I can order inhibitors.'

'In … hibitors?' She thought for a moment. 'I'll fetch some tins of pineapple chunks.'

'Not tinned—they're heat sterilised. Heat destroys the inhibitors. It must be fresh.'

'Okay, I'll get fresh. Coffee in ten minutes?' Emma turned to leave.

'Yes, thanks.'

Gavin continued with his work until he heard people talking in the main hall of the factory. He walked along the corridor and into the hall. Jim and Walter chatted as they extracted a new valve from a brown box.

'Hi,' Gavin said when he caught sight of Jim.

'Everything going all right?' Walter asked.

Gavin raised a positive hand. 'Yes, I've started protein assays of the latest batch.'

Walter gave Gavin a flat-lipped smile. 'Fine.'

'Good—good.' Jim sounded pleased but he had his mind on his new valve.

To get their attention, Gavin fetched the bottle of enzyme and plonked it on the bench beside the new valve. 'This isn't regular commercial enzyme is it?'

Jim stopped fiddling with the valve. 'Eh … that's right—it isn't.'

Jim and Walter exchanged uneasy looks.

Walter cocked his head. 'Is that a problem?'

'No problem, but if you plan to scale-up, how will you maintain future supplies?'

Jim seemed relieved and replied, 'I see. Yes, well, enzyme supplies won't be a problem because our enzyme is self-generating.'

Gavin shook his head. 'What?'

Jim shrugged. I don't know how but that's the end result.'

Gavin laughed aloud. He thought he'd just heard the silliest comment ever about an enzyme. Even sillier than some of exam howlers he'd read in student answers.

Disappointment took over when he thought his fears had come true. A crackpot project that would collapse as soon as he started.

'Enzymes are proteins. They aren't alive. They can't self-generate.'

Jim shrugged. 'Well, maybe you'll have a better explanation.'

Gavin chewed his bottom lip. 'What do you mean?'

Jim racked his mind for a moment. 'About fourteen months ago, Emma and I were on a weekend break at our holiday home in Oban. We were walking along the shore one morning when we came across a dead seal, a young one.'

Walter added, 'That winter, a number of seals washed up on beaches around the Scottish coastline.'

Jim continued, 'It had been in cold water and decay hadn't started. We hauled it up to the car and took it back to the cottage. When we moved it into the warm kitchen, it decayed rapidly, and to avoid a mess, we placed it in a large zinc bath.

'By evening, it had reduced to a fluid soup, and we recognised that something novel had occurred. I put some of the fluid into a pot with fish bought from the fishmonger. Within ten minutes, the fish, including bones, had reduced to a thick soup.'

'Why did you do that?' Gavin asked.

'I thought I could produce an animal feed supplement for the farmer along the road,' Jim replied.

Emma added. 'In exchange for fresh eggs and vegetables.'

Jim continued, 'Then, I did some crude kitchen tests and discovered the exceptional functional properties of the fish soup.'

Gavin furrowed his eyebrows. 'So, the source of enzyme is where, exactly?'

Jim shook his head. 'No idea. In the big fridge, we have a large tank and the enzyme is busy digesting scrap meat from the butchers. The cold slows it down.

'Every week, we set up a fresh batch with more scrap meat and seed it with one tenth of the soup from the previous batch. We filter the soup, chill it, and that's our enzyme solution. I suppose it came from the original seal.'

Gavin nodded to show he understood. 'Okay, sounds as if you have bacteria from the dead seal producing your enzyme. Re-seeding with new meat keeps the bacteria growing and producing fresh enzyme.'

Jim tapped a finger on the bottle. 'Part of your job is to characterise our enzyme, identify the source and grow it on a larger scale.'

'Why did you choose the black fiddle fish?' Gavin asked.

Jim replied, 'Local fishermen in Oban gave me black fiddle for free because they can't sell the dark flesh in the market. Fish is fish. I don't mind the colour. When I tried the enzyme on a black fiddle fish, the dark flesh became off-white. Result!'

Emma slipped into her outdoor coat. 'I'm off to fetch fresh pineapple for Gavin.'

'Pineapples?' Jim asked.

Gavin replied, 'I'll extract some crude inhibitors from pineapple to provide an emergency spray for accidental splashes.'

'Good idea. You're right. The enzyme attacks skin like the blazes.' Jim rolled up his sleeve to show a circular red scar on his underarm and wrist. Emma came over to look.

Jim rubbed his scar. 'On that first night with the seal, I splashed some of the soup on my shirt sleeve. I didn't feel it stinging me until I had a bath—then it burned like hell.'

Emma examined his scar. 'I didn't know about that.'

Jim patted her on the shoulder. 'Darling, you worry if I spend too much time in the loo.' Then, he turned to Walter. 'Come on, let's get this valve installed.'

Gavin retreated to the small laboratory where he sat down, sighed loudly and buried his face in his hands. Panicky spasms clenched the pit of his stomach.

Unknown bacteria, unknown enzymes, no safety procedures. *What am I doing here? I have to bail out.*

The idea of extracting enzymes from dead tissue had always bothered him. He got most of his enzymes from a commercial bottle, and even though some of them were deadly, he didn't feel they were dangerous when they came out of a bottle.

A lion tamer doesn't step into the ring with a strange lion. The nasty looking scar on Jim's arm gave a stark warning. Every fibre of his professional training warned him to walk away.

He thought about asking Christine to phone Jim and say he'd contracted double pneumonia and couldn't continue with the work.

SeaPro would find another biochemist. He imagined Christine speaking on the phone. The picture made him feel much better.

Then, he recalled the wonderful smile on Emma's face each time she greeted him. Memories flooded his mind and drowned his concerns.

Seventeen

As they prepared the new valve, Jim resumed his conversation with Walter about the damage young Davy had caused. The lad hadn't cleaned the tanks and residual solid sludge had split a valve seal.

Since his pet had run off, Davy had spent every spare minute trying to find the dog. Now, Davy hadn't been around for several weeks, and all of the tanks need cleaning.

Jim cursed Davy for leaving without telling anyone, and suspected his homeless sister might have found a new squat for the two of them.

Davy's sister had caused trouble recently when Emma told her to stop hanging around the factory.

Walter shook his head dismissively. 'Davy knows next to nothing about the process. At worst, he might have stolen some tools.'

Jim raised a bunch of keys. 'I'll change the locks on all the doors, just as a precaution.'

Emma called out from the office. 'Jim … Mr Horissey from Mascarri's office is here.'

'Right, I'm on my way.'

Jim stamped into the boardroom and slammed the door shut. Instead of charging SeaPro for his time, Tony Mascarri had received a share in the company. Now, several weeks had passed without any word.

Jim glared at the man in front of him. 'I don't know you.'

The man offered his business card. 'Jacksan Horissey, partner, with—'

'Where the hell is Tony?' Jim snapped.

'I'm afraid, he's still away on business,' Jacksan replied.

'When will he return?' Emma asked.

Jacksan turned to face her. 'I can't say, exactly.'

Jim scowled. 'Why is he not returning my calls?'

'His mobile is in his desk. He doesn't have it with him.'

Jim demanded, 'What have you learned about the work he did for me?'

'I've spoken with the food research institute. They sent final reports directly to Mr Mascarri. He processed their invoice and we have duly paid.'

Jim shouted, 'Where are my reports?'

Jacksan delved into his briefcase, and pulled out a report. 'I found this one in the safe.'

Jim pulled the file out of Jacksan's hand. He closed his eyes briefly as he gripped it.

'When he's sober or straight, or whatever the hell you call it—tell him to phone me immediately.' Jim spoke in a voice that ordered, *get out of my sight*.

Emma opened the door, and Horissey left the office.

With a look of trepidation, Jim flicked the pages of the report. If the product had mediocre properties, it would never compete against traditional food ingredients.

He sat down and opened it. Emma stood behind him to look over his shoulder. A couple of minutes later, he skipped to the concluding pages.

He held the report up high and roared, 'My stuff is the best. It's brilliant.'

Emma leaned down and kissed his cheek. 'Well done.'

He stood up and hugged her. 'I've hit the jackpot. This calls for a celebration. Call the partners. Don't tell them anything—just invite them to our house tomorrow night for a drink.'

She cuddled against him. 'I'm so pleased for you.'

'Thanks for all the *savoir-faire* you do with the partners. If it weren't for your charm, they would have pulled out long ago. We're a great partnership, you and I.'

'Yes, we are.'

'I know our marriage isn't as fulfilling as you would like. But—'

She put her finger on his chin. 'Don't say that. Our marriage is fine. I have everything I need, and much more than many women.'

'You know what I mean, don't you?'

'The physical side isn't important to me. I can do without it. No marriage is perfect.'

He reached out and rubbed her arm. 'I do love you the best way I can.'

Emma smiled. 'I know you do. I'm happy with what we have.'

'We should let Shawlens know he's working with top-quality goods.'

*

Jim told Walter the news, and together they went to the lab. Gavin read the summary, then raised his head and smiled. 'Congratulations.'

Excited, Jim raised his voice. 'We need to hurry along the patent work. It has to be secured before I enter discussions with the finance people and government departments.'

Gavin agreed. 'It won't be too long before people start to sniff around.'

They all laughed at Gavin. The smell of fish hung in the air and he hadn't intended a pun.

'Can you schedule in a bit more time?' Emma asked him.

Gavin gazed into her eyes and dismissed all thoughts of backing out. 'I can schedule more time if you can afford the fees.'

'Yes, yes—go ahead. The others will agree now we have this golden report,' Jim enthused.

Walter, Emma and Jim returned to the office. Emma made coffee.

Jim switched off the kettle. 'Let's go now for a celebration drink.'

Emma switched the kettle back on. 'I'm still waiting on Paris to return my call.'

Jim pleaded with his eyes. 'They can wait.'

Emma shook her head. 'No, they can't. The muntok white harvest is on now. The price should tumble. I need a better price to offset the high price I paid for the asta black. You know that supply is erratic for those peppers and the price can bolt.'

Jim conceded. 'Of course, you're right. We can't ignore our spices and condiments business. We still need our bread and butter. Make sure delivery dates are confirmed in writing.'

Gavin declined to go for a drink as his experiments were nearing completion.

Walter and Jim strolled to a local bar ten minutes from the factory. They barely gave a second glance to the large SUV parked across the road or the woman and two men inside.

Emma brought two cups of coffee into the lab. She sipped her coffee as she stared at the flashing lights on one of Gavin's machines.

Gavin cocked his head. 'I would have taken a message for you.'

'Just let them go. Men need space from time to time. Chris was the same.'

'I wish I'd found out when you divorced him.'

Emma sipped more coffee, hesitant to re-visit that part of her life. She thought about leaving the room. 'I'm glad we didn't get back together.'

'Why?'

Emotion sapped her voice. 'It would have crushed me if you'd hated me as much as Chris did.'

'I couldn't hate you.'

Emma had sensed him drifting from her. Little negative things he'd mentioned, concerns about the process and whether it would work, and how she would feel if it failed. She decided that opening up a bit more would pull him in a little closer.

'I didn't think Chris could hate but he got so desperate for a family. When it didn't happen, we went for tests. It turned out he had a good BCMPT.'

'What's that?'

'I thought you were a biochemist,' she teased.

'It's not a biochemistry acronym.'

'It's a bovine cervical mucus penetration test. They tested how well his sperm could penetrate a tube of bovine cervical mucus. His sperm were A1. Other tests showed my cervical mucus was the problem. Superglue, I remember the consultant's description.'

'That must have been quite a shock?'

'They might as well have told me I was dying from cancer. At first, Chris seemed to understand. We did ask about IVF.'

'Did you give it a try?'

'Too expensive and no guarantee.'

'I can't imagine how painful that must have been.'

Her expression indicated no hope and she sensed his sadness. 'Our world just shattered. All of his brothers and sisters have children. I felt totally helpless and depressed. I made everyone around me suffer. I lost interest in keeping myself and my home.'

'Oh … Emma, I can't imagine you like that.'

'I almost lost my job at the bank. As I told you, Chris started to drink. One night, we fought, and he punched me. We both came to the same miserable point.'

'I'm sorry I spoke.' Their eyes locked together.

Emma felt relieved to have told him. In a way, she wanted him to know she'd been punished for the pain she'd caused eighteen years ago. In another way, she'd pulled him back to her side. Just where she wanted him.

*

A man in the SUV received a call from his colleague to report on the movements of Jim and Walter. Then, he and the woman left the vehicle and walked across the road to the factory. The man spoke to Emma who showed them to the laboratory.

'Good evening, Dr Shawlens,' the man said when he entered the room.

Gavin shook his head with surprise. 'Titch! I might have guessed it would be your crowd.'

Gavin knew Russell Titchmann from equipment suppliers, M.Y. Barta. He shook Gavin's hand. Emma left them to talk.

Titchmann visited Kinmalcolm regularly to sell equipment and consumables. Gavin despised Titchmann's lavishness, his well-tanned, bald head, manicured fingers, diamond earrings and diamond cufflinks.

Gavin didn't like his methods. Titch regularly pumped technical staff at Kinmalcolm to find out who had new research money to spend. Who had new projects starting up.

'I'd like to introduce my new colleague, Maria Munsdale.'

Maria handed her business card to Gavin, and he noted that Maria C. Munsdale BSc was an area sales manager.

She topped out at over six-foot tall with broad shoulders, a chubby face, a short pageboy hairstyle and large dangly hoop earrings.

'I'll be handling this important part of the country for M.Y. Barta. Please phone me anytime, day or night. I always give excellent service.' She released his hand, slowly.

The woman had an artificial seductive voice, which began with an insulting purr then developed into a dirty promise.

The tips of her fingers brushed the palm of his hand, and Gavin knew she'd just made a pass at him.

Titch rubbed the top of one of the machines. 'Any problems with our equipment?'

Gavin shook his head. 'No complaints but it's still early days.'

'Excellent. This project has such great potential. We want our equipment to make a good contribution. Is there anything else we can provide, ex-demo, of course?' Titch asked.

Gavin smiled. 'I have everything I need.'

'I know Jim and Walter are anxious about the patent. Is it coming along all right?'

Gavin hesitated. 'Erm … it's okay.'

Titch drew a salacious grin. 'Maria is a biochemist, and very willing, if you need a pair of technician hands to speed things along. I see you don't have Christine here to help with the basic stuff.'

Gavin contemplated the smirk on Maria's face and imagined her more suited to sumo wrestling than technical support. 'No thanks.'

Gavin felt wary of their familiarity and thought Jim and Walter must have sought advice from Titch before they contacted the University.

Gavin wondered if Titch had recommended him to Jim Patersun? It might be better not to know if he had. He didn't want to owe Titch any favours.

Maria used one hand to stroke the other. 'Dr Brian Herding says my hands-on work is excellent.'

Gavin turned to face her. 'I'll bet he did.'

Titch moved closer to Gavin. 'Will you be running the function tests, or are you having them done outside?'

'Why do you need to know?'

Titch took a catalogue from his briefcase and placed it on Gavin's bench. 'We can supply the equipment. Maria could calibrate it and do some of the tests for you.'

Gavin flapped his fingers to reject their catalogue. 'Don't bother with that. I won't need any equipment.'

Titch surveyed the apparatus on the benches. 'Okay, I understand perfectly.'

Shit! That was a mistake. Titch had fished for information, and now he knew an outside company had done the function tests. It wouldn't take much for him to find out where.

The two reps left when Gavin told them he had work to finish off.

In his mind, they knew too much about the SeaPro process already, and he didn't want to be the one accused of passing on more details.

Gavin had always been cautious with Titchmann. Something about him didn't fit right. His spoken English seemed too perfect.

His expensive suit, Gucci moccasin shoes with tassels, Gucci interlocking Gs trouser belt, hand-stitched silk shirt and jewellery—all seemed too flash for an equipment rep.

He could just be an extravagant idiot, or he could be a commercial spy. Heck, the man could be an international criminal.

With such blatant opulence, he could be all three. He stood out as markedly different from all the other reps who visited Kinmalcolm.

Eighteen
Presnensky District, Moscow

The largest meat processing conglomerate in Russia, MeatPromena Inc, had a palatial head office in central Moscow. At his desk, chairman of the board of directors, Aleksandr Potersky drew on a Sobranie Black Russian while he contemplated his next meeting.

Potersky had multiple chins and receding short white hair. His puffy skin bulged over his collar and he carried a massive gut.

Too many years of hard drinking had enlarged his liver, and his yellow-tinged skin signalled impending organ failure.

He had spent most of his professional life in the Kremlin working for the KGB and its successor, the FSB. He boasted of a long history of hardness in dealings with adversaries and enemies of the State.

A dull and murky atmosphere haunted his office. A thick coat of cigarette tar and smoke particles covered the wood panels, curtains and ornate ceiling decorations.

Files, maps, and charts cluttered his desk. He had two ivory-coloured Bakelite telephones that were stained with nicotine.

Aleksandr stubbed his cigarette on a dinner-plate glass ashtray, which already overflowed with gold foil filters. A rapid knock on the door echoed in the room and then a young woman entered.

'Professor Nikolay Zavarok is waiting outside.'

Aleksandr rose from his seat and walked to the door. 'Show him in. Make sure we are not disturbed.'

A moment later, he raised his arms high and met his old friend at the door. 'Welcome Nikky,' Aleksandr called in a hoarse voice. They hugged, kissed each cheek and locked their arms for a moment.

'Why is it you have the prettiest secretary, eh?' Zavarok asked.

'Oh, Tirina! She has looks but bitches every minute about her tiny flat. She thinks I still work the old miracles. How is your lovely Galeena? Is your boy still at university?'

'Good … Dmitri has done well at university. I am pleased with him,' Zavarok said.

Zavarok had served as a colonel in the old Soviet GRU. He had completed many successful operations that had pleased his superiors.

At forty-nine years of age, he had retired from fieldwork and concentrated on analysis for Russian military intelligence.

With a PhD in biological sciences from Moscow University, he had started his career at the secret Academy of Military Aviation, and for a time he worked in the Institute of Advanced Cosmic Biology.

At five foot ten, Zavarok towered over Aleksandr. He occupied a powerful-looking body, and his strong square face showed signs of harshness from more challenging times as a covert agent. He had specialised in biological warfare and had made several vital captures for the Soviet Union.

'You have read the reports from the White Knight team on this SeaPro technology?' Aleksandr asked.

'Yes, the team have done well.'

'You are too modest, Nikky. It's brilliant work. You should be congratulated at the highest level for setting up your White Knights in the UK.'

Aleksandr waddled around his desk to his chair, which creaked painfully when he eased back into the depression created by his backside. 'The highest importance has been attached to this fish process. We have been waiting for this technology for a long time.

'Our scientists have tried endlessly to overcome horrid fish smell. We have great fishing fleets and vast processing factories. Above all, we have greatest need.' Aleksandr pounded a clenched fist on his desk.

Zavarok observed strain on the old man's face. 'I understand.'

'I'm sure you do. That's why I must ask you to come out of retirement, travel to Scotland, and bring this technology home to me.'

'With respect, I have been out of the field for three years. Surely the TCT would—'

Aleksandr raised a hand. 'I wish I could send the TCT. They have an excellent record for avoiding international incidents.'

The Technology Capture Team had received most of their training from Zavarok and operated well as a team. Aleksandr paused, turned to the side window and gazed longingly at the Moscow River for a minute.

'Titchmann reports that timing is critical. We must be certain the process is complete before we take it. A biological specialist must assess progress and make the decision. Too soon would be a disaster if the work is incomplete. Too late might make capture impossible.'

'Has Titchmann made any further progress?'

'He identified a scientist completing the patent work.'

'Good. That person is a key.'

Aleksandr handed over a file, which had a photograph of Gavin Shawlens stapled to the outside. 'He's academic, single, financially stable but sexually bland. A loner of little consequence. I sent Katriana to bed the man but Titchmann does not believe she will snare him. I need you to take command.'

Zavarok inspected the photo, smiled and shook his head. Katriana was a massive woman with broad shoulders and a large chest. Shawlens didn't look desperate enough to bed a walrus, and the only way she would control him would be to sit on him.

Zavarok tucked the file under his arm. 'I'll contact Titchmann and get an update.'

'You will have full co-operation from every quarter. Contact me direct if necessary. I have permission to move mountains for this process.'

'What about security?' Zavarok asked.

'FSB have people in Scotland. Titchmann will arrange for you to meet them.'

The two men shook hands, hugged and then Zavarok walked to the door.

Before Zavarok reached for the doorknob, Aleksandr said, 'Nikky, I am brutally honest with you. *Demokratsiya* and our new economy are disappointments. New *biznizmeny* become billionaires and spend huge fortunes while our old and poor are destitute.

'Our great fishing fleets must have this technology. Cost is no object. Bring it home. Do this for me, Nikky.'

Nineteen
10 Downing Street, Westminster, London

The large wooden door creaked while it eased open. The Prime Minister's permanent private secretary entered the cabinet room. The Prime Minister leaned forward on his leather-covered chair.

Then, he glanced back to see the time on the Napoleon-style mantel clock on the marble fireplace behind him.

Beside him, his ministerial red box sat open with various papers scattered in and around it. At his side, Ian Soburman, Minister for the Department of Environment, Food, and Rural Affairs (DEFRA).

'Prime Minister. Sir James Barscadden is arriving,' his PPS announced.

The PM looked up from his papers. 'Ask him to wait … no, don't bother. Show him in.'

James Barscadden stepped out of his chauffeur-driven Rolls Royce and walked at a brisk pace to the entrance to No. 10 Downing Street.

The police officer on duty rang a bell to alert the porter, who opened the shiny black door to allow Barscadden to continue inside without breaking his stride.

Waiting for him, the PPS smiled courteously and then escorted Barscadden to the cabinet room before opening the door wide and announcing the visitor.

The Prime Minister and Soburman welcomed Barscadden with firm handshakes. The two politicians returned to their seats at the cabinet table. Barscadden took a seat opposite the Prime Minister.

'Coffee, James?' the PM asked.

'Yes, thank you.'

'Coffee for three, please.'

The PPS nodded and closed the large door.

'You know the Minister for DEFRA?' the PM asked.

'Yes, of course.' Barscadden kept his eyes on the PM and didn't acknowledge Soburman. They didn't like each other.

'How are you these days?' the PM asked.

'Fine, my business is growing, despite the best efforts of your government.' They all smiled.

'You said you wanted to discuss fishing policy, so I've asked Ian to join us.'

Barscadden didn't want anyone from DEFRA involved. He rearranged his agenda.

'Yes, I am considering an expansion into the fishery sector. Can you fill me in on this quota system business?' He turned to look at Soburman.

'Certainly, the UK fishing policy is governed by EU Common Fisheries Policy. Every year, they regulate the quantity of fish through a system of quota allocations.' Soburman spoke with a clinical tone.

'All fish?' Barscadden asked.

'Not all. Mostly white fish, cod and haddock. We share out our quotas amongst the UK skippers,' Soburman replied.

'Is it working well?' Barscadden asked.

Soburman gave a quick sideways squint to the Prime Minister, for reassurance, before he continued. An attempt to demean Barscadden because the information wasn't confidential.

'No. The Sea Fish Industry Authority tell me that the UK fleet is overfishing by around twenty percent.'

Barscadden asked Soburman. 'Why is that?'

Soburman read from a paper. 'Skippers say they need eighty-five grand per month for wages and boat costs. Some months, they may get less than sixty. They raise their income with black fish.'

'Black fish?' Barscadden raised his eyebrows.

'Black market fish,' Soburman replied.

'What measures have you taken to conserve fish stocks?' Barscadden asked.

Soburman shifted around in his chair. 'To protect employment and conserve fish, we have a process of decommissioning boats. Early retirement for skippers.'

The PM tapped a finger on the table. 'We pay them to scrap their boats—it's expensive.'

Barscadden returned a flat smile. 'Excellent. Just the picture I need to help me with my decisions. Thank you for that.'

The coffee arrived, and the three talked about the state of the economy in general. Barscadden engaged the PM's eyes. 'I do have a personal matter I wish to discuss with you while I have your attention.'

As a seasoned politician, Ian Soburman took the hint and gave them the room.

'I felt sorry to hear about your so-called cabinet colleagues.' Barscadden referred to recent political in-fighting troubles.

'You don't know the half of it, believe me. If I get another stab in the back, my liver will fall out.'

Barscadden had supported the PM's rise in politics, and they had been friends for many years. The PM trusted him.

'Not helpful,' Barscadden agreed.

'That's politics. Anyway, enough of my burdens. What can I do for you? Bearing in mind that I have the least power in this ramshackle Government.'

Barscadden opened his hands, palm up. 'I have news that will help you.'

'Go on.'

'At the present time, the British fleet is on the rack, and you're having problems controlling quotas. Yes?'

The PM agreed. 'Yes, but it is self-inflicted.'

'Other countries are encroaching on our fishing beds. Am I correct?'

'It's an on-going battle with Brussels. I would need to treble the number of fishery protection vessels to win that one. Not a cheap option.' The PM's expression confirmed a lack of success.

'What if I could get the British fleets back to full employment?'

'Don't tease me. I don't need it.'

'I'm serious about this.'

'In political terms, it would be enormous for the country. Financially, it would be a great boost for the economy. I fear you're going to ask me for a miracle.'

'Not this time, but it will require a careful political manoeuvre. Not a great one.'

'Go on, please.'

Barscadden spoke eagerly. 'My people have developed a process to convert non-quota fish into a high-quality food ingredient. Fishing fleets will be sent to fish non-quota fish. Markets are large, and stocks are vast. In particular, we have identified stock called the black fiddle fish. It is a deep-sea fish.'

The Prime Minister stood and clapped his hands. The prospect of a major boost to the fishing industry would be of enormous importance. He walked along the length of the cabinet table and around to his friend. They shook hands.

'James, what do you need to make this happen?'

'I want to ensure Britain retains the lead. The problem, as always, is the EU. They have a hefty tax on non-dairy food ingredients. The legislation is under review by trade committees. If we can exclude fish-derived food ingredients from this tax burden, then our product would have a significant future.'

The PM smiled, impressed.

Barscadden felt proud of his clever ploy to obtain protection for a product before its value became known.

The PM asked, 'Is that all?'

'Yes, that's all.'

'I'm sure I can persuade the Minister for DEFRA to support the protection of these vital food ingredients.'

'With as little briefing as possible to avoid a race to develop similar products.'

The PM smiled. 'Of course.'

'Thank you, Prime Minister.'

With a smile on his face, Barscadden retrieved a small jar of light-yellow cream from his jacket pocket. The name on the gold-coloured label read, Adipicene TR.

'Please, give this to your good lady wife.'

The PM's eyes lit up. 'Ah! The mystery cream.'

'For a wonderful lady.'

The PM marvelled at the small jar in his hand. 'Elizabeth is truly besotted with this. Her skin was always quite ruddy in places. Now, it's silky soft with no wrinkles or blemishes. James—you should have this on the market.'

'I so wish. It's enormously expensive to scale-up. Small scale it must remain for the time being. Anyway, thank you for your time.'

Barscadden left the cabinet office and walked past Soburman without looking in his direction.

When Soburman returned to the office, he found the PM with a deep frown on his face.

Soburman glanced back at the door. 'He is a bit of a cold fish.'

'What do you know about a fish called the black fiddle? For some reason, I recall that name but can't remember why.'

Soburman raised a hand to cover his mouth. His heart raced and the hairs on the back of his neck made him uncomfortable.

Hesitantly, he replied, 'You may have … come across that name … in security files relating to Beauford's Dyke.'

'Why on earth would a fish be reported in security files?' the PM asked.

'During the Second World War, German submarines probed the British coastline and attacked fleets fishing on the continental shelf.

'The fleets were sent to fish deep sea stock on the slope off the continental shelf because German U-boats kept away from the steep slope.'

'What has that got to do with the black fiddle fish?'

'The fleets found enormous stocks of black fiddle fish but they were of no use because the fillets are dark grey.

'Wartime boffins tried to produce white flesh using crude genetic and chemical mutation. The files contain grotesque photos of their experiments. Fish with two heads and the like.'

The PM glanced at the time. 'Is there a point to this story?'

'The boffins did increase reproduction fifty-fold so females could lay millions of eggs but the flesh remained a dirty grey.

'They returned thousands of mutant fish to the natural breeding grounds. When the war ended, the project ran down, and fish recaptured up to forty years later seemed perfectly normal.'

The PM asked, 'If a business planned to exploit this fish, would we have any concerns?'

'None, as far as I know. In fact, black fiddle fish have been found in the stomachs of seals washed up on the beaches.'

Soburman didn't volunteer that studies had been authorised to investigate unexplained deaths of seal, whale and dolphin found washed up on Scottish beaches.

'What's the connection with Beauford's Dyke?' the PM asked.

'As you are aware, Class One containment canisters were dumped in Beauford's Dyke during the fifties and sixties. It's a deep trench off the coast of Northern Ireland. Survey vessels monitor the dump and black fiddle is one of many fish found in the Dyke.'

Soburman didn't add that many Class One canisters dumped in Beauford's Dyke contained viral warfare agents that were resistant to destruction by conventional methods.

Isolated from hot springs and geysers, they possessed natural indestructibility and had been engineered to ensure the lands of an aggressor would remain contaminated for decades.

'Are the canisters still safe and sound?' the PM asked.

'As far as I know. Surveys haven't reported any problems with canisters.'

The PM frowned. 'It's probably all right then, safety wise?'

'As far as I am aware.'

Soburman chose not to say that survey vessels had only ever located, and subsequently monitored, twenty-two percent of canisters dumped in Beauford's Dyke.

Soburman smiled as he thought, *Barscadden, if you're going after the black fiddle fish, you'll have your arse well and truly kicked.*

Twenty
University of Kinmalcolm

Noise in the enzyme technology laboratory was greater than usual as a centrifuge and a fume cupboard competed to make the loudest racket. Christine Willsening, perched on a stool beside a spectrophotometer, grew more and more frustrated.

Almost six-thirty in the evening; everyone else had gone home. She slapped her hand on the bench, and scowled at a computer screen message: PROGRAM FAILED: INVALID PARAMETERS.

The machine had stopped running her procedure and required re-programming because someone had tried to modify the procedure without any idea of what to do. The instruction manual had disappeared years ago, and Christine tried every trick she knew to get the machine back on-line.

Emma Patersun knocked loudly then peered around the laboratory door.

Christine swivelled around on her stool. 'Can I help you?'

Emma raised a large brown envelope in the air. 'I'm looking for Gavin Shawlens.'

Christine stepped off her stool. 'They've all gone to a seminar. Can I take a message?'

Emma's expression signalled disappointment. 'I'd like him to look at this tonight.'

'I'm sorry, Dr Shawlens is having dinner with the speaker after the research seminar.'

Emma frowned. 'Okay, I'll probably drop by his flat and leave this with Kim.'

Christine spoke cautiously. 'Erm … Kim isn't good with documents. She's been known to tear them up in a temper.'

Emma raised her brows. 'Good God.'

Christine sighed loudly, and approached Emma as if she were about to reveal a confidence. The two women hadn't met until now. Christine scanned the writing on the brown envelope and the penny dropped. 'Is it SeaPro work?'

'Yes, it is.'

'Hi, I'm Christine. Gavin's technician.'

'Emma Patersun. Nice to meet you.'

'Kim's a horrible little bitch. Very possessive and tends to go ballistic when another female visits his flat. I thought I should warn you—if that's important.' Christine shifted her eyes to the envelope.

'I had no idea.'

With dramatic use of her hands, Christine gestured. 'Two months ago, he went off with flu, and I had to collect a PhD thesis from his flat. He was poorly, and I only offered to make him coffee. Kim chased me out of the kitchen so fast, my feet didn't touch the floor.'

Emma glared with concern. 'They must be close.'

'People tell him she's an evil bitch but he won't hear a bad word against her. She's a simple type, and he's her meal ticket.'

Emma stared at her envelope and couldn't hide her shock. 'I see … okay, thanks.'

'Look, Emma, he has to come back here for his jacket. If you leave your envelope with me, I'll give it to him.'

Emma's envelope contained a list of questions and comments on a draft patent application from her patent agent. She'd thought they might sit down over a light dinner and go over the report.

Emma left the building more quickly than she'd entered. She told herself that an emotional involvement with Gavin was out of the question. In her car, she reflected on what she wanted. *This is stupid, I'm married to a good man*, she thought.

Jim Patersun always treated her well, she had money, a great house in affluent Newton Mearns and a good car.

They hardly ever argued, and he liked to treat her to wonderful weekends in Paris, London or Barcelona. He let her run his spices and condiments business with minimal interference, and she loved her independence.

They made a great business couple but slept in separate bedrooms. Jim Patersun was not, had never been, and would never be—romantic.

Emma felt annoyed. Gavin had told her nothing about Kim, and by the sound of it, maybe Kim wasn't such a good catch. Disappointment filled her mind. She'd thought Kim would be someone similar to herself. Kim sounded exactly the opposite.

*

Lecturers, final year students, and research workers thronged Kinmalcolm's large science lecture theatre for their fortnightly research seminar. Professor Julie Blackhest drew her talk on industrial enzymes to a close. The audience showed their appreciation with loud applause.

Dr Charlie Jimison chaired the seminar. A short man with a bald head who regularly fidgeted with his frizzy, grey and white, caveman beard.

He rose from his seat in the front row as the applause died down and thanked Professor Blackhest for an interesting and informative talk.

Several in the audience asked questions and Julie dealt with them effectively. Charlie brought the seminar to a close. He asked the audience to join him in thanking Professor Blackhest for stepping in at the last minute to give her talk.

Many smiled appreciatively as they filed past Julie, Gavin, and Charlie Jimison at the front of the lecture theatre.

The Blackhest role model enthralled the females in the audience: successful scientist, Armani clothes and an attractive, sexy smile. She oozed enough palpable charm to mesmerise the males.

Charlie introduced Julie to Gavin, and when they shook hands, she smiled warmly to let him know she liked him. Julie had her presentation stored on a USB stick, and Gavin fetched it for her before he went back to his office to collect his jacket.

While they waited, Charlie discussed dinner options. Julie expressed a preference for Italian.

Charlie drove them to the *La Pagitalia* restaurant in the centre of Glasgow. The compact restaurant boasted stone-covered walls and flag-stoned floors, which gave the room a cool and airy ambience. Subtle wall lighting added a touch of warmth, and a glazed roof overhead gave a view of the night sky.

'What's it like working for Barscadden?' Gavin asked.

Julie swept her hand through her mop of dark copper-red hair, cut in a slicked-back style to emphasise her piercing emerald green eyes and perfect skin.

She smiled provocatively. 'It's good. As head of R and D, I enjoy the life of an academic and all the perks of a company executive.'

Charlie showed his prejudice. 'I expect you're on an obscene salary.'

'Oh, I never look at my salary line these days. The monthly bonuses take my breath away.'

Charlie shifted his eyes to Gavin. 'Of course, money is the foundation of all corruption.'

Gavin ignored him and turned to smile at her. 'I know Barscadden started with nothing, but he must be extremely wealthy now?'

Julie gave Gavin a warm smile. 'What is wealth? Barscadden has two chauffeurs, two pilots, a captain and crew. He has a mountain of responsibility, relentless business stress and chilling isolation. I have friends with no money or power but they have a happy and fun-loving family. In my eyes, they have the real wealth.'

Charlie's eyes reflected irritation as he turned and jerked an index finger aggressively at one of the waiters. Julie and Gavin raised their eyebrows to each other while the waiter ignored him.

His behaviour confirmed her earlier assessment—hostile male chauvinist.

A carafe of house wine arrived with the menu.

Gavin and Julie discussed the merits of squid cooked in its own ink before deciding on fresh mussels steamed in garlic sauce for a starter. Gavin pondered over the steak with veg and potatoes for his main meal. Charlie decided on a simple lasagne.

Julie shook her head. 'Gentlemen, surely we can be a bit more adventurous?'

She caught the attention of the headwaiter, and he arrived at her side. 'The roast halibut sounds, interesting, can you tell me more?' she asked as she sank her attractive eyes into his face.

The waiter told her exactly how the halibut would be cooked and presented. She checked the faces of her two companions. Gavin nodded and smiled. Charlie appeared uninterested.

'Roast halibut for three. A bottle of your best Sauternes, lightly chilled, please, to go with the halibut.' She smiled sweetly.

'Most certainly. An excellent choice if I may say.'

The waiter whipped the menus from the two men, and then eased the menu from her fingers.

'Sauternes? Isn't that a dessert wine?' Gavin asked.

'Yes, but it will go lovely with this fish—trust me.'

*

Charlie found it difficult to communicate with Julie. He saw a pushy woman rather than a successful and attractive scientist. It didn't take long for Charlie to discover himself surplus to requirements.

She ignored him, undermined him, challenged his views, and he got the message. Julie had smiled at Gavin so many times; Charlie thought she had a facial defect.

Charlie hadn't invited Julie to give a seminar. His scheduled speaker had dropped out at short notice and had organised Julie to take his place.

Charlie hurried his main meal, and apologised for not wishing to stay for sweet or coffee. When he left them, he felt relieved to be on his way. He had nothing in common with her and didn't like her superior attitude. As he put on his jacket, he glanced back at the table and saw their heads nodding closely in conversation.

Neither of them glanced over as Charlie walked out. He paused at the door to reflect. She had said her seminar topic would be on protease enzymes. And that her PhD student had worked on the enzyme bromelain. He had thought of Gavin Shawlens as a suitable dinner companion because of his work on bromelain.

Twenty-one
City Centre, Glasgow

When Charlie called it an early night, Julie felt relieved. Now, she could concentrate all her attention on Gavin. She had a question that needed an answer, and she wanted to hear what his answer would be. Julie put her hand on his wrist and gave it a little shake. 'Come on, you haven't smiled much tonight—let me see a smile.'

His half-smile stretched to a full open smile and he laughed with her. 'I'm enjoying your company.'

'I've read all your research papers. Your work on protease enzymes is impressive.'

'Thanks, I'm sorry, I haven't come across your work but your seminar tonight was excellent.'

'In industry, we don't publish much because of confidentiality issues. Anyway, how is your research coming along at Kinmalcolm?'

'It's good. I'm working on a plant protease called bromelain. It has novel therapeutic properties.'

Her eyes widened. 'Sounds interesting—tell me more.'

'I think it can be used to disperse blood clots that cause heart attacks and strokes.'

Julie raised her eyebrows. 'Really? If that's so, why isn't it on the market?'

'Only big pharma have money for the clinical trials to prove efficacy, and if they did, what would happen? People would eat fresh pineapple. There's no profit for them.'

Julie leaned forward, opened her hands palms up in front of him. 'You know, I'm always on the lookout for novel protease applications. We're working on a new food ingredient for use in soups, gravies and that sort of market.'

Gavin's face lit up. 'Snap! I'm also working on a new food ingredient. From fish. It has brilliant functional properties—' He stopped and a worried expression formed.

Julie noted his concern. 'It's okay. I understand. In industry, we're always paranoid about our secrets.'

She glanced to the side to watch a woman opposite kissing her partner. *Careful now, softly, softly, catchee monkey.*

Gavin frowned. 'Sorry ... that work is confidential. I can't say anything.'

Julie held his gaze. 'Understand completely. On the department tour, your laboratory impressed me. Well-equipped space, plus two postdocs and a technician. You must have a large research grant to support all of that?'

Suddenly, he became flustered. 'Yeah, erm ... excuse me.' He rose from his seat and hurried to the men's room.

Julie watched him walk away and shook her head with disappointment. Any academic with funding for three staff would be overflowing about research awards.

When he returned, he changed the subject back to the meal. His avoidance of a discussion on his funding only served to fuel her curiosity.

Every research academic she knew complained constantly about lack of research funding. It annoyed her that a research funding offer wouldn't hook Gavin Shawlens. She needed to re-think her plan. 'Did you ever consider working in industry?'

'The biotech industry?'

'Yes, you would have an opportunity to influence politicians and captains of industry. I regularly meet the science advisor to the Cabinet Office, and I help politicians develop their science strategy.'

She sounded boastful but saw from his expression that she hadn't offended him.

Gavin asked, 'Do they ever act on your advice?'

'The thing about politicians, they're not scientists. Most of them are as dense as horse shit and only half as clean. They need advisors to guide them and they'll listen to someone they think doesn't have an axe to grind.'

'So, you keep your axe behind your back.'

Julie smiled and gave him a look of encouragement. 'Actually, I chair an influential think-tank for science development and I'm recruiting new members. The remuneration and expenses are generous for just one or two days each month. I could use your expertise.'

'I hate politics. The political crap at Kinmalcolm is way more than enough torture for me. No thanks.'

Julie stared intensely at her wine glass for a few moments, and thought, *Scrap that then. Okay, one more chance. Either you get on the boat, or you drown.*

New approach, she decided. As if taking off a coat, she slipped out of her professional scientist facade and into her elegant inner persona.

A charming glow replaced her sharpness, and relaxation unfolded over her protective tension. The wine had done its job and they felt at ease with each other.

Constantly primed to deal with male chauvinist pigs, Julie felt wrong-footed by Gavin who appreciated her success without hang-ups, suspicions or innuendoes. She liked him and wanted him to join her team—willingly.

Her voice softened and her body relaxed in her chair. 'Do you have many female academics in your department?'

He sounded disappointed. 'We only have two female academics.'

'Do they do their job well?' she asked.

'Very well, and run a home, and look after a family, and keep a hubby happy.'

She raised her eyebrows. 'Seems you understand your female colleagues.'

'I grew up with an older sister. She and her friends liked to have me around. I became an honorary member of their girly gang. It was good.'

'You were their playboy?'

He laughed. 'I did play along. I remember one girl, Doreen, had a big sister called Margaret, who worked in a fabric and haberdashery shop. One day, while the girls peered in through the shop window, they sent me into the shop to tell Margaret I needed to get felt!'

Julie smiled at his revelation. 'I'm sure you loved the attention.'

'Well, it was good for learning the ropes. I don't say I fully understand them but I'm comfortable with sagacious women.'

'I'll take that as a compliment.'

Gavin leaned closer. 'Forgive me, for this is going to sound crass but your skin is exquisite.'

Her skin appeared flawless with a light luminous glow, lightly bronzed rather than tanned and radiant rather than shiny. With a coy expression, Julie said, 'Thank you, kind sir.'

'Do you have great genes, or is it a beautiful skin secret?'

Often, she received compliments from attention seeking males about her Versace jewellery, John Galliano outfits or Armani trouser suits. Rarely, did anyone comment on the one aspect of her appearance that deserved the greatest compliment.

Observation is a key skill in science. Struck by his appreciation, Julie decided on another strategy to hook Gavin Shawlens.

'How old do you think I am?'

He examined her skin more closely. 'When I first saw you this afternoon, I thought you were … no more than thirty. Since talking with you tonight, I think you're about thirty-two, maybe thirty-three.'

'I'll be forty-eight next month.'

'Agh!' Gavin gasped and inspected her eyes for tell-tale signs.

He shook his head. 'Sorry, but I don't believe that for a second. That's an old trick. If you want to look younger, tell everybody you're fifteen years older than you are.'

She smiled. 'Gavin, it's the truth.'

'How can that be even remotely possible?'

'We developed a wonderful skincare product called Adipicene TR,' she replied.

'Well, it must be a magic potion.'

Julie reached into her bag, brought out a small bottle of cream and handed it to Gavin. The gold label gave the manufacturer as Barscadden Research Foundation.

With a proud voice, she nodded to the bottle. 'Originally designed to stop skin cancer; it has a brilliant side effect.'

Gavin examined the bottle for ingredients. There were none.

She continued. 'It renews skin and eliminates wrinkles. I once had five-two-eight on both eyes but not anymore.'

Gavin threw her a bemused look. 'Five-to-eight?'

'Crow's feet measurements, my boy. Five lines, two millimetres wide, by eight millimetres long.'

'Shit. I've been telling students that anti-age skin creams are useless. Am I wrong?' he asked as he returned the bottle.

'Our product alters the ratio of collagen and elastin in skin. Collagen is lost as we grow older, and dastardly elastin pulls skin together, causing wrinkles. As you know, collagen is only produced when needed to repair damaged skin.'

'So, your product stimulates skin cells to produce new collagen?'

She smiled. 'Yes. Skin fills out. Wrinkles disappear.'

'Fantastic.' Gavin raised his eyebrows and sounded impressed. 'Adipicene TR seems like a clever metabolic solution.'

'You do accept that this is all confidential? I would hate to face you in court.'

'Of course, don't worry. I harbour tumultuous secrets, too. Secrets I don't even dare think about—or I would have nightmares.'

Julie's jaw dropped. She pushed back in her chair and raised her eyebrows at his revelation.

'So long as we're clear.'

'Is it in the shops?' Gavin asked.

'No. This small bottle costs twenty grand, and it only lasts four weeks.'

'Wow! Do people pay that?'

'Yes, because it works. We make twenty-six bottles each month. All repeat orders, of course.'

Gavin thought money for a moment. 'Think what you could make if you priced it at a hundred.'

'Scale-up is far too difficult. The problem has thwarted my best biochemists. I'm looking for someone to input fresh ideas.'

Gavin narrowed curious eyebrows. 'Is it an enzyme or a hormone?'

'I can't say more unless you sign a confidentiality agreement. I would value your input. You would be well remunerated for your time.'

Julie felt confident about her offer.

He rubbed his chin while he thought. 'Sounds like a fascinating problem.'

Come on, take a big bite, you know you want to. Julie tilted her head downward and glanced up at him while she leant her head on her hand.

'Just think, if you made the breakthrough we need for scale-up—you would become a god to countless millions of women, including me.'

'I'm tempted, seriously, but I'm so busy with too many other things.'

A loud grunt echoed in her mind as she straightened her posture. 'Fine, not a problem.'

She broke eye contact and stared at the wall behind him. Her patience nearly exhausted. Disappointment filled her mind and she prepared to bring the evening to a close.

'BARSCO isn't known for health care. How did you get them to develop this Adipicene TR product?' Gavin asked.

When she spoke, her voice had hardened. 'The company owns a private clinic in London. We have extensive medical facilities at our disposal.'

'Does BARSCO provide good health care for its staff?'

'Not only staff but also family. One of my people, Andrew Portcairn, almost lost his mother to a failing heart. Her heart surgeon couldn't do anything for her. We whipped her into the BARSCO clinic for an emergency heart transplant. How many life-changing perks do you get at Kinmalcolm?'

'Where did you find a heart for an emergency transplant? The waiting lists are so long.'

She snapped. 'Private sector clinic. Private sector waiting list.'

'Impressive. I can see why people want to work for BARSCO.'

Proudly, Julie enthused. 'The clinic was my baby. I had to fight tooth and nail with sceptical colleagues. Now, of course, they use the clinic themselves.'

'Well done, you. The glass ceiling in science is hard for women scientists.'

He'd hit a nerve and Julie reacted. 'You know nothing about the glass ceiling, believe me.'

An offended look dropped onto his face. 'I do. It's the same for me. I have to deal with a grass ceiling.'

She raised her voice. 'What ceiling? Did you say *grass*?'

'Yes. I'll never get promoted because I don't play golf.'

She shook her head. 'It's not the same.'

'And we boys don't have women's lib screaming in our corner.'

Her eyes widened and she snapped up from a slouched posture to stiff-backed. 'Women's lib is vital for professional women. I'm a good scientist and don't want to hide the fact that I have breasts.'

'I disagree. Obviously, about the women's lib, not about your science or your breasts.'

A waiter swooped into the midst of the tension to clear away dessert plates and cutlery. He told the barman table sixteen would explode any minute.

Twenty-two

An awkward silence hung in the space between them. Julie reeled back in shock while adrenaline rushed through her entire body. Was Shawlens a pig in sheep's clothing? Her hand shook as she restrained it from giving him a slap across the face.

Her features sharpened and her eyes menacing. 'Watch yourself, Shawlens. I'll rinse your dirty snout with this wine.'

Gavin drew a sheepish expression. 'Nowadays, women's lib is more destructive than constructive.'

Julie rose up. 'So, you are a dirty chauvinist pig after all.'

Gavin spoke in a whisper. 'Hear me out. If you still think I am, I'll go to the toilet, strip off and walk out of here naked.'

Other diners glanced over and talked about them. Slowly, Julie sat down and eyed him with suspicion. 'There might be a tiny thing worth laughing at for a second.'

'Men like to be treated as men as well as scientists. I want the same for women. But I don't want female scientists to be any less female.' He paused to think.

'Go on.'

'Women are more caring, more understanding and more appreciative. Women add balance to the human race. I'm sad when I see a professional woman become a pseudo-male. Gain equality and fight discrimination.

'Males have to fight religious discrimination, race, golf and other prejudice. But don't ever give up your femininity for women's lib. Please.'

Gavin had spoken genuinely as he explained his point. His eyes pleaded like a little boy who wanted his way.

She relaxed. 'I understand your point, but it's hard out there.'

'I know but it doesn't mean you give up being a great female to be a great scientist. And you are a great female.'

'Would you have the same opinion if your boss was a woman?'

'I would be happy with a female boss provided she remained feminine. Trouser-suited, shirt-and-tied artificial

117

males confuse me. I have a technician, Christine, and she is a great scientist with a wonderful femininity.'

'Shawlens, you sail too close to the wind. You have no idea how dangerous that can be in this big bad world.'

'Men have simple minds. Women must keep things simple for us. Don't you agree?'

They clinked their wine glasses. 'Okay, truce—you can keep your clothes on.'

Julie ordered more coffee, and they settled back into a more relaxed atmosphere.

'Why did you choose to work in industry?' Gavin asked.

'My first degree is in economics and my first job was in the City.'

'The City?' Gavin raised his eyebrows.

'The City adds great wealth to this country. More than a hundred billion is turned over every single day,' Julie said with pride.

'That's huge.'

'I worked for a merchant bank in corporate finance, mostly on management buy-outs and venture capital.'

'Sounds like heady stuff.'

'Once you understand money basics, it's all quite predictable. Money makes money and good deals have good hallmarks. It becomes routine to make a good deal. Risky deals look risky, so you must work hard to calculate risk. Bad deals always have a bad smell.'

'Did you make a fortune?'

Julie detected slight criticism in his voice. 'Yes, I did.'

Gavin turned her wrist to look at her large Cartier La Dona gold watch. 'I see.'

Julie gave him a tight-lipped smile. 'I worked hard. I got rewarded for my efforts.'

Gavin thought for a moment. 'Why did you leave the City?'

It seemed the next logical question but caught Julie unprepared. She'd let her guard slip and allowed him to control the conversation.

Now, she looked away to the side but failed to hide a flicker of uneasiness in her eyes. For a moment, she hesitated and then decided to take him further into her personal life.

'I worked in a sector with thousands of males, and less than thirty females. Severe sexual harassment was a way of life. A strong relationship exists between money and sex, and people making tens of millions in a day gain great potency and power.

'Some took huge risks with vast sums of money. They lived on a knife-edge, and if they lost money, they often took solace in viciously descriptive verbal sexual abuse.'

Her voice lost its confidence.

Gavin fidgeted with the cup and saucer on the table. 'I had no idea it was like that. Sorry for asking.'

She sensed his discomfort and followed through. 'Some dealers' jargon disrespected females. They called a successful dealer a high swinging dick. When someone made money on a deal, and others wanted to know, they didn't say let us in on the deal, they'd say lift up your skirt, and believe me—that's polite language.'

'Oh, shit. That's horrible.'

Julie saw his reaction and felt sure she had him in her grasp. *Come on, Shawlens, you could be so useful to me*, she thought. He lifted her hand, comforted it in his hands. 'I can't imagine how disgusting that must have been.'

'It's more covert now due to sex discrimination but old traditions die hard. It left me mentally drained and I decided to get out of it.'

'It takes a lot of courage to change discipline. Why biochemistry?'

'I met Barscadden through the job. We had a few business lunches. A serious problem cropped up and he helped me find a solution. I joined BARSCO and returned to university to study food biochemistry. I worked my way up to research director and I've never looked back.'

With eyes full of admiration, Gavin squeezed her hand gently. 'Well done.'

At last, now I've got you, she thought. They swapped mobile phone numbers, and she admired his wristwatch, an Omega Aqua Terra chronometer.

Julie excused herself and headed for rest room. She had received a text reply from her personal assistant.

While she leaned heavily on a row of built-in hand basins, dark memories of her time in the City re-surfaced. She remembered the male colleague who'd objected to her meteoric rise in their company. He'd set Julie up for an illegal deal.

When the deal finalised, he cornered her in his office and raped her savagely. Then, while she called the police, he told her about her illegal deal and threatened to say she'd offered sex to keep his silence.

When she put the phone down, he told her he would be gentler, next time. Traumatised, she had relived the nightmare every night for months after. Then, she met Barscadden and they became close platonic friends.

On a weekend visit to his country home, she woke in the middle of the night with a scream of terror. Barscadden rushed to her room, sat on the edge of her bed, and listened while she recalled her nightmare.

He wiped her tears, straightened her bedcovers like a devoted brother, and promised to ease her heartache.

Three weeks later, Barscadden phoned Julie and told her she needed to face her rapist one more time. He told her the man would arrive at her office at one-thirty in the afternoon to apologise for what he'd done to her. To make amends, he would help her better manage her work time.

Julie had waited apprehensively, watching every minute on the clock. She'd planned what to say to him, word for word. In no uncertain terms, she would tell him she didn't want a time manager. The appointed time arrived, and he didn't show up. Julie cursed him but felt relieved.

A plain brown box arrived in the afternoon mail. Julie unwrapped and extracted a large egg timer. The card attached had 'Time Manager' in bold letters. She examined the timer. Instead of sand, the glass contained powdered grey ash with numerous specks of white bone-like material.

Julie regained her thoughts in the rest room, and read the reply from her PA. She couldn't believe her eyes.

She telephoned her PA and gave further instructions before she returned to the dinner table, refreshed, calm and collected.

Gavin had paid for the meal in her absence. They gathered their things and fetched their jackets. He helped her into her coat and asked, 'Shall I have them call you a cab?'

'Yes, please. I'm staying at the Excelsinor.'

They sat together near the door to wait for the taxi. 'Well … many thanks for your talk. Heavens, that reminds me. I've got your USB stick.'

Gavin retrieved it from his pocket and handed it over. Julie twirled the stick in her hand, and gave him a mischievous look to imply he'd tried to look at the contents.

He shook his head. 'I didn't look.'

'I know you didn't because it has state of the art encryption.'

Julie glanced at her watch twice in quick succession and flashed a look of concern at him.

'Sorry, I didn't realise you were in a hurry.'

'How long will it take to get to the Excelsinor from here?'

'About twenty minutes.'

'Oh, that's fine. The in-house movie is one of my favourites. I'll have a nightcap, a packet of cashews and curl up with my pillow to watch the movie.'

Her eyes pushed out to embrace him but she got no reaction.

The barman called over, 'Your taxi has arrived.'

Gavin opened the door for her. 'Which movie is it?'

'*Terminator* with Arnold squashed-his-nuggets.'

'It's a classic.'

In a coy, seductive voice, she whispered, 'A classic don't-watch-alone movie.'

Hell's bells this is hard work, she thought as they left together in the taxi.

Twenty-three
Excelsinor Hotel, Glasgow

In the early hours of the following morning, Julie stared intensely at Gavin as he slept soundly in the king-sized bed in her hotel suite. She felt confused. The text she'd received in the restaurant told her that a search of research funding databases showed no funding awards for Dr Gavin Shawlens.

How could he lead an expensive research group without funding? If Shawlens had private wealth, he kept it well hidden.

His work on the SeaPro patent made Shawlens a critical asset, and Julie wanted to be certain he could be trusted with such a valuable prize.

To monitor his contacts and conversations, she planned to insert a comms module in his phone. While he slept, Julie gave his mobile to her PA in the next room.

Her PA popped her head through the connecting door and waved for Julie to come through.

'What's the problem?' Julie asked.

'No space in his phone to fit a comms module. Also, and I'm not an expert, but his phone looks seriously high tech.'

'What options have we got for just now?' Julie asked.

'As an alternative, I can fit a simple GPS tracker in his Omega watch.'

Julie shook her head. 'A tracker doesn't give me what I want.'

'It's useful to know his location. We could spot any suspicious activity if he's selling out to another company.'

'You're sure you can't make space for a comms module?' Julie asked.

The PA showed Julie the exposed back of Gavin's phone. 'This isn't a simple battery I could swap out for a smaller one. It's a special combination-module battery. If I replace it with a regular battery, the phone won't function as normal. More likely, if the module is missing, it won't function at all. This is advanced stuff.'

'We don't have much time. Okay, put the GPS tracker in his watch. Find out more about this module battery thing in his phone.'

*

Despite a long night, Julie showered and dressed before seven. An hour earlier, she had asked Gavin to leave. Quietly, she sipped coffee, picked at the food on her breakfast tray, and put Shawlens out of her mind. Her PA joined her and they discussed arrangements for her next meeting.

A sunshine and showers day had settled over Scotland. Julie drove to Glasgow airport and settled in a private lounge seat overlooking the single runway, so that she could watch out for Barscadden's Lear jet.

Just after nine-twenty, she caught sight of his plane approaching a domestic pier. She made her way to the VIP arrivals hall to wait.

First, she spotted his characteristic brisk walk and then his face. He carried a medium-sized Globe-Trotter Heritage suitcase. 'Morning, Julie.'

He didn't stop walking, so she adjusted her pace to match. 'Good morning, Sir James.'

'How did your talk go last night?'

Julie stretched to keep up with him. 'Excellent. Well received.'

'What time is our meeting?'

'We're due at his home at eleven-thirty.'

Barscadden raised his case to show he'd brought a change of clothes. 'If you'll take me to your rooms, please.'

'How did your meeting go with the Prime Minister?' Julie asked.

'Very well indeed, but I gave him my last jar of Adipicene TR. Is a new batch underway?'

'I'll check with the guys at the Rehab factory.'

Barscadden raised his eyes. 'What about Europe? They have plenty of criminals there. Could we not extend the Rehab programme to Europe?'

'It would be WRATH's call. Peter would need to bring them into the country. It seems to be easy enough for illegal

123

immigrants to get in. It should be possible for WRATH to bring in a few criminals. I'll ask him to look at it.'

*

Julie drove him to her hotel in a hired Volvo saloon car. They went straight to her suite. Inside, he walked around to inspect the room.

Julie understood what to do. 'Would you care for anything to eat or drink?'

'Do they serve lapsang souchong?' Barscadden asked.

'Yes.'

'A pot of that, please.'

'I'll see to it.' Julie left the room. She knew what her boss liked and had brought a supply of his favourite tea.

When she returned with a waitress carrying a tray, Barscadden had dressed to appear as a low-ranking, elderly, accountant. Complete with an old briefcase, grey hair-piece, grey moustache, spectacles, washed-out shirt and jaded business suit.

Over tea, they caught up with office work. At the appointed time, they walked to the hotel car park, and she drove him to their meeting in a different car hired by her PA. A white four-door family saloon, appropriate for a low-ranking company car.

Twenty-nine minutes later, they arrived in the driveway of Jim Patersun's home in Newton Mearns.

'Good afternoon, Mr Patersun. Jayne Mitchell, and my assistant, Charles Norfolk. Nice to meet you, finally.' Julie smiled.

Jim opened his door wide to allow his visitors inside. They shook hands and exchanged business cards. Their cards stated that Jayne R. Mitchell and Charles K. Norfolk represented Birtmappe Bank Plc.

'Come through.' Jim swept his arm to show the way.

Julie said as she passed, 'Thank you for seeing us.'

Jim gestured them toward the sofa. 'Sit down, please. Would you like a drink?'

She replied, 'No thanks.'

Barscadden shook his head.

Jim sat in a chair opposite.

124

She opened a folder on her knees. 'As I explained on the telephone, Mr Mascarri contacted us regarding capital finance for your project. We've been trying to contact him without success, so I decided to contact you directly.'

'I'm not certain what Mascarri told you. He's out of town at the moment.'

Julie smiled. 'Mascarri painted a favourable outline of your project but details are scant. He had agreed to provide a business development plan.'

Jim Patersun explained the expected capital cost of his plan. They discussed the likely annual profit after tax and long-term plans for expansion.

She consulted a spreadsheet. 'I would be keen to see a final business plan, together with an independent product evaluation report and, of course, the patent application.'

'The product report and draft business plan are available. The patent will require two more weeks.'

Julie gave a positive sideways glance to her colleague. 'Sounds good.'

Jim seemed keen to get to the bottom line. 'Ballpark figures. What share in the company would you want for providing the capital investment?'

Julie glanced at her colleague and leaned back against the sofa.

He took up the conversation. 'In a new company created to produce and sell your product, we would require thirty-five percent with forty-eight percent retained by you and your associates. The remaining seventeen percent would be held by a guardian angel.'

Jim glowered. 'Guardian angel?'

He pulled out a business card and handed it to Jim. 'We feel the new company will need security and muscle from a major player in the food industry. To prevent abuse from large food companies. We recommend BARSCO.'

Jim handed back the business card and rose from his seat. 'No way. No thanks.'

'Neither ourselves nor BARSCO would have control. Your forty-eight percent would be a controlling interest.'

Jim shook his head. 'I would rather see it fold than become a cog in a conglomerate.'

Barscadden raised his voice a notch. 'Your chances of survival in this business would be much greater.'

Jim turned to face Barscadden. 'Sorry, but I don't see it that way.'

Anxious and annoyed, Jim stood at his lounge door and opened it wide. Blackhest and Barscadden rose from the sofa and exchanged looks of disappointment.

'In the current financial climate, no finance house could possibly consider the risk without a major angel on board to ensure fair play for your product. It's a difficult market,' Barscadden said.

'I don't want a big company with all its corporate baggage, thank you.' Jim ushered them to the outside door.

As she walked past Jim, Julie asked, 'Will you at least put our proposal to your associates?'

'The only key associate is my wife and she's not here.'

'Can we put our proposal to Mrs Patersun?' Julie asked.

Jim shook his head. 'No. She's in Paris on business.'

Barscadden and Blackhest exchanged looks of surprise to give Jim the impression that they suspected him of dealing with another company.

'She flies over to Paris every two weeks to exchange contracts with our spice business suppliers. Nothing to do with this project. I'll talk over your proposal with her. If we want to talk further, I'll call you.'

'Please, contact me at any time,' Julie said as Jim closed the door on them.

In the car, Barscadden and Blackhest stared out through the windscreen at the dense thicket surrounding Patersun's garden.

'I'm disappointed with him. I thought he would see the need for a guardian.'

She agreed. 'Small-time businessman. Spices and condiments. He doesn't understand the food industry.'

'Could his wife change his mind?' Barscadden twisted in his seat to look at Julie.

'Interesting—that he lied about his wife. She does indeed have a trip planned to Paris, but at this moment, she's at their factory. He doesn't want us to speak to her. I think his mind is set in stone.'

'He is incredibly naive if he thinks ingredient producers will not fight back.'

Julie started the car. 'It's unfortunate but we've given him an opportunity to join us willingly. His choice.'

Barscadden grimaced for a moment. 'I'm glad I came to meet the man. He's not a great inventor or even a good designer. Just a weak-minded opportunist who lacks the vision to turn this great process into the success it deserves. No great loss to the world.'

Julie shrugged. 'When the product report becomes known more widely, a queue of competitors will line up to take it from him.'

'The easy way didn't work. Sadly, we must do it the hard way. Are you prepared?'

'Took a bit of doing but everything is in place.'

'Good girl. I desperately want this product. I have great plans for this business. The Prime Minister is behind me. I will deliver a great boost for the country. I will have all manner of politicians eating out of my hand. I cannot allow anything to get in my way. Nothing must be left to chance.' He patted her wrist.

'Of course, Sir James. I will move heaven and earth, if necessary.'

Twenty-four
Saffron Walden, Essex

In the small town of Saffron Walden, like many towns, breakfast time produced varying degrees of pandemonium as clock hands moved ever closer to the next minute.

Kineerdly Beechgrove, a handsome Georgian house, stood resolutely oblivious to the demands of clocks. It overlooked an archaeological site at Repell Ditches where two hundred Saxon skeletons were found.

The grand house boasted six bedrooms, a triple garage, a square breakfasting kitchen, and an acre of mature back and front walled gardens.

A sumptuous home for Nicholas and Penelope Orcherd and their two daughters. Nick and Penny stood at five foot seven, but with heels, Penny liked to appear slightly taller than Nick.

Every inch an attractive and easy-going thirty-four-year-old, and a natural blonde, Penny wore her hair shoulder-length, and spoke with a rich, husky, voice.

Nick, older at forty, thin-faced but handsome with sharp upper-class features. He kept his hair short and neat and liked to look good in well-tailored, immaculate smart-casual outfits, mostly Barbour country gent styles.

Both born into privilege, they kept themselves trim and fit with competitive matches at their local tennis club where they played both singles and mixed doubles.

The Orcherds ran a successful antiques business from a large shop in Saffron Walden.

Penny Orcherd's head bobbed back and forth while she struggled to serve breakfast to her girls, cook for her husband, prepare packed lunches, check school satchels and explain childcare arrangements to her sister, Cassandra, on her mobile.

Nick sat back in his chair with his thick brogues resting on a wooden stool, dressed in his 'Lord of the Manor' beige flannel trousers, brown and country-green check shirt, and matching light-brown tie. He had his head buried deep in *The Times* newspaper.

'Yes, Cassie, I'll pick up the girls tomorrow morning. I know, I know but it's a piece that we simply must bid for on behalf of a wealthy private collector. He collects evil *objet d'art.* Obscene and disgusting pieces.

'This piece, Lot 479, is particularly vile, but that's his taste. I wouldn't have it within a hundred miles of my shop— ghastly thing. All right, darling, see you tomorrow, love to Robin, tootle-oo, bye, byeee.' She moved quickly to rescue two slices of toast from incineration.

'Mum, do you have to go?' her oldest daughter, Camilla, asked before she plunged a chunk of sausage into her mouth.

Penny moved around her breakfast table to dispense food onto plates. 'Sweetheart, this important object will never come to the market again. It's awfully important for both of us to be there.

'Bidding will be hectic, and you know how difficult it is for one person to keep an eye on all the other bidders. Daddy spent most of last week checking the authenticity. Now, it's up for auction and an important client has asked Daddy to do his bidding.'

'Everyone's mum and dad is going. It's not fair,' Camilla declared loudly.

Penny said, 'Aunt Cassie and Uncle Robin will collect you from school. They'll take you to your concert.'

Camilla thumped the table with her upright knife clenched in her fist. 'It won't be the same.'

'*Camilla.* I have explained. Now, that's the end of the matter. Nick!'

Her voice summoned Nick to exert his parental authority. He peered around his newspaper to face his daughter.

'Uncle Robin will video the whole concert. I'll see how well you do when I get home.'

Camilla headed out of the kitchen, and her little sister followed like a lost puppy. Penny followed them and stopped in the hallway. Her eyes tracked Camilla's footsteps up the stairs.

'Get out of those trainers, my lady. Now.'

When Camilla came back down the stairs, she wore her black school shoes and a hard-luck smirk.

'Tell Aunt Cassie I'll phone tonight. You can tell me all about your concert.' Penny opened the front door.

A people carrier arrived at the bottom of their drive and blasted its horn twice. The two girls gathered their school bags and blazers. Then, they shot out of the house and ran to the car, which waited to take them to their private school.

Three neighbours took turns to operate the school run. Penny followed them out to tell her neighbour that her sister would collect them from school.

'Bye-bye, darlings. Have a nice day at school. Byeee,' she shouted as the car pulled away from the kerb.

A few minutes later, Penny and Nick sat at the table and finished off their breakfast.

Penny shook her head. 'I'm going to lock those bloody trainers away during the week. She thinks it's such a hoot but I was the one who got a frightful ticking-off from the deputy head.'

Unconcerned, Nick smiled back. 'I'll speak to her.'

'How is the car running?'

'The brakes are still too sticky. This is a good, long run and should loosen them up. If they haven't improved, I'll take it back to the garage.'

'Look here, just you tell that service manager chappy, you know, the tall one with the PC ears. You're not pleased with his work.'

'PC?'

'Prince Charles.' They shared a smile.

'Sticky brakey thingies are simply unacceptable in a top-of-the-range car. The manager chappy should know this—for goodness sake.'

Later, while Nick drove them to their shop, Penny telephoned her house cleaner and informed her of the jobs she wanted done.

Beverly, their shop assistant, waited at the shop entrance and greeted them with her normal chatty manner.

*

At two-thirty in the afternoon, they closed the shop early and made preparations for the four-hour journey to Birmingham.

Their comfortable Volvo XC90 Executive took the strain out of their drive, and Nick Orcherd felt much happier with its brakes. Penny used Google maps on her mobile to obtain directions to Pershore Street.

When they arrived, they pulled into a concrete multi-level car park. Nick parked on level three and then opened the tailgate to take out two large sports bags.

He locked the car and then they took the stairs up one level, but before they entered level four, they watched through the glass door panels for three minutes.

When he felt comfortable, they walked briskly to a dark-blue Ford Transit high-roofed van with dark-blue tinted rear windows. Nick opened up the back door, they got inside and he switched on a battery-powered strip light.

Penny removed her Nicholas Kirkwood tri-tone leather pumps and put them into her sports bag. 'Oh, I forgot to tell you, Beverly sold the Clarice Cliff lotus jug.'

Nick removed his corduroy jacket and folded it into his bag. 'The Lucerne Orange pattern?'

'Yes. She put a solid three hundred profit on it.' Penny smiled while she folded her Vivienne Westwood red label jacket.

'That's splendid.' Nick unbuttoned his shirt and removed it.

'I said her commission would be ten percent. Is that all right, darling?' Penny removed the rings from her fingers and placed them in a small box with other jewellery.

Then, she pulled her crepe de chine blouse over her head. Nick helped her untangle when it caught on her bra. He untied and removed his brogues. 'Of course, I'm happy with that.'

'I'm pleased with Beverly—she's a good egg.' Penny unzipped her skirt, wriggled, and allowed it to drop on the floor.

Nick smiled while he unzipped and slipped out of his trousers. 'She has an incredible knack for giving customers the impression the objects are her personal property, and she can't bear to sell them. Hooks them every time.'

Penny folded her skirt neatly and placed it on the pile of clothes in her bag. 'Darling, I want to go down to the stables day after tomorrow.'

'For evening stables?' Nick extracted new clothes from his bag and then paused for a moment to look at her body, covered only by underwear.

Penny saw him looking and posed like a model for a moment. He'd bought her the underwear for her birthday, or rather, she'd chosen it after a prolonged search, and he'd paid.

'Yes, darling. I know, it's an enormously big decision but I'm absolutely thrilled to bits.' She gave him a flirtatious look.

For several months, they'd pondered over an investment in a racehorse called BabyBlue Gilt. A friend had purchased the yearling filly at the Tattersalls sales in Newmarket.

He laid half of the purchase price to four joint owners in a syndicate. The syndicate had an option to complete the purchase after the end of season as a two-year-old.

Penny buttoned up her plain white cotton blouse. 'You haven't seen her, have you, darling?'

'Not yet.' Nick pulled on his shirt.

'Come with me to evening stables. You'll fall in love with her. She has these wonderful eyes, the tallest ears and luxurious hair. Her legs are just awesome pillars.' Penny pulled her skirt up to her waist and zipped it up.

'You're impressed.' Nick did the cuffs on his shirt.

'She's a dream. If the stables develop her speed and stamina, she'll win a classic.' Penny unfolded her coat.

'I'll have to see her, then.'

When they'd dressed in their new clothes, they pulled a tarpaulin over their sports bags and climbed into the front of the van.

Nick sat in the driver's seat and drummed his fingers on the steering wheel while he sighed at the windscreen.

Penny tried to reassure him. 'What's the matter, darling?'

'I'll just be glad to get this one done.'

'I know. Lot 479 is a risky one, but don't worry, sweetheart. If it gets too nasty, we will walk away quickly.'

'I know.'

'Do you want me to carry the pistol?' Penny asked.

'Do you mind? These pockets are too deep.'

'Give it to me. I'll put it in my bag. Now, don't fret, sweetheart. It'll soon be all over.'

Twenty-five
Birmingham, West Midlands

When they arrived at their destination, they found themselves in a run-down and battered district known as Rablocky Estate, where deprivation and poverty were day-to-day struggles for many of the residents.

Badly constructed tower blocks, not even fit for rats, gave very basic shelter and accommodation.

Nick and Penny discussed their plan to acquire Lot 479. When they felt ready, she picked up her folder. He adjusted the position of his cap, locked the van and then they walked over to the nearest tower block. They passed a group of children who taunted and shouted abuse as they approached the entrance to the tower.

In the graffiti-defaced entrance, they walked around bundles of litter and piles of rubbish. A nauseating smell of urine stung their senses. Penny pinched her nose as she walked past.

The floor of the filthy elevator had numerous flies crawling over faeces, vomit, used condoms, syringes, empty cans and old newspaper. With a shudder, Penny shook her head and they decided to use the stairs.

Carefully, they stepped past endless piles of dog faeces while they climbed the stairs to the fourth level. They walked along the open deck walkway, looking at door numbers, until they reached the flat they wanted.

The door had suffered many beatings in its time. A wooden panel had been kicked-in, pushed out and then covered with brown cardboard.

The aluminium door handle hung loose, and the wood around the lock bore deep gouges from past forced entry. The name on a piece of paper pinned to the door read, Jason Pidgin.

Naively, Nick pressed the buzzer button and then tutted loudly when it made no sound. Penny frowned at him—he should have known better.

He knocked on the wooden part of the door. From inside the flat, they heard shouting. No-one answered, so Nick banged harder on the door with the heel of a clenched fist. The noise inside quietened.

The door opened slightly and a man peered through the gap. He saw a uniformed policeman, and an official dressed in a light-coloured raincoat, plain skirt suit, and white blouse.

She carried a dark-brown folder cradled in her arm. A foul stench took its chance and rushed through the gap. Penny coughed to clear her throat.

The man screeched. 'What ta feck da ya want?'

'Mr Jason Pidgin?' Penny asked.

'What da ya bloody want?'

'Mr Jason T. Pidgin?' she raised a more forceful voice.

'AYE!' he shouted and rolled his eyes to the night sky.

'This is Constable Hamers, and I am Mrs Bolwest. I'm your probation officer.'

Nick showed his warrant card, which bore the name Constable A Hamers, and Penny showed a probation officer ID card for Mrs J C Bolwest. Pidgin examined the cards carefully.

'Bolwest, right ... right, ah wiz told that already. Feckin' hell, I'm jist out of ra pokey, two bleedin' hours. See ya tamorrow.'

He tried to shut the door but Nick pushed it back open.

Penny shook her head to disagree. 'I want you at my office now ... to do the paperwork.'

'Feck that—tamorrow'll da it.'

'No. I don't want you doing something stupid tonight, and then saying you didn't know it was against your probation conditions.'

Pidgin reached out his hand. 'Gimmee the feckin papers.'

He knew the drill. He had to be told formally of his probation conditions, and then sign the forms. He also knew the location should be specified on the form and that it went against procedure for her to do this at his house. His little test to find out how tough she would be.

'My office. Now,' she bellowed.

Nick stepped past Pidgin and peered inside the living room. A woman stood there, shaking and sobbing.

She dabbed a wet towel against her forehead to wipe the blood from her face. The left side of her face swollen and red, her lower lip bled, and a heavy limp suggested a lot of pain.

Her t-shirt had ripped at the neckband, and her torn skirt had pulled around so much, the back zip had moved to the front of her body.

Her bare legs showed bright-red scratch marks on her knees. Their arrival had been timelier than they knew.

Three small children with dirty, matted, and greasy hair, ran around half-naked. The woman, probably in her mid-twenties, appeared fifteen years older. Nick turned to Penny. 'I think I'll have a look around.'

Pidgin blocked his path. 'Right … right, feckin 'arassment. Okay, aye'll get ma jayket.'

Pidgin pushed the woman into their kitchenette, shut the door behind him, and then grabbed her throat. He stood face-to-face with her and agitated his fist at her head.

In a harsh voice, he threatened. 'Ya stay put—ya stupid bitch. I'll deal wi ya whin aye git back.'

She cowered when he feigned a vicious swipe at her head. Pidgin slammed the door shut, and followed Penny along the walkway to the stairs.

Nick followed Pidgin. 'Your wife's in a terrible mess.'

Pidgin shrugged. 'Jist 'er usual.'

When they reached the van, Nick opened the back for Pidgin to climb inside. Nick got into the driver's side, and Penny sat in the passenger's seat.

Pidgin settled himself down with his back against the sidewall and stretched his legs as the van moved off. Penny turned round to face him. 'Looked to me like someone beat her.'

Pidgin glanced out of the tinted back window. 'She's pissed. Can't feckin walk strayt. Stupid bitch, she fell *again*.'

'Fell?'

Pidgin turned to face her. 'Aff been on remand fur three month an she's denying ma feckin rights! Ever 'eard enthing so fecking stupid?'

She regarded his face, and asked, 'Tell me something, completely off the record. Not saying you have ever raped anybody but if you could help me understand the mind of a rapist. Why do you, sorry, *they* do it?'

He shook his head. 'Easy, 'tis just animal, lions do it, dugs do it. Yer lion don't ask a skirt for a date, dis it? Dugs don't piss about kissin' for 'alf hour. Yer bitches like it rough, just like wild animals.'

Penny smirked. 'I know some ladies do like a little bit of rough.'

Pidgin smiled as he swayed with the motion of the van. 'Well, Bolly, if ya needs a good seeing to. Am yer animal.'

Penny reached into her handbag. 'My name is Mrs Bolwest, if you don't mind.'

Carefully, she raised a gas compression pistol and waited until he looked out of the back window.

'BANG!'

A one-inch hard plastic ball hit Pidgin's head, which cannoned against the van sidewall. He slumped to the side, unconscious.

'I liked that bit of rough,' she said to Nick as she turned to sit correctly in her seat.

Nick stopped the van and went to check Pidgin's carotid artery. He examined the mark on his head, just a shade above the right eyebrow where the ball hit his skull. As he got into the driver's seat, he frowned. 'Penny, you must be more careful.'

She smiled and shrugged at him.

He flashed a look of reprimand. 'That shot could have taken his eye out.'

'Trot on, Nicholas.'

'I'm just saying … you should be more careful.'

She raised her voice. 'Trot on.'

Nick drove back to the car park, and to the same spot where they had collected the van. He got into the back of the van and secured Pidgin's hands behind his back.

Next, he taped a cloth gag around his mouth and secured his feet together with large plastic ties.

He used body straps to secure Pidgin's torso and legs to the side of the van. Then, he retrieved a bottle of chloroform and a gauze pad from his sports bag.

Finally, he changed out of his police uniform and into casual clothes.

Penny adjusted the driver's seat in the Volvo while Nick replaced the two sports bags in the boot. She pressed a switch to wind down the driver's side window. They kissed briefly through the opening.

'You're sure he's gone baw-baws?' Penny asked.

'Out like a light and tied up tighter than a drum.'

'Have you got everything out of the van?'

'Yes.'

Penny laughed. 'Don't forget the jolly lolly.'

'I won't. Safe journey home and love to the girls.'

'I'll see you at Heathrow, darling, bright and early. I love you, byeee.'

Nick watched her drive away and then returned to the van. He searched his phone for a number and spoke to a man with a broad Scottish accent.

'Vilegon Fertilisers.'

'Hello. Lot 479 is ready to join the Rehab AVC programme.'

'What's your ETA?'

Nicked checked his watch. 'I'll be at the factory gate in five hours.'

'I'll be ready for you.'

Twenty-six
M6 Motorway, Central England

It took Nick Orcherd twenty minutes to find the M6 and head north. With care, he observed speed limits and motorway regulations. Five miles south of Penrith, he pulled into a motorway service station for coffee and biscuits.

While there, he checked on Pidgin and found him conscious, seething with rage, but quiet and well secured. With chloroform and a pad, he put Pidgin back to sleep for the last lap of his journey.

Nick let out a sigh of relief as he turned into Miltonbrae Street. A secluded street in an industrial area on the south side of Glasgow.

One side of the street had a row of small factories. On the opposite side, a perimeter wall five metres high, ran around a large secured private estate to protect thirty-eight factory units.

Nick steered the van toward a massive wooden gate at the entrance to the estate. The door opened slowly on large ball bearings housed in a steel track.

One guard waved him inside, while another with a clipboard noted the vehicle registration number and logged the time.

'How many visitors?' he asked.

'Just me, for Vilegon Fertilisers,' Nick replied.

'They're expecting you. Drive on.'

'Thanks.'

Nick drove to the Vilegon Fertilisers building and around a corner to the fire exit door. The fire exit door opened, and light flooded the area around the van. A man stepped out. 'Hello, I'm Hugo.'

Nick frowned. 'You're not the usual chap.'

'Correct first time, squire. He's moved on. I'm here now,' Hugo replied with a strong Scottish accent.

Nick moved around to the rear of the van. 'Switch the light off, please.'

'No worries, squire.'

Hugo had a shaved bald head, a chubby face and a neat pencil moustache. He wore green combat fatigues and steel toe-capped boots.

Pidgin hadn't moved an inch during the journey. He stared at the two men with violent red eyes, revealing an underlying madness, ready to explode. Hugo recoiled at the stench of urine.

'Lot 479 for the Rehab programme,' Nick announced.

'Whew! That's strong. Need to get him changed before he smells the whole place out.

Nick raised his brows. 'Is this your first delivery?'

Hugo pinched his nose. 'The first one smelling like a dead tart's knickers.'

The smell had become pungent in the small van. Nick put Pidgin to sleep again and then they manhandled him onto the tarmac.

Unceremoniously, they deposited him inside the door, closed it and switched on the light.

Nick spoke in a tone that suggested he'd finished his work. 'Okay, then.'

Hugo took hold of Pidgin's upper body. 'Surely, you can give me a hand to get him up to the lab.'

Nick shrugged. 'I don't mind.'

Nick felt embarrassed. Normally, he would about turn and leave because that's how the previous guy handled arrivals. Although Pidgin appeared thin and light, they struggled to lift him up the metal stairs and along a metal gantry to three connected rooms that Hugo called 'the labs'.

Wood and glass panels surrounded the rooms. White wood panels from ground to waist height, and glass panels from waist height to the ceiling.

From the metal gantry walkway, they shuffled into the first room. A general preparation area and office for technicians. They carried Pidgin to the middle room.

A technician, dressed in blue scrubs and white boots, leapt from his chair to open the glass partition door, so the two men could continue their shuffle into the room.

The set-up reminded Nick of a small hospital ward. The area held four beds, and beside each one, a trolley bristled with equipment for gases and electronic monitors. They heaved Pidgin up onto a vacant gurney.

'What's he on?' the technician asked.

'Chloroform,' Nick replied.

Hugo secured Pidgin's wrists and ankles to leather restraints on the gurney. 'I'll get these clothes off and wash him down.'

Nick scanned the room. He had never been further than the doorstep, and had a limited idea of the Rehab programme.

They left Pidgin and returned to the prep room, which served as a kitchen and a small laboratory. The technician returned to his seat, stretched out his legs, and read his magazine.

'Stuart, this is the delivery man. Delivery man, this is Stuart.'

They nodded to each other. Nick stood at a glass partition and gazed beyond the middle to the end room. He saw an operating theatre with a large circular mirrored light above an operating table. Curious, he studied the metal trolleys around the table and the trays of instruments.

Hugo smiled. 'You seem bewildered, squire.'

Impressed, Nick scanned all around. 'First time, I've seen the operation, so to speak.'

The two men smiled at the unintended pun. Hugo handed a brown envelope to Nick. 'There's fresh coffee and sandwiches if you're interested.'

'Thanks, I could use a coffee.'

'Check your cash before you go. No comebacks here, squire.' Hugo cut through Pidgin's clothes.

Nick placed the wads of notes in his jacket pockets. 'All in order, thanks.'

Stuart saw Nick's bewildered face and asked, 'You do know what we do here?'

Nick glanced at Pidgin. 'Actually, I've delivered these people with the same mindset I have when I drop my car off at the garage. I know something of what is done but not the detail.'

'They should have told you, in case you ever need a service.'

Nick turned around to look at Hugo. 'Why would I need a service?'

'If you need a new heart next week, what'll you do? Join the queue and pray. We supply BARSCO's private clinic with organs from these Lots. Obviously, if any member of Gyge's Ring needs a new part—we can jump the queue. Good, isn't it?' Hugo beamed with pride.

Surprised, Nick asked, 'Transplants? Is that possible?'

'It is with our universal donors,' Stuart replied.

'Universal donors?'

Stuart explained, 'Ever since the first transplant in 1905, when a French doctor transplanted a pig kidney to a man, the problem with donor organs then and since, has been the human immune system. It attacks and rejects a donor organ.'

Nick filled a mug with coffee and selected an tuna sandwich. 'How does it know an organ is a donor organ?'

'The immune system detects foreign protein on the surface an organ. We perfuse donor organs with enzymes that chop off the identifying surface proteins to produce clean blank surfaces.

'When the organs are transplanted, the recipient immune system doesn't find foreign proteins and doesn't attack the new organ. The recipient populates the blank organ with its own proteins and the new organ is never rejected.'

Hugo added, 'We call it rehabitation. From each Lot you deliver, we take the good parts and rehab them back into the community as replacement organs.'

Nick nodded as though he understood. 'Rehabitation? Of course, it makes more sense to me now.'

With a new feeling of pride, Nick walked around the middle laboratory. On a bed farthest from him, lay the body of a woman. Equipment obscured her, so he hadn't noticed her before.

When he leaned closer, he saw that tubing connected her to a life support machine beside her bed. Her wrists and ankles were bound to the corners of the bed.

'Whoa,' Nick shouted and jumped backward when the woman's eyes followed him.

Hugo glanced over. 'Startle you, did she?'

Embarrassed. Nick shrugged. 'Silly thing. I thought we only did men.'

'She is Lot 471. Don't let her eyes bother you. I don't think there's anything at home.' Hugo pointed a rotating finger into his head.

Except for a crumpled white towel on her chest, she lay there naked. Nick's eyes flared on inflamed crisscrossed scars, which tracked along her legs, arms, and body.

Nick swallowed some coffee. 'Why is she naked?'

'We have to keep her tap scars clean and free from infection.'

Hugo joined Nick and pointed to an old newspaper cutting attached to the wall near her bed.

'Did you read about them in the press? Two ex-schoolteachers, enjoying retirement, killed by two young women. The old schoolteacher tried to fend them off. But the women bashed his skull until it resembled a mashed pulp. His wife died in hospital.'

'I remember that case. Awful.'

Hugo examined her scars. 'They stole a few notes from his wallet. A neighbour heard breaking glass, summoned the police, and they found the women in the kitchen, drinking alcohol and cleaning blood off their clothes.'

'Is she one of the women?'

'Yes. We're expecting the other one in a few weeks.'

Nick pointed at her scars. 'What are these for?'

'She's on a special programme to produce a hormone we need for the Adipicene TR product. That's where we tap her body for the hormone. Not unlike tapping a rubber tree for the latex,' Stuart said as he inspected a leg scar for signs of infection.

'Adipicene TR?' Nick asked.

Stuart replied, 'It rejuvenates skin, removes wrinkles, blemishes and all that stuff.'

'Does it work?'

Hugo enthused. 'All the bosses use it. We can't get enough of it. There just aren't enough violent females around for us to meet the demand. Professor Blackhest thinks we'll need to shop abroad.'

'What's planned for Lot 479?'

Stuart consulted a sheet of paper. 'Heart and lungs are already paid for. I'll perfuse them tomorrow. The kidneys and eyes are booked. There's an interest in his pancreas and liver. I think there are four or five other parts on the list. A good proportion of him will go back into the community.'

Nicked emptied his coffee mug. 'Gosh. I'm glad I came upstairs to find out what happens to the Lots.'

Hugo said, 'Remember, if you ever need a spare part, you only have to ask Mr Bromlee. We look after our own—always.'

*

Nick drove the van to Glasgow airport. He parked it on the top floor of the multi-storey car park opposite the terminal building. Then, he caught the first red-eye flight to Heathrow where he met his wife.

He had so much to tell her about the Rehab programme. On further reflection, he decided not to tell her about the female Lots and the procedure for producing Adipicene TR.

Twenty-seven
Glasgow Airport

A crisp, dry, morning welcomed travellers heading for Glasgow airport. They thronged the terminal buildings, struggling with luggage and hyperactive children, heading off for the May bank holiday. An unfounded rumour of long queues at airport security had circulated like a bad smell.

Gavin Shawlens felt conspicuous queuing with excited families and interesting couples. He tried to look like a businessman but his casual clothes and worn holdall undermined his facade.

He bought a coffee and sat down to reflect on the reason for his trip. Strange circumstances, to say the least.

Three days earlier, he'd been summoned to Professor Crawford's office.

Crawford gave him an email he'd received from Paris. It announced that Gavin's research work on bromelain had been made a late addition to a shortlist of new research developments in an EU research funding competition.

A small French pharmaceutical company, Bionartine SP, had sent the four-page email. They gave details of a dinner cruise reception for finalists, and an opportunity to meet senior company staff. Tickets for two had arrived by courier.

Crawford echoed Gavin's annoyance about the short notice but the grant award amounted to 200,000 Euro.

Reluctantly, Gavin agreed to travel to Paris and attend the awards ceremony.

He stared into his white polystyrene coffee cup, and his mind wrestled with the ongoing poor work from Sharon Bonny.

Her research project had stalled and she seemed content to mark time. He wanted to cancel her contract but his HR advisor warned him it would be too costly.

He became conscious of someone standing beside him. 'Gavin, what are you doing here?' Emma asked.

'Emma!'

She stood alone, and he moved his holdall off a seat onto the floor. Emma placed her overnight bag beside his and sat down beside him.

He glanced at his watch. 'I'm flying to Paris in twenty minutes.'

'Amazing. I'm on the Paris flight too.'

He felt self-conscious at the coincidence. 'A pharmaceutical company invited me to a reception in Paris.'

'What seat number are you?'

He checked his boarding pass. '14C.'

'I'm 6A. If there's a spare seat at the back, we can sit together.'

The Boeing Super 737 wasn't full, and when they had settled into their seats, Emma asked, 'Have you been to Paris before?'

'First time to Paris. I've been to Compiegne, and I've been to Marseille on conferences.'

'It's beautiful. You'll like it. How long are you going for?'

'Fly back tomorrow evening. My research has been shortlisted for an award. There's a reception tonight to announce the losers.'

'Good luck.'

He sounded cynical. 'It's just an EU gesture to make UK scientists feel included in EU research funding.'

'A change of scenery will be good for you.'

'Are you having a short break?'

Emma shook her head. 'I'm popping over to sign contracts with one of our spice suppliers. It's a formality. I go every two weeks with a new contract because the price fluctuates week by week. We argue about the prices over a lovely lunch, and then we sign. It's fun.'

*

They stared at different parts of the plane while it rattled down the runway. Gavin thought hard about what he wanted to say before he spoke. 'What do you have planned after your meeting?'

'Some shopping. I love the shops in Paris.'

'The company is hosting a dinner cruise on a Bateaux-Mouches something.'

Her eyes opened up. 'That's a five-course dinner and river cruise on the Seine.'

'It's for two, so if you'd like, I could—'

Emma's eyes darted to the safety of the window and distant clouds. She thought quickly and found an excuse. 'I expect it'll be formal dress?'

He read out the invitation. 'Gentlemen, tie, jacket, no jeans. Ladies, evening dress. I'm sure you would be fine as you are.'

She shook her head. 'I'm not prepared for an evening dinner.'

She had dressed for business in her two-piece dark-blue skirt suit and cream blouse. No way would she attend an evening dinner in her day suit.

They settled down to read. Gavin perused a research paper on protease enzymes, and Emma flicked through a women's health magazine, which featured an article on hormone replacement therapy.

Their flight arrived on time at Charles deGaulle airport. Emma told him about CDG's curious circular structure with gates spread out like the points of a clock.

They had cabin luggage only and walked quickly through security and passport control.

Gavin negotiated other passengers to stay at her side. 'Where are you staying?'

'I'm booked into the Fortel Estoile near the Arc de Triomphe.'

'I've not got anything booked. Is it a good hotel?'

'I always stay there.' She reached a revolving door and waited.

'Okay, we can share a taxi.'

'Certainly not.' She stepped smartly through the door.

Gavin felt embarrassed. Maybe he'd presumed too much. He hesitated to follow her. She waited for him on the other side and beckoned for him to hurry.

'A taxi is at least seventy Euros. I have a pass for the Air France bus, which stops off at the Arc. You can buy a ticket on the bus. Driving in Paris is tough but not many argue with a bus pushing its way through.'

They had moved one-third clockwise around the circular structure to gate thirty-four. Through the gate, they crossed a road to find the Air France bus to Paris city centre, already three-quarters full and a queue forming. Now, he understood why Emma hurried.

Throughout their bus journey, he didn't speak to her because all the passengers chatted in French, and he felt acutely foreign.

The bus arrived in Avenue Carnot beside the Arc de Triomphe. They stepped from the vehicle into bright sunshine, covered by a brilliant light-blue sky.

Gavin gazed at the Arc. The sun warmed his back, and he welcomed the heat to chase the air-conditioned chill from his body.

'Magnificent, isn't it?' Emma stood beside him.

Gavin pointed to the top. 'Looks like tourists up there?'

'Yes, an elevator runs to the top. If you're fit, you can take the steps.'

As they walked on, Gavin glanced at the fast traffic whizzing around the Arc. 'I see what you mean about the traffic.'

'That's mild. You should see it at rush hour.'

They made their way to Rue des Acasias and along to Hotel Fortel Estoile.

'Bonjour, Madame Patersun. Wonderful to see you again. I have your room ready.'

'Bonjour, Nathalie. I have a colleague with me today, Dr Shawlens. Do you have a room for one night for him, please?' Emma asked in fluent French.

'Certainly. Dr Shawlens, please, complete the card.'

She'd judged correctly and spoke to him in English with a heavy French accent.

Emma pointed to the card. 'My company will pay for Dr Shawlens. Add it to my account, please.'

*

In their respective rooms, they unpacked their things and felt relieved to be on their own for a while. Gavin lay out on his bed and stared at the ornate ceiling.

Talking with Emma had sparked off a flood of memories. An hour later, Emma knocked on his door.

'Settled in?' she asked as she cast her eyes over his room.

'Yes, it's fine.'

'It's a lovely day. Shall we go up the Eiffel Tower before lunch?' she asked.

'Yes, I'd love to. What's your agenda for this afternoon?'

'Meet the suppliers at two. I'll be finished by four. I spoke to Jim. He's playing cards tonight with Walter and friends. I'll stay over and join you for dinner.'

In the warm afternoon air, they turned left for a short walk along Rue des Acasias, then a left into Avenue de la Grande Armee and then forward to the Arc de Triomphe.

They went down steps to Argentine Metro station and then took the Metro to Trocadero.

They walked along a marble passageway and through the magnificent twin buildings of Palais de Chaillot. Before them stood the Eiffel Tower, tall and proud.

They strolled down steps, through gardens with spectacular fountains and across a wide bridge over the Seine to stand underneath the Tower.

From the Tower, they spent an hour admiring the magnificent views. Emma pointed out landmarks and added little bits of history. When they returned to ground level, they sat under a shady tree.

She bought a cheese baguette and a glass of cold beer for his lunch before she left for her meeting.

With his mind wrapped up in Emma Patersun, Gavin hadn't noticed a man who'd followed and photographed them since they'd arrived in Paris.

The photographer wore a beige baseball cap, black bomber jacket and a long-lens camera hung from his neck.

Twenty-eight
Paris, France

Later that evening, Emma knocked on Gavin's door. He gasped when she walked into his room and twirled around on the soles of her shoes. The move showed off her black, halter neck, satin dress with a bodice made of fine lace.

The rich material flowed elegantly, just an inch below her knee to show off her tanned and sculpted legs. She carried a pale blue satin shawl over her arm. Her purse and shoes were a matching shade of deeper blue. Her makeup seemed barely noticeable.

'How do I look?' she asked.

'Wow!'

'I'm glad you approve.'

'Stunning, absolutely stunning.' He leaned close and kissed her cheek fleetingly.

'I'd seen this outfit before, and today, I decided I wanted it.'

Gavin wore a dark-blue blazer, tired but not untidy. His white, short-sleeved shirt, light-blue tie and light-grey trousers were better turned out.

While he locked his room door, he watched her walk along the corridor, adjusting her shawl. He fixed the beautiful vision in his mind.

As they waited for the elevator, Emma straightened his tie and dusted off his shoulders. Gavin grinned pensively while she smiled at him. His pupils dilated, and a light-red flush formed just above his collar.

She liked his transparency, and always knew when he felt up or down, sure or unsure. She knew all his tells, and at this moment, they told her he felt embarrassed.

She moved close to him, kissed his cheek and then wiped away a faint lipstick mark with her finger. As their bodies came close together, their hearts raced.

Gavin pulled in a deep breath. Emma felt an ache down in her groin, which she'd not felt for a long time. Emotions soared until she stepped back when the elevator opened with perfect timing.

*

They arrived at the Bateaux-Mouches landing stage at Pont de L'Alma with thirty minutes to spare. Excitement filled their minds as they joined a large bustle of people, milling around, and waiting to board many boats offering evening cruises. Merry foursomes, light-hearted sixsomes, and many courting couples had gathered.

A romantic atmosphere filled the evening air. Slowly, they shuffled with the crowd, along a railed boardwalk and up a gangway.

Gavin stood close to Emma, and they held hands to maintain contact against the pressing crowd. At times, when the crowd nudged, their warm bodies pressed against each other.

Their cheeks brushed as they held onto one another. Body contact and soft skin brewed a powerful aphrodisiac. Her favourite perfume filled Gavin's senses with stimulating essences of vanilla, jasmine, and peach.

Eventually, they boarded their boat, Le J S Mouche. A long boat enclosed with a glass roof and glass sides. Along the sides of the boat, lay tables set for dinner.

Three musicians in evening dress played piano, harp, and violin. A waiter escorted Gavin and Emma to a table set for two.

A bright-yellow linen tablecloth covered the table, which had been set for a five-course meal. A silver ice bucket on a silver tray near the middle of their table, chilled a bottle of white wine.

While they soaked up the ambiance, they nibbled *Hors d'oeuvres* from a silver platter and sipped blackcurrant Kir. The menu card, in French, had tick boxes for the starter and main meal.

Gavin's total French amounted to *Je ne parlez Francais, parlez vous Anglais*. He watched Emma place a tick at Grenouilles Provencale for Entrees, and Fricassee De Homard for her main meal.

'This is excellent. What are you having?' she asked.

'Um … not sure just yet.'

Emma noticed another of his tells. His left hand rubbing hard on the side of his head whenever he felt uncertain. They turned together at the same time and smiled. She'd rumbled him and his eyes yielded as they laughed away his fluster.

'The starters are salad, duck, snails, frog legs and fillet of sole. The main courses are fillet steak, quail, venison, salmon, lobster, roast turbot or duck.'

'I'll have salad and fillet steak.'

Emma challenged him with her eyes. 'Are you sure? Try the quail.'

He pursed his lips. 'Okay, I'm in your hands.'

'You're still my baby, and I'm—'

'Good evening.'

A pompous-sounding waiter arrived to collect their menu cards. He stood impatiently while she helped Gavin complete his card.

When he marched off, they giggled to each other like two children told off by their teacher.

After another glass of Kir, the entrees were served and the boat started on its mini-cruise up and down the Seine.

Nervousness between them evaporated and they rekindled the magic that had once bound them together.

Enchanting music and soft lights flirted with Emma's mind. Gavin's close attention fuelled her feelings.

When young, she had shared a great deal of her heart with Gavin, and he'd handled the responsibility well. While she gazed at the flowing Seine, she thought about Jim Patersun and her life.

Anguish took hold as she realised she could open to temptation. She thought, *this is stupid. What am I doing here*? With an effort, she purged the teenage lust from her mind.

'I can't understand why you're not married to a wonderful woman.'

'Find me a wonderful woman.'

Emma smiled with satisfaction. It pleased her he didn't think Kim wonderful.

'There must have been lots of girls in your student days.'

152

'When I fall in love again, it will be with the right person and this time it will last forever.' He sounded more harsh than he intended.

Emma felt the dig sharply but saw in his eyes he regretted saying it. She sipped her wine and glanced at a young couple walking hand-in-hand along the riverbank.

The boat passed the Eiffel Tower, and Emma stared at it while deciding whether she might spoil the evening.

'Why didn't you bring Kim?'

'I couldn't bring her to this.'

'Doesn't she mind being left on her own? I know I would.'

'She's not by herself. My sister is looking after her.'

It concerned Emma that Kim needed looking after. 'Is she all right?'

'She'll be fine. Kim loves my niece, Kirsty. More than me, I think.'

'That's nice. Is Kim fond of children?'

He sipped some wine. 'Yes, I think Kim would have been a good mother.'

'Maybe that's what she needs to help her settle down.'

'Probably, but it's too late for her now.'

Emma frowned with surprise. 'Surely, she's not too old?'

He shook his head. 'She's not old, it's just that ... well ... I've had her sterilised.'

Emma almost choked on her food, and he patted her back while she gasped for air. She gulped her wine.

She swallowed more wine to clear her throat. 'That's not funny.'

Gavin shrugged. 'Well, I can't have my flat overrun with puppies.'

'Puppies? I don't understand. I thought Kim was your flat-mate?'

'Kim has four legs and a tail. That's flat, isn't it?'

'Kim is a pet? Really ... Gavin. Sometimes, I wonder if your brain is fully connected to the real world.'

'Well, I can't tell people I live with my pet dog. So, she's my flat-mate.'

Emma remembered her conversation with Christine Willsening. 'Someone told me she was a bad bitch?'

'She's not bad, she's a typical Westie. Like wee Whisky.'

Emma pushed her knife and fork onto her plate. One hand clasped over her mouth while her other patted her chest. She closed her eyes, and when she opened them, they went wide and dewy.

'Oh my God—wee Whisky. I haven't thought about him for ages.'

When he and Emma had first met, her family had a white West Highland terrier dog called Whisky. He and Emma spent many evenings walking and chasing the dog in the local park.

Gavin smiled as he remembered. 'Whisky was a smart cookie, wasn't he?'

Emma tilted her head toward him and smiled. 'I loved that little dog with all my heart.'

'Remember that Tuesday afternoon when your parents took your sister to a clinic in Edinburgh? We spent the afternoon in your house.'

She smiled. 'Whisky crept under my bed and growled at you all afternoon. That was so funny.'

She squeezed his hand. They peered into each other's eyes to remember that afternoon of teenage love.

The cheese and coffee arrived at their table when a short man and a glamorous woman took position beside the harpist. The man pulled a microphone close to his mouth and spoke in French.

Emma perked up. 'He's the host, and he's going to announce the awards.'

Gavin paid no attention. He expected these awards were fixed. The host rambled on and on for quite a while.

A roar of clapping hands erupted while three members of a table got up and made their way toward the host.

Hands continued to clap as the trio posed for photographs with an envelope confirming their award.

The host launched into a second chatter while the ecstatic trio returned to their seats. A pair of photographers took more photos of the winners hugging and kissing.

Emma grabbed hold of Gavin's wrist. 'He said pineapple.'

Gavin heard his name before the clapping drowned further comment from the host. The host nodded to Gavin and his hand beckoned Gavin to join him.

The clapping thundered on as Gavin returned to his seat with his award. Several photographers followed behind him and made their demands in French, which Emma translated, 'Hold up the award letter.'

'Smile. Heads together.'

'A celebration kiss.'

'Once more.'

*

The late evening air cooled and refreshed their bodies while they walked along Avenue de New York to Place de Varsovie. Many people milled around as they walked through Jardins du Trocadero and up to the large marble square of Palais de Chaillot. They stopped to look back at the Eiffel Tower. Brightly lit in a blue-black sky.

From there, they walked to the Metro station at Trocadero, and then took a taxi back to the hotel. A small Citroen overtook their taxi and raced down the road, packed with young people, who sprawled out of the windows and the sunroof, tooting their car horn and screaming loudly.

Gavin threw a puzzled look at Emma. 'Did they get research funding?'

She smiled. 'They are letting Paris know one of them will be married tomorrow.'

Later, in their hotel bar, they sipped Irish liqueur. Gavin re-read every dot and letter of his award.

Emma encouraged. 'Obviously, if there's a clot-busting drug to be had, they'll want it. Well done.'

She kissed him on the cheek and not a fleeting peck. Then, she cuddled in, leant her head on his shoulder and squeezed his arm against her body. His mind snapped up and he thought more clearly.

'Yeah ... that's exactly it. What drug?'

'What do you mean?'

He explained, 'Bromelain is a natural plant enzyme that could digest blood clots. There is no drug. Why would they

155

invest money in a product with no profit potential? They can't make any money.'

Twenty-nine

Gavin regarded Emma's face while they talked but his mind roamed a million miles away. He couldn't pay attention to her. He'd done that to her before and spoiled the moment.

Jim and Chris had done the same thing. Emma believed it to be a male thing. Men could only focus on one big thing at a time and it took all of their attention.

In one of her magazines, she'd read that it had something to do with cavemen needing total focus on killing a wild animal for food.

Anything less than total focus meant the animal took the caveman for its dinner. She'd read that man-eating animals had removed almost all of the genuinely sensitive men from the planet. This time, she said nothing and thought it best to leave him with his thoughts.

'I'll say goodnight, then. I'm quite tired.'

Gavin's mind stayed lost in mixed thoughts and emotions while they waited for the elevator to arrive. 'Thanks for tonight. I would have been a mess here on my own.'

'First, I was a baby snatcher, now I'm a babysitter.'

They paused in the corridor outside Gavin's room. Emma kissed him on the neck below his ear, wished him sweet dreams and then turned to go to her room.

'Oh … erm, I bought you a gift this afternoon, for helping me out. I'll give it to you at breakfast.' Gavin opened his room door.

'A gift. What is it?' Emma held his door open while he went inside and searched through a clutter of papers on his dressing table.

She allowed the self-closing door to shut and stood beside him. He found a rolled length of thin card and opened it to show her.

A vivid watercolour drawing depicted a view from the back of people walking on Avenue de La Grande Armee toward the Arc de Triomphe.

In the centre, a couple walked together holding hands. He'd bought it from a riverside artist.

Emma took the drawing from him and put it back on the dressing table. A wave of nervous energy coursed through his body. She took his hands and drew him close.

'Hhhh ... he said he'll be famous, one ... one day ... it'll be w-w-worth a fortune.'

His hesitant voice sent an emotional charge through her body. She saw love in his eyes and wanted to bathe in the feelings she had cherished before.

She reached out for a hug. 'Hold me.'

He took her in a firm embrace, eased his fingers through her hair and then rubbed the top of her neck. 'I love you so much.'

Emma breathed deeply as they wrapped themselves in each other's arms. She rested the side of her head on his shoulder. Tears rolled down her cheeks. 'I know ... I'm so sorry. You were only a little boy and I broke your heart.'

The tenderness of his soft fingers fired deep sensual feelings. Her mind raced back to the nights of exciting pleasure when she'd kissed him as an inexperienced teenager.

She drew her head back and their eyes met. 'Tell me our sweet love is still alive.'

He took her hand, kissed the back, the soft palm and then slipped the tips of two of her fingers into his mouth.

Her wet cheeks passed her tears onto his cheeks while her lips brushed over his on their way to kiss the side of his neck.

Quivers in his lips produced pulses of excitement in her body, and she felt a powerful ache low in her pelvis.

An intense thrill forced juice to flow, and her pants became warm and moist. She hadn't felt such pleasure for a long time. They hugged each other and searched for guidance on what they wanted to happen.

Memories flooded back, inhibitions dissolved and they wanted their old passion once more. Emma's tear-filled face fired his emotions and tears scampered down his cheek.

Fleetingly, he peppered kisses up her neck, the top of her ear and then he rolled his tongue in her lobe to send a thrill down her spine.

Their heads pushed strongly into each other with powerful kisses meant to join their hearts.

'Oh, I've missed your touch so much.'

*

Under his duvet, naked, their kisses alternated between soft and fleeting to forceful and urgent.

'How is the lovely Vicky?' he whispered.

'Vicky!' They kissed more until she needed to breathe. 'Vicky left me when I left you.'

'Ahhwll.' He squirmed when she took a grip.

'Oops ... I'm sorry, Percy. My nails are too long. I haven't done this for ... oh yes.'

Emma had trained the inexperienced teenager in the art of lovemaking. The art of making love to Emma. Her vagina had been pet-named Vicky after Victoria Falls on the Zambezi River because of the fluid that flowed from her when they made love. At the time, Gavin had been doing Southern Africa in his geography class.

Gavin's penis had been pet-named Percy for no other reason than it made them laugh and eliminated his embarrassment.

Emma enjoyed multiple orgasms before they climaxed together. They separated, panting for breath. Their bodies radiated surplus heat and moisture.

His duvet discarded, they lay on his bed, relaxing until their sweat became cold and damp. Gavin retrieved the duvet, and they cuddled together to warm their bodies.

Emma had trained him well, and he'd been a good student. His training had stood the test of time. He remained true to her first rule, the lady always comes first, and her second rule, the lady always comes again.

'Damn. The bed is wet. I thought you said Vicky had gone.' He inspected a large damp patch on the bottom sheet. Emma offered a simple smile.

'I'm glad this isn't my room. Yuck. Hand me some tissues.' Emma lay back with her knees up and legs wide open.

She pushed down on her womb to force out his milky coloured fluid. For a moment, she studied the fluid on the tissue. 'Do you have a microscope in the lab?'

'Yes. An electronic one with the latest ultrafine controls.'

She smiled. 'I'd like to see your sperm.'

'Fine, but you'll have to cut those nails.'

'For the microscope controls?'

He shook his head. 'For the sample collection.'

They laughed and kissed before he got up to pee. Emma leapt off his bed and followed him into the bathroom.

'Quick, quick, I need to go too.' She scampered into the room.

Gavin stopped his flow of urine and moved over to the bidet. 'Ah, now I know why the French invented the bidet.'

Once he'd done in the bathroom, he fetched two towels and put them over the damp patch on the bed.

They wrapped the duvet around themselves, then cuddled and kissed each other tenderly until they fell asleep.

*

Emma opened her eyes as dawn broke over Paris. She lay for a while and examined fine details on his face. Gently, she moved a whisper of hair from his eye. Her fingers hovered imperceptibly over his temple. She savoured the strong echoes of satisfaction from her groin.

Gradually, uncomfortable feelings became too much to ignore. Dried sweat made her skin feel sticky, and the tops of her legs felt tacky from the fluids that had seeped from her body during the night.

On her hand, she could smell a strong aroma. Time for a warm shower with lots of shampoo and soap.

When Gavin opened his eyes, he felt disappointed she'd gone. While he showered, he reflected on the previous night and tried to anticipate Emma's reaction.

An hour later, he knocked on her door, and without speaking, they made their way to the breakfast room. In an uneasy, atmosphere, Emma seemed a different person.

Jim Patersun had called her first thing in the morning, and she'd told him a pack of lies. Now, a strong sense of guilt filled her mind, and she struggled to deal with her betrayal.

In the hotel foyer, Emma paused and suggested they go for a walk before breakfast. On the street, in the cool early morning sunshine, they walked past shopkeepers busy preparing their shops for opening.

While they strolled, the reality of her life came into sharp focus. Her good life with Jim Patersun asserted itself, and she had no intention of giving it up for Gavin.

'I have no regrets about last night, but it *was* just a rush of lust and excitement. I'm not starting an affair with you.'

'It was my fault. I'm sorry. I didn't mean … for us to start an affair or anything.'

'I'm married to Jim and that's not going to change. You will forget about last night. The evening swept us back to when we were kids.'

With the air clearer, they returned to their hotel for a continental breakfast. They'd booked return flights for six in the evening.

Most of the day they spent at the Louvre, wrestling with their thoughts and wondering how they would be able to work together.

Gavin settled on the idea that he should pass the SeaPro project onto one of his postdocs. Brian Herding or Sharon Bonny. On second thoughts, not Sharon Bonny.

He imagined that a continuing stand-off relationship with Emma would bring new torment and despair to his life.

They walked around a small park to the east of the Louvre before returning to their hotel to collect their things. Gavin's feelings had crystallised.

He would withdraw from the SeaPro project. He couldn't continue to see Emma and not want her.

He feared a return of the deep melancholy that had consumed him before. In a strange way, making love to her had helped him to chase away the dark shadows haunting him. For the first time in almost eighteen years, he felt he could let her go and move on with his life.

While they waited in the departure lounge, he turned to Emma. 'I can't do it. I can't go on seeing you every day. I'll step back from SeaPro.'

Her eyes glared. 'Are you leaving us in the lurch?'

'My postdoc, Brian Herding is a good enzymologist. I'll give him all the help he needs to take over and complete the work on your project.'

'Jim will be furious. He'll think something happened in Paris.'

Emma sounded angry and thought that Gavin had decided to do this because she'd made it clear she wouldn't have an affair with him.

'I'll tell Jim I've got pneumonia. I can't carry on with the project. Brian will take over.'

She nodded. 'Fine. It's probably for the best. Jim would see through you in a minute. I don't want him wondering about us in Paris together. You make damn sure you're convincing when you tell him.'

Thirty
Glasgow Airport

Gavin and Emma hardly spoke during their flight to Glasgow. They flicked through magazines while troubled thoughts circled in their minds.

At the security desk, the border control officer asked if they were travelling together. Then, he asked them to wait to one side.

He picked up a telephone and made a brief call. Almost immediately, a man and woman arrived at the security desk, and the officer handed their passports to the man.

'Mrs Emma Patersun?' the man asked.

Surprised and confused, she replied, 'Yes.'

'Police. I'm Detective Inspector Packerman and this is Detective Constable MacBane.'

They showed their warrant cards. DI Packerman stood an inch taller than Gavin, and carried sixty pounds overweight.

His shirt strained to hold his surplus in place and his protruding belly pushed his trousers down. He had short grey hair.

The DC's dark red, mid-neck length, hair, seemed in need of a wash. The same height as Gavin but thin and gaunt with dark-brown rings around her eyes.

Dark nicotine stains on her fingers, and a strong smell of cigarette smoke, suggested she chain-smoked. Her plain black suit and white open-necked shirt would have benefitted from a quick once over with a steam iron.

DI Packerman extended his arm to show the way. 'Come with us, please, and you too, sir.'

The DI led the way and the DC brought up the rear. Gavin and Emma felt embarrassed as other passengers whispered and stared as if two terrorists had been arrested. The officers took them to a small room used for body searches.

The room contained a wall-mounted telephone, one table and four chairs. A uniformed policewoman waited inside near the door.

Packerman pulled a chair away from the table for her to sit. 'Please, sit down, Mrs Patersun. I'm afraid I have bad news.'

'Oh God—what is it?'

Packerman spoke softly. 'I'm sorry, but I have to inform you that your husband, Mr James Patersun, has been found dead. I'm very sorry for your loss.'

'Oh God! Not my Jim,' she screamed.

Emma took a sharp intake of breath and bowed her head. She sobbed, and fumbled in her bag to find a handkerchief.

Gavin moved a chair closer and sat down beside Emma. He looked up at Packerman. 'When did it happen?'

MacBane addressed Emma. 'He was found dead this morning in your garage.'

Between sobs, Emma glanced at Macbane. 'There … must be … a … mistake. I spoke to him first thing … this morning.'

'At what time was that?' MacBane asked.

'Just after seven, UK time. He was fine.'

Packerman consulted his notebook. 'There's no mistake but I will need you to formally identify the body.'

The woman police officer sat down at Emma's side, ready to comfort her.

Gavin asked, 'What happened?'

Packerman watched Emma closely. 'We've not completed our investigations but it might be suicide.'

Emma raised her head, wiped her eyes. 'Suicide? That's impossible.'

Packerman asked, 'How was his state of mind when you last saw him?'

Emma raised her voice with hope. '*Suicide* is out of the question.'

'Why do you think it was suicide?' Gavin asked.

MacBane consulted her notes. 'Mr Patersun was found in his garage at eleven fifty-five this morning. We estimate time of death at nine-thirty this morning. Mr Patersun didn't leave a note but beside him they found this newspaper.'

MacBane unfolded a tabloid newspaper. She opened it at page four and spread it on the table. It contained a photo with a short caption underneath. The caption read:

KINMALCOLM LECTURER SCOOPS 200K EURO AWARD.

In the text below the picture, it read, *Dr Gavin Shawlens and his girlfriend Emma Patersun attended a special dinner in Paris to receive the award.*

The photo showed Gavin and Emma entwined and kissing on board the Bateaux-Mouche boat.

Emma stared at the photo, shocked at the implication. She cupped her face with her hands, closed her eyes, and thought, *oh my God—what have I done?*

When she put her hands down, a nervous smile had snapped onto her face. Her reaction to fear and tension.

Since childhood, she had always made this smile whenever she'd been caught misbehaving or taking things that didn't belong to her.

The police officers looked on with concern but she couldn't shift the smile from her face.

Gavin raised his voice. 'Hold on, Inspector. This is all wrong.'

Emma stood and turned toward the door. Her shaking hand pointed. She took a deep breath. 'I want to go home.'

*

In the police car, Emma and Gavin sat silently as they struggled with the shock. When they arrived at her home in Newton Mearns, they found police cars and vans parked in her large drive. In the evening darkness, bright floodlights bathed her house and gardens.

Uniformed police officers meandered around the gardens, chatting and calling to each other. People in white forensic overalls carried plastic bags to and from a portable office.

For a few unnerving moments, the loud chatter faded while Emma and Gavin climbed out of the car.

Packerman escorted them into the house and through to the living room. Emma dropped her bag and jacket on the floor, collapsed onto her sofa, and curled into a ball.

She buried her face in her hands. She didn't want eye contact with anybody while she sniffed tears back up her nose.

A woman police officer stood on guard at her living-room door.

'Mrs Patersun. What were you and Dr Shawlens doing in Paris?' Packerman asked.

Emma sat up straight and moved her hands to her knees. Colour had drained from her face. She rubbed her hands on her skirt to wipe sweat from her palms.

Her voice sounded weak and tense when she replied, 'I attended a business meeting ... with our French suppliers ... I met Gavin in the departure lounge.'

Gavin chimed in. 'I'd been invited to attend the awards reception. We didn't set out to go there as a couple. I asked Emma to join me after we met at the airport.'

'There was no reason for me ... not to go with him ... we work together. I called Jim. He knew. He agreed.' She sounded defensive.

For the first time, Emma noticed that MacBane wrote everything down in her notebook.

'I'm sorry if this is painful. Were you and Dr Shawlens having an affair?' Packerman asked.

Emma closed her eyes and lowered her head. Tears ran down her face.

Gavin scowled at Packerman. 'Where did that idea come from?'

MacBane put the paper on the arm of the sofa. 'News seems to be painting it that way.'

Gavin shook his head. 'It's totally wrong. No-one interviewed us. They made it up.'

Emma blinked rapidly to regain her focus on the newspaper. 'Where did this newspaper come from?'

'I expect your husband bought it this morning,' MacBane replied.

Emma shook her head. 'Never. He wouldn't waste money on tabloids. Look over here.'

Emma pointed to a rack filled with broadsheet newspapers. 'He's a businessman, an investor. He buys quality newspapers for the financial pages. Tabloids—never.'

'Who found him?' Gavin asked.

'Mrs Jackson. She's in severe shock and under sedation,' MacBane replied.

Emma frowned. Her cleaner, Mrs Jackson, had discovered Mr Jackson after a heart attack, and had taken the trauma in her stride.

'Mrs Jackson did bring a newspaper but not this one, and it wasn't delivered by your postman. It's certainly a mystery,' Packerman said.

Emma rubbed her forehead. 'Suicide is impossible for me to grasp.'

'Why?' Packerman asked.

'He never quit anything in his life. Jim wouldn't quit. Why now?'

Emma rejected the idea that Jim had killed himself. He'd always been strong and spiritual. Suicide isn't a solution he would ever consider.

Packerman asked, 'Were you having marital problems recently?'

Emma clenched her hands tight. 'No, Inspector, we weren't. We get on well.'

'You got on well. Were you not in love with your husband?' MacBane asked.

Emma faced MacBane with an offended look. 'I loved him in my own way. We were never in love. We were good partners.'

Emma cupped her head in her hands. The reality of Jim's death took hold, and her mind tried to imagine what the aftermath of his death would mean to her.

MacBane finished writing and repeated, 'Good partners.'

Emma switched her gaze to Packerman. 'If we had marital problems, I would be up to my neck in lawyers with sharp scissors, aiming to cut me out of his business, and out of his life. That would be Jim's reaction to infidelity.'

Packerman and his DC exchanged raised eyebrows to note a point of significance.

'You seem certain he wouldn't take his own life.' Packerman exchanged eye contact with MacBane.

'Look, Inspector, business was his life. He would never abandon it for anyone, including me.'

The two detectives seemed more relaxed with Emma, and she felt more confident to maintain eye contact with them.

Packerman stood in front of his DC and they spoke in whispers.

When he turned back, Packerman asked, 'How long have you been married to Mr Patersun?'

'Eight years.'

'Obviously, you know him well?' MacBane asked.

'Yes, of course,' Emma snapped.

MacBane asked, 'Please forgive this intrusion but did you have normal sexual relations with your husband?'

Emma's jaw dropped and she glared at the detective. 'How *dare* you,' she shouted as guilt flooded back into her mind.

Thirty-one

Emma stood and faced Packerman. Her face reddened with anger, and her arms flailed as if she wanted to get away. She turned and stepped over to the French windows.

Packerman followed. 'Please, answer the question.'

Emma turned to face him with her eyes blazing fiercely. 'Yes, Inspector, normal. Not often, but perfectly, perfectly, normal.'

Gavin asked, 'Inspector, how can that be relevant?'

Packerman leaned closer to Emma. 'The circumstances suggest that Mr Patersun was a sexual asphyxic.'

Both detectives watched her reaction. She didn't understand and her bewilderment showed. The two detectives noted genuine confusion on her face.

Gavin rose from his seat and drew a sharp breath.

Emma's face contorted with concern. 'A what?'

Gavin went to her side, placed his hands on her arms and walked her back to the sofa.

MacBane looked up from her notebook. 'Were you not aware of his preference for sexual asphyxia?'

'What is she talking about?' Emma asked Gavin.

'Dr Shawlens? Did you know?' MacBane asked.

'I know *what* it is. I didn't know that side of Jim Patersun.'

'Gavin, what are you talking about? What is it?'

Gavin took both her hands in his and locked eyes with her.

Packerman spoke softly. 'Mrs Patersun, your husband was found hanged by a rope.'

She screamed once more. 'Oh my God!'

Gavin wrapped an arm around her, and pulled her close, but she pushed herself free. Packerman waited a moment for the information to sink in. He noted her tense jaw, rapid breathing, ankles and knees locked together, and head shaking.

Packerman spoke as sensitively as he could. 'He used a hand towel to protect his neck from rope burns, and he had a table close by for him to stand on comfortably. We found a clock on the table and a quick release knot in the rope to prevent accidental strangulation. But it seems he didn't release the knot in time.'

Emma closed her eyes as the image formed in her mind. 'Why? What for?' she asked as tears rolled down her cheeks.

MacBane said, 'We found your husband naked. Sexual asphyxics obtain sexual arousal by fighting loss of consciousness. They watch the clock. They know how long they can dice with death.'

Emma pushed away from Gavin and stood face-to-face with Packerman. 'What do you mean, quick release? He couldn't do knots. He did his shoe laces too softly. They always came loose.'

Packerman spoke slowly. 'Sometimes … a miscalculation results in tragedy. Sometimes, heartbreak is too much to bear.'

MacBane asked, 'Have you ever had any indication of this behaviour before?'

Emma's face blanked with disbelief. She covered her mouth with the palm of her hand as she paced around the room, searching. She didn't believe Jim could hide such a secret. Dryness strangled her voice, and she struggled to make a sound. Gavin fetched a glass of water for her.

In a low voice, Emma replied, 'What do you mean, indication?'

MacBane consulted her notebook. 'Have you ever found towels with brown rope marks or items such as a clock or a coffee table out of place or left in your garage?'

Emma turned to look at Gavin. 'What rope? I don't think we've got rope.'

'When the forensic team has finished with it, I'd like you to examine the rope and confirm whether or not you've seen it before,' Packerman said.

She struggled to say, 'I … I … can't believe Jim would want to do this … thing. This is so different from what I know about him.'

Packerman drew a curious expression. 'Why do you say that, Mrs Patersun?'

'Inspector, he'd not risk death for sexual satisfaction. He just wouldn't.'

MacBane sounded callous. 'It's strange what some people do for sexual satisfaction. The partner is often the last person to find out.'

'Not Jim. Sex was low down his priorities. He didn't need it … his business meant everything to him.'

Packerman saw that Emma needed time to recover from what she'd just been told. He suggested they all have a break. The two detectives huddled in a corner of the room for five minutes. They re-assessed their approach and allowed Emma time for reflection.

Packerman returned and took up the interview. 'My mind is still open until I receive the forensic report, but it seems you are telling me your husband wouldn't risk his life. If that is so, and he didn't die by asphyxic suicide or accident, what do you think happened to him?'

Emma glanced back at Packerman with her mouth gaping as his logic gathered in her mind.

Gavin raised his voice. 'Jesus, this is a nightmare.'

MacBane asked, 'Do you know of anyone who would want your husband dead?'

'I don't know.' Emma shook her head. 'No-one.' Then, she returned to the sofa.

MacBane raised her voice. 'Are you sure? Take your time to think.'

Emma squealed with frustration, leant her elbow on the arm of the sofa and cradled her head in her hands to cover her eyes. Her head ready to burst with tension.

Packerman called another break to help everyone's nerves. He asked if the woman police officer could make tea for everyone.

Packerman sat down in an armchair and leant forward to face Emma. He gave her an apologetic hand gesture. 'Look, Mrs Patersun, I'm a stranger in your life. I know nothing about you, your husband or this household. I don't know for sure what happened here. I need to ask all sorts of obtuse questions to find a lead. If I explore every possibility, then I may come across something. Surely, you want me to get to the bottom of this?'

'Of course, I do.'

'There may be something you don't think important. But it may be a key for me. I don't know what that is. I have to push and pull every angle, pleasant and unpleasant, until that key falls at my feet.'

'I understand. It's just too much for my mind all at once.'

Gavin asked, 'Inspector. Is this a murder investigation or what?'

Packerman turned to face Gavin. 'I have to wait for the pathologist to make his report. Until then, I'll keep an open mind.'

Emma sprang to her feet and walked over to a photo of Jim on her mantelpiece. Terrible thoughts gathered in her mind. 'Oh, Jim, what happened to you?'

The police officer arrived with a tea tray.

Thirty-two
Newton Mearns, Glasgow

Emma sighed, and wiped tears from her face as she stared at a photo of her husband. Gavin went to her side to comfort her. The two detectives drank their tea while they walked out through the French windows and onto the patio. MacBane ditched her tea, lit a cigarette and took a deep draw. They watched their forensic colleagues, busy at the far end of the garden.

They discussed inconsistencies that didn't fit the pattern of accidental death by a sexual asphyxic. A survey of Jim Patersun's wardrobes convinced them the man would have been neat and tidy.

Elsewhere in his house, they found his clothes folded neatly. But near his body, his clothes lay piled in a heap on the garage floor.

On the polished table, there should have been foot scuffmarks and dirt from the garage floor, if he'd stood on the table to prepare the noose and towel. However, they found no such signs.

Also, no fingerprints at all on the clock, and the clock wouldn't be placed on the table in case it fell off. Importantly, the clock he'd used had no alarm. Typically, they'd find a kitchen timer or clock with a loud alarm. They didn't find semen or marks on his penis to indicate strong masturbation.

Also, they also found no sign of rope wear, or indeed, much disturbance of dirt on the wooden beam used for the rope. No rope fibres were found on his fingers. They did consider that Jim Patersun had attempted it for the first time and it went wrong.

The two detectives mulled over the possibilities. Suicide, accident, or a clever murder. They started with the most obvious motive. A large financial gain for a sole beneficiary who conveniently had a cast-iron alibi. They judged Mrs Patersun capable of a clever murder, particularly if Jim Patersun planned to divorce her for infidelity.

On her sofa, Emma and Gavin sat together and hugged. MacBane nudged her boss to turn his head and look inside at the pair. Packerman agreed. Shawlens and Patersun were obviously an item.

MacBane nipped her second cigarette, and the detectives stepped back inside the house. Packerman pointed to the large cedar conservatory at the bottom of the garden. 'Does your land extend beyond the conservatory?'

'Yes. We planted the dense thorny shrubs out there for greater security.'

'Has your husband ever been threatened by criminals?' MacBane asked.

Emma shook her head. 'I don't think so.'

'Did any of his business associates worry or frighten him?' Packerman asked.

'No. I would have known if he had any trouble like that.'

Packerman extracted a black-and-white police photo from a buff coloured folder. It showed the head and shoulders of a man, together with a police reference number in the foreground. He gave it to Emma.

'Do you know this man, socially or through your business?'

'I've never seen this man before.' She glanced at it and passed the photo to Gavin.

Emma felt relieved at the change in tack. The intense pressure had delayed her grief, and she wanted privacy to think about Jim.

Packerman pressed, 'Are you sure?'

'Yes, Inspector—I'm sure.'

'Do you know the name, Joe McCaughey?'

'No.'

'Have you ever heard your husband talk of Joseph R McCaughey or heard the nickname, JR? Please, take time to think carefully,' Packerman said.

Emma shook her head. 'I'm sorry, Inspector, those names mean nothing to me.'

'Are you certain?' he asked.

'Perfectly,' she replied, confidently.

'Inspector.' Gavin handed the photo back.

MacBane took back the photograph. 'We know Joe McCaughey. He's a career criminal with a long sheet for burglary and violence.'

'What does he have to do with Jim?' Gavin asked.

'That's what I want to find out,' Packerman replied.

The DI pointed through the French windows. 'Joe McCaughey was found just inside the thicket at the bottom of your garden.'

'You caught him here?' Gavin raised his voice, excitedly.

'No, we didn't catch him. He was found dead this afternoon,' MacBane replied.

'Dead.' Emma shouted and slapped a hand to her chest.

Packerman said, 'Do you have anything to say about that, Mrs Patersun?'

She covered her eyes with her hands. 'I ... I ... can't believe this is happening to me.'

Her heart raced and she felt faint.

Packerman raised his voice. 'We think he was killed there on Tuesday night, sometime before midnight.'

Gavin sat back in the sofa. 'Jesus. That's awful.'

Packerman consulted his notebook. 'What were you and your husband's movements last Tuesday evening?'

'Tuesday night. I've ...Christ. I don't know ... Tuesday night?' Her mind struggled to think back.

Packerman padded the air with his hand. 'Take your time.'

'We were here ... we had Walter and Anne. They came over to play cards for a while. When they went home, Jim wrote a letter to the bank. I went to bed.'

'What time did your friends leave?' MacBane asked.

She shrugged. 'Ten-thirty ... eleven, maybe.'

Emma struggled to deal with the thought of a dead criminal in her garden. She felt threatened. She worried the police wouldn't believe she knew nothing. Emma became anxious, and felt she might be moments away from losing control of her mind.

'Have you lost any kitchen utensils recently?' Packerman asked.

Gavin saw her distress. He got up and stood in front of Packerman. 'I think that's enough for tonight.'

Packerman raised his hand at Gavin. 'Please answer the question.'

Emma strained to keep her focus. 'What do you mean?'

'Kitchen equipment, knives, that sort of thing,' MacBane replied.

Emma shook head and her eyes revealed she didn't know.

'Can you check now, please?' MacBane asked as she led the way to the kitchen.

Once there, Emma cast her eyes over the equipment drawer. To her mind, everything seemed normal. She opened her hands in the air. 'I have no idea.'

'Do you have a two-pronged fork? The type used for carving meat?' Packerman asked.

'Yes. I'm sure we have one.'

'Where is it?' MacBane asked.

Emma opened another drawer and rummaged for a moment. 'Here it is.' She reached to pick it up.

'Don't touch it,' MacBane snapped.

MacBane put her hand in a plastic glove and then lifted the fork into a large plastic evidence bag. She didn't look enthusiastic as she shook her head gently at her boss.

With her voice trembling, Emma said to Gavin, 'I can't take any more of this.'

Gavin stood between Emma and Packerman. 'Please, Inspector, can you continue this tomorrow? It's late. This is hard.'

Packerman moved past Gavin. 'There is one more photo I need Mrs Patersun to look at.'

From his folder, he pulled a black-and-white photo, larger than the previous photo but poorer in quality. The picture had been taken from a high position, looking down.

It showed a woman in a dark t-shirt. She had light-coloured, shoulder-length, hair. She wore tight fitting jeans that were frayed at the bottom. Her trainers seemed old and grubby and had split at the sides.

'Who is this, Mrs Patersun?' Packerman asked.

Emma raised her head to look. 'My front door.'

'Yes, it's from your CCTV. You cannot see her face because of her hair and the camera position, but otherwise, do you recognise her?' Packerman asked.

MacBane raised her voice a notch. 'It's vital we speak to this woman. She may have crucial information.'

Emma shook her head. 'I'm sorry ... I don't know her.'

The two detectives exchanged looks of frustration. MacBane sighed loudly at Emma.

'Are you certain?' MacBane asked.

Packerman said, 'The woman's behaviour in the video suggests to me she wanted to speak to someone in the house.'

He felt sure she wanted to speak to Emma. The criminal, McCaughey, had been stabbed in the neck with a two-pronged fork. It would have been bloody, and the DI didn't expect the murder weapon would have been returned to the drawer.

That left this unknown woman as a possible witness to what happened to Jim and or McCaughey.

Gavin examined the photo. He gained a distinct and familiar feeling, which he quickly dismissed. Sometimes, he came across people who reminded him of former students, and experienced vague recollection of memories. He said nothing.

'Have you noticed any petty theft from the house in the past six months. Food or clothing, or anything like that?' MacBane asked.

Emma raised her voice. 'No—No—No!'

'She looks destitute.' Gavin handed the photo back to MacBane.

Packerman turned to Gavin. 'Interesting, you say that. I think this woman has been living rough in the thicket out there. There's a sheltered hideout just beyond the conservatory.'

'Are you saying we had squatters?' Emma asked.

MacBane read from her notebook. 'We found a home-made sleeping bag, personal belongings, clothes, toys, large black plastic refuse bags, tins of food, bottles of water and an old black quilted jacket.'

Packerman asked, 'Know anything about any of these items, Mrs Patersun?'

Emma shook her head. 'Nothing ... I know nothing. Have you not given me enough to worry about?'

'Why was she camping out on your land, Mrs Patersun?' Packerman asked.

'Enough!' Emma shouted as she ran out of her living room and bounded up the stairs to the bathroom. They heard her retching into the toilet bowl.

MacBane called up the stairs. 'Who is this woman, Mrs Patersun?'

'Come on, Mrs Patersun. If she wasn't stealing from you, why was she hiding?' Packerman called up the stairs.

Packerman's face reflected frustration as he gathered his things.

MacBane turned to Gavin. 'There's a neat and tidy little den out back. Forensic people estimate it's been in use for a while. It's unusual for a tramp to live so close to a house and not steal anything ... unless she stayed there for a purpose.'

'Tonight is the first time I've been in Emma's house. I'm sorry, I don't know anything.'

'Now, the tramp has disappeared, and it's most unlike a tramp to abandon all her junk.'

Gavin shrugged at MacBane.

Packerman shouted up the stairs. 'Mrs Patersun. I will find this woman. I will find out the truth.'

'Get out of my house. Get out!' Emma shouted from the bathroom.

Packerman raised his voice. 'Don't leave town, Mrs Patersun. Uniformed officers will remain outside while the garage and back gardens are cordoned off.'

The detectives and the uniformed officer left the house. Gavin started up the stairs but Emma came down. Her face distraught, she'd smudged mascara over her eyelids.

They stepped into the living room and sat on the edge of the sofa.

'It feels like a bomb has gone off. My life is totally destroyed.'

He rubbed his chin with concern. 'You should have your lawyer here tomorrow. In case Jim was involved in something illegal.'

'I know in my heart he wasn't involved with crooks. But now I think about him, he did spend a lot of time on his own in the conservatory.'

A look of alarm sprang onto her face.

'What is it?'

Her jaw dropped and she sighed. 'The boy, Davy, from the factory.'

'What about him?'

'His older sister is homeless. Jim wanted her to stay with Davy at the factory. I said it was too risky having a young female sleeping there. Please, God, he wasn't seeing her behind my back.' Emma covered her eyes with the palms of her hands.

Gavin rubbed her shoulder. 'This is an awful nightmare.'

'My head is splitting. Can you get me a painkiller? There's ibuprofen in the kitchen cupboard, above the toaster.'

Gavin fetched the ibuprofen and a glass of water. 'What do you think was going on?'

'I don't believe Jim committed suicide because of that Paris photo. He'd want to have it out with me. But this sexual thing, I don't really know. Somehow, he must be involved with this woman, and this dead man. I can't believe all of this went on behind my back. The police must think I know about them.'

As they hugged, Gavin's thoughts returned to the woman in the CCTV photo. Her face had only been partially visible in the photo.

He focused his mind on her head and shoulders. Could she be a former student? While he concentrated hard on her face, he brought the photo to life in his mind's eye.

He watched in slow motion as she raised her head. Her hair parted from her face when she glanced up at the camera. Her eyes stared at him, and an ice-cold shiver ran through his entire body.

Thirty-three
Victoria Harbour, Greenock
Ten Weeks Later

On a warm, sunny day in mid-July, the board of SeaPro gathered to decide the future of the company. A sombre atmosphere reflected sadness and insecurity surrounding their project. The boardroom and the pilot plant equipment had grown dull and dusty from neglect and lack of use.

Walter accepted the role of acting chairman. He opened the meeting with a brief lament on Jim Patersun's life. Jacksan Horissey agreed to stand in for Tony Mascarri as the company accountant.

Walter and Jacksan had met earlier to decide the way forward. Walter had received a generous offer from BARSCO, and they agreed to seek approval by the board.

'... and Jim was our driver. He drove the project and we all enjoyed the ride. But, today, we must decide whether the company can go forward or not.' Walter said.

Emma wanted to get the meeting over with as soon as possible. The past ten weeks had been the most difficult of her life.

The police investigation had been relentless. Jim's business affairs proved more complex than she could imagine. The police questions reminded her constantly that she had betrayed him.

Her grief had been delayed, and she had been unable to sleep soundly for many nights. She felt drained and exhausted. Only once, a few days after Jim's death, had she spoken to Gavin. Emma felt that he'd abandoned her to face the police alone.

'Where are we now with the patent?' Jacksan Horissey asked Gavin.

'I've sorted all the issues raised by the patent agent. It can be submitted to the patent office next week,' Gavin replied.

'Would you be willing to take up the reins?' Jacksan asked.

Gavin shook his head. 'I'm not a businessman. I don't have the time.'

Walter chimed in. 'No-one can replace Jim's commitment.'

Jacksan held up a document. 'It's tragic, but I think we must sell the process to someone who can make the dream come true. I have an offer from BARSCO, which I think we should consider.'

Walter glanced and Emma and imagined she had no appetite for a boardroom battle.

'What's the condition of the production equipment?' Gavin asked.

'The last run through the process was well before Jim died. Davy hasn't been around so the equipment needs to be deep cleaned and serviced,' Walter announced.

Gavin chimed in. 'The buyer will want to check the equipment.'

'Can you supervise a clean-up and check the equipment?' Jacksan asked Gavin.

Gavin replied, 'Walter and I can do that next week.'

Jacksan wrote down some notes. 'It seems we have a strategy for going forward?'

Walter spoke softly. 'It hurts me to say this, but I propose we consider the offer, and if we find it acceptable, we sell the process and the pilot plant.'

'I second that proposal,' another board member said.

'Any counter-proposals?' Walter scanned the assembled faces.

No-one spoke, and with a look of betrayal on her face, Emma hurried out of the room.

'Is there any other business?' Walter asked.

With no reply, the meeting broke up, and a few of the members walked around the factory for one last look at the equipment. Walter went to the office to find Emma.

'Emma, how are you holding up?' Walter asked when he saw her wrought face.

Her voice weary, she replied, 'Soldiering on. Nothing else for it.'

'Are the police any further on?'

'Not really. My garage and garden are still cordoned off. They think I knew the dead man and the tramp living in the woods. They keep asking me over and over about them.'

Walter shook his head. 'They're barking up the wrong tree.'

'They're hunting for Mascarri. He's in serious trouble and they're sure his disappearance is linked to Jim's death. They're also searching for Davy and that woman. If any of those three turn up, the nightmare will kick off again. Waiting for that to happen is the worst part.'

'Anne and I want to be there for you. Just call us, please. Don't let this bother over the business upset you. None of us are capable of taking it on. You know that.'

Emma hugged Walter and thanked him for his support.

Walter flat-smiled at Gavin as he passed him in the corridor.

Gavin had been unavailable for eight weeks and only recently returned. A week after Jim's death, the Lambeth Group sent him to Manchester to investigate a university professor suspected of fraud.

Gavin ambled into the office to join Emma. His expression apologetic.

'I called you a few times, but you didn't answer. I called the lab. Christine told me you were away but she wouldn't tell me where.'

Gavin didn't like to lie to her but he couldn't tell her the truth. 'I had to do some research for the government. A bio-terrorism thing. It's always drop everything and come right now when they have problems to be sorted. I didn't take my mobile, sorry. I spent most of the time isolated in a bio-containment building.'

'It doesn't matter now.'

'I heard what you told Walter. The stress must be unbearable.'

Sounding exasperated, Emma ran her hand through her hair. 'My nerves are wrecked. I'm sick with worry. I've never done comfort eating. Now, I can't stop. I've put on twelve pounds.'

'Don't worry. When all this bother is over, you'll get back to your normal self.'

'I hope so.'

'It's difficult, but you need to hang on.'

Emma raised her eyes to glance at the ceiling. 'The police are pushing so hard. I don't have any answers. I feel so helpless. I just wish one of the missing people would turn up and tell the police what happened.'

Gavin put his arms around her and cuddled her while she rested her head on his shoulder.

'On top of all that, I have lawyers trying to untangle Jim's finances, which he spent a lifetime building into a complex web.'

Gavin drew back, and they separated. 'You could do without this hassle.'

Emma gave out a loud sigh. 'I don't blame them. They want to move on. Fine. I'll be glad to see the back of it anyway.'

Gavin leant close to kiss her on the lips but she pushed him back.

'I'm sorry. I didn't mean to do that.'

Emma hung her head. 'I haven't yet buried my husband. They haven't released his body.'

Without saying another word, Emma collected her jacket and bag then stood in the empty processing hall. Tears filled her eyes while memories of Jim filled her mind.

She remembered him busying himself in the factory. Working with Walter, laughing loudly in the office and explaining the process to young Davy.

Distraught, she searched her bag for a packet of paper handkerchiefs. When she found them, she marched out of the building.

*

Two weeks passed before Gavin and Walter could agree a time to clean the equipment. When Gavin arrived, Walter had already connected water and power to the six stainless steel tanks, lined up side-by-side in a row.

On top of each tank sat a stainless steel lid, and attached to each lid, a stirring motor. The motor connected to stirring paddles inside the tank.

Walter searched through his toolbox. 'We have to check the stirrers before we fill the tanks, so that any adjustments can be made while the tanks are empty.'

Walter climbed the metal staircase and along the gangway. He listened to the stirring motors while Gavin started each motor in turn and raised the revs.

Walter announced, 'The spindle in tank number four is freewheeling. The stirring paddles aren't connected to the spindle.'

'Okay. What do you need?'

'I need a size twenty-six Allen key for the nuts on the stirring gear. You look for one down there. I'll look for it up here.'

'When did you last use one?' Gavin asked.

'Davy had one. He used to slip down through an inspection hatch and tighten the nuts when they worked loose.'

'Where did he keep his stuff?' Gavin asked.

Walter strode past Gavin. 'In his cupboard.'

Gavin followed and they walked toward a cupboard near the office.

'Davy was homeless, so we allowed him and his dog Boggin to sleep in this cupboard.' Inside, they found a makeshift bed, old clothes and an upside down crate for a table.

On the crate, lay a cup, a knife, a fork and a dinner plate, which hadn't been washed for a long time. Gavin lifted the blankets on the floor and found three dead rats.

Walter sounded frustrated. 'It's not here. Little sod has taken it with him.'

With the tip of his shoe, Gavin moved the rats. 'Need to get rid of these.'

Walter huffed and fussed. 'I'll have to make a new key from a piece of hexagonal rod.'

Gavin mooched around while Walter made a new key. Then, he called on Gavin. 'You'll need to help me hoist the lid.'

Walter pointed at the stirring gear on the tank lid. 'Davy was thin enough to slip in and out of the lid hatch. We'll need to lift the lid so I can use the ladder to climb down inside.'

They walked to the fourth tank and Walter opened the lid hatch. A small funnel of light streamed into the upper part of the tank. They peered inside and strained their eyes against the inky blackness.

Walter frowned. 'Can't see properly, but the paddles are off the spindle all right.'

Gavin pointed inside. 'Looks like sludge lying at the bottom. We'll need to clean it out.'

Walter walked past him. 'I'll take off the bottom inspection plate and make sure the spindle is free before we hoist the lid and spindle. If we bend the spindle taking it out, it will be a bitch getting the paddles back on again.'

Gavin stood beside tank number four. Walter went down the stairs, collected his toolbox and then peered inside the ten-inch porthole on the side of the tank. It remained too dark to see anything through the thick plastic cover.

The porthole sat on a raised boss head with a metal ring. Six bolts secured the thick plastic cover to the boss head.

Walter called to Gavin, 'The sludge has stuck the bloody inspection plate. See if you can find a torch. I need to see inside.'

Walter removed all the bolts and the metal ring but the plastic cover wouldn't budge. He wedged a screwdriver between the plate and the boss head to lever off the plate.

Gavin called out. 'Can't find a torch.'

'*Aagghh!*' Walter jerked himself back from the tank and crashed his head against an upright metal support for the stairway.

He collapsed in a heap on the ground, holding his head.

'Are you all right?' Gavin called while he jumped two steps at a time down the stairs.

He stopped sharp when he caught sight of a boy's face jutting out through the porthole. A chunk of his face had stuck to the plastic plate and hung by a strip of facial skin. Walter vomited violently onto the floor.

'Oh God! Is that Davy?' Gavin asked.

185

The boy's face had decomposed but his eyes stayed open because the eyeballs had swollen. Gavin replaced the glass plate and secured it with one bolt.

In shock, Walter sat on the floor and propped himself against the metal upright. He had a small cut on the side of his head. He waved Gavin away, not wanting his help.

Gavin returned to the tank, hoisted the lid clear and then rigged a portable light. It lit the inside of the tank, and revealed its macabre sight. A torch and metal brush lay at the boy's side.

It appeared as though his flesh had turned to fluid, and drained to his legs where it leaked out to form a large pool of white material. His head had stuck to the porthole and kept his body sitting upright.

Gavin stared at the white material. He sniffed the air inside the tank but didn't pick up any odour. He stepped back from the tank.

His heart thumped, and a fearful grimace contorted his face. He shook his head. The tank should be stinking with the smell of death.

Thirty-four

With shock on his face, Gavin peered into the tank. His mind raced back to the vivid image of the dog at Fairfells. The odourless pool of white material, and the unexplained destruction of the black and white mongrel dog.

Walter joined him. His voice trembled when he asked, 'What on earth did that to him?'

'Why was he in the tank?'

'He's got his torch and brush. He must have been cleaning the inside ready for the next day. That's why we allowed him to stay here.'

'He's been in here *all* this time. The tank should stink.'

Walter pointed inside the tank. 'What the hell's that white stuff there?'

Gavin tried to remember the Lambeth Group report on the samples he'd taken from the dog. No bacteria, no viruses, just fragments of protein.

'Looks as if he's been digested just like the fish.'

Gavin turned to look at Walter. 'Surely, he wouldn't drink your enzyme solution.'

'Never. He knew how nasty it could be. Jim showed him the burn on his arm.'

'The product then?' Gavin asked.

'We all tried the product. We used it in lots of food preparations to check for fish taste. The boy had plenty. So did his dog.'

'His dog?' Gavin glanced over to the cupboard.

'What?'

Gavin hurried back to Davy's makeshift home. He'd noticed a white rim around the boy's cup. If coffee or tea had dried out, it would have left a brown ring.

Gavin inspected a thick white powder residue in the cup and then examined the dog's bowl. He picked up the red plastic dish. 'Look at this.'

Walter examined the bowl. 'What's that got to do with anything?'

'What happened to his dog?'

Walter shrugged. 'Boggin disappeared a week or more before the boy.'

'Was that around the beginning of March?'

'March, probably. Yes, I think it was about then.'

Gavin rubbed his temples as if trying to ease a headache. He recalled the dog at Fairfells Pet Centre. 'Was his dog a black-and-white mongrel with white speckled ears, long hair and white front paws?'

Walter's jaw dropped. 'How the hell do you know that?'

Gavin took the cup and bowl into the lab where he set up a test-tube rack with four test-tubes. 'Fetch the milk from the fridge.'

Walter frowned. 'That's for our tea.'

Gavin faced him. 'I need it.'

With care, Gavin scraped the white powder onto a sheet of plain paper. Then, he poured an equal volume of milk into each test-tube.

With a spatula, he transferred the same amount of white powder into three of the test-tubes, and then mixed the powder with the milk.

Walter shook his head. 'What the hell are you doing?'

'This is a crude test to show up any residual enzyme activity.'

Walter shook his head. 'I checked every product for residual activity.'

'We'll know in a few minutes.'

'Know what?'

Gavin lifted and examined a test-tube. 'If there's active enzyme in that powder, it will clot the milk.'

'You're wasting time. I'm telling you, I checked every batch.'

Gavin stood impatiently. He took out each tube in turn to give it a shake. Within seconds, large white specs of clotted milk stuck to the sides of the test-tubes.

Then, the milk curdled, and large clumps of white milk protein settled to the bottom of the test-tubes. The fourth tube, a control with no white powder, remained unchanged.

Gavin examined the glass tubes. 'The powder contains active enzyme.'

'That's bloody impossible.'

'It's just turned this milk to cottage cheese in less than a minute. It's active,' Gavin replied, then stood back.

He didn't expect the outcome to be so conclusive so quickly. He'd grown used to doing experiments that yielded the results he had predicted, but this unknown enzyme seemed unpredictable, and the idea scared him.

Gavin regarded Walter with accusing eyes. Walter, an engineer with experience of building ships, had learned food technology from reading one book.

Gavin suspected Walter had cut corners with the procedure to save money on running costs. 'You didn't use enough heat to deactivate the enzyme.'

Walter raised his voice. 'I bloody well did. I followed the deactivation procedure to the letter.'

'Get me samples of all product batches.'

'That was the last of the milk.' Walter shook his head.

Gavin pointed to the door. 'Go and get more.'

*

When Walter returned, Gavin repeated the test on all twenty-two batches of product. He found strong enzyme activity in all batches over six months old, and no activity in batches less than four months old.

Gavin rubbed his forehead, deep in thought. 'The final heat step in the process should have destroyed the enzyme. Somehow, with enough time, the enzyme has recovered its activity.'

Walter sat down and covered his eyes with the palms of his hands. In his mind, he saw a vivid image of young Davy, trapped in the storage tank with his face at the porthole screaming for help. Walter's hands hid his tears but not his sniffing and snorting to prevent water running down his nose.

Walter rubbed his face. 'I don't understand how this could happen.'

'Neither do I. It doesn't make sense. Think of what happens when you cook an egg. When heated, egg protein changes from clear fluid to a rubbery white, solid, protein. Understand?'

Walter sighed. 'Yes.'

189

'Think of uncooked egg proteins as rolls of double-sided adhesive tape. When egg is cooked, egg proteins unroll to become long, flat, sticky ribbons. All the ribbons stick together to form a mass of cooked, rubbery, white egg protein.'

Walter frowned as he tried to understand. 'Heat unravels the proteins into long chains.'

'The heat step in your process should have unrolled the enzyme so it became another ball of sticky tape with no activity.'

'But I never used less than the recommended amount of heat … *never*.'

'For the enzyme to regain its activity, it would need to re-roll and refold back into its original shape. That is impossible. You can't make rubbery cooked egg go back to uncooked clear egg white.'

'Will I end up like Davy?' Walter asked.

Gavin gave Walter a reassuring pat on the shoulder. 'Not if you ate fresh product. Digestive proteases in your guts would have chopped the unfolded enzyme into harmless building blocks.'

'So, it's older product that has regained its activity?' Walter rubbed the bridge of his nose.

'Yes, reactivated enzyme has blitzed its way through Davy's body. The white sludge is digested body protein. Poor kid. The same thing happened to his dog.'

'How do you know that?'

'The dog turned up at a pet centre. They asked me to have a look at it. Same white fluid. Same absence of smell, and same destruction of the body.'

Walter ambled into the office and sat down to think about Davy. First, his friend Jim, and now Davy. He wondered if the project had been cursed.

Gavin remained in the laboratory. His scientific brain worked through the implications. The SeaPro enzyme seemed like the discovery of a lifetime. If his idea proved correct, and the enzyme did regain its activity, then all life-science textbooks in the world would need to be re-written.

Walter wanted an answer. He returned to the laboratory. 'What are we going to do about this?'

Gavin hadn't decided. 'Right ... well. It's obviously ... an industrial accident.'

Walter pulled out his mobile phone. 'I'll call the police.'

Gavin shook his head. 'Not yet.'

Walter frowned. 'Why not?'

'We have to postpone the discovery for a day or two.'

'That's crazy.'

Gavin pointed an accusing finger at Walter. 'If this goes public—forget the patent—forget selling the process. There might be criminal charges to face.'

'Oh ... *bloody hell*,' Walter yelled.

'We can explain this but our explanation has to be watertight. I need to do some experiments to find out why this happened. Otherwise, no-one will believe it to be accidental. A couple of days, a week at most.'

'What about Emma? She was fond of Davy. She thinks he's gone off with his sister. She should know what's happened.'

'I'll tell Emma, but not a word to anybody else. Wash away that vomit before you go.'

Walter sounded annoyed. 'What about the rest of the clean-up?'

'Can you finish it off on your own? I need to figure out what happened.'

'I suppose I'll have to manage on my own.'

Gavin needed time to think. He imagined Emma's reaction to the news and decided to wait. He hoped she would understand his compulsion to find out what happened.

For now, he had to protect this discovery from slipping out of his hands.

His mind locked onto a vision of solid, rubbery, egg white, flipping back to a clear, runny, fluid. Over and over, he thought, *impossible but it's the only answer*.

Thirty-five
University of Kinmalcolm

Gavin strained to keep his eyes focused. He'd had little sleep during the three days since Walter had found Davy's body, and he'd neglected his appearance. Mentally, he flew as high as a kite as he explored the properties of the SeaPro enzyme.

He'd worked all day and asked Christine to stay late to help finish his experiments. At six in the evening, after a short break for a meal in the University refectory, they strolled back to their lab.

He opened the lab door for her. 'Thanks for helping out. I need this work done quickly.'

'No problem. I didn't have anything planned.'

'Well, I owe you dinner out next week. Somewhere nice, your choice.'

A man arrived just after the door closed. He peered through the glass panel.

Gavin turned back and opened it a few inches. 'Can I help you?'

A bald-headed man in a black leather jacket pushed through the door, knocking Gavin backward. A second man entered the lab. Tall, he had short dark hair, wore a dark-grey suit and a light-grey shirt. He drew a pistol from inside his jacket.

Christine dashed to a wall telephone and lifted the receiver.

The bald man ran to her, grabbed the phone out of her hand. 'Niet!'

Gavin raised his arms above his head. 'What do you want?'

The bald man beside Christine pulled a pistol from inside his leather jacket and motioned with it for her to back away from the phone.

The tall man asked, 'Dr Shawlens?'

'What's this about?'

The tall man extended an open hand. 'SeaPro. Give me all the process details.'

'SeaPro.' Gavin repeated and shook his head. 'I don't ... keep process details here.'

The tall man pointed the pistol at Gavin's head. 'Give them to me—now.'

Gavin squeezed his eyes shut. Said nothing.

The tall man fitted a suppressor to his Makarov PMM handgun. He stood apart from Gavin, raised his arm to shoulder height, and aimed at Christine's head.

With shock on her face, Christine struggled with the bald man. He took a firmer grip of her arm.

After seconds, that seemed like minutes, the tall man sensed he hadn't frightened Shawlens nearly enough.

He jerked his arm and fired a shot into a computer monitor. It imploded and showered glass fragments on the floor close to Christine and his comrade.

Alarmed, Gavin shouted, 'All right. The details are on a USB stick.'

The tall man extended an open hand again. 'Give it to me.'

Gavin shifted his eyes to the floor. 'Nothing is allowed off-site. It's kept at the factory.'

'Lies.' the tall man leant forward and pistol-whipped Gavin. His fingernails and the gun butt scratched Gavin's face.

The tall man pointed his gun at Christine. 'Do you want her to die?'

His comrade grabbed her hair, ready to force her onto her knees. She turned and kicked him hard in the groin. He collapsed in a heap, squealing in Russian and writhing in pain.

The tall man fired a shot at Christine. Her body recoiled, and her outstretched arm crashed against racks of test-tubes on the bench beside her.

A stool lay in her path, she fell backward over it, and landed heavily on her neck. Test-tubes rolled off the bench and down on top of her. She lay motionless.

As the tall man turned to aim his gun, Gavin grabbed a glass beaker from a nearby bench, and threw it full force at his head. It smashed against his skull, sending liquid into his eyes.

Gavin scampered out the door and along the corridor. From behind, he head the men shouting in what sounded like Russian while he ran down the fire-escape stairs.

Frantic, he burst through fire-exit doors at street level, and then discarded his lab coat.

When he reached the main road, he stopped running. Lots of people on the street made him feel less threatened. As he recovered his breath, he glanced back at the building. No-one had followed.

Bent over, to catch his breath, he wiped blood from his face with the side of his hand. He straightened up and headed for the nearest police station.

He cursed himself for leaving his mobile phone and car keys in his office.

He stopped short and tremendous fear flooded his mind. The gunmen would go after Emma for the process details.

With his SEM phone, he could have contacted the Lambeth Group to get support.

Unfortunately, he hadn't stuck to their protocol, which required him to carry his SEM at all times. It took him ten anxious minutes to find a taxi.

*

Gavin let out a loud sigh of relief when the taxi made its way up the drive leading to Emma's house. In the twilight just before dusk, her house appeared tranquil and beautiful.

Emma came to the door to meet him. She smiled to the policeman on duty to confirm that she knew the visitor.

When Gavin approached, she saw anxiety on his face. Then, the cuts on his cheek. Had he gotten into a fight?

He followed her inside and closed the door behind him. Emma fetched a first aid kit, attended to his cuts and tried to calm his trembling hands.

'What happened to you?'

He waved a dismissive hand. 'Better call the policeman.'

The officer took off his cap and scanned Gavin's face. 'Are you all right, sir?'

'I'll be fine.'

The policeman sat on the sofa beside Gavin. Emma perched on the chair opposite.

194

'I've just come from my work at the University of Kinmalcolm. I'd been working late with my technician, Christine Willsening, when—'

Gavin stopped as a vision of Christine falling to the floor caused him heartache. An intense feeling of guilt slapped his mind when he realised he'd run off and left her alone. He gripped his knees to stop his hands shaking.

'Take it easy, sir. Just try to relax. Start from the beginning.'

Gavin's voice trembled. 'Two foreign-sounding men ... Russians, I think. Broke into my lab and demanded details of the SeaPro process.'

Emma raised her voice. 'Our process.'

'Yes. They knocked us about ... then ... then. Christine kicked one of them, and—'

Emotion sapped his voice.

'Take your time, sir. Would you like a drink of water?'

Emma hurried to fetch a glass and handed it to Gavin.

'Drink it slowly, sir. You'll feel much better.'

Gavin engaged Emma's eyes, composed himself, and continued. When he got to the part about the tall man shooting Christine, Emma squealed, 'Oh my God.'

'Is she wounded?' the policeman asked.

'I ... don't know. I ... had a chance to get away.'

A strong feeling of shame took hold when he admitted he'd fled. He turned to Emma for support but she turned away.

Her jaw dropped, and she raised her hand to cover her open mouth.

'When was this, sir?'

'Forty ... maybe forty minutes ago.'

'Sir, did you call the police?'

Gavin lowered his head and shook it gently.

'An ambulance?' Emma asked.

Gavin shook his head again. The policeman frowned with disappointment.

'They want your process,' Gavin said to Emma. 'They'll come here next. I had to get here first.'

'Well, sir, let's hope it's not too late for your technician.'

The officer stood and went into the hall to use his radio. Gavin remained seated. He bowed his head, cradled it in the palms of his hands, and rested his elbows on his knees while he thought about Christine.

His imagination provided vivid pictures of her rolling around in a pool of blood and crying out for help. He felt stupid and incompetent.

He should have phoned for help and then called Emma. His mind had become saturated with all the credits and fame he would receive when he revealed the miracle enzyme.

When the police officer returned, he stood in front of Gavin. 'Just you sit tight, mate. The CID are on their way here.'

'How is Christine?' Emma asked.

The officer kept his focus tightly on Gavin. 'Look, mate, why don't you tell me what really happened?'

Gavin looked up at the officer. 'What do you mean?'

The officer bent forward and pointed to the cuts on Gavin's cheek. 'You know what I mean.'

'I don't.'

'Did she give you a bit of grief? Is that it, mate? Is that what happened?'

Gavin tried to stand up but the officer pushed him back onto the sofa.

'You sit right there, mate. You're not going anywhere.'

'What are you saying?'

'You can explain it all to CID. Just sit still for now.'

Emma asked, 'What happened?'

The officer kept his focus on Gavin. 'Did she tease you then change her mind? Before you knew it, you were punching and kicking. Look, mate, it happens all the time.'

'The Russian shot her.'

The officer turned to Emma. 'We have reports of a serious sexual assault.'

Her jaw dropped. 'Gavin!'

'Look, mate. You didn't call the police because you assaulted her. Didn't you?'

In the moments that followed, Gavin's mind ran wild. If these two men twisted Christine's attack to look as though he'd done it, he would be arrested and out of the picture long enough for them to take Emma. Her life would be in danger.

The officer turned to speak to her. 'The girl is still unconscious. When she—'

Gavin braced himself against the sofa, and with his left leg, he made a powerful sweep to slap the sole of his foot on the officer's ankle. The policeman's legs swept away to the side and he fell.

Gavin had leaned forward to put power into the sweep, and the policeman's jaw connected with the top of his knee.

Emma gave out a loud gasp. Gavin rose to his feet, and Emma knelt beside the fallen officer.

'He's out cold.'

'These people will kill you for the process details. God knows, I should have helped Christine. I've been foolish but I had to get here before them.'

Emma put her arms around him and gave him a hug.

'If I'm arrested, it'll take too long to explain.'

'What do you want to do?'

'I have to get you to a safe place before the police take me.'

Emma fetched one of Jim's jackets for Gavin and then collected her bag.

Gavin moved the officer into the recovery position to minimise any complications.

'We'll take your car. Leave your mobile—they can track it.'

'Where can we go?' Emma asked as they dashed to her car.

For a moment, they sat Emma's BMW 5 Series saloon, facing each other. Gavin revved the engine to warm it up.

The headlights lit up the driveway. The sun had set for the evening, and a cold wind blew in from the west.

'I'll contact the government people I work for. They'll sort this mess out in no time.'

A silver Mercedes sped up Emma's driveway and screeched to a halt. It blocked Gavin's path. Gavin strained to see through their headlight glare. Then, he spotted the passenger. The tall man who'd shot Christine.

They all froze and stared at one another. Then, the Merc driver's door opened and the leather-jacket man put his foot onto the ground.

The tall man got out from the passenger side. Gavin revved his engine hard.

'Dr Shawlens, this—' the tall Russian called out.

Gavin accelerated the BMW and rammed the Merc driver's door, crushing the driver's foot between his door and the car sill. The man gave out a piercing screech when the door crushed his shinbones.

'It's them,' Gavin shouted at Emma while he drove past the car and into the shrubs.

Moans ripped the evening air as the injured man recoiled in pain. The tall Russian came around the back of his car while Gavin drove over low shrubs and bushes then down the driveway.

The tall man ran to Emma's side and hit the passenger window with the butt of his pistol. The glass shattered into thousands of tiny fragments.

The pistol followed through and scratched the back of her hand as she protected her face.

The BMW's wheels screeched when Gavin swerved down the driveway. The Russian rebounded from the car and fell to his knees.

When he recovered, he took aim and fired three shots. The first bullet missed the car, the second pierced the boot, and the third hit the rear light cluster.

At first, Emma didn't notice her hand bleeding. She stared at the attacker through the rear window.

One of the blue veins on the back of her hand had received a deep cut. It stung fiercely and her eyes welled up.

Gavin pulled out of the drive, brought the steering under control, and floored the accelerator.

Cold air rushed through the broken window and the chill made them shiver. Gavin drove the BMW through the back roads out of Newton Mearns.

Twenty minutes later, they merged into traffic in East Kilbride, near Glasgow.

Gavin pulled over to the side of the road when the BMW stuttered and ran out of petrol. Emma wrapped a handkerchief around her hand and they continued on foot.

As they walked, Emma replayed images of the attack. The thought of someone firing a gun at her weighed heavily in her mind.

A feeling of dread gripped her when she thought about Jim, and the way he died.

Thirty-six
East Kilbride, Glasgow

The day had been sunny and warm, but after nine, the evening air turned cold. Gavin and Emma alternated between fast walking and jogging. Emma pulled up, and they stopped for a rest. She leant against the window of a clothes shop. Her tortured face reflected jagging pain.

'Are you all right?' Gavin held her elbow.

'Where are we going?'

'We can't go to my flat. I'll find somewhere for us to rest.'

'Honestly, Gavin, I feel ill. We need to do something now.'

He swivelled his head to get his bearings. While driving, he'd thought about the risks of returning to his office for his car keys and SEM phone.

If he could contact the Lambeth Group, they would send people to help him and provide security. They'd plucked him out of serious trouble before when he'd been on an investigation.

Gavin wiped his closed mouth with his hand. 'I'll need to go back to my office and get my phone.'

'I left mine because you said they'd track it.'

'Your phone has a network SIM card. Mine has a secure encrypted module. It's an SEM phone.'

'Encrypted.' Emma stared at him.

'Yes. The government research I do is secret, high security.'

'Call them on a public phone.'

'The SEM connects with a special socket on a satellite. There's no phone number for people to hack.'

'Call their office.'

'It's not that simple. The SEM authenticates me to them.'

You don't understand, he thought. They'd given him the SEM for just this type of emergency, and even though he wasn't on a Lambeth Group investigation, they would run to help him.

If Emma found out what he did for the government, she would become a security risk, and the Lambeth Group made security risks disappear.

'Well, I can't go any farther. I'm too weak.'

Gavin scanned the area. 'Brian Herding lives in Busby. He could put us up for a while. Give me time to think.'

'I've heard that name. Who is he?'

'One of my postdocs. Do you remember when we came back from Paris? I said he could take over the SeaPro project.'

Gavin flagged a passing taxi, which took them to a street in Busby where Brian rented a flat. Home and alone but not fully dressed for visitors, Brian opened the door wide and let them in.

'Hi,' Gavin said as he walked past him. Emma followed.

'Gav, what are you doing here?'

Gavin stepped aside to allow Emma to pass. 'This is Emma Patersun.'

'Hello, Emma, lovely to meet you. SeaPro, isn't it?' Brian offered a hand.

Emma shook his hand and smiled. Brian looked up and down her body with a naughty-boy smirk.

'Can you put us up for tonight while we sort something out?' Gavin asked.

'Yeah, no problem,' Brian said as he scanned the marks on Gavin's face and Emma's blood-stained hand. 'What happened?'

'Car accident,' Gavin replied.

'Seriously? Is that why the cops were looking for you?'

'What cops?' Gavin asked.

'Cops came here earlier to ask me if I knew where you were,' Brian replied.

'What did you tell them?'

Brian shrugged. 'What I knew. You were working late at the lab.'

'That's fine.'

Emma unwrapped the handkerchief on her hand. 'I need to rest.'

Brian examined her wound. 'Can I get something for that?'

She grimaced. 'I'd be grateful. I feel a bit rough.'

Brian fetched his first aid kit, and led Emma to his kitchen to clean her wound. He examined the cut. 'It's nasty. You need an anti-tetanus jab, if you haven't had one already, and stitches.'

'Tomorrow. I need to rest now.' Emma sounded weary.

'Are you sure?' Brian asked.

'If you don't mind,' she replied.

Brian showed her to his spare bedroom.

When he returned, he asked Gavin, 'What have you done?'

The two men sat at Brian's kitchen table and drank wine. Gavin told him about Emma but held back what had happened. 'Look, it's late. Let me get some rest. I'll decide what to do in the morning.'

Emma stretched out on the bed and thought about the attack. She imagined Jim hanging in the garage and she believed the men planned to kill her as well.

If it would put an end to her nightmare, she would close her eyes and let it happen. Her mum, dad, sister and husband, all dead. A powerful feeling of loneliness made her want to join them.

*

The following morning, Emma stirred just before seven when traffic noise grew louder in the street below. From the stale smell, she guessed the bed hadn't been aired for a long time.

She shuffled over to the window, and opened the curtains to allow daylight into the room. Then, she slipped into the bathroom, washed and dressed. She joined Brian in the living room.

He gave her a wide smile. 'Morning, how's your hand?'

She flexed her fingers. 'Good morning. Better, thanks.'

'Is Gavin awake yet?'

'Not yet. I'll give him a few more minutes.'

'So, what happened yesterday?'

Emma hesitated. 'Gavin should explain. I'll get him up.'

When Emma sat on the bed beside him, Gavin woke. Brian followed her into the room and offered to cook breakfast for all three.

202

He recommended his famous Bri's Fry. Although not hungry, Gavin accepted the offer, but Emma couldn't even think about fried food.

Brian went off to prepare breakfast while Gavin washed and dressed in the bathroom. In the kitchen, the noise from an old microwave drowned out the news from the radio.

Gavin joined Emma in the lounge.

Emma had decided what she wanted. 'Let's get this sorted. Contact the police.'

'But someone twisted the truth about Christine's attack.'

Emma shook her head and raised her voice. 'I don't care. People tried to kill me. I want the police to deal with it.'

'I could contact Packerman. We know him.'

She agreed. 'Do it now.'

Brian's house phone hung on the kitchen wall so Gavin went through to ask if he could make a call.

Overnight, he'd decided he would try to get in contact with the Lambeth Group. However, he had to do his best to keep their existence secret.

Gavin lifted the handset. 'I need to speak to the police about what happened yesterday.'

Brian nodded but didn't leave the room. Gavin waited and stared at the phone. He planned to call the Home Office. They would ask for confidential information to verify his status with the Lambeth Group. Gavin held the handset to show Brian he wanted privacy.

Brian ignored him and carried on cooking. 'I have a police contact. Nice guy, detective um … what's his name? His number's here … somewhere. Ah, here it is. DS Collins. I'll call him if you want.'

'Okay. Let's do that. Tell him I need to speak to Inspector Packerman.'

Gavin shuffled back into the living room and sat beside Emma.

'Did you call them?'

He gave her a flat-smile. 'Brian is calling Packerman. He'll know what to do.'

'Good. We need professionals to get this thing sorted.'

Brian popped his head through the doorway. 'Okay, folks. DS Collins is on his way.'

'Thanks.' Gavin raised an appreciative hand.

Brian came through to the living room. He held an egg turner, and wore a novelty kitchen apron, which depicted the body of a muscular, bronzed athletic man, wearing a short red tartan kilt low on the hip, standing in front of a sea loch surrounded by green grass. Emma smiled. Gavin frowned.

'So, are you going to tell me what this is all about and why the police are looking for you?'

'Yes,' Gavin replied.

Brian turned back to his kitchen. 'Hold on a minute, breakfast is nearly ready.'

Five minutes later, the smell of fried food filled the flat. Brian invited Gavin and Emma into his kitchen.

On the table, sat three mugs of coffee, a bag of sugar, a carton of milk, butter and marmalade.

On one plate, he'd set a pile of toasted bread. On another, he'd stacked fried bacon, eggs, mushrooms, sausages, and potato scones. Gavin and Emma sat down at the table.

'I thought we should have a breakfast party. Help yourselves.'

Emma smiled. 'I'll bet all the girls love your apron.'

Brian pointed a finger at Gavin. 'Think we should get one for him?'

Gavin side-glanced Emma. 'Don't even think about it.'

Brian pointed to the food. 'Come on. Tuck in.'

Emma studied the greasy food on the plate and it turned her stomach. She took one slice of toast and drank just half of a mug of coffee to ease the nausea she felt.

Brian asked Gavin, 'What happened to your face?'

Gavin ran his fingers over his cheeks. 'A while after you left the lab, Christine and I were attacked.'

'Attacked. You're kidding.' Brian's jaw dropped with alarm.

'Two thugs forced their way into the lab. One of them shot Christine.'

Brian pushed his knife and fork onto the table and reeled back in his chair with shock. 'Jeese-us. Is she *dead*?'

'I don't know.' Gavin sipped his coffee.

Brian shook his head. 'For God's sake.'

Gavin felt guilty. He hoped he wouldn't need to say he'd ran out and left Christine.

Brian took a couple of minutes to get through the shock. 'Wait, hold on a minute, this happened in our lab?'

'Yes, just after six o'clock.'

'Six o'clock! What about the cops?'

'What cops?'

'DS Collins was here when I got home. Asking about you. I told him you were still at work.'

'When was that?' Gavin asked.

'About five-twenty. He said he'd go straight back to the lab.'

Gavin stood up and reached for Emma's hand. 'We need to go, now.'

Brian's front door burst open and slammed hard against the wall. The large man, whose shoulder had forced the door, stumbled while he tried to stay on his feet.

Another two men entered the flat and darted over to Gavin and Emma. A fourth man followed. Tall, he wore a dark-grey suit, light-grey shirt, and tie. He closed the door behind him.

'Hey, DS Collins, what the hell's this?' Brian shouted.

'Mr Herding, you called me. I got here as quick as I could. I thought they might be holding you hostage,' the tall man replied.

Gavin and Emma recognised him.

The tall man showed Brian a police ID card bearing the name of Detective Sergeant N Collins.

He pointed at Gavin. 'We want him for killing Christine Willsening.'

Gavin struggled with the man holding him. 'That's a damn lie.'

'Christine.' Brian repeated.

The tall man pointed at Gavin. 'She named him before she died. We tried to arrest him at this woman's house but he killed a police officer, and they escaped.'

Brian shook his head at Gavin. 'Oh Jesus.'

Gavin shouted to Brian. 'It's a pack of lies. They're not policemen.'

The tall Russian pierced Gavin with his eyes. 'Will you come quietly?'

Brian stepped in front of the tall man. 'Maybe I should go with you to the police station.'

The Russian shook his head. 'I will come back later for a statement.'

Brian closed his eyes for a moment. 'I don't know about this.'

His eyes flashed back and forth between Shawlens and the tall Russian.

Gavin struggled while a man put rigid handcuffs on his wrists.

The Russian's men hustled Gavin to the door while he called out, 'They killed Christine. They'll kill us.'

Brian grimaced. The police ID seemed genuine but the accent? Collins wasn't from Glasgow, not even Scottish, Polish maybe.

The other men appeared more like thugs than policemen. Then, Brian realised there were no female officers. There should be at least one woman officer to arrest Emma.

Brian headed to the cupboard for his jacket. 'Wait. I'm coming with you.'

The Russian turned his back on Brian, pulled a suppressed Makarov handgun out of his jacket, turned and shot Brian at point-blank range in the forehead.

Brian catapulted back and landed heavily on the floor. The back of his head shattered, sending blood and brain tissue across the floor.

Emma screamed, and her captor slapped her face.

Gavin slipped down onto his knees with his head bowed. He clamped his eyes shut, and he felt blood draining from his head as if he might pass out.

The man holding onto Gavin pulled him back onto his feet.

The tall Russian leant into Gavin's face. 'You should keep your mouth *shut*.'

Thirty-seven

Nikolay Zavarok's men marched Gavin and Emma to the street. A black Mercedes SUV with blacked out windows, waited with its engine ticking over. Inside, it stank of stale cigarette smoke and diesel fumes, and set Gavin off in a fit of coughing.

They drove to the docks at Port Glasgow on the Clyde estuary and parked at a manned entrance gate. A customs officer approached the car.

The driver got out and spoke to the customs officer. They met halfway, and the customs officer glanced over to the car. He seemed satisfied with what he was told, waved them on, and went back into his office.

The driver parked the SUV close to a Russian ship, *Pechorna*, where the crew were busy loading second-hand cars for shipment to Russia.

Zavarok led the pair along the deck to the wheelhouse and then into a narrow corridor underneath the bridge. Zavarok stepped into a cabin. He moved to one side to allow Gavin and Emma to enter.

Inside the cabin, two sailors argued in Russian. One wore a peaked cap and a dark-grey sweater over a grubby shirt. The other wore an unzipped boiler suit over an old t-shirt.

When Zavarok entered, they stood and then cleared empty food wrappings from the table in the centre of the cabin. The air smelled strongly of stale food and stale clothes. Several bluebottles buzzed around the confined space.

Zavarok started a heated conversation in Russian with the Captain. The three FSB agents waited in the corridor and lit cigarettes.

The Captain and the engineer left the cabin with angry-looking faces as they pushed past the FSB agents.

Zavarok's voice reverted to English with a strong Russian accent. 'Sit down, please. My name is Nikolay Zavarok. Do as I say and you will not be harmed.'

'What are you going to do with us?' Gavin asked.

Zavarok smiled. 'Business, Dr Shawlens, just business.'

'What do you want from me?' Emma asked.

Zavarok turned to Emma. 'Russian people need your discovery, Mrs Patersun.'

Gavin's voice weakened. 'You didn't have to kill innocent people.'

Zavarok frowned. 'If you gave up details yesterday—no death today.'

Gavin turned to Emma. 'I wish I'd given up the damn files.'

'Give me them now—our business is done.'

A bit too eagerly, Gavin replied, 'I don't have details on me.'

'No matter. You worked on patent. You will build new factory for us in Russia.' Zavarok turned and prepared to leave.

Gavin shook his head. 'A factory! No chance.'

Zavarok stopped in the doorway and cocked his head. 'If you do this, you go free. I give you my word.'

Gavin slammed a defiant hand on the table. 'I'm not going anywhere.'

'You will go to Russia—now.'

Silence hung in the air while Gavin rubbed his chin. 'I'll go to Russia but leave Emma here. She knows nothing about the process.'

Outside the cabin, Zavarok regarded Emma. He'd seen the bond between them. 'Dr Shawlens, you'll need female companion.'

'I'll make it work for you but only if Emma stays here.'

'Gavin!' Emma strained her voice. She read in Zavarok's eyes that she wouldn't walk free either way.

'If you don't want her—she will die. Is that what you want?'

The Captain returned to the corridor to argue for more time. A further shipment of cars would arrive later that evening.

Zavarok pinned him against the wall, rebuked him loudly and then shoved him back along the corridor.

Gavin thought he could delay the sailing. 'I need plans and materials from the pilot plant. Not far from here.'

Zavarok returned to the open door and raised suspicious eyebrows. 'What materials?'

'Custom specialised enzyme. It's the key.'

Zavarok shook his head. 'You cannot leave here. Police are searching everywhere.'

'Without the enzyme—there is no process.'

Zavarok searched Emma's face and saw she understood what he meant. 'You tell me what and where.'

Gavin gave details of the USB drive that he kept at the factory, along with instructions to collect five litres of enzyme solution.

Zavarok beckoned an FSB agent waiting in the corridor. 'Take them to end cabin. Find warm clothes.'

The agent moved Emma and Gavin along the narrow corridor to a smaller cabin, which contained two folding bunkbeds on one side, a narrow table in the middle, and a bench on the opposite side.

A small lightbulb hung above the table and swayed with the motion of the ship. Emma sat on the bench and leant her elbows on the table.

Gavin sat on the lower bunk and bent forward to avoid his head hitting the upper bed.

He felt despondent and inadequate. Three times, he'd behaved in an asinine way. Two of his friends had died and he'd almost invited them to kill Emma.

His mind alternated between a horrific picture of Christine lying on the lab floor and a vision of Brian lying in a pool of blood. His hands shook. He wanted to weep for them but he held it back.

Emma caught his eye. 'Don't feel bad. You're a biochemist, not James Bond. You don't think like these people.'

He ran his hand over his hair and down his neck. 'I thought I knew what to do but I've made such bad mistakes.'

She moved around the table to sit beside him.

At times, his clandestine work with the Lambeth Group involved risk and great danger. Danger he found exhilarating but never for him alone, for the team.

He always had a safety net, someone at his side to keep him out of the fire. In an emergency, the Lambeth Group always stood ready for rescue, support and backup.

This situation had turned out so differently, and it made him feel helpless. Thoughts of revenge gathered and the vivid image of Davy in the tank snapped into his mind.

'I'll make these bastards pay for what they've done to Christine and Brian.' He spoke with the certainty of someone who knew he could carry out the threat.

Emma sat back from him; surprised by the tone of his threat. 'Don't speak like that.'

'They want this for their people … I'll make sure their people get their share … their share of the pain. Horrible— unbearable pain.'

'Gavin, you're frightening me.'

Rage burned in his eyes, and a look of dread settled on Emma's face. She sensed something he hadn't told her. He'd always been an open book to her and she could read him easily. She knew he held something back.

*

Sir Christopher Aden-Brown had a traditional office on the third floor of Peel Building at the Home Office in Marsham Street, London. He'd led the Lambeth Group for six years.

In a meeting with the Vice-chancellor of the University of Darlington, they sat at a leather-covered coffee table, positioned between two brown leather Queen Anne high-back wing chairs. For the past forty minutes, they'd engaged in a full and frank discussion.

Aden-Brown's PA rang through, which annoyed him because he'd told her he was not to be disturbed.

He hand-gestured an apology to the Darlington v-c, rose from his chair, and strolled over to his desk to answer the telephone.

'Irene. What is it?' he asked, and his voice relayed his irritation.

'Sir. I'm sorry to interrupt your meeting, but Alan Cairn is here. He says it's *very* urgent.'

Sir Christopher braced himself. Alan Cairn, the Director of the Centre for Protection of National Infrastructure, always calm and confident, and not one to interrupt a meeting unless he had something critical.

A satisfying glow flickered in his mind. He enjoyed having MI5 mandarins come running to his door when they needed the Lambeth Group.

'Very well, show him in.'

'Yes, sir, right away.'

Aden-Brown turned to his visitor. 'Look, Giles, I'm awfully sorry. Something urgent has popped up. Can you, please, reschedule another meeting with Irene? We still have details to discuss.'

They had just finished shaking hands when Irene opened the door. The two men passed each other on the doorstep.

When Irene closed the door, Alan Cairn and Sir Christopher sat down at the coffee table.

Cairn sounded slightly out of breath. 'Is Gavin Shawlens on the grid?'

'No, he's not. Why do you ask?' Aden-Brown held Cairn's gaze.

Cairn relaxed a little and caught his breath. 'There's a flap on in Glasgow. Shawlens is in the middle of it.'

'What kind of flap?'

'Apparently, Shawlens got attacked in his laboratory. Two people died.'

'Is Shawlens dead?'

'He's missing. A policeman, and one of Gavin's people, Brian Herding, both executed, apparently.'

'Executed. For what reason?'

'If Shawlens isn't on an operation for you, then that is an excellent question. Something has blown up in his face. At this moment, I don't know what.'

'Where is Shawlens now?' Aden-Brown sat straight in his chair.

'Unknown. The police are scouring the country for him. I have Special Branch and MI5 looking for him.'

'How can he be missing? Why haven't you tracked him down?'

With an annoyed look, Cairn shook his head as if Shawlens had done something wrong.

Aden-Brown sensed bad news. 'Don't tell me. Not again.'

'We found his SEM phone in his office.'

'Damn fool. I've warned him about keeping his SEM with him at all times.'

'We'll find him—if he's still alive.'

'What do you know about the attack?'

'His technician, Christine Willsening, was knocked unconscious. She's recovering and my people are interviewing her to find out what happened.'

Aden-Brown sounded concerned. 'This doesn't make sense. His research has no value to anyone.'

'Has he done any classified work recently?'

'Shawlens hasn't done anything classified for more than six months. I sent him to Manchester recently, but that was a low-profile conflict of interest investigation, which he completed without a hitch.'

'I had to be sure he wasn't on an operation for you.'

Irene rang through. Aden-Brown answered. 'It's for you.'

He held the handset until Cairn joined him at his desk.

Aden-Brown went back to his chair beside the coffee table and poured more coffee into his cup.

After a few minutes, Cairn joined him at the Queen Anne chairs. He didn't sit down.

'We have a lead. Willsening has identified one Nikolay Zavarok, Russian security.'

'*Russian* security, That does sound ominous.'

'What could Zavarok get from Shawlens that would interest the Russians?' Cairn asked.

'Shawlens has knowledge of Lambeth Group operations. Secrets that could bring down the government. In the wrong hands—political napalm.

'This changes things.' His eyes sharpened on Cairn. 'You had better retrieve Shawlens before he disappears into the belly of Mother Russia because our masters will not be pleased with what comes shooting out the rear end.'

'I'm on it.' Alan hurried to the door.

Thirty-eight
Kensington, London

In the large bathroom of her luxury executive flat in Kensington, Julie Blackhest posed naked in front of a full-length mirror. She had risen from a warm and relaxing bath, and the aroma of luxury oils filled the room.

After she examined her trim body in the mirror, she wrapped a soft fluffy towel around her hair. What she saw, pleased her, as she patted herself dry with a soft bath sheet.

She heard the telephone ring and reached for her white housecoat. Her friend Donna answered the phone.

As Julie tied the belt around her waist, a gentle knock sounded on the bathroom door. A hesitant voice spoke. 'It's for you, Julie.'

Julie gave Donna a reassuring cuddle as she took the handset from her. 'Thanks. Could you pour me a glass of red wine?'

A male voice spoke, 'Secure line, please.'

Julie pressed a button on a small box attached to her telephone charger-cradle. A pair of small lights flashed red on the device. While she waited, she unravelled the head towel and gave her hair a good rub.

The frequency of flashing slowed until they stopped. It took twenty-seven seconds to secure her line.

Julie walked with the handset close to her ear. 'Line secure.'

Donna handed her a glass of Shiraz. Julie thanked her with a wink and a loud double click sounded on the line.

'Hello, Professor Blackhest, it's Ronnie at WRATH control. I'm monitoring Shawlens.'

'What's happened?'

'Can you confirm your GPS tracker is in his wrist watch?' he asked.

She took a sip of wine. 'Yes.'

'Shawlens has been static for the past three hours.'

'So what?'

'GPS puts him *in* the river Clyde near the docks at Port Glasgow.'

'Damn. Wait—he might be on the water. Send someone to obtain visual.'

'Already in hand.'

'How long before you have eyes?'

'Twenty minutes,' Ronnie replied.

'Okay, thanks for the update. Contact me when you have more.'

His voice dropped a notch. 'There's one more thing.'

Julie took a large swallow of wine. 'Go on.'

'There is an extensive police search for Shawlens.'

'Why?'

'Not known, but everybody and their dogs are out searching for him.'

Julie stood to attention and her mind sharpened into focus. 'Inform your Ring Leader immediately.'

'Understood.'

'Blackhest out.'

Julie made two phone calls while she dressed. She also asked Donna to pack overnight travel bags.

While Julie and Donna made their way to Gatwick airport, a standby pilot filed a flight plan for the BARSCO Lear jet.

Forty minutes after their arrival at Gatwick airport, the jet soared into the sky, heading north to Scotland.

In flight, Julie made a call, using a secure communications briefcase. Thirty-five minutes later, as they flew over the Scottish lowlands, a blue light flickered on her communications briefcase.

This time, Peter Bromlee made contact with her. 'Hello, Julie, I'm at Miltonbrae Street.'

'Pete, what do you have?'

'Good, bad, and bloody confusing. My man on the pitch reports a Russian ship making its way out to the Clyde estuary. Given GPS on Shawlens, I'd say he's on board. We're checking the ship, details soon,' Peter replied.

'Russians! What's the latest on the police search?'

'That's the bad. A female technician got attacked in his laboratory. Police suspected Shawlens for sexual assault, but the technician explained Russians had attacked them. Police had Shawlens under control at Patersun's house but now they have a policeman shot dead there.'

Julie jolted with surprise. 'A botched abduction. Are they stealing my SeaPro process?'

'That's not all.'

Julie closed her eyes to prepare for more bad news. 'Go on.'

'Dr Brian Herding worked for Shawlens. They found him dead in his flat, shot in the head. Eyewitnesses put Shawlens and a woman at the location.'

Julie sighed. 'What an utter mess.'

Peter sucked in air noisily. 'Are you ready for the confusion?'

'Fire away … if you must.'

'Police, Special Branch, and MI5 are each deploying resources to look for Shawlens.'

Panic gripped her voice. 'Why? Not for the SeaPro thing, surely?'

'Obviously, police want to know what happened to their man at Patersun's house, but Special Branch and MI5. What do they want with Shawlens?'

Julie knew WRATH had opened a file on Shawlens and had found nothing. 'Shawlens was clean as fresh snow.'

'Not completely. His satellite phone should have red-flagged him. What is an academic doing with a satellite comms module? We should have followed up more quickly. Clearly, there's more to him than we can see.'

Julie detected a reprimand in his voice, and they both knew she'd been lax in her evaluation of Shawlens. She'd been slow to tell WRATH about the satellite comms module on Gavin's phone.

'I see that now.'

Concern controlled Peter's voice. 'What worries me is that all of this is under the radar. There is no media and no publicity. It's all on a strict need-to-know basis.'

'Shawlens. I can't believe he's a player. Who the hell for?' she asked.

'Good question. I thought SB might be on us but not MI5. I know we're not on their agenda.'

Julie felt threatened. 'We desperately need a heads-up on Shawlens.'

'Agreed, so I've called in a massive favour to find out what's going down.'

'Anything from your other Ring members?' she asked.

'My Ring member in SB can't shed any light on the sat phone. Her guess, if it's official and not private security; it must be specialist undercover.'

'Oh God. I don't like the sound of that.'

'Neither do I. We must retrieve Shawlens. He's a direct link to you, and the tracker you put in his watch is a direct link to WRATH.'

'Maybe MI5 are on the Russians?'

Peter sounded unconcerned. 'I doubt it. The Russians have sailed merrily away. The three agencies are spinning around chasing down all known contacts. They don't know where he is. If SB or MI5 were on the Russians, they would be chasing the ship, not chasing their tails.'

'Who gave Shawlens that fancy phone, if it's none of them?'

'It has to be one of them. Maybe the Russians ditched his phone when they took him and that's why the services can't find him.'

'What's our status if we have to intervene?'

'My men will board the ship and eliminate Shawlens. How do you feel about that?'

'Fine. Dump him overboard. Have you briefed the Ring Master?'

'Yes. He agrees with me. I'll tell you more when I see you.'

'Okay, Pete. I'll see you in about forty minutes.'

Thirty-nine

Julie and Donna held hands to give each other strength. Julie's distress made Donna fearful and upset. They hugged each other for a few minutes.

'Phew. Thank goodness for the GPS tracker. Remember this, Donna. Listen to what people tell you but always go with your gut instinct.'

'I'll remember. I promise. Will you be okay, now?' Donna replied.

Julie put her arm around Donna's shoulder. 'Don't worry. This is a big special game we're all playing. Everything will be fine.'

Donna took her iPod from her bag. 'Can I listen to my music?'

'Of course, you can.'

Donna listened to the Beatles *Abbey Road* album. She played the tracks over and over. Julie watched as Donna mouthed the lyrics.

*

Julie and Donna arrived by taxi at the WRATH factory in Miltonbrae Street on the south side of Glasgow. The large wooden gate opened, and the taxi stopped just inside.

Julie informed the guard she had business with Vilegon Fertilisers. The guard started to give directions but the two women headed off in the correct direction so he gave up.

Once inside, they stood in the main hall to absorb the milieu and gain orientation. The shadowy outline of large pieces of machinery dominated the centre of the hall, and the atmosphere seemed unwelcoming.

Most of the hall hid under a cloak of darkness, except for a long table near the machinery in the centre of the hall, lit by portable lights.

Smaller tables jutted out from the main table to provide additional space for equipment and maps. WRATH associates busied around the furniture, examined papers, checked equipment and talked on mobile phones.

Others sat at communications briefcases similar to the one Julie carried. Confidently, she strode to Peter Bromlee.

He saw them approach and gave parting instructions to his Ring member before turning to address Julie. 'Hello, ladies.'

'Pete,' Julie replied and then turned to Donna. 'Would you make tea and coffee for everyone, please?'

Donna smiled, gave the overnight bags to Julie, and ran over to the small kitchen at the end of a row of glass-partitioned offices.

Peter and Julie watched her for a moment.

'How is she doing?' he asked.

Julie shook her head. 'The terror on her face when she wakes up from one of her nightmares—makes my heart thump.'

'It'll take time but she's a strong girl. She'll pull through.'

'I know. She's a lot better than when I first got her. Anyway, what's the latest?'

Peter gave Julie a detailed update on all the current intelligence. She examined an aerial photograph of a Russian ship, and Peter used a large map to show her how the *Pechorna* headed down the estuary under direction of a coastguard pilot. He checked at his watch and confirmed the pilot would leave within the hour.

'They'll sail up the west coast to the north of Scotland and around to the North Sea.'

He received a note from one of his men; reporting the *Pechorna* travelling at ten knots and low in the water.

'They'll pass through the Minches. Strong currents funnelling through the Minches will slow the ship to a crawl of maybe five or six knots.'

'Is that when you'll get aboard the ship?' Julie asked.

'Yes. I've established a forward post at our training centre near Cape Wrath.'

The irony that the *Pechorna* sailed toward their training centre amused Julie.

'Do you have enough people?'

'No. I have two jobs in midstream, so WRATH personnel are stretched. I've given instructions to deploy eight Ring associates currently undergoing final evaluation.'

'Are we all right for time?' Julie chewed on her lower lip.

'No problem with time. They'll not reach the Minches until tomorrow night.'

Hugo Hurrigan, a senior WRATH Ring member, joined them. 'Then, most of them will be vodka tonic.'

Julie hugged him. 'Hello, Hugo. It's good to see you.'

'Nice to see you again, Julie.' Hugo smiled.

'So, you think takeover will be straightforward enough?' Julie asked.

Hugo cocked his head to the side. 'Yes, boarding on the fly is the main challenge.'

Hugo showed a picture of Gavin Shawlens to Julie. 'I understand we have to eliminate this threat and recover a tracker in his watch.'

Julie nodded. 'Be sure to grab a confirmed kill image for me. I want to be sure.'

Peter received a call on a secure line. He signalled to Julie that this was a call from the favour he'd called in.

When the discussion ended, he shouted to all Ring members and associates. 'Stand down! Stand down! Everyone. Stand down and await further orders.'

With perfect timing, Donna entered the hall with a trolley of teas, coffees and biscuits. Everyone made their way to the trolley.

Julie and Peter retired to a quiet corner of the hall. Peter revealed the news he'd received from his friend in the UK Special Forces Support Group.

'A team of Special Boat Service Marines, from Black Group, have been scrambled to board the Russian ship and recover Shawlens.'

'Black Group?

'Specialists in boarding ships at sea.'

'Are we in the picture?' she asked and held her breath.

'No. This is *all* about Shawlens.'

She raised her eyebrows. 'Who the hell is he?'

'Do you remember two years back? You came across a name, the Lambeth Group.'

She racked her mind for a moment. 'I recall I didn't find out who they were.'

'They are specialist university researchers that police complex research and technology projects. They're linked into MI5 and the Home Office.'

'Impressive.'

'Apparently, Shawlens is their top life-science boffin. He knows where Lambeth Group bodies are buried. They think Russians are trying to kidnap Shawlens to get at Lambeth Group secrets. By the way, it's their satellite phone but the idiot doesn't have it with him.'

'Thank God. Why are they running around in circles?'

'It's taken them all this time to join up the dots. Shawlens' technician identified a Russian agent, so they know where he is now. We must get your tracker out of his watch before they trace the technology back to us.'

Julie sucked in air. She sensed the situation spinning out of control. With an effort to keep calm, Julie rested her hand on Peter's arm. 'Cards on the table, Pete. Can WRATH drag my sorry arse out of the fire?'

Peter engaged her eyes. 'Cards on the table. My first duty is to protect Gyge's Ring. You're a valued Ring Leader. I'll do my best to protect you. But if the Ring is put at risk, you know what I must do.'

'Of course. If it comes to that, promise me, you'll take care of Donna. I don't want her to be left alone in this world.'

Forty
The Minches, West Scotland

The *Pechorna* maintained a steady nine knots as it passed the Eileen Trodday lighthouse off the north coast of the island of Skye. The helmsman chatted with the communications officer in the wheelhouse.

An FSB officer sat with his feet up on a table and read a newspaper. They listened to a weather report and reminisced about the times they'd sailed through murderous weather.

Occasionally, a full moon peeked through the clouds to provide a spectacular illumination of the sea.

The engine clonked and clunked in the still night, and metal plates creaked and groaned with regular monotony as the vessel ploughed through a two-metre swell.

The *Pechorna's* speed had dropped to six knots when two high-speed inflatable raiding crafts (IRCs) crept up on the port side.

In the lead raft, four SBS Marines prepared to board while their driver, at the back of the IRC, concentrated on matching the speed of the ship.

The four marines, Jambo, Wolfie, Shortcut, and Bennie, had practiced boarding at sea many times. Only Jambo and Wolfie had experience of boarding a hostile ship at night in choppy seas. Shortcut, the least experienced, hadn't been blooded. Jambo led the team.

As they made final communication checks, Jambo and Bennie identified themselves as Alpha team. Wolfie and Shortcut as Bravo team. They wore black Nomex waterproof assault suit overalls, and black three-hole insulated Balaclavas under their MK7 combat helmets with integrated mini-cam video for live feedback.

Noses and eyes, visible through the Balaclava holes, they'd blackened with non-reflecting make-up. Their hearts raced when they drew up parallel with the ship.

The backup IRC, with one driver in control, took up position twenty metres behind the first. Each man carried two magsteps. Powerful electro-magnets that resembled rubber flashlights, but square shaped, so boot heels could fit securely into the corners.

Jambo threw a black rubber-coated grappling hook and rope ten metres up to the bulwark. The rope had large knots at one-metre intervals for grip.

He pulled the rope tight, switched on the first magstep, and waited for the next swell to push up the ship.

Jambo signalled his team to start counting. The powerful electromagnets had sufficient power to support the weight of a man plus kit for twenty minutes.

On the next swell, Jambo used the rope to pull himself up to stand on the step. He climbed the rope and constructed a magstep ladder up the side of the hull.

Fifteen long minutes later, all four men clung to the rope and stood on a magstep. Splashes from the sea washed over them.

Cold sea, muscle fatigue and heat loss made their hands stiff. Adrenaline kept their hearts hot and minds sharp.

The *Pechorna* pushed up and down through the water and it felt like a funfair ride. The rubber raft moved back from the ship.

Their hearts thumped when Shortcut slipped off his step. He dangled on the rope until his foot found it again. The backup IRC drew up close but Shortcut waved it back.

It took five more minutes for Jambo to reach the bulwark edge. He signalled to his team, *someone on deck*. Without warning, Shortcut's step lost power and dropped into the sea. He clung to the rope while the weight of his kit pulled him. He slipped down to the knot below.

Jambo retrieved a small Beretta 92FS suppressed pistol from his chest holster, flicked the safety, and re-holstered. He climbed the rope and popped his head over the edge.

A seaman stood on the deck, trying to urinate over the side. When he spied Jambo, he received a slug into his forehead.

Six minutes later, all four marines crouched on deck while they consigned the seaman to the deep without ceremony.

They extracted equipment from their waterproof backpacks. Each man had been equipped with the same set of weapons, explosives and communications equipment.

Each man carried a Heckler & Koch sub-machine gun with integrated suppressor, sub-sonic ammunition for ultra-silent operation, and six magazines.

Each had a Beretta 92FS handgun hidden in a chest holster.

In side pouches, they had ammunition clips, flash bang grenades, standard grenades, one torch and one Blackhawk knife. Other pieces of kit, they had stashed in various pockets.

Jambo and Bennie made their way to the wheelhouse, darting from one shadowy area to the next until they found the metal steps and handrail leading to the wheelhouse.

Jambo climbed the steps while Bennie covered his back. Jambo rubbed through the dirt on a glass panel and peered into the wheelhouse. A seaman sat at wheel, and another man (security) sat with his feet up on a table.

Music from a radio broke the monotonous drone of the engine. The sound of the Bee Gees resounded around the wheelhouse.

Jambo turned his attention to two doors, which led out of the wheelhouse, one open wide and one closed. The open room housed radio communications and the other contained radar and navigation.

Jambo told Bennie what he'd seen, and they agreed on the likelihood of other men in the side rooms. They planned their attack accordingly.

Jambo burst into the wheelhouse, sub-machine gun forward and menacing. With soft sounds—'ttzipp—ttzipp', he fired two slugs into the FSB security man.

The seaman at the wheel jerked his hands up.

Bennie dashed over to the rooms leading off the wheelhouse. The open communications room lay empty, so he turned around and kicked the second door inward with one forceful stab of his boot. He trained his gun on a seaman sitting at a satellite TV.

Instinctively, the seaman clasped his hands on top of his head. Bennie steadied the door with one hand and waved his gun to direct the seaman outside.

Bennie shouted pre-prepared Russian phrases. His accent poor but his meaning clear.

'Freeze.'

'On the floor.'

'Now.'

Both seamen scampered down on the deck. Bennie secured their hands and feet with large plastic ties then taped their mouths. Jambo covered the door.

Bennie removed a Makarov handgun from the FSB officer's holster. Jambo closed the curtains on the two doors and then examined the PA system.

When they'd secured the seamen, he relayed his status to Bravo team.

*

A weary-looking seaman climbed a metal ladder leading from the front cargo hold, through the circular housing and crane gear, and around the foremast.

When he stepped out of the housing onto the deck, he stopped to light a cigarette.

He didn't see Shortcut standing in the shadows with his back pressed against the housing. When he collapsed, he didn't know he'd been shot through the back of his head at point blank range.

Wolfie and Shortcut rolled the dead body over the side. Wolfie patted Shortcut on the shoulder, leant forward, and whispered, 'Well done.'

Shortcut had worried about his first kill but did it without hesitation or ceremony. Exactly as in training. When they'd completed their preparations, they made their way to the wheelhouse to join Alpha team.

Wolfie hung back and allowed Shortcut to walk in front of him into the wheelhouse. He raised his hand high and gave a thumbs-up signal to Bennie and Jambo.

They both congratulated Shortcut on his first kill.

Wolfie extracted a remote-control handset, extended a short aerial and pressed a grey button. On a small, red LED screen, the number 1 appeared. He pressed a black button then the number 1 disappeared.

Wolfie repeated the process two more times and then he pressed a red button. Incendiary devices exploded in the forward cargo hold and thick billowing smoke streamed out of the hold vents.

Jambo held a small digital voice recorder to the PA system microphone. He switched the system on and pressed play on his recorder.

A voice shouted in excited, panicky Russian.

'Fire in the forward hold. All hands on deck.'

'Fire in the forward hold. All hands on deck.'

'Fire in the forward hold. All hands on deck.'

Bennie broke the glass cover on a fire alarm button. The klaxon blasted out its warning tones. Jambo switched on all the deck lights to illuminate the deck and all the holds.

The front hold appeared well ablaze with extensive smoke billowing onto the deck.

Seamen scurried about, extracting hoses and activating pumps, while the klaxon blared. It seemed like unbridled chaos but the well-drilled seamen attended the fire effectively.

The Captain and first mate stormed into the wheelhouse. The door slammed shut behind them. The sight of four black-clad figures stunned them.

Then, they noticed the dead FSB security man whose blood formed a large dark-red pool on the deck.

'What happened here?' the Captain yelled.

Jambo pulled out a photo of Gavin and showed it to the Captain. 'Shawlens.'

The Captain shrugged. 'I know nothing about him.'

Bennie knelt down beside the seamen on the floor. He extracted his Blackhawk knife and pressed the blade hard against the throat of the first seaman.

'Wait.' The Captain held up his hand. 'Two foreigners below, end cabin.'

The Captain pointed at the floor to indicate the location of the cabin.

Jambo and Bennie left the bridge to find the cabin. An FSB officer, hurrying to the bridge to find out what happened, lunged at Jambo. Bennie killed him with a single head shot.

Moments later, they took position at the starboard end of the accommodation corridor. The centre cabin door opened. An FSB officer stepped out. He saw Bennie and slammed the cabin door shut.

Jambo ran to the door and pulled it wide. The FSB man had drawn his gun but Bennie cut him down before he could raise his hand and pull the trigger.

Bennie checked for a pulse while his headcam transmitted images of the face back to the SBS Commander.

Jambo pulled at the handle on the starboard end cabin. Locked. Bennie fired a burst on the lock, which shattered and showered the corridor with tiny fragments of hot metal.

He found Emma and Gavin huddled inside.

'Shawlens?' Bennie asked.

'Yes.' Gavin replied and jumped to his feet.

Bennie pointed to Jambo. 'Follow him.'

Emma followed Gavin and felt relieved to hear an English voice. Jambo pulled her out of the cabin when she didn't move quickly enough. No time to waste in a hostile zone.

In the corridor, she appeared ready to burst out crying, so Jambo covered her mouth with his gloved hand. He shook his head at her and his eyes told her to keep quiet.

Gavin and Emma followed Jambo up the stairs to the bridge. Bennie remained in the corridor with his sub-machine sweeping from side to side.

*

In the wheelhouse, Wolfie reported to the SBS Base Commander and then held his radio handset in the air. He told the Captain that a Russian-speaking person would give him instructions.

The Captain stopped the fire klaxon and issued instructions over the PA system. When they had the fire under control, he told his crew to gather beside the central cargo hatch in full view of the bridge.

In the cabin corridor, the portside end cabin door creaked open and a handgun poked out. Bennie fired a burst from his MP5SD and the door slammed shut. Bennie spotted a small porthole above the door.

He retrieved a flash-bang grenade, blasted the porthole with his sub-machine gun and popped the grenade through the hole.

Two seconds later, the grenade blasted a deafening boom in the metal cabin. Bennie opened the door and killed the man inside.

He radioed Jambo and told him he'd cleared the three cabins. Then, he checked the body while his headcam video transmitted the scene back to the command centre. He stepped out of the corridor and glanced along the gangway.

An angry mob of seamen gathered on the deck. They wielded metal pipes and tools as weapons. Bennie radioed Jambo and told him the crew had improvised weapons in their hands, but he hadn't seen any firearms.

In the wheelhouse, Emma let out her tension. She screamed at the blood and the dead man on the floor.

Gavin took Emma in his arms and turned her away.

Jambo rested a friendly hand on Gavin's shoulder. 'We'll soon have you folks back on the mainland.'

While he held Emma in his arms, Gavin peered out of a window and focused on a distant point of the moonlit sea. His mind surged with what he expected would happen next.

Face the music with the Lambeth Group and Alan Cairn. Face everyone at Kinmalcolm with the death of Brian and Christine. His work with the Lambeth Group finished. His research funding finished. His job at Kinmalcolm finished.

Forty-one

The Lossiemouth RAF command centre received an EVAC message from the Jambo on the *Pechorna*. The SBS Commander announced that his lads were preparing to move out. The command centre staff cheered and applauded.

The commander ordered a Chinook HC3 helicopter from Special Forces Flight to move up to the Russian ship, now drifting with the sea current.

The Chinook, with its night enhancement package for low-level night flight, had maintained a shadow position eight kilometres behind the ship, where it had deployed the two IRCs.

The Chinook hovered above the rear deck, and the air loadmaster crewman unwound forty-five metres of steel winch rope from the personnel winch above the forward door.

Jambo and Bennie stood on the cargo deck, beside the Captain, and faced the crew. Wolfie and Shortcut took Emma and Gavin to the poop deck. The wind blew strongly and the steel rope billowed back and forth with the stiff breeze.

Emma froze when she saw Shortcut attach a flimsy red and yellow extraction sling to the hook. It had a simple padded chest strap and narrow straps for legs. She stepped backward and shook her head.

Gavin tapped Wolfie's arm. 'The Russians have a USB data stick with government secrets. I need to get it from them.'

Gavin followed Wolfie, and when Emma saw them leave, she shouted, 'Wait, don't leave me.'

Gavin glanced back, and despite the terror on her face, he padded the air with his right hand, fingers open.

'Uugghh!' she shouted at him when he turned away.

Shortcut held the sling open for her.

She shook her head. 'I can't.'

'Move up or stay here,' Shortcut shouted over the noise from the helicopter.

Terrified, Emma stepped forward and Shortcut fitted the sling. Before she had time to think, he signalled, and the chopper hoisted her upward.

She gripped the rope for dear life as her body twirled like a top and her legs flailed in the wind.

Wolfie led Gavin to the cabins and they searched the bodies. Gavin stopped and stared at Zavarok for a moment. Wolfie stepped forward and searched Zavarok.

'This it?' He held up a blue USB stick.

'Great, that's everything,' Gavin replied.

He took possession of the USB stick and picked up the bag containing bottles of enzyme solution.

When they sat in the safety of the Chinook helicopter, Emma and Gavin appeared overwhelmed with relief. They wore communication helmets to protect their ears from the engine noise.

Their eyes and facial expressions showed them to be unharmed when they gave the air loadmaster a thumbs-up sign—good to go.

When the crew had stored the winch gear, the Chinook peeled away to its holding position, eight kilometres behind the *Pechorna*.

Shortcut and Wolfie watched the Chinook veer off into the night sky and then they joined their mates on the cargo deck. The crew edged closer to Jambo's position, ready to pounce.

'Show them,' Jambo shouted.

Shortcut pulled around his backpack and retrieved a package about the same size as a large book. He showed the Captain an electronic detonator device flashing a red light. The label read, *Composition C-4*.

Shortcut showed the Captain a remote control device in his hand before he threw the package down into the nearest hold.

Jambo finger pointed at the Captain. 'My mission is over. I'm leaving. If you attack me, I'll blow a large hole in your ship, understood?'

Wolfie and Bennie secured one end of a rope ladder to the deck and threw the other end over the side. An IRC moved up to the vessel, and the driver caught hold of the rope ladder after a couple of attempts.

One by one, the four SBS men went over the side, down the ladder, and onto the IRC. Each man embraced the driver and clasped hands with each other to acknowledge their success.

The IRC veered sharply away from the *Pechorna* to rendezvous with the Chinook for their extraction. Ten minutes later, the four Marines boarded the helo, and Jambo sat beside Gavin and Emma.

They flew to RAF Lossiemouth and landed on the designated pad for refuelling. Emma, Gavin, Jambo and his men hurried over to a large hangar, where hot drinks waited. Two Special Branch Officers, both in suits and overcoats, met them.

Gavin and Emma drank coffee with one of the officers while Jambo spoke to the other. When the Chinook had refuelled, Jambo wished Gavin and Emma good luck.

Emma thanked and hugged Jambo for saving them. He re-joined his men on the chopper.

Gavin and Emma followed as the SB officers led them to another helicopter pad, where a small Lynx helicopter waited to take them on the next leg of their journey home.

The helicopter-landing pad at the Southern Hospital in Glasgow. The senior SB officer called ahead to inform his colleagues in Glasgow of their ETA.

*

Ten minutes from landing, the senior officer called again to update when wheels would touch the ground. Throughout the flight, he twice tried to make conversation with Gavin.

He wanted to know what had happened, and what Gavin had told Zavarok about the Lambeth Group.

Both times, Gavin brushed him off because he didn't want to talk about the Lambeth Group in front of Emma. But he proved so inept at putting the man off that Emma picked up on his refusals.

She raised her eyebrows and wondered what Gavin didn't want to tell them.

While the Lynx descended to the hospital landing pad, Gavin peered out through a window. An ambulance waited to collect them.

With the ambulance he saw two men in plain clothes, a doctor in a white coat and a nurse carrying a Red Cross medical suitcase.

When they landed, the nurse ran over and escorted Gavin and Emma into the ambulance. The two SB officers veered off to speak to their colleagues. The noisy Lynx took off, hovered above them for a minute, and then peeled away into the night.

With the Lynx as a distraction, the two men knocked the SB officers unconscious then dragged them over to the grass verge.

The doctor got into the back of the ambulance, and the two men got into the front. The ambulance drove past the car park, adjacent to the landing pad.

In the car park, they passed two empty cars with three bodies lying on the ground between them. They'd been held at gunpoint, knocked unconscious and secured just before the Lynx landed on the pad.

In the ambulance, the doctor and nurse busied themselves with medical examinations, pulse rates, blood pressures and temperatures.

The nurse removed Gavin's Omega watch. The medics asked a stream of questions and neither Gavin nor Emma thought to ask why they'd been driven away from the hospital.

*

Twenty-six minutes later, the ambulance arrived at the WRATH factory in Miltonbrae Street. The ambulance entered the compound, swung over to the factory and around to the car park on the east side of the building.

The doctor remained in the ambulance, which left by the same way it had come. The nurse led Emma and Gavin through a fire exit door, where Peter Bromlee met them, just inside the building.

Peter introduced himself, shook hands with Emma and Gavin, and then led them inside the darkened factory. 'Dr Shawlens and Mrs Patersun. I'm pleased to see you both unharmed.'

'Where are we?' Emma asked.

Peter regarded the bag Gavin carried. 'I see you recovered all your belongings.'

The nurse handed the Omega watch to Peter who inspected it for a second and then put it in his pocket. Gavin handed over the carrier bag, which contained the bottles of enzyme.

'Everything,' Peter demanded.

Gavin retrieved the USB stick and held it in his hand.

'Excellent work,' a voice called out from the shadows.

Julie Blackhest stepped into the dim light. A WRATH associate, John Deakin, took the USB stick from Gavin and handed it to Julie.

'Julie, what on earth are you doing here?' Gavin asked.

Emma surveyed all around. She realised they'd not been rescued. A strong sense of confusion and betrayal filled her mind.

Julie inserted the USB into her notebook computer and attempted to open the protected file. She threw an annoyed look at Gavin. 'Please, don't force me to be painful.'

'My initials, GFS, then twenty-two, eighty-eight, then … plasticine.'

Julie laughed. 'Plasticine! Well, playtime is over for you, my boy.'

She opened the file and surveyed the contents for a minute.

She nodded positively to Peter. 'Good. That's everything.'

Bromlee issued orders to his WRATH team. 'Take them upstairs. Pack up your gear.'

Two WRATH associates manhandled Emma and Gavin toward a metal staircase that led to upstairs laboratories.

'Who's Julie? Who are these people?' Emma shouted at Gavin.

Gavin's face twisted with confusion while he tried to understand what just happened. Emma saw his disappointment. Gavin knew something; something he hadn't told her.

'Julie?' Gavin called out.

Julie turned her back on the pair and walked toward an office. It was time to wake her friend Donna who was fast asleep on a couch.

'The process is fatally flawed,' Gavin yelled after her.

232

The racket of people talking, moving and folding equipment, dropped to a whisper.

Gavin shouted, 'I'm the only one who knows how to fix it.' His voice echoed in the large hall.

Emma's jaw dropped as she stared hard at Gavin. Her face blank with disbelief. Streams of thoughts cascaded in her mind. *What has been going on behind my back? What has he done?*

Julie stopped and turned back from the office door. 'I did wonder if you would own up about what happened to Davy.'

Emma glared at Gavin. 'What happened to Davy?'

The thought that Gavin had been involved in Davy's disappearance came as a massive body blow. Emma couldn't put words to the betrayal she felt. She fought hard not to pass out as nausea drained her.

A black wave surged over the back of her head. Her legs buckled, and the man holding her just managed to stop her collapsing to the ground. He helped her back onto her feet.

Stunned and confused, Gavin couldn't speak and think fast at the same time. Julie couldn't know about Davy. No-one knew about Davy, except Walter MacDougill, then he understood. 'Walter!'

Julie smiled. 'A smart enough businessman but not strong on technical points. Thank goodness you explained everything to him in great detail. Sorry to burst your little bubble but you're not the only one who can fix it. I did like the egg analogy, by the way.'

'Shawlens! You two-faced bastard,' Emma cried as saliva splattered from her mouth.

Emma tried violently to wrestle herself free, but the exertion pushed her over the top, and she passed out. Two men carried her up a metal stairway and into a suite of laboratories.

John Deakin had been a WRATH associate for six months. Slightly shorter than other associates at five-six, he made up for that shortfall with a fit and sturdy looking body.

John approached Bromlee. 'Searching for Shawlens and Patersun will intensify. It might be better if their bodies were found and it all stopped.'

The WRATH Ring Leader thought about John's proposal. His friend in the Special Forces Support Group would be furious if Shawlens remained missing.

The panic over Lambeth Group security would not cease until they had his body. Emma Patersun, on the other hand, would yield at least ten bottles of Adipicene TR.

'What do you have in mind?' Peter asked John.

'A stolen car, quiet country lane, exhaust hosepipe. They couldn't face the music, alcohol, pills, suicide—case closed.'

'Okay, you have a go, but leave Patersun here.' Peter turned and called out, 'Hugo, bring Shawlens back.'

Hugo pushed Gavin into a chair. Peter placed paper and a pencil on a table. 'Let me explain how this will work. Within the hour, both of you will be dead. If you write a convincing suicide note, I promise, Emma Patersun will die without pain.

'If not, she'll die in severe stress while you watch. I have no particular preference. So, what is it to be?'

Gavin glanced at the faces watching him. Armed, they exuded danger. Nothing could save him or Emma from certain death.

Defeated, he wrote the note. Peter had given him no choice. Gavin imagined Emma screaming in pain, swearing and shouting at him as she suffered. He couldn't bear it.

As he wrote, he thought about his sister, Siobhan and his niece, Kirsty. Strong lights in his life, he loved them dearly. Profound sadness filled his mind as he knew he would never see them again.

His thoughts drained him, and he felt exhausted. If someone had put a pistol to his head, he would have closed his eyes and let it happen.

*

In the upstairs labs, a technician opened the door into the first room. He told the men to put Emma on a gurney and strip her naked. On the cold metal, she regained consciousness but couldn't resist with her wrists and ankles strapped.

When they'd finished, they parked the trolley near to a bed where another naked woman lay motionless and strapped to the bed. Connected to various tubes and bottles, she had numerous angry-looking crisscrossed scars on her body.

The sight turned Emma's stomach. Strapped to the bed, she could do nothing to save herself. Not that she cared much anymore. Since Jim's death, she felt she marked time until she would suffer the same fate as him. An ugly death.

Forty-two
Southside, Glasgow

John Deakin and Hugo Hurrigan took Gavin outside to a waiting Renault car. They cruised around for ten minutes until Hugo spotted an old Ford he could steal.

John and Gavin watched Hugo pull away in the stolen car.

John pointed ahead. 'Overtake the Ford, then, at the end of the road, turn left.'

'Where are we going?' Gavin asked.

'Concentrate on following my instructions.'

The stolen Ford followed the Renault, and they made off through the streets of Glasgow. John gave directions and said nothing else.

The two cars moved out of the yellow glowing streetlights of Glasgow city and into the inky-black darkness of the countryside.

For fifty minutes, they drove on the A809, heading north. Gavin stared off into the distance with a blank expression.

They passed a quiet country area known as Carbeth, and turned off the main road onto a farm track. They followed the track for fifty metres. Then cut off into a small field, which ran steeply downhill.

'Stop here.'

John dragged Gavin out of the car and signalled for Hugo to drive on.

Hugo drove the stolen Ford into the field. He bounced the car off an old dry stone wall on the edge of the path.

He aimed the car at a Scots Pine tree, and braced himself for a minor collision.

The Ford came to a dead stop with the engine still running. Hugo stepped out and used his torch to inspect the damage.

John and Gavin waited until Hugo made his way up the field to join them.

Hugo swivelled his head to admire the dark and lonely countryside. 'This is a good spot.'

John nodded. 'I've done this before.'

John held a gun on Gavin as they made their way to the crashed Ford. Hugo carried a bottle of whisky and a black plastic refuse bag.

John pushed Gavin onto the driver's seat, and forced him to place his fingerprints on the steering wheel, gearstick and controls. He pulled the wires apart and the engine stopped.

Hugo extracted a piece of garden hosepipe, old rags and disposable gloves from the bag. He made Gavin place his fingerprints on the hose.

Next, Hugo wrapped the rags around the end of the hose and wedged it into the end of the exhaust pipe. After he'd made it secure, he led the other end of the pipe to the window of the rear passenger door. He jammed the pipe in the window.

John took the whisky bottle, steadied himself in the car, and with his other hand, squeezed Gavin's jaw open.

'Need any help with him?' Hugo asked.

John shook his head. 'I've got it covered.'

Hugo started back up the field. Against the faint light from the car courtesy lamp, Hugo watched John pour whisky down Gavin's throat.

Gavin offered no resistance, and the whisky bottle moved up and down at regular intervals. Hugo watched for a minute and then continued up to the Renault car.

'Aagghh!' Gavin moaned.

'Shut up,' John snapped.

*

None of the whisky went down Gavin's throat. It poured down the side of his face, down his neck, down his body, and collected in a pool in the seat of his trousers. The cuts on his face stung.

A graze on his ribs burned viciously when whisky seeped into the wound. The bucket car seat caused a puddle of whisky to form at his backside. The alcohol burned the soft skin on his backside and his scrotum blazed as if on fire.

When Hugo had moved far enough away, John whispered, 'Listen carefully. I'm John Deakin. I'm a Special Branch officer, undercover. When I leave, wait fifteen minutes, then contact Special Branch on this number.'

John slipped a small piece of paper into the breast pocket of Gavin's jacket. 'The Carbeth Hotel is one mile back down the road. Call the number and tell them who you are. They'll collect you. *Don't* call the police.'

'I know the local police aren't safe.'

John looked up the field to see Hugo stood watching and waiting with his arms folded.

John shifted his eyes to Gavin. 'Bring the troops to Miltonbrae Street. I'll protect Emma. Remember, fifteen minutes. Ask for a change of clothes. One loose cigarette and you're toast.'

Gavin's eyes darted to the hose in the rear window. 'Will I be okay?'

John threw the empty bottle into the passenger seat. 'I've taken care of it. Now, slump to the side and don't move a muscle. Hugo is watching.'

John joined the wires, and the engine started instantly. Fumes poured into the Ford. He walked back up the field, stepping on stones to avoid leaving footprints. Hugo had started his way down the field to meet him.

Gavin sat rigid. The car fumes nauseated him more than the whisky. John had set the air vents on the car facia to point at the driver with the blower set on full to force fresh air over Gavin's head.

Hugo watched a small stream of fumes billow out from the door window where he had jammed the hose. 'Okay?' Hugo asked John.

'Perfect, he's out cold,' John replied as they walked through the grass.

Hugo stood at the top of the field and watched for two minutes. He wanted to be sure the engine didn't stall.

'That should do him.' Hugo slid into the passenger seat in the Renault.

John drove away, but Hugo grabbed the steering wheel when he heard the engine cut out.

Hugo cocked his head to the side. 'Wait, the bloody car has stalled.'

'He's already dead,' John said.

'Come on,' Hugo reached to release his seat-belt.

'We don't need to do any more.'

'What do you mean?'

'The whisky will finish him off,' John replied.

Hugo sat back in his seat. 'Well, if it doesn't, the heroin will.'

'What Heroin?'

Hugo held up a black pouch. 'I had a heroin syringe ready for an overdose. No point wasting it, so I put it in the whisky. Enough to drop a dinosaur.'

John smiled. 'Brilliant. Job done.'

When the Renault drove off, Gavin climbed out of the Ford, and dropped to the ground, coughing. The whisky ran down his legs.

His backside and genitals flamed in the cold air. He struggled onto his feet and leant against the car with his legs firmly closed. Unsure if he would be able to walk.

He felt a mixture of anger and relief. John had helped him but they'd still roughed him up some. And even though John had made sure none of the whisky went down his throat, it burned his privates.

Scared and irritated, Gavin checked the dashboard clock. He had a while to wait yet, and wait he would. He didn't want to mess up his reprieve. He hoped John would keep his promise and protect Emma.

Forty-three

John and Hugo returned to the Miltonbrae Street base. While they drove, Hugo told John more about WRATH and its work. Proudly, he told John about the Rehab AVC programme and the Adipicene TR ingredient they would extract from Emma Patersun.

John listened carefully. It was what he wanted to hear. His decision to go undercover had been the right call, and the more he heard about WRATH, the more determined he became to stop them.

John had been recruited as a WRATH associate six months ago. The crisis had overridden the rigorous selection process, but John had played his cards well, and the Shawlens situation catapulted him into the Ring.

John had seen and heard enough to know that Miltonbrae Street harboured the evidence needed for Special Branch to bring WRATH down. His painstaking investigation had reached a successful climax.

'Report,' Peter Bromlee asked when Hugo and John walked into the hall.

'Shawlens has committed suicide,' John replied.

Hugo nodded his agreement.

'Well done, lads.' Peter patted John on the shoulder.

Julie and Donna stood beside their bags. 'We're ready to go,' Julie said to Peter.

Peter said to John. 'Do you mind taking Julie and Donna to the airport?'

John glanced upstairs to the labs and wondered about Emma Patersun. He thought about the note he'd given Gavin Shawlens. Quickly, he tried to work out new timescales.

Peter raised his voice. 'John!'

'Of course not,' John replied.

*

Gavin hurried along a country road and found the hotel John had told him about. He burst inside and made his way to the public phone. He drew looks of concern from the locals.

One man, playing solitaire, shouted over to Gavin, 'If it's a taxi you want, I'll take you.'

240

Gavin shook his head and then cradled the handset between his head and shoulder while he retrieved John's piece of paper.

An elderly couple sitting near the telephone moved to another seat. The stench of whisky made the man cover his nose and the woman shook her head in disgust.

A female voice answered the phone.

'My name is Gavin Shawlens. I've been told by John Deakin to call this number.'

'Dr Shawlens, where are you?' the woman asked.

'I'm at the Carbeth Hotel, north of Glasgow. I need a change of clothes, and shoes, size seven.'

'Stay there. We'll be with you as soon as we can. Do not call anyone else.'

Gavin put the handset back and let out a sigh of relief. He made his way past the bar to the gent's toilet. The barman sized him up.

'Are you buying a drink or what?'

'White coffee, please,' Gavin replied.

Gavin paid for his coffee and waited beside a window near the door. He covered his eyes with the palm of his hand and sighed deeply in the darkness.

John Deakin had saved his life. Would he return in time to save Emma? They'd parted on bad terms and he'd seen hatred in her eyes. He regretted not explaining what happened to Davy, and what he knew about the process.

Jim, Davy, Christine, Brian and then Emma. Their faces swept into his mind and scorned him. He didn't want to be the only one alive. He didn't want sympathy. He didn't want all the sadness that would follow. The troubled faces in his mind told him he didn't deserve to live.

*

Forty-eight minutes later, a black Jaguar XJ saloon swept into the car park. A woman driver with one male passenger in the back seat. Gavin watched through the window as the woman climbed out of the car, fetched a holdall from the boot, and approached the hotel.

She didn't speak as she faced him and handed over the holdall. Gavin took it and returned to the washroom to change.

241

While Gavin undressed, he glared at the floor. The driver's face reminded him of the woman in the black-and-white photo DI Packerman had shown him in Emma's house.

In that photo, her face had been partially visible, and at the time, Gavin had tried to focus on her face to bring the picture to life in his mind's eye.

In his thoughts, he had watched her raise her head to look up at him. When her hair parted and revealed her face, her eyes stared at him. He didn't believe what he thought he'd seen because it was impossible.

Now, the driver had brought the face in the photo back into his mind. The face in his thoughts wore a tight-lipped smile. Gavin clamped his eyes shut. *Impossible*, he thought.

Gavin dressed in a hurry, returned to the driver, and handed the bag of old clothes to her as they headed through the car park.

In the back seat of the car, Chief Inspector Tom McKean introduced himself and Helen, his plain-clothes police driver.

As the car drove off, Tom asked, 'Has Lambeth Group security been compromised?'

'No. The Russians weren't interested in the Lambeth Group. They were trying to steal a food technology process.'

'Food technology?'

'Yes, a process invented by Emma Patersun's company, SeaPro. I've been working on the patent. Now, it has been stolen by the people who kidnapped me.'

Tom liked what he heard. 'That will be welcome news in London.'

'What happened to the Special Branch guys at the hospital?'

'Overcome. The two who brought you and three other officers waiting at the hospital. Overcome by people unknown. Thankfully, they're alive and receiving treatment.'

'Thank God.'

Tom glanced at Gavin's face. 'What happened to you?'

Gavin explained the events that had unfolded and then finished by handing John's note to Tom who opened it and read the message.

WRATH base, Miltonbrae Street, Glasgow.

Patersun—imminent danger. Hostage rescue—urgent.
Scrap police support—senior rank corrupt.
Rescue insertion, east wall, south fire exit, await my signal.
J S Deakin SB0257698.

Tom frowned, sighed and rubbed his eyes. The message supported Gavin's story. It confirmed senior police corruption and meant that police armed response units couldn't support the rescue.

'How many hostiles on site?' Tom asked.

'They were all packing up their gear to leave. I spotted only two or three who weren't getting ready to leave. Guards, I think.'

'John must believe a rescue is achievable without police support.'

Imminent danger ruled out the SAS hostage rescue team. McKean decided that Special Branch would need to rescue Emma without police support.

He called the Scottish Counter Terrorist Intelligence Section, and apprised them of the hostage situation. They agreed a rendezvous in Miltonbrae Street.

Helen drove the Jag there, and stopped about twenty car lengths from the entrance to the factory complex.

Gavin confirmed the location. She cut the engine and switched off the lights. While they waited, Gavin asked about Christine Willsening.

'Zavarok didn't aim to kill her. She was knocked unconscious when she fell over. She has recovered and she's fine.'

'Oh, thank God. I'm so grateful she didn't die.'

'She identified Zavarok from our database We tracked his movements to Greenock then to the *Pechorna*.'

'Zavarok had police helping him?'

Tom agreed. 'Yes. Police confusion about your attack on Christine was deliberate. Zavarok had help from a senior police officer. We'll track him down.'

'Was it the same people who overcame your two agents?'

Tom drew a deep breath and let it out slowly. 'Good question. John Deakin is undercover investigating a criminal gang called WRATH. If they intercepted you at the hospital. They received up-to-the-minute intelligence. We must have a leak.'

'Could be the same person who helped Zavarok.'

'I won't find that out until I get hold of someone to interrogate.'

'Zavarok killed Brian Herding.'

'Special Forces have evened up that score. Herding's death and your kidnapping have drawn a veil over the diplomatic mess. Someone in Moscow will be getting their fat arse kicked.'

'Good, that's the right outcome.'

'So, this new technology of yours must be valuable. The Russians took a huge gamble, and now these WRATH criminals have taken an enormous risk to interfere with our rescue and steal it from you.'

Helen interrupted. 'Excuse me. We have company.'

A slow-moving dark-blue van, with its lights extinguished, stopped about six car lengths behind them. A faint torchlight flashed twice in the dark cabin.

Gavin wanted to hurry along to the van but Tom restrained him. All three climbed out of the Jag and staggered unsteadily like drunks out for a good time.

The news about Christine had lifted Gavin's spirit. He prayed for more good news about Emma.

Forty-four

Krystal Pallork stepped up and down on the spot to keep her blood moving. A cold wind blew her black, chest-length, hair onto her face, and she'd developed a nervous head flick to throw the long tresses off her face.

For the tenth time in the past hour, she pulled out her bright-red lipstick, and refreshed her lips. She used thick lipstick and heavy makeup to ensure none of her punters wanted to kiss her lips.

Krystal worked as a late night butterfly at her usual pitch in Miltonbrae Street. A desolate street populated with a string of factories and offices on one side, and a large wall-enclosed industrial precinct on the other.

The precinct, known locally as 'the compound', contained various factory buildings and storage facilities.

Krystal twitched and tugged her clothes, uncomfortable in her uniform of sheer black stockings, short, skin-tight skirt, loose, gaping satin blouse, and black blouson jacket with loose flapping cuffs.

If thugs tried to drag her into their car, by grabbing her jacket, she could easily allow the garment to be pulled over her head.

On cold, wet nights, Krystal worked in a brothel known as BJD's Health & Relaxation Club. Always warm and dry, the club offered a safe place for her to conduct her business, and the punters were easier to control.

A couple of welcome drinks helped lubricate her joints, and she had fun with the other girls, sharing stories about their clients.

On the street, there were no good times, just money and sex, but all her money stayed in her purse. Krystal never deluded herself into thinking she provided a service to lonely men.

She cringed when prostitutes spoke on daytime chat shows 'of service to the community'. Krystal hated men who used prostitutes for selfish, aggravated and often violent sexual exploitation. Krystal made no excuses to anyone. She suffered it for hard cash.

*

'Hello, Donny.' Tom McKean entered the van and shook hands with CTIS Detective Inspector Donny Johnstone.

Tom introduced Dr Gavin Shawlens and his driver, Helen. Donny shook hands with them and then introduced his team of seven men from CTIS.

'I understand it's a hostage situation,' Donny said.

'Yes. One woman held by an illegal security group called WRATH,' Tom replied.

'Don't know them. Are we waiting for ARUs to arrive?' Donny asked.

'There's a rat in the job. An armed response unit will flag the opposition, so no.'

Donny shook his head. 'If I'd known there was no ARU, I would have scrambled a second team or called for SAS backup.'

Tom spoke confidently. 'The situation is imminent. I have a man inside, and he made the call. No more than four hostiles, and he'll protect the hostage. He has provided us with an insertion point. When he's ready, he'll let us inside and pinpoint the targets. Then, we crunch some skulls and Bob's your uncle.'

Donny thought for a moment before he replied, 'Okay, that feels better.'

Gavin sketched out what he could remember of the factory layout. One of the CTIS men opened a box and lifted a grapple rope and hook.

'Boss, are we going over the wall?'

'Good point.'

They talked over the options. It would be easy to scale the wall but movements of security guards and dogs would be a problem. Tom suggested the front door so that security guards could be controlled in the gatehouse.

'How?'

Tom pointed along the road. 'A good old Trojan skirt.'

Donny and Tom stepped through a panel door between the driver's cabin and the rear of the van. Donny peered along the road through night vision glasses. He returned a smile.

Tom told Helen to go with one of the CTIS men and recruit the street woman working along the road.

Krystal Pallork had no choice in the matter, co-operate or get arrested for prostitution. She ambled up to the large wooden gate entrance and pressed the gatehouse intercom.

'What do you want, Krystal?' Hamish MacRhoan barked through the intercom.

Krystal fidgeted, knowing Hamish could see her on his CCTV monitor.

'Hamish, I need to use the bog. Last night's curry—it's in a bloody hurry.'

Krystal peered into the camera while she stepped up and down and wrapped her arms around her body.

'Get lost.'

'Come on, ya prick. It's poking oot ma arse. It's no good for business.'

'What's in it for me?'

'You're on for a free punt.'

'Now you're talking.'

On the other side of the massive wooden gate, Hamish slipped the bolt on the panel door and pulled it inward. It creaked and groaned in the still night.

In a split second, a CTIS man moved past Krystal and held the muzzle of his Browning 9mm semi-automatic tight against Hamish's forehead.

Two CTIS sergeants followed and took Hamish under control.

Krystal smiled and ambled back along the road to her pitch.

'Bloody hell, what's this about?' Hamish yelled.

'Shut it.'

The others slipped through the door and into the gatehouse. They crouched down below window level. The newly built gatehouse stood ten metres square, brick built to window level and surrounded by glass panel windows giving an all-round view.

A CTIS sergeant pulled Hamish into the gatehouse to face Donny Johnstone. Everyone had crouched down into a squat position.

'What do you want?' Hamish asked.

Donny replied, 'Co-operation, friend. We're going to raid one of your crooked factories.'

Tom showed a warrant ID card to confirm his position in Special Branch.

Donny spread Gavin's sketch on the floor. 'Well, Hamish, I'm interested in that factory unit. What's their business?'

'Vilegon ... they're small-scale specialised fertilisers.'

'How many have signed in?' Tom asked.

Hamish flicked through the pages of the logbook and did the arithmetic. 'Should be five people over there now.'

'How many normally work there at night?' Tom asked.

Hamish rubbed his chin. 'Sometimes none. Sometimes, one or two arrive at odd hours, work for a while then leave.'

'Seems a strange setup?' Donny shifted his attention to Tom.

Tom waved a dismissive hand. 'It's a cover operation.'

'They're not factory workers—that's for sure.'

Tom cocked his head at Hamish. 'What do you mean?'

Hamish chewed his bottom lip. 'They're all hardnuts.'

Tom asked, 'How do you know?'

'Three weeks ago, we had a break-in. Kids stealing copper pipe from the plumbers merchant in C-block. My mate stumbled on them, called and I ran down.'

Hamish hesitated. Donny grabbed his jacket lapels and pulled him forward. 'Spit it out.'

'Two of these Vilegon guys arrived at my back and took over. Gave the kids a severe beating. One kid died at the scene, another died in hospital. The locals are outraged about what happened. We've had protests, verbal abuse and all sorts of trouble. I've had threats from the local hard men. I've lost count of the number of smashed windows.'

'Have the Vilegon thugs been charged?' Tom asked.

Hamish's lips quivered with fear as he hesitated to say more.

'Go on,' Tom demanded.

Hamish rubbed the back of his hand across his lips before he spoke. 'A police inspector took me to one side. Told me we had to say the kids fell off the roof or we'd go down for manslaughter.'

Donny and Tom exchanged looks to acknowledge the bent officer they were after.

'What was his name?' Tom asked.

Hamish shifted his gaze to the floor. 'He didn't tell me his name.'

'How did they know about the break-in?' a CTIS sergeant asked.

'All of the factory units are patched into the gatehouse radio link. They tell us if they want to leave or are expecting a visitor or have an emergency. Anyone can listen in.'

'Hamish, you've been helpful. Now, I want to see a plan of their factory,' Donny said.

He spread the plan out on the floor, and all of the men gathered to get a good understanding of the layout. Tom recalled Deakin's instruction.

Wait at the southeast fire exit for his signal. Donny planned how each pair would approach, and where they would rendezvous to wait for John Deakin's signal.

When he was ready, Donny turned to Gavin and Tom and gave them a thumbs-up. He organised them into four pairs, and each pair left the gatehouse in ten-second intervals.

Tom had paired with Donny, and as he prepared to leave, he tilted his head in the direction of the gate, and whispered to Gavin, 'You go and sit with Helen.'

Gavin slipped out of the gatehouse. He crept through the panel door and then stepped onto the road. He gave out a sigh of relief.

When he looked up and down the road, he saw the CTIS van and the Jag to his right. To his left, he saw the prostitute on the ground trying to crawl off the road. Gavin hurried along the road toward her.

Gavin's alarm soared when he saw blood streaming from Krystal's head and down her neck. He helped her to her feet, and they stumbled off the road and into a dark recess in the wall. An old fire exit that Krystal used as her place of business.

Gavin scanned her injuries. 'What happened to you?'

'Two … bastards … battered me.' Pain pinched Krystal's voice.

'Jesus, you need to go to a hospital.'

'Nah … all you get … stupid forms, stupid questions.'

'You need medical care.'

Krystal doubled over in pain and then straightened up. 'Good hot bath, I'll be as right as rain.'

She wiped blood from her nose. When she attempted to stand straight, she flinched and winced. Gavin helped her to stand steady until she could move.

'Did you get a number plate?'

'No car. They came over the wall on a rope. Called me "a fucking bitch". They beat me and ran across the road, there.'

'Over the wall. Were they wearing combat clothes?'

'Yeah, that's them.'

Gavin felt numb as he inspected her bloodied and beaten body. A wave of panic hit him when he realised the men were WRATH.

He heard an engine revving, and then he saw the CTIS van drive through the big gate. He backed into the dark recess and hid. His mind blanked with fear. He had no idea what to do next.

His legs gave and he slid down the door and sat on the ground. He rested his trembling hands on his bent knees while he stared straight ahead.

Helen had no time to react when the back door of the CTIS van flew open. A man dressed in combat fatigues pointed a pistol at her head.

He tied her up and then ran in front of the van to open the gate while his mate drove the van into the factory.

*

Donny Johnstone, his CTIS men, and Tom McKean died in quick succession. They had no chance with WRATH already aware of their intention. Each pair had slipped out of the gatehouse and into the dark shadows of the next building where silent headshots from close range killed them.

They didn't know WRATH had overheard the entire conversation in the gatehouse. Peter Bromlee's mole in Special

Branch had discovered Tom McKean's contact with Gavin Shawlens, which in turn exposed John Deakin.

The mole also told Peter that Tom McKean had contacted CTIS for backup. Peter ordered his mole to delete the SB logs, so no-one would know that Shawlens contacted McKean or that the CTIS team had gone to the Miltonbrae Street factory.

Quickly, WRATH moved the bodies into the factory and stacked them unceremoniously in a heap. Later, they would render them into fertiliser by the same process used to dispose of body remains after organs had been removed for Rehab.

Their disappearance would remain a mystery but no trace would ever be found. They took Helen to the laboratory, stripped her naked, and strapped her to a gurney; ready for her body to supply Adipicene TR.

Forty-five

Gavin ran away from Miltonbrae Street. Streams of hopeless thoughts weakened him. *Emma is dead* screamed through his mind and he felt suicidal. His heart thumped hard and tears streamed down his face.

This entire life-and-death trauma felt totally alien. He'd neither the experience nor the confidence to think straight under great pressure.

He thought about trying to contact the Lambeth Group but they worked hand-in-hand with Special Branch and MI5. Hope disappeared and Gavin felt like the last person running alone on the planet.

Like he'd fallen down a deep sinkhole, and a dark and crumbling underground cavern had become his world.

A strong feeling drew him home. Not far from Govan where he'd grown up, he remembered one place where he might find the means to end the nightmare.

He changed direction and headed into the heart of Govan town.

While Gavin leant on a shop doorway, he sucked in large breaths. He rubbed his chest to ease a crushing pain.

He'd run too fast for too long. The surroundings were familiar, and he walked on unsteady feet to a building he knew well from his youth.

Gavin needed the means to carry out what he wanted to do. He had no choice but to scrape the outside of the barrel.

His breathing came in hard pants, and sweat tacked his shirt to his back as he stumbled into an old public bar called 'The Baldy Heed'.

A traditional dark and gloomy bar with cracked linoleum floor tiles, and wood bench seats in cubicles. It had a long bar and a row of slot machines along one wall. Unchanged for decades, it needed redecoration sixty years ago.

Despite a national smoking ban in public places, many drinkers smoked openly and a pall of cigarette smoke clung to the ceiling.

To regain his breath, Gavin rested on the bar with his two arms outstretched. At the far end, he spotted two pool tables surrounded on three sides by wood benches.

A group of drinkers watched and cheered the pool players.

Gavin straightened himself and strolled unsteadily down the aisle, between the bar on his left side, and the cubicles on the other side.

Gavin's eyes searched the faces peering out from the cubicles. Local men and women eyed him with suspicion. He remembered a few faces from his school days. People he'd avoided at school because they were trouble.

The barman watched as Gavin stumbled toward the pool tables. More and more sets of eyes bore down on Gavin's weary figure. It seemed like a scene from an old cowboy movie, except Gavin Shawlens was no John Wayne.

He continued until he approached the nearest pool table. Two men played for a beer glass stuffed with money.

Before Gavin could speak, a large bald-headed man in a dirty white singlet grasped a handful of Gavin's hair from the back.

Gavin flinched as thick fingers closed tight on his hair. The smell of alcohol punched Gavin's nose. One of the pool players, Drew McKerr, glanced at Gavin.

'What are you doing here?' Drew asked as he stood straight and leant against the pool table with one arm outstretched, holding his cue upright.

Drew nodded to the bald man who released Gavin before he returned to his seat.

A long time ago, Gavin and Drew had grown up together in Govan. They'd been close friends until their paths took radically different directions.

Gavin had been the kid picked on by bullies and called names because his father was an Elvis impersonator. Gavin was the sissy who hung out with his sister and her friends. So, he'd always fought bullies and name-callers.

One day, after school, he took on two bullies at once. He'd been on the receiving end of a beating until Drew waded

253

in to even the odds. They became friends, and no-one dared bully Gavin again.

Drew had survived twenty-odd years of gang fighting, unprovoked attacks, revenge beatings, counter attacks and attempted murders.

His reputation as a hard man remained intact even when he 'retired' and left the gang scene to younger thugs. Women in Govan called him Steve because his face reflected the actor Steve McQueen.

Gavin stood beside his old school pal. 'I need a gun.'

'A gun? Didn't think students were *that* bad.' Drew and the people around the pool table laughed.

Gavin swallowed hard. 'Can you help me out?'

'Why?' Drew asked while still concentrating on the game.

'Something I need to do.'

'Why, for the second and last time?'

'I've got a friend in a real mess. I need to get her out,' Gavin replied.

Drew lined up his next shot. 'Forget it—you'll lose your toes.'

Gavin raised his voice a notch. 'Some bastards grabbed Emma Baxster.'

He used Emma's maiden name and hoped Drew would remember her.

'Emma, from the bank?'

Gavin glanced furtively to the side. 'Yeah.'

'What? Is there a bank job on the go?'

Gavin rested both hands on the pool table. 'If I had a gun and someone to back me, I could sneak in and get her out.'

'Get a ton of cops to play with your robbers.'

Gavin's expression hardened. 'They've killed two cops.'

Drew raised his voice. 'Two dead cops? That's serious shit.'

'Can you help me?'

'The only sneaking I'll be doing … is out that door at closing time when big Jake kicks my arse. If you need a car or a phone, no problem—that's my business. Otherwise, get out of my sight.' Drew positioned himself for a shot.

Gavin covered his face in his hands, and sucked in a deep breath. When he removed his hands, a hopeless expression drained the vitality from his face. 'Right. Sorry. I'm just … ugh. Not thinking this properly.'

Gavin turned and dragged his tired legs toward the door. He felt stupid and belittled for thinking he might convince a gang of drunken misfits to follow him on a suicidal fight.

'What are you gonna do?' Drew called out after he'd missed his shot.

Gavin hurried along and wanted to be away quickly. 'I'll phone the cops, fire brigade, and bring everything to their door.'

Drew called out, 'Scunner, give him a phone that works.'

Scunner walked with Gavin to the door. He reached inside his pocket, pulled out a Blackberry mobile, and then put it back.

Next, he retrieved a Samsung smartphone from another pocket and murmured, 'Not getting that one.' Eventually, he pulled out a grey Nokia.

Scunner examined Gavin's face. 'I was in the same geography class as you at school.'

Gavin shook his head, he didn't recognise Scunner. 'Sorry, I don't remember you.'

'I sat at the back but I remember you. Boring the tits off everybody with your stupid questions.'

Gavin guessed Scunner had become a petty criminal. No point asking him how he'd got on since leaving school.

Scunner pulled out another phone. 'Okay, this one's got limited range. You'll need to be close to a base station. Where are you going?'

'Miltonbrae Street.'

'The compound in Miltonbrae Street?'

'Yeah, that's where they've got Emma.'

'Who's got her?'

'A gang with a stupid name, Vilegon,' Gavin replied.

Scunner raised his voice. 'Vilegon in the compound?'

Gavin shrugged. 'Yeah.'

Scunner stopped in his tracks and shouted to the entire pub, 'VILEGON's back.'

The pub fell silent. Drew shouted to Gavin. 'Those bastards wearing combat fatigues?'

'Yeah,' Gavin replied.

A melee of noise and bustle filled the whole pub. It seemed that everyone started talking and shouting at the same time.

More people hurried to the pool tables to listen to Drew who stood on a bench and raised his voice for all to hear.

Drew pointed to a man near the front. 'Tooter, go and get the McKuchnie brothers. They might be in The Wee Hoff or up in slinky Lizzie's pit. Find them.'

A dozen hardnuts gathered and brandished kitchen knives and machetes. Drew skimmed his eyes around them.

The large bald-headed man in the singlet, staggered back onto his feet. Drew pushed him back into his seat. 'Sit doon, mate, you're far too pissed.'

His eyes moved to Janice Dunn, a thirty-year-old brunette, who wore a black t-shirt and dark-blue jeans. She stood at the edge of the group and saluted with her index finger. Drew returned the gesture.

Gavin marched back to the pool table and walked around the group.

A man in his mid-thirties with a thick mop of blonde hair stepped in front of the group and turned to face them.

With his index finger, he pointed at the people standing in front of Drew. 'One-potato, two-potato, three-potato, four, five-potato, six-potato.' Then, pointing to himself. 'One-potato more.'

Gavin arrived at Drew's side and asked, 'You know the Vilegon people?'

Anger set on Drew's face. 'Too right. We have a score to settle with those bastards. Some of our kids broke into that compound to nick some copper pipe.

'Two of them came back with their brains crushed. Janice Dunn's son and the McKuchnie brothers' cousin. Other kids took a battering. One kid lost all his teeth and an eye.'

Drew got down from the bench. He beckoned a tall and muscular ex-army man in his early forties with arm tattoos and cropped red hair.

Drew opened his hands, seeking advice. 'What do you think, Mark? We're on the hop. The bastards will disappear again if they've scrubbed two cops. How do we score here?'

'No option. It'll need to be something we all know,' Mark replied.

'*Ring-Bang,*' Drew and Mark shouted while they high-fived each other.

A roar of laughter resounded in the bar. Drew inspected the weapons on view and then turned back to his mate, Mark. 'We'll need decent tools for this job.'

Mark shifted his attention to Gavin. 'How come two cops bought it?'

The background chatter dropped. Attention focused on Gavin and he felt it. 'I'm not sure. I went with the cops to the compound. We were in the gatehouse looking at the Vilegon factory layout when they told me to get off the pitch.

'I'd just got out onto the street when the bastards took them by surprise. Nabbed the police van parked in the street. Just scooped it up and took it behind the wall.'

Mark said to Drew. 'Sounds like a tip-off or they got a heads-up from the gatehouse.'

'Did they bolt after?' Drew asked.

'No. I waited for a while. They're still there,' Gavin replied.

Mark furrowed his brows for a moment. 'So, they've whacked two cops, no backup arrived and they're sitting pretty. That's a filthy inside cop job. Vilegon will be as cool as a dead man's balls.'

'How many at Vilegon?' Drew asked

Gavin stared hard at Drew. 'Two, maybe three.'

Gavin's mind flew into a panic. He felt wretched for lying to them but didn't want to frighten them with the truth.

They seemed more focused on exacting revenge rather than on how he and Emma became entangled with Vilegon.

'Okay, that's good for us.' Drew stepped up onto the bench and shouted, 'Has anyone been working for Mr Jelly?'

'Me,' John Birnie raised his hand. Nickname Burnit—a fitting epithet for a known arsonist.

'Right, Burnit, go tell him what we're about. Get some lemons and strawberries but none of that bloody blackcurrant stuff.'

Burnit, overweight and lackadaisical, dragged his body slowly. Drew jumped down from the bench and slapped him on the back of the head. 'Move it.'

*

It seemed like a lifetime to Gavin but only two hours had passed since he entered the bar. The hastily assembled Govan team gathered under a dim streetlight at the south wall of the compound, farthest away from the gatehouse.

Drew had brought Micky, one of the kids attacked on the fateful night. Two of the team passed time by throwing small stones at a streetlight.

Gavin and Drew were armed with pistols and had sixteen rounds of ammunition between them. In total, the team had six pistols, two sawn-off shotguns, and one hand-held mini-crossbow. Drew and Gavin stood together.

Three others stood in a huddle. Mark, Scunner, and Jan. The two McKuchnie brothers hung around Kech and Sanny who stood with a ladder they'd stolen from a window cleaner's van.

Tooter and Con searched for more stones to throw at the streetlight. They all waited impatiently for Burnit, the last member of the team.

Gavin watched Jan. She seemed distraught, rubbed her hands frequently and blew warm air into them. The heartache and anger of her son's funeral still fused on her face. Her shoulder-length hair hung thick and chunky.

Drew caught Gavin's stare. 'Don't worry about Jan, she's granite. She just wants to get her boot in first.'

Gavin shook his head while he watched the guys fidget and throw stones at streetlights like a bunch of delinquents. Worry terrorised his mind. The stupid lies he'd told them, the dead Special Branch team, and the merciless WRATH people. His thoughts fuelled a terrible panic and he thought, *We're all going to die—in a bloody massacre.*

Forty-six

It would soon be midnight. The cold night air provided a sobering effect for those who needed it, and invigoration for those ready to fight. Drew handed out a new packet of twenty cigarettes and everyone lit up except Gavin and Con. It didn't surprise Drew when he got the packet back empty.

Con kept them amused with a constant supply of jokes and stories. The guys had heard all of them before but his antics as he told them made them smile.

They all turned to look when they heard hurried, plodding footsteps. Burnit puffed and panted while he scurried along the road. He carried a white-and-red picnic cool-box.

Drew asked, 'What did you get from Mr Jelly?'

'The tight bastard wouldn't give me any good stuff. This is all past its sell-by date. I had to hunt for a box to keep them cool,' Burnit replied, in between gasps for breath.

Mark took the box from him. 'What did he give you?'

'Two lemon, two raspberry, two blackcurrant.'

'I said no fuckin' blackcurrant. We'll blow ourselves up. Bastard. Okay, we're just waiting for Micky.'

Gavin squinted at the box. 'Why the picnic cool-box and the jars of fruit?'

'Don't you know Jelly?' Drew asked.

'Never heard of him.'

Drew told Gavin about Mr Jelly. 'The army trained him to work with explosives. He got wounded in Iraq and disabled out of the army. With only a few years' service, he gets almost no cash support, so he boosts his income by selling explosives on the black market.'

'What's wrong with blackcurrant?' Gavin asked.

'Mr Jelly pays our kids to steal sticks of gelignite from quarries so he can extract the nitro-glycerine. He sets the nitro in gelatine mixed with jam preserves and re-packs it in five-hundred-gram jam pots.

'The jam colour indicates the amount of nitro. Lemon contains the least, blackcurrant the most. The pots are stable at room temperature for a week then they need to be kept cold to keep the gel set.

'The more nitro, the faster they become unstable, which makes blackcurrant fucking dangerous, especially when past its sell-by date.'

Gavin's eyes went wide. 'How do you set it off?'

'A built-in detonator of enriched nitro-glycerine, fixed in superglue, on the inside wall of the glass jar. Break the glass with force and the shock fires the nitro. *Boom,*' Drew explained.

'Bloody clever.'

'Bloody splat if you drop one of these buggers.'

Micky Kirby popped his head over the wall and whispered down to Drew, 'The guard is heading back.'

Drew punched a clenched fist into the palm of his other hand. 'Right, we know what we're here for. Let's top an tail these bastards.'

The McKuchnie brothers positioned the ladder against the wall. Drew steadied the ladder and climbed up and over the wall. Gavin followed and they knelt down to wait for the others.

While they waited, Gavin mopped sweat from his forehead. His hand trembled and sheer panic locked his face.

He should have told the truth. He should have told Drew how good these Vilegon people were. He should have told Drew how many armed Special Branch officers had died.

Drew pulled Gavin behind a large Rhododendron bush and they stood toe-to-toe. He slapped Gavin hard on the face. The force knocked Gavin to the ground where he lay on his side. Drew bent down toward him and whispered in a restrained but harsh voice, 'Get a grip.'

Gavin shook his head. 'Can't … can't do it.'

'Remember when we were kids in Govan, playing ring-bang-scoot?'

Gavin thought back and recalled the posh tenement building. The residents kept it spotless and complained about kids loitering and playing football.

Drew pointed a finger at Gavin. 'You were the only one of us with the guts to ring-bang running up the stairs instead of down. Remember, old MacPherson opened his door and kicked your arse. You had no fear then.'

'I was a kid.'

'This isn't a kid's game. We'll likely get our skulls crushed. Govan boys take it as well as dish it. You deserted Govan but Govan hasn't deserted you. It's still in there.' Drew pressed his finger into Gavin's chest.

Gavin took in a deep breath, let it out slowly. 'I was never good at fighting. That's why Siobhan made me join the judo club.'

'If you really want Emma Baxster, get your balls on the table.' Drew offered his hand to pull Gavin to his feet.

They returned to their place to watch the others scale the wall. Gavin placed his hand on his gun. He stepped over the line, kill or be killed.

Con lingered near the place where Drew and Gavin waited. In a world of his own, he did a little shimmy dance while he whispered a tune to himself.

Con sang, 'Well, why do you wanna throw mince pies at me for. If they don't mean what they say. You make me boke, you make me fart, then you shout a lotta things that cut thru my heart. Oh why do you wanna throw mince pies at me for.'

Gavin stared at Con. 'I know him.'

Drew glanced over at Con. 'Surely, you remember wee Alec? He gave you a hiding the night you got your blue belt.'

'Oh shit. Alec Ferginson? I remember. The judo grading at Bellahouston Sports Centre. He caught me with a *uri-gari* and dropped me like a ton of bricks. What happened to him?'

'Six months after the judo grading, Alec was on his way to the judo club. He carried his judo kit in his mother's old brown vinyl shopping bag. He stopped at a newsagent's to peer in the window at the cheap plastic toys and mouldy old sweets.'

'I remember that shop.'

'A cop car drew up, and two cops got out. They towered on either side of wee Alec and tried to take hold of his bag. Alec had never been in trouble before and had no idea what to do. He put his bag behind his back.

'He didn't understand what they wanted and felt scared he'd lose his judo kit. He couldn't afford another one. Frightened like a cat, he ran, and they caught him in an alley.

They emptied his judo kit onto the mud and wiped their feet on it as they walked away.'

'Bastards.'

'Alec started crying and kicked one of them in the leg. The two cops turned back and cracked his skull with their batons. By then, a crowd had gathered, witnesses, you know, so they picked him up, lifted a half-brick from the alley and put it in his bag. They arrested him for attempting a smash and grab.'

'From a sweetie shop. Really?'

'He got eighteen months in the prison psych ward.'

Gavin's jaw dropped. 'That's horrendous.'

'So, now he's called Con. Convict he was. Confused he definitely is. Condemned to a shit life, no doubt about it. Conman, maybe? He gets invalidity from social security. You choose.'

'Did nobody speak up for him?'

'Cops told his mother to keep it shut, or she'd be assessed unfit, and all her kids would be taken into care.'

Gavin shook his head in disgust. 'That's terrible.'

'It's normal for people like us. That's why we hate cops.'

'Not all cops are like that.'

'Around here, it's safer to assume they are.'

Gavin glanced at Con. 'Are you sure he's okay to be doing this?'

Drew smiled. 'Con will be fine. Keep out of his way when he swings his machete.'

Forty-seven

Inside the compound, the team gathered around Micky Kirby, and he told them how to avoid security in the compound. His job done, Drew told him to scarper.

Keeping a tight group, they shuffled cautiously between buildings, blended into shadows and avoided spot-lit areas monitored by cameras. Gavin and Drew settled in a corner shadow, facing the gatehouse. Drew handed his mobile to Gavin.

'Gatehouse. MacRhoan speaking.'

Gavin raised his voice. 'Mr MacRhoan, don't speak, and keep your hands up in full view. Your life depends on that. This is Gavin Shawlens. I came with the cops earlier tonight. I'm back with a lot more people. I'm watching you with field glasses. Nod if you understand.'

Hamish peered out through the gatehouse window.

'MacRhoan. Are you fucking stupid? I said nod up and down if you want to live.'

Hamish nodded.

'Good, now nod for yes or shake side-to-side for no. Does Vilegon have someone watching out over their factory?'

MacRhoan nodded.

'Good. Now switch off all the surveillance cameras. Tell your mate to tie up and muzzle your dog. Then, both of you get down on the floor. Be very careful, or this time, you'll be the first one to die.'

Drew's phone vibrated, and Kech reported, 'The guards are secure on the gatehouse floor. MacRhoan says a Vilegon watcher sits in the front office looking out over the square.'

Drew replied to Kech, 'Put the phone on loudspeaker so the guards can hear. Give the phone to Con.'

Drew spoke slowly and carefully. 'Con, son, I need you to stay with the guards. If what they've told us is good, I want you to let them be.

'If it's shite, I want you to make sure they'll qualify for invalidity benefit. Now, Con, you're the world expert. It's up to you to decide how much invalidity benefit they should get.'

Con knelt down beside MacRhoan. 'Okey-dokey. I'm the smokey, doing the hokey-kokey.'

Con reached down into his trousers and drew out a twenty-eight-inch curved machete. Hamish's eyes flared with fear.

Black, crumbling rust covered the big blade and sprinkled onto the floor. Con picked off a few black flakes and flicked them away.

The broken and filthy handle left a grubby brown mark on Con's hand, which he wiped onto his jeans where it left a dark stain. Completely blunt, the blade had large flattened dents on the cutting edge where it had been used as a hammer.

Con raised the machete above his head and practiced a blow to land just above MacRhoan's ankle. The handle slipped and he judged badly. Con broke Hamish's skin, tapped the bone and made him squeal against his gag.

Con switched the machete to his left hand. He pointed at the two men with his forefinger in a telling-off fashion. With wild facial expressions, Con rhymed. 'Fiddly dum and fiddly dee. If it's shite for dinner—then it's chops for tea.'

Kech spoke on the phone to Drew with more information from MacRhoan. 'The watcher stretches his legs for ten minutes every hour or so. He has a silent alarm and a handgun. All seven of them are armed, including the watcher.'

'*Seven.*' Drew whipped his head to face Gavin.

Drew told Con to put on MacRhoan's cap and jacket and then stand about in the gatehouse with his official face on. Next, Drew told Kech to bring the layout of the factory.

Kech returned to the group with a building plan, and they all gathered around to plan their attack. Gavin identified the front door and reception area on the south wall.

He pointed to the west wall. 'Those are offices with doors. The front entrance opens to a reception area with stairs leading to the upper floor. A metal stair leads to a metal walkway along the length of the east wall. Off the walkway, you'll find three laboratories, each interconnected and each with a door from the walkway.'

Drew circled his finger over the entrance. 'What's here?'

'A door, which leads to the main hall. Half of the hall reaches up to the roof, and the upper floor covers the other half. The hall has big pieces of industrial equipment, tables, and sacks of fertiliser. A car park sits adjacent to the east wall,' Gavin replied.

Drew marked a cross on the right side.

'Fire exits?' Mark asked.

'Three. North wall—centre, east wall—north end, and east wall—south end,' Gavin replied.

Drew marked them on the plan.

'Stairs open or covered?' Mark asked.

'Metal staircase, open guard rail.'

Mark frowned. 'That's a bastard—no cover.'

Drew said to Gavin. 'Okay, we'll take the front door, and head up the stairs.'

The others agreed that Gavin should head up the stairs.

Drew pointed to the east wall. 'Mark and Janice, blow the fire exit door on the east wall, north. Kech and Sanny, blow the door on the east wall, south. Scunner and Tooter, blow the northwest-office window. If we all huff and puff together, we'll blow the fucking place down.'

'What if I see a bastard?' Sanny asked.

Mark raised his voice. 'Shoot it for fuck's sake. If they've killed cops, there will be no comeback on us killing them.'

Apprehension infected the team. All of them were up for getting even with Vilegon, few of them had thought about killing people.

None of them felt sure that they'd escape comebacks for killing Vilegon thugs. They had all sounded murderous back in the pub but now they had doubts.

Anger in Drew's voice. 'They kicked the living daylights out of wee Gary and Declan. Just you think back to the funerals we all attended.'

Jan scowled at them. 'I'll do them myself if you empty bastards won't do it.'

With a confident expression, Mark said, 'Look, these bastards will run to the doors to repel attackers. They can't cover every door, so some of us will get in. Then, they'll have to turn their backs. They're fucked. I've done this hundreds of times in the army killing house.'

Drew faced Mark. 'You'll need to crack the watcher. Make sure he doesn't hit his alarm. We'll wait until he comes out. Burnit, go with Mark and then get transport organised for a fast getaway.'

In the gatehouse, the two guards lay on their backs. Con marched around them singing and rhyming.

'Hump, two, three, four. Hump, two, three, four. Humpty Dumpty leaned on the walls, so Humpty Dumpty got kicked in the balls. By all the king's horses and all the king's men, who hurt Humpty Dumpty again and again and again.'

He marched around and around and, occasionally, stopped to give another rhyme or song.

'Kissing girls is painless, it tends to make me brainless, but I won't have to do it if I sneeze, and she can do the same thing with her tease.'

'Hump, two, three, four. Hump, two, three, four. There's silence in the banks, they've taken all my money, and didn't say a thanks.'

*

Drew and Gavin concentrated on the watcher when he stepped out of his office. He put his alarm in his top pocket, lit a cigarette and then turned left. Drew rang Burnit to give instructions. 'Left.'

Burnit slipped backward from the corner along the side of the wall. Mark stood stiff as a board with his back against the wall at the corner.

'Ten metres,' Drew whispered to Burnit.

Burnit scratched the brickwork with a coin. Mark turned his head. Burnit raised five fingers, spread out. He opened and closed them twice.

'Five metres,' Drew said.

Burnit scratched the brickwork and gave Mark the update. The watcher's boots crushed grit against the concrete pathway.

Mark's heart pounded. Adrenaline rushed through his body, causing sweat to bead on his forehead. He repeated over and over in his mind that the guard would shoot him dead if he didn't make the first hit count. *Him or me—him or me—him or me.*

The guard arrived at the corner. He heard a noise from behind, he stopped, turned around and cocked his head.

A figure in a peaked cap approached from the opposite end of the building.

'Where's your dog?' the watcher called out.

Mark swung around the corner and plunged a sabre into the man's back, through his heart, and out through his chest. The man's legs buckled, and he fell to the ground when Mark pulled the sabre out of his body.

Blood spurted out of his chest, and a pool of blood formed. His body made a horrible gurgling sound as it expelled the final splurges of blood.

'Oh, baby-Jesus, mammy-daddy,' Burnit squealed when he saw the man's eyes blinking at him.

Burnit collapsed to his knees, and spewed-up a spectacular fairy fountain flow as his stomach ejected a half-digested concoction of cheap beer, pizza, potato chips and white bread.

He crawled over to the wall and leant against it. His face white, he held his head with his eyes clamped shut.

Kech took off the peaked cap and hurried to Burnit's side. He noticed the watcher's eyes, now blinking slowly. Kech helped Mark drag the body around the corner and into the shadows. Mark extracted the alarm and took the pistol from the man's shoulder holster.

Any other killing method might have given the watcher time to raise the alarm. Satisfied, Mark and Kech returned to the group and told them that Burnit was out of it. No-one seemed surprised or angry.

Drew gathered the team around him. 'For the ring-bang to work, we need perfect timing. I've got five minutes past one. What have you got, Mark?'

'Six past one,' Mark replied.

'I've never done time.' Tooter shrugged.

Gavin shook his head. 'No watch, they took it.'

Kech tapped his watch. 'Eh. I've got half past seven.'

Sanny's elbow dug Kech in the ribs. 'It's always half past seven on that stupid kid's watch.'

Janice shook her head. 'Time's a drag.'

'Scunner?' Drew asked.

'What time is that?' Scunner asked Mark.

Mark grabbed Scunner's wrist to look at his watch. 'It's a fucking show-off watch, fake diamonds—no fucking numbers.'

Drew's jaw dropped. 'Two good watches. We'll be fucked if we don't get the timing right.'

Mark smiled. 'Relax. I'll fix up a conference call.'

Mark organised a mobile-phone conference-call to connect them all. Each phone received a text from the service provider, containing a call access number and a text that when opened made the connection to the conference call.

When they had all connected, Drew spoke first. 'Right, everybody, keep your ears on your phone. I'll tell you when to make your move. Anybody spies a problem, or needs help, yell out. Let me know when you're in position. I'll start a countdown for the ring-bang.'

The pairs scurried off their separate ways, making occasional quiet comments into their mobiles. Gavin and Drew surveyed the entrance door.

With care, Gavin placed one jar of the blackcurrant jelly at the door. He crept back while Drew prepared to sight his shot. They waited in the shadows.

Beside the east wall car park, the open ground had a tarmac surface and provided no cover for hiding. The McKuchnie brothers placed their raspberry jar against the fire exit door and took up position in bushes twenty paces away.

When each group had reported ready and waiting, Drew spoke into his phone. 'Okay, Mark, ring the bell.'

Mark activated the watcher's alarm.

Drew shouted, 'Once for the honey, twice for the whore, thrice to get even. BANG the fucking door.'

Forty-eight

Three violent explosions drowned out the gunshots. The air filled with smoke and debris. A fire alarm shattered the silence in the gatehouse. Con danced around, excited, with his hands flapping as a large button on the control panel flashed bright red.

He shouted at the flashing button, telling it to stop its nonsense. When it didn't, he slapped it and switched it off.

At the southeast door, Kech had fired a mini crossbow bolt at their jar and missed. He turned to his brother. 'Get the bolt.'

'Aye, that'll be fucking right. D'ya think my brain zips up the back?'

Kech tossed the crossbow. 'Fucking stupid kid's crossbow. I could've thrown the fucking jar.' He searched around for a stone to throw at the jar.

Scunner and Tooter climbed in through the blown northwest office windows. Then, they crouched down on the floor.

Mark and Jan burst through the northeast fire door and drew a hail of sub-machine-gun fire. Jan dived inside to the floor and scurried behind a bag-filling machine. Mark remained outside.

Two Vilegon men in combat fatigues were using equipment in the centre of the hall. A stench of blood and guts filled the air. They'd loaded the dead Special Branch officers into a grinding machine.

The working machines made a bone-grinding noise. The noise stopped suddenly when one of them released his pressure on a control button. He reached for his weapon and fired at the door.

The two Vilegon men hid behind the machine. Mark ducked in, fired a shot at them and then ducked back out.

Janice crawled along the north wall. She used a bagging machine on her left side for cover.

Gavin and Drew stepped through the broken front door, crept along a short corridor, and climbed the metal staircase.

The two men in combat fatigues appeared below them and to their left, ten long paces away. Their attention focussed on the north wall.

While Gavin and Drew climbed the stairs, they saw inside the grinding machine hopper. Blood splattered the walls and bodies had been loaded into it. The horrific sight shocked and repulsed them.

One Vilegon man rolled over to the offices along the west wall. He kicked in the middle office door before dropping to the floor.

Gavin and Drew could no longer see him.

The next twenty seconds produced a pandemonium of noise, shouting and gunfire.

Drew took aim and fired at the Vilegon man beside the grinding machine.

The bullet clipped his shoulder. He crashed against the machine but stayed on his feet. As he turned, he sprayed the stairway with a barrage of bullets, many of which ricocheted with bright-yellow flashes off the metal stairs.

Mark stepped into the gaping hole of the fire exit and shot the man in the head. Janice got to her feet and with her sawn-off shotgun pointing forward, blasted one shot into the middle office.

Glass and splinters of wood showered the floor. A burst of return fire from the Vilegon man in the office caught Janice, and she catapulted back against the wall, leaving a splurge of blood as she slipped down.

A third Vilegon man emerged from a toilet under the stairs. He ran out into the centre of the hall and fired single shots at Gavin and Drew, which hit the wall above their heads.

The man who'd gone into the middle office darted out to join the one from the toilet. They stood back to back, one with his gun trained on the fire exit where Mark hid, and the other trained on Gavin and Drew.

They moved closer to the metal stairs.

Gavin and Drew raised their hands in the air.

A fourth Vilegon man came out of the upstairs labs and moved along the walkway toward Gavin and Drew.

A loud bang hit the southeast fire-exit door, and everyone turned their attention there.

The Vilegon man on the walkway slipped over the rail guard, slid fast down a metal ladder to the ground, and ran over to the fire-exit door. He positioned himself against the wall, beside the door and checked his machine gun.

Another bang thumped the door hard. The man facing Gavin and Drew demanded they lose their weapons.

Gavin threw his Colt Peacekeeper revolver down on the landing behind them, and Drew laid his Smith & Wesson semi-automatic pistol at his feet.

The Vilegon man fired a short burst of gunfire above Drew's head.

Gavin and Drew ducked down fast. Drew fell forward against the metal guard-rail and Gavin grabbed Drew's jacket to stop him falling off the stairs. A jar of blackcurrant in Drew's pocket, popped out, bounced off the stairs, and fell to the ground where it splattered two metres from the two Vilegon men below.

The jar exploded, throwing lumps of concrete floor and dust in all directions. The force blasted the two men to the other end of the hall.

The blast threw Gavin and Drew back and showered them in dust and tiny fragments of concrete. A few glass shards tore their clothes.

Drew snatched Gavin's Colt from the landing and gave Gavin a backup Smith & Wesson from his back waist belt. They ran up the stairs, along the walkway and crashed into the first laboratory.

*

Outside, Kech and Sanny threw more stones at their jar, still waiting at the fire-exit door. Kech picked up a half-brick while Sanny threw another stone at the jar.

The fire door sprang open, followed by a hail of machine-gun fire. A Vilegon man pushed the door out into the car park. The yellow flames from his machine gun shocked the two brothers.

A bullet hit Kech in the arm and spun him around before he fell to the ground. His brother dropped to the ground and froze.

The explosion made the Vilegon man glance back indoors. Had a grenade taken out his mates? A single bullet blew off the entire back of his head. An easy target against light from inside the factory.

Mark stood flat against the east wall with his arm outstretched, holding his pistol. He whistled to the two brothers who stood quickly. Mark checked the dead man, lifted his sub-machine gun and then slipped inside.

Carefully, planning his move as he had been trained to do in the army, Mark calculated that two men remained and he figured them to be upstairs.

He darted past the large hole in the floor, assessed the blood-splattered Vilegon men, and confirmed they were dead.

The strong stench of explosive, together with a thick smell of burnt human flesh, caught Mark's throat. He needed to swallow several times. He'd experienced it before, so it didn't bother him.

His eyes connected with Scunner when he raised his head above the wooden partition to look through the shattered glass and into the hall.

Mark snapped his fingers and pointed Scunner to go to Janice. Scunner opened the office door and did as instructed. Janice bled from her chest but remained alive. Scunner stared at her blood.

Tooter joined him, and they carried her out through the northeast fire exit. They met up with the McKuchnie brothers, and the five struggled along the building toward Burnit. They swore at Burnit, kicked his backside and told him to find transport.

Forty-nine

In the gatehouse, Con answered a telephone call from the local police station. The police office had received reports of fire alarms, loud bangs from the factory, and the crackle of fireworks.

Con stood petrified and pale-faced. His grip almost crushed the handset. Panic locked his mind and he struggled to find words.

While he danced a jig, he blurted out. 'My piddly dee, it's a grocer's loaf, you see, with frozen chips and chocolate dips, and six of them for me. My piddly dee, it's time for me to pee.'

The officer shouted and demanded an explanation. Con wore a sheepish expression as if he'd been told off. He put on his best aristocratic voice with a prominent slur and matched it with his best serious expression.

'We're having a bit of a party here, don't you know. I haven't heard any firecrackers but I may have farted once or twice. It's the beans you know, they're packed with executive farting powder, don't you know. That's how you get to become a big noise around here, don't you know.'

'Are you bloody idiots high on drugs again?' the officer shouted.

Con replied in an edgy voice, 'It's a blackened decker, honest boss, cross my heart and hope to fly.'

The policeman shouted, 'A what?'

'A blackened decker, boss, a drill. Dee! Are! Eye! Ell! Comprendo! Momento! I think you're round da bendo. Wake up when I'm farting. Next time, I check. You better be smart, or I'll have you wiping my arse with your tongue. You stupid half-baked excuse for a numpty,' Con shouted, then put down the phone.

*

Gavin and Drew crouched just inside the first lab. They peered into the middle laboratory. It resembled a hospital ward with four beds. Gas cylinders with tubes connected to machines on trolleys, and a bank of monitors on castors, attended each bed.

'What the fuck,' Drew hissed to Gavin when he saw three women strapped to metal bars on separate trolley beds. Gavin shrugged.

A regular pattern of clicking and beeping noises came from machines while they cycled through their various activities.

The metal staircase behind Gavin creaked. His heart pounded, then eased when he saw Mark making his way to them.

Drew shook his head and mouthed, 'No sign of anybody.'

Mark replied with hand signals that five were down and two must be in there.

Crouching, Drew pushed open the connecting door to the middle room. Mark shuffled inside, and knelt low with the Heckler & Koch pointing forward.

His head cocked while he stared down the gun-sight. Drew followed and jerked his weapon from side to side. Gavin watched their backs as Mark scanned the scene.

When Mark signalled, Gavin rushed to Emma and untied the straps on her arms and legs. She wore only a loose, white, full-length cotton gown.

Wide-eyed, she grabbed his arm and almost burst into tears. He placed his hand over her mouth to keep her silent. He nodded to Helen to let her know she would be released.

Mark focused on the end room, which resembled an operating theatre with a large table in the centre and circular lighting above.

Unlike the open room where he stood, this one had partitions and cubicles, which made it impossible to see if anyone hid there.

Helen joined Gavin and Emma, and they backed up toward the connecting door. Drew undid the straps on the third woman.

Naked, except for a small cloth, she didn't move. Drew's stomach turned when he saw her scars and the tubes running out of her body.

He glanced at Gavin, and signalled the woman couldn't move on her own. He stepped backward into the centre of the room beside Mark. Carefully, they backed out.

Gavin guided the two women through the door. Drew and Mark faced the end room, weapons at the ready, walking backward.

Mark's laser-sharp eyes caught sight of movement in the large mirror above the operating table. He blasted the wooden partition. The sixth Vilegon man, dressed in blue medical scrubs, crashed against the operating table as he tried to stand. He fired his sub-machine gun and sprayed wildly toward Mark.

The bullets shattered the glass partitions and ended up in the ceiling. Before the man could straighten himself, Mark sprang forward and sprayed bullets into his head and chest, killing him instantly.

Unexpectedly, the woman in the bed sat up as if woken by the shots. She pulled at the tubes that tracked down her nose and mouth. A slimy yellow material covered the tubes. She jerked them out of her head.

Then, the woman grabbed the tubes in her arm and yanked them out. The tubes sprayed out their contents, and she threw them to the side.

She stared at her legs in shock then with a gut-wrenching noise, vomited along the length of her bed.

A yellow slime, tinged with crimson red, drooled down her jaw and onto her neck. She threw her legs around to the side of her bed, and pulled out the tubes connected to her rectum and vagina. She screamed with excruciating pain.

Finally, she stumbled to her feet, took two steps and then fell onto her knees. Her legs weak and bloated. Unsteady, but determined, she got up. Blood streamed down her legs and onto the floor.

Her rescuers mesmerised by the horrific state of her body, and the devastated expression on her face. She stumbled past Drew and Mark and fell to her knees once more. Drew grabbed her arm and helped her onto her feet.

With one last surge, she rushed past the two women, aiming for a row of large, double-doored steel lockers. Gavin lost his balance and stumbled as he got out of her way.

The end locker door sprang open. A Vilegon technician in blue scrubs emerged with a pistol. He shot the woman in the chest when she lunged at his locker.

Mark shouted at Emma, and tried desperately to clear a line of fire.

Drew froze as his eyes race down the barrel of the pistol to the man's curled trigger-finger.

Gavin crashed down on his backside and fired upward as the man's face came into view. Gavin's bullet entered the side of the man's head, travelled upward and blasted a section out of the top of his skull.

Blood splattered up to the ceiling as he collapsed to the ground.

The man fired his pistol before Gavin's bullet hit him, and the bullet zipped past Drew's ear.

Helen and Emma screamed and grabbed each other.

Gavin stared at the man while his body twitched away the last spark of life. Everyone froze for a few seconds.

Mark recovered first. 'Party's over, folks. Time to go.'

*

Outside, Burnit had broken into a parked van, and while the others piled into the back, he hot-wired the engine. With the back doors swinging open, the van screeched over to the big gate. Mark leapt out to drag it open.

Gavin helped Helen from the van and led her into the gatehouse. It was the closest he'd been to her face, and he stared at her for a few seconds.

Her hair and face remarkably similar to the woman in the photo that DI Packerman had shown him at Emma's house.

Helen's resemblance felt uncanny, scary. She was the spitting image of the woman in the black-and-white photo. Or, his mind had played tricks, because it couldn't be the woman he thought he'd seen in his mind's eye.

Drew cut the guards free and they stood beside Helen. Then, he grabbed the gatehouse first-aid kit, and gave it to Con to take to the van.

Con squinted at Helen in her hospital-type gown. 'The sun has got its hat on, hip-hip-hip, hooray. The sun has got its hat on, and it's time to fly away. Bye—bye.'

Drew faced Helen. 'You owe us your life. There's no CCTV. Tell them we wore balaclavas. You didn't see any faces.'

Helen nodded her thanks and agreement.

Drew turned to the two guards. 'Keep your mouths shut.' Then, he flicked a thumb back towards Con. 'If you think he's bad, his sister is *ten* times worse. Believe me—you don't want her chopping bits off you and your family.'

Drew climbed into the back of the van. Sanny grabbed the first-aid kit from Con and tended to his brother's arm. Mark closed the back doors and got into the front of the van.

'*Go,*' Drew shouted, and the van sped off into the night.

In the back, Gavin cut through Janice's t-shirt, and Sanny tossed gauze bandages to him to stem the flow of blood from her shoulder. Two bullets hit her. One grazed her arm and the other hit her shoulder.

The bleeding from Kech's arm soon stopped and he relaxed. Drew banged on the wall of the cabin. 'Mark? Phone Doctor Jon. Tell him we've got incoming. Tell him it's Janice.'

Drew knelt beside Gavin and asked, 'How bad is it?'

'She's lost a lot of blood.'

Con stared at her blood while she lay on the floor. Her breasts swayed gently with the motion of the van. Worried about her dignity, Con took off his jacket and covered her chest. Her eyes opened. Drew leaned closer to her. 'How do you feel?'

'Did we get even?'

'Better than even.'

Fifty
Paisley, Renfrewshire

The following morning, Gavin slapped his hand on the side of the bread delivery van to let the driver know he and Emma had slipped out the back door.

Gavin gave a grateful wave to the driver as Emma swivelled her head to get her bearings. 'It's not far from here.'

She checked her watch, nine-thirty. Thirty-three hours had passed since they'd fled from Miltonbrae Street. While police swarmed around Govan, Gavin and Emma recovered in Drew's flat.

Drew's wife gave Emma fresh clothes. When he thought the coast was clear, Drew organised the bread delivery van to help them slip away from the area.

It had been an emotional rollercoaster for Emma. While strapped to the trolley bed, she had raged against Gavin's betrayal. Then, like a knight in shining armour, he'd come back to save her from disgusting torture.

She'd watched the technicians in blue medical scrubs work on the woman. They'd laughed and taken pleasure in telling Emma what they planned to do to her body.

While they recovered in Drew's flat, Gavin told her everything he knew about Julie Blackhest, the flaw in the process, the discovery of Davy, and the SB rescue attempt.

She told him about their rehabitation of organs and the extraction of hormones from the woman. He had saved her from a horrible fate, and her intense relief eclipsed her anger.

The van had dropped them close to a small warehouse on the outskirts of Paisley. A store where Emma and Jim kept supplies of spices and condiments. Gavin broke a window, climbed inside, and opened the front door for Emma.

Gavin waited beside brown sacks and bales, stacked to head height in the main hall, while Emma opened the half-glass door and entered the office.

Poor ventilation in the building produced a dry and distinctly fusty smell from the fine dust in the various sacks.

Emma sat in the chair behind her desk and made up her mind. 'I've had enough. This has to end right now. I've never had anxiety and nausea this bad. Its making me ill.'

He sat on the edge of her desk and stared at the telephone. 'I don't know who we can trust.'

She reached for the telephone and raised her voice. 'Stop it. I'm not waiting. We should have given ourselves to the police last night but I didn't want Drew and his wife to get into trouble.'

Gavin tried to reason. 'There is a rat in Special Branch. He killed his fellow officers and he'll be even more desperate to keep us quiet.'

'I cannot go on like this. I'm at my wits end. I don't care what it takes. Contact Packerman.'

Gavin conceded. 'Okay. I agree, But not by phone. It will be safer to stop a uniformed patrol officer rather than call the police.'

'Fine, whatever. Let's do it, now.'

They left the warehouse and joined a busy throng of pedestrians on High Street. Twenty minutes later, they spotted a parked police patrol car manned by two uniformed officers.

In the backseat, they spilled out their story. The officers reassured them as they listened. The policewoman called her local station, and received instructions to wait for backup.

The policewoman rubbed Emma's arm. 'Try to relax. It's over. You're safe now.'

Eighteen minutes later, an unmarked black van parked behind the patrol car. The policeman stepped out of his vehicle and met a man in a light-grey business suit.

The policeman returned to the front of the police car with the man.

'Dr Shawlens, this is Superintendent Smythe. I've seen him many times at area HQ. He's a senior in Special Branch.'

'Henry Smythe. I've been working with John Deakin. Come with me, please.' He indicated with his hand that they should transfer from the car to the van.

The policeman turned to Smyth. 'Sir, we're supposed to stick with them.'

'I know. Escort us to area HQ, blues and twos, if you please,' Smythe replied.

Gavin and Emma slipped inside the back of the van.

Smythe went back to the two police officers waiting in their patrol car with the engine running. The policewoman wound her window down, and Smythe crouched down at the window.

'Have you radioed ahead?' Smythe asked.

She turned to face him and nodded. 'Yes, more uniform are on their way.'

Smythe extracted a small, snub-nosed, suppressed handgun and shot both police officers through the head at point blank range. Calmly, he got into the front of the van, and it pulled away from the police car, just as pedestrians discovered the police officers had been shot.

When Emma and Gavin had climbed into the van, they stepped over a woman sat in the back with her legs stretched out. The woman smiled at Emma as she passed.

Gavin glanced at her as he stepped over her legs.

'Uugghh!' He gasped as he sat down.

His jaw dropped. His eyes widened as he glanced back at the woman. No doubt in his mind. It was the woman in DI Packerman's black-and-white photo.

The hair and the shape of her face, no mistake. Long hair covered much of her face. She lowered her head to keep her face covered. The woman stared ahead and pulled her knees up to her chest. Tears dripped from her face and onto her jeans while she sniffled.

Emma rested her head against the van wall, and closed her eyes.

Gavin's heart raced as he tried to think of what to say. If he'd got it wrong, Emma would punch his face for being stupid. If he had it right, then it made no sense.

It felt like no more than ten minutes on the road before the van stopped. Then, Smyth turned around in the passenger seat, and said, 'Sit where you are. We won't be a minute.'

Smythe and his driver alighted from the van.

The back doors opened and the driver helped the woman out.

When the van door closed, Gavin whispered to Emma. 'Did you see her face?' I think she's the woman in the photo that Packerman showed us at your house.'

Emma pushed up and stretched over the driver's seat to look through the windscreen. Smythe and the woman had their backs to her.

Emma sat down. 'I could only see the back of her head. A car has arrived probably to take her away.'

A few minutes later, two different men got into the front of the van. When Gavin saw their faces, he recognised the passenger, Hugo Hurrigan.

Gavin's heart sank and he nudged Emma.

Hugo smiled at Gavin. 'Hello, Dr dead man walking.'

He showed Emma and Gavin a pistol in his hand, and told them to behave.

Gavin got onto his knees and stretched to look out through the windscreen before Hugo shouted at him to sit down. Gavin sat back and tried to understand the snapshot he'd seen.

Julie Blackhest had her arm around the woman as if consoling her. She used a large handkerchief to wipe tears from the woman's face.

Before Gavin dropped back, the woman turned her head to look at the van. A gust of wind blew her hair. For a fleeting second, Gavin caught a glimpse of her face. He slid down onto his backside, his jaw dropped, and he stared at the floor. *Oh my God—it can't be.*

Emma remembered the driver with his red hair and pockmarked face. He wore a smart suit and pretended to be a businessman. Hugo called the driver Minty.

Forty-three minutes later, the van swung sharply onto a long uphill road on the outskirts of Eaglesham village where offices and light industries occupied a small estate.

They stopped at an isolated two-storey office building at the end of the road. Minty got out of the van, and although the area appeared deserted, he scanned all around before he opened the back door for Gavin and Emma to get out.

Hugo opened the office door. 'Inside.'

The building had two levels. On the ground floor, numerous computer desks, filing cabinets and metal storage cupboards. Hugo led Gavin and Emma upstairs. He opened an office, walked inside. 'Company for you, squire.'

John Deakin sat on the floor. His face bruised and beaten.

Gavin cocked his head to look more closely. 'John.'

John raised his arm to show his left hand handcuffed to a large iron pipe, which rose through the floor in the far left corner and passed along the floor to a heavy-duty cast-iron radiator.

Hugo handed handcuffs to Minty. 'Cuff them to the pipe.'

When Gavin and Emma had been secured to the iron pipe, Hugo said to Minty. 'You go back with the van. I'll wait here for the boss.'

Hugo followed Minty out the room before he closed the door.

Emma remembered John from the factory. Gavin told her about his part in the Special Branch rescue. They nodded to each other. 'I'm glad you made it out, Emma.'

'What happened?' Gavin asked.

John drew a deep breath and let it out slowly. 'When I got back to the factory, I had to do a taxi duty for Blackhest. When I returned, Hurrigan went berserk. He knew you had survived. Someone in our office tipped them off when they picked you up at Carbeth. They killed the rescue team—every single one.'

Gavin recalled the images. 'I know. Their bodies were dumped in a crushing machine. Sickeningly cruel.'

'I'm alive because they've been trying to find out if I know the identity of their person in Special Branch.'

'Do you know Superintendent Henry Smythe?' Gavin asked.

John dropped his head and slumped his shoulders in disappointment. 'Oh, sweet Jesus, not Henry.'

'He handed us over to Julie Blackhest.'

John shook his head. He would have trusted Smythe with his life. 'I can't believe it. I've worked with Henry for eight years. I thought he was as straight as they come.'

Emma threw a look of concern at Gavin. She pointed at a video camera up in the corner of the wall opposite. 'Good call. Now they know we can identify Smythe as a traitor.'

Gavin stared at the camera. 'They already know we can identify him.'

'There is no chance of rescue—is there?' Emma asked John.

'I worked undercover. No-one knows they brought me here.'

'Why did they bring us here?' Gavin asked.

'Not to kill us. They could have done that anywhere.'

Emma puffed out her cheeks and blew air through the lips. 'Don't you guys get it? They're going to rehab our organs.'

Fifty-one
Eaglesham, Renfrewshire

More than an hour passed before Gavin heard the sound of people walking up the stairs. Julie Blackhest stepped into the room, followed by Hugo Hurrigan and Peter Bromlee. Hugo extinguished his cigarette.

Julie wandered around the room to satisfy herself they had no means of escape. She cast a condescending eye over the three dishevelled figures handcuffed to the radiator pipe.

John announced. 'Hello, a final visit from the princess of darkness, or is it madness.'

'I'm pleased to see you are all well,' she replied.

'Come for a kidney, or can we offer you a new brain?' John asked.

Julie checked her watch. 'Nothing of the kind. In fact, you will be released in twenty-four hours with all your organs intact.'

John said to Gavin. 'That's rubbish—we're dead meat waiting for the butcher.'

Julie tutted loudly and scowled. 'Idiot. If I wanted you dead or put in the rehab programme—you wouldn't be sitting here like the three stooges.'

'Why twenty-four hours?' Gavin asked.

Julie shrugged. 'The balloon has gone up. MI5 is on our tail. If killing you could change that, believe me, I would do it in a heartbeat. We need time to organise secure exits for all the Ring Leaders. Twenty-four hours, then it will be impossible for you to find us.'

Peter said, 'When we've disappeared, someone will send a message to the police. They'll come here for you. So, just relax and sit it out.'

John side-glanced Gavin. 'Lies. She's not going to let us live.'

'Do you need anything to drink?' Julie asked.

Emma licked her lips. 'I'm parched.'

Julie frowned at Hugo. 'Oh, for God's sake, man. Fetch the milk you've got downstairs for your tea. Share it out, then run down to the supermarket for water and sandwiches.'

Hugo fetched a bottle of milk and three brown polystyrene cups. Peter poured milk into the cups and Hugo handed them out one by one.

Gavin and Emma drank the cool refreshing liquid and drained their cups. John drank more than half and then sipped the remainder.

Instinctively, the hairs on the back of John's neck sprang rigid. He noticed Bromlee had been more careful than necessary pouring the milk, and the smirk on Hugo's face as he watched them drink—told it all.

John peered into his cup. Attached to the bottom and sides, he saw many large white lumps. Then, he jabbed the cup at Gavin's face. 'What the hell's that?'

Gavin took the cup and peered inside. His jaw dropped, and he looked up at Julie. 'Oh Jesus … Julie, please … you didn't. Say you didn't.'

'What?' Emma scanned the inside her cup. 'It's just sour milk that's clotted.'

Gavin shook his head. 'It's not sour … there's no sour smell.'

Julie frowned. 'Indeed, the milk has clotted.'

Gavin engaged Emma's eyes. 'She's laced the milk with Jim's enzyme. It clotted the milk.'

The fear in his eyes frightened Emma. 'There's nothing much in mine or yours.'

All three focused on Julie's face.

John shouted, 'Have you poisoned us? What are you playing at?'

Julie shook her head and tutted. 'I am so unhappy. This last farewell isn't going to be pleasant, after all.'

Julie walked over to a window, stared outside and waved to a woman waiting in her car who waved back.

Julie explained, 'Of course, Gyge's Ring won't be sacrificed for you pitiful idiots. We will grease the political monkeys in our money-grabbing government. Provide proper pensions for a few of our top enforcement officers.

'Believe me, when serious money flows, the high and mighty know exactly how to butter their bread. People with power but no wealth are easily led with wads and wads of money. They won't ever need to fiddle their expenses again.'

Gavin thought of the boy Davy and his dog, Boggin. 'God help us.'

Julie sounded upbeat. 'Nevertheless, I am indebted to you for this needle sharp lesson. I've been lax but this sloppiness isn't me. It will never happen again.'

Gavin pleaded. 'If you have any compassion, kill us quickly, please.'

Julie rolled her eyes. 'I'm sorry to lose you, Gavin. With your Lambeth Group position, and my support, you would have reached truly great heights.'

'Why is it only my cup that's clotted?' John asked.

Julie smiled. 'Well, now … you see … it's all quite scientific. I couldn't resist a little experiment. I've given you thirty millilitres of enzyme.'

'You've got twenty,' she said to Gavin, and turning to Emma. 'You've got ten.'

'Why have I got ten?' Emma asked.

Julie stood in front of Emma. 'Because the less you get, the longer it takes, and the more *pain* you will endure. If my calculations are correct, you'll watch these two die before it's your turn. Normally, I would allow ladies to go first, but you're not a lady. You are an evil bitch and you'll receive *exactly* what you deserve.'

'*You* are the evil bitch,' Emma screeched.

An image of Davy filled Gavin's mind and his pleading sounded desperate. 'Oh God! Don't do this—please.'

Julie laughed in his face. 'Stop behaving like a wimp. This is your big chance to find out what it's like to be *in* an experiment. Feel free to record any useful observation for the video.'

Hugo had left the room. When he returned, he brought three black body bags, two pairs of black arm-length rubber gloves and two pairs of black Wellington boots.

He placed them all on a table beside the door. Then, he placed the keys for the handcuffs on top of the body bags.

'Good to go.' Hugo confirmed to Peter.

John addressed Julie. 'When we meet in hell, I'll make sure your torture is long and painful.'

Julie stopped in her tracks, and her face became severe. A faint redness appeared on her neck. Her eyes blazed as her inner bitch sprang up to the surface.

'Are you really that dense? Every day, millions of people suffer drug abuse misery, thousands are traumatised by burglary, and every ten minutes, someone is raped, molested or battered in this country. Wake up—you stupid man. This *is* hell!' Julie shouted back at him.

Emma shouted, 'God will never forgive you.'

Julie jabbed a finger at her. 'Patersun, *shut up*. I won't have any moral crap from you—of all people.'

Gavin shook his head in disbelief. 'Julie, this is sadistic. This isn't you.'

'Gavin, it's not you that … ugh! This is for *her*,' Julie shouted and pointed at Emma.

Julie lunged at Emma with a clenched fist. Her eyes raged, and she stopped herself at the last second from throwing a punch at Emma's head.

She stood back, and instead, she pointed an accusing finger at Emma. 'I want her to die in excruciating pain.'

'Why me?'

Peter stepped in between Julie and Emma, took hold of Julie's arms, and moved her backward. 'Come on … leave it.'

'What have I ever done to you?' Emma shouted.

Julie screamed over Peter's shoulder, 'I *hate* you.'

Then, in a steadier but emotional voice, Julie announced, 'With every nerve cell in my brain, I hate you. I'll cheer when I watch the video of you screaming in pain. If I could, I'd rip the skin off your face for what you did to your sweet little sister.'

Fifty-two

Peter held Julie in his arms. She closed her eyes, bowed her head and tried to calm herself. Emma's face paled with shock and she struggled to speak.

Then, she shook her head. 'My sister is dead.'

Julie raised her voice. 'You're about to die. What's the point of lying? You know she's alive.'

'Donna *is* alive,' Gavin's voice sounded a note of confirmation.

Julie said, 'Yes, she's handicapped with a mental age of ten but very much alive.'

Emma grabbed Gavin's arm. 'They're lying. Dad told me she died.'

'She *died* to hide your family shame,' Julie shouted at Emma, then said to Gavin. 'They didn't want a handicapped child—so what did they do. They hid her in a cheap and dirty care home to live with the scum of the earth.'

'Why are you saying this?' Emma screamed.

Julie switched her attention back to Emma. 'She's a beautiful woman now, perfect, except her brain stopped developing before her teens.'

'Why are you tormenting *me*?' Emma shrieked, then buried her head in Gavin's chest.

He put his free hand under her chin and raised her head until their eyes met. 'Emma. I'm so sorry … I should have said something to you.'

Memories of Emma's sister flooded back to him. Guilt consumed his mind for not telling Emma he thought he'd recognised her.

Packerman's photo of the woman living rough near Emma's house had appeared so much like Donna. He felt sure he'd recognised her in the van but he couldn't tell Emma he thought her sister had come back from the dead.

Emma peered into his eyes. 'You've *seen* Donna?'

'It was Donna in the van, wasn't it?' Gavin asked Julie.

'Yes, it was.'

Emma pushed Gavin away. 'No, it couldn't be. Dad told me he buried Donna in the family plot.'

'I recognised Donna but I couldn't tell you she'd come back from the dead.'

Emma cried with a force that pushed out from her heart.

Gavin tried to comfort her. 'I couldn't believe it was Donna. It wasn't possible.'

Julie regained her composure. She watched Emma's reaction, and the strength of the Emma's emotions surprised her.

Emma said to Gavin. 'Please, believe me. My father told me Donna had died. I don't understand what's been going on.'

Julie said, 'When your father died, payments to Donna's care home stopped. They put her out into the community to fend for herself. The Salvation Army helped her find her father's grave. They took what information Donna had, and found out you were married to Jim Patersun. They wanted to place her with you but Donna refused.'

'Why? I loved her.'

'Fear,' Julie replied.

'I don't understand.'

Julie sucked in a deep breath and held it for a moment. 'She has the mind of a little girl. She's so frightened you'll send her away. She says she must have upset you because you never once visited her in that care home. She thinks it's her fault you didn't visit her.'

Emma dug her nails into her temples and sobbed. Her throat constricted as if she would choke and her body trembled. Gavin tried to hold her but she pushed him away.

Emotion gripped Julie's voice. 'She hopes that someday you'll forgive her. Open your arms and tell her you want her back. She wears a green t-shirt, jeans and trainers most of the time because that's what she wore when you last saw her.'

Emma remembered the graveyard, the tramp and the little posies. 'Oh, my dear God. I saw her at his grave. Ohh!'

Tears welled in Julie's eyes. 'She crossed your path many times but you ignored her. At your father's grave, you cut her heart so deeply, she cried for weeks. But she didn't give up, she kept going back.

'Waiting for the day when you would forgive her and take her home. Every single night before bed, she prays her heart out, asking you to forgive her. She wants so much to tell you she's sorry she upset you.'

Emma whispered up to the ceiling. 'Donna. I've let you down so badly, I've—'

Peter said, 'You ignored her again in the van. That will be the last time.'

A tear ran down Julie's face. 'When she told me her story, I sat with her and we wept for most of the night. I promised myself you would suffer for what you've done to her. When I show her your body tomorrow, she'll begin to forget you and she'll start a new life.'

Julie stood beside the window and stared out at her car. She waved at Donna.

Emma cried uncontrollably while her brain searched her memories of the scruffy woman she'd seen in the cemetery. She held Gavin's arm in a grip so tight, he flinched as her fingernails dug deep.

Julie continued to gaze out of the window. 'She's a lovely ten-year-old girl in the body of a woman. She has a warm heart, she's eager to please and eager to help. How anybody could hurt her.'

'What happened?' Gavin asked.

Julie turned around to face Gavin. 'On the streets, she suffered horrible abuse. She survived because she'd grown used to being molested by care home assistants and lecherous patients in care home hell.'

Upset and sickened, Julie paused. 'I so hate this life. The vermin who ran the care home turned a blind eye as their care assistants raped and abused young and old. Poor girl never ever enjoyed a proper bath.

'They used a communal washroom to wash their bodies from a hand basin with just a flimsy plastic curtain between each sink. It didn't protect Donna from groping hands.

'Care assistants watched from behind, laughed and leered while they washed. Just put yourself in that position for one minute. How she survived, I'll never understand. I couldn't.'

'Why didn't my dad stop this?'

Julie replied, 'Donna said she told her dad what they were doing to her. There's only one small blessing. For some reason, she didn't become pregnant, and has been spared the trauma of abortion. A vicious time in her life but she has survived, and that says a great deal about her.'

Emma sobbed while tortured images of Donna troubled her mind. Her heartache magnified to an unbearable level.

Peter grinned. 'The men who attacked Donna as busy providing rape support. The yellow oil seed rape in numerous fields all over the country.'

'Vilegon fertilisers,' Gavin asked.

Peter raised his voice a notch. 'Vile gone fertilisers.'

'Donna helped them on their way. She waited patiently for them to regain consciousness before she started the grinding machine. That girl didn't flinch one bit as she pressed the start button. Steady as a rock, despite spurting blood, crunching bones and piercing screams.'

John chimed in, 'Taking revenge has turned her into a cold-blooded killer.'

Julie faced him with an unconcerned look. 'Revenge is therapeutic for the soul—believe me.'

Gavin recalled the black-and-white photo of Donna on Emma's house CCTV and asked, 'How did you find her?'

Peter said to face Gavin. 'When my people dealt with Patersun, she stumbled onto the scene.'

John interrupted. 'That's rich. You killed Jim Patersun. How evil is that?'

Peter ignored him and continued, 'She lived like a frightened rabbit near the Patersun house. Watching, trying to pluck up the courage to knock on the door. Intensely afraid of being sent away.'

Emma felt the oxygen had been sucked from her lungs.

'Where is she now?' Gavin asked.

Julie replied, 'WRATH took her for rehab. But when I heard her story, I took her under my wing. I'll be the big sister she never had. Now, she travels everywhere with me and she'll never be alone.'

Julie moved nearer to Emma and spoke in her usual confident voice. 'I believe, now, that you didn't know your sister was alive. You don't know this but Donna has been looking out for you.

'She killed a vicious burglar as he prepared to rob your house. Stabbed him in the neck with a carving fork. She saved you from a disgusting experience that she knew all too well.'

Emma's shoulders shook with guilt for failing her sister. She damned herself for not recognising Donna in the cemetery.

Never once had she checked the girl's face. She tore into herself for not sensing the presence of the baby sister she loved.

'Is she outside there in your car? Let me see her for a moment. Please … please, do this, I'm begging.'

Julie retrieved her mobile, searched through her videos, and held her phone screen in front of Emma.

The image showed a head-and-shoulder's photo of Donna with her light blonde hair flowing over her bottle-green t-shirt. She appeared bemused. Emma scanned the image.

Julie pressed a key, and the photo transformed into a short video clip. Donna swayed her head to throw her hair back from her face. She smiled sweetly, said her name, giggled and seemed embarrassed.

With her fingers, she pulled her cheeks apart and crossed her eyes to make a funny face. Then, she asked Julie if she would like tea and cake. Julie could be heard replying, 'Yes, please. Tea and toast and chocolate cake.'

Donna's face lit up, and she said, 'I'll make it—I'll make it.' Then, she waved her hand, turned away, and was gone.

Emma sobbed, touched the screen, and whispered, 'Oh. Sweetheart. I love you so much. I'm so … so … sorry, I wasn't there when you needed me.'

The video drained Emma's heart. Donna's voice sounded exactly as she remembered it. She closed her eyes and tried to remember every second.

Julie spoke softly. 'She still has terrible nightmares that wake her up soaking in sweat but I'll displace those horrors with happy times. In two weeks, I'm taking her to Disneyland. She's so excited. So am I—if I'm honest.'

'Please, find a way to tell her our father lied to me. I didn't know anything about the care home. I would have killed him if I'd found out. If I'd known, I would have taken her home.'

Julie strolled to the door then turned to the three sad people seated on the floor.

'I'll give you some beautiful thoughts to take with you. I have a spacious and luxurious bathroom. When I took Donna home for the first time, she spent two hours in the bath submerged in bubbles and perfumes, playing with fancy bottles of shampoo and listening to her Beatles. Did you know she's a crazy Beatles fan?'

Emma couldn't speak but remembered her sister singing Beatles songs.

'That night, she slept in her own bed; in her own pretty room as Beatles songs soothed her broken heart. Her eyes sparkle again, and now she has a new love in her life. A little white Westie puppy that she calls Whiskers.'

Gavin said to Emma. 'She's got wee Whisky to look after her.'

Peter followed Hugo out of the room, and said, 'Come back in ten hours and collect the video. Transport the bodies to Patersun's spice warehouse in Paisley.'

Julie followed Peter, then turned back for one last look. 'You understand how this will play out. The enzyme attacking your body will get on with its job. That can't stop. Face your deaths together. Support one another as best you can. Die with dignity, and rest assured, we will all move on—to better things.'

Julie pulled the door shut.

Fifty-three

Grey clouds assembled and dulled the afternoon sunlight. Many living in Eaglesham hoped the rain would hold off until they'd cut their lawns. The shadowy room grew darker, except for one corner where a patch of sunlight lit part of the wall.

Emma sat with her knees pulled up to her chest, staring down at the floor, just as Donna had done in the van.

Gavin stared at the ceiling. 'I wish I'd said something to you in the van. It just seemed too incredible to be Donna.'

Emma sat quietly with her eyes closed.

John said to Gavin. 'If you had, then she would be sitting here with us, waiting to die. At least, she'll have a life.'

Emma still didn't speak, not while the emotional trauma of what her parents had done to Donna exploded in her head. Unexplained memories raced back to her mind.

Arguments she'd heard but didn't understand. She remembered hearing her parents fight over Donna. Remembered fragments of whispered conversations her mother had with other people about Donna. So many veiled things that didn't make sense at the time, but now were crystal clear.

'What's this enzyme Julie gave us? What does it do?' John asked.

Gavin didn't want to tell John or Emma about the dog at Fairfells or young Davy in the factory. The reality would feel painful enough without the worry of anticipation. *Keep it simple, change the subject*, he thought.

Gavin replied, 'It will cause a heart attack.'

John frowned. 'That's not too bad. A villain I once arrested after a chase, had a heart attack, and he just keeled over.'

Gavin asked, 'Is Barscadden psychopathic?'

John sighed. 'He fits the profile. He's charming and optimistic on one side. Emotionless, guiltless and vicious on the other.

'Cunningly, he manipulates those in Gyge's Ring with a continuous stream of conniving lies and deceit. They don't see him running complex circles around all of them.'

'How can he do that? Julie Blackhest is an intelligent woman.'

'Psychopaths create a mystery that's appealing. They have great powers of persuasion. He could sell ice cubes to an Eskimo.'

Gavin's shoulders drooped. 'I suppose he's difficult to resist.'

'People like Barscadden, always have grand plans, massive confidence, and great enthusiasm for their underlings. Without fail, people follow a charismatic leader.'

'I still don't understand how he can take in smart people like Blackhest.'

'Barscadden drew other like-minded psychopaths into Gyge's Ring. That's why it works so well. They're all blind, morally and emotionally. They believe wholeheartedly in what they're doing. The rehabitation of organs is their version of doing good work for the community.'

'How did they manage to get away with that?'

'No bodies, no forensic, no murder investigations. Most of the victims are still on missing person files but spread all over the country.'

'Why would Barscadden choose such a path?'

'I have no idea. I know from his file that as a young teenager, Barscadden suffered physical and sexual abuse from his father and his uncle. His mother suffered violence at the hands of both men, and they used her as a free whore for their mates.

'It ended when his father died from a fatal stab wound. His mother confessed, and despite a deeply moving and harrowing account of her husband's abuse, she received a jail sentence and died in jail. The uncle has never been found. I suspect Barscadden killed both men.'

'That's horrible. Doesn't excuse his evil but does explain what influenced his choices.'

'So, this heart attack that's coming. What'll happen? Pain in the arm, radiating up to the chest sort of thing?'

'How do you feel at the moment?'

John grimaced. 'Bit of discomfort in my stomach, otherwise, no different.'

Determined not to spell out what would happen, Gavin changed the subject. 'How did you discover WRATH?'

'An IT specialist at the National Police College at Bramshill worked on a database of solved and unsolved rape cases. She discovered hundreds of sex offenders also listed on the missing persons database.'

'Too many to ignore.'

John shrugged. 'Bells rang. Then, the IT clerk and her datasets got moved well out of the way. People were told it was faulty set-up parameters.'

'Covering their tracks.'

John agreed. 'Special Branch took an interest. We traced an inspector who pulled the cover-up. Tapped into him. Found that someone much higher up had instructed him.'

'Who was that?'

John shook his head. 'Don't know. It might have been Henry Smythe but he's only a Super. I'm sure they have someone at Chief Super or Assistant Chief Constable level.'

'So, you went undercover to flush him out?'

'Surveillance led us to Bromlee. I agreed to go in as a WRATH associate. We wanted the inspector's boss but I learnt all about Gyge's Ring. I discovered the power and influence it commanded. Bromlee led us to Barscadden. We had a good picture.'

'Why didn't you bring it all down sooner?'

'They have high-ranking police officers on their side. Probably senior civil servants and politicians in the Ring. I needed fireproof evidence before I could pull the chain on any of these people. Too soon, and they have the power to snuff you out.'

'Saving us blew the whistle before you were ready.'

John grimaced. 'They panicked in London when the Lambeth Group thought you were heading to Russia. That accelerated everything. We all got caught on the hop. I should have taken control earlier. My call, my mistake.'

'With Henry Smythe working for them, you couldn't succeed.'

'I guess so. Nothing we can do about it now.'

John sighed, and his voice signalled his disappointment with the turn of events. He grasped Gavin's arm. His face paled and his eyes glared.

'What is it?'

John struggled with the handcuffs. 'My back is sore. Wow! I feel hot—all over. Is this a heart attack?'

'Try to keep calm.'

John blew out a large puff of air. 'I feel extremely nervous like I've been told off by the boss. Not good.'

John rocked back and forth. Perspiration bloomed on his forehead. His free hand pressed hard into his chest while the other hand pulled hard against the handcuff.

He gulped his breaths and tried to stand up. Then, he tried to get off his knees. He faced the wall and pulled on the cuff.

Gavin watched, aghast and helpless. An image of young Davy paralysed his mind. He told John to lie down flat and take pressure off his heart.

John did so and drew his free hand over his forehead to show how much he'd sweated.

Gavin watched John's body writhe and struggle. 'It's adrenaline.'

'Whew. This is hellish. I hate this feeling.' John's face pinched with fear.

'I know.'

'Aagghh, my heart,' John screamed, then doubled-up.

Gavin clasped his free hand on John's shoulder. A minute passed then John relaxed but still pale with shock and wet with sweat.

John wiped his face. 'My heart's battering ten to the dozen. I'm having a heart attack.'

Gavin grimaced. 'It's a severe palpitation.'

'*Christ.* My back, aagghh … bloody pain, aagghh … God,' he screamed in panic.

Tears ran down his cheeks. He sat with his back against the wall until he fell over onto his side and lay still.

Gavin pushed onto his knees, he leant over to see John's glazed eyes and terror on his contorted face.

With rapid breaths, he spoke hurriedly. 'Ma … ma … arm, ugh. Can't move. I'm parr … parr … lysed.' He stared ahead and slid his legs up and down on the floor as if running.

Gavin guessed John had suffered a stroke. He helped him sit upright and rested his back against the wall.

John's head flopped and drooled uncontrollably. 'Can't— swallow. I'll choke.' He spat white fluid onto the floor.

More fluid ran down his chin and neck.

John tried to speak but the words wouldn't flow. 'I'm no—'

John struggled with his handcuffs. With erratic breaths, he vomited two mouthfuls of white fluid onto the floor between his legs. All three stared at the fluid as if it had no right to be there.

'Ugh,' John moaned in pain then collapsed in a semi-conscious heap.

'John! Talk to me,' Gavin shouted.

'Is it over?' Emma asked.

Gavin wondered how Emma would react when his turn came?

John drifted in and out of consciousness. At one point, he emptied his bladder, and the evidence showed on his trousers and the floor beneath him.

Gavin and Emma watched while John struggled through his final death throes. He spoke with a deep coarse voice as if he had a severe throat infection.

His voice box teetered on the point of collapse. On one of his hard coughs, he spat four teeth onto the floor.

'… no pain.' He tried to smile but his face took on a hideous contortion.

A puzzled expression formed on Emma's face.

Gavin said to Emma, 'After a trauma, the brain secretes endorphins. Painkillers to stop the barrage of pain swamping the brain.'

'I *get* it.' Emma snapped. She didn't want details.

John turned on his side and pulled his right hand against the handcuffs, which cut deeply into his skin. Blood covered his sallow-coloured flesh when the cuff gouged deeply.

Gavin realised what he wanted to do. 'John—don't.'

'Am … ugh.'

John turned his body around to face the wall and sat as close to it as possible. Then, he pushed his feet flat against the wall and strained against the handcuffs.

With an almighty push, he sprang his legs as straight as he could. A sharp crackle echoed in the room, followed by a dull thud.

The bones in his hand shattered, and he landed slap on his back in the middle of the room.

The push left him exhausted. Slowly, he turned his ailing body to face the table near the door, which lay two paces away from his head. Inch by painful inch, he dragged himself to the table.

Dampness and fluid trailed across the floor. John lunged upward to grasp the leg of the table with his good hand. Then, he collapsed face down on the floor. He rested for a few minutes, stretched again and grabbed the table leg.

Once he had it, he pulled it forward so it toppled over his body. The body bags and keys fell to the floor. The keys landed on a body bag ten inches away from Gavin's foot.

Emma closed her eyes while the final tremors of life left John's body. She said nothing to him before he died and had lost her will to live.

Determined to go down fighting, Gavin wedged the toe of his shoe against the body bag and dragged it to him. He persevered and dragged the bag close enough to reach the keys.

When they'd freed themselves, Gavin checked John's pulse then shook his head. They hugged each other tightly. Then they put John's body in a bag and zipped it up.

Downstairs, Emma rushed to a telephone in the office but found it disconnected. Hugo had locked the front door, so Gavin smashed a window and they climbed out.

Fifty-four

Cool air refreshed their lungs as they struggled out of the office and onto the road. Gavin spotted a supermarket at the bottom of the long street. They set off at a run but then Gavin stopped short and stiffened his body.

He closed his eyes, arched his back, and pushed his stomach out with his hands resting on his hips. Pain and anguish sapped his strength. His back flinched with a sharp jagging pain.

Emma backtracked to his side, and shouted, 'Come on.'

'You go. I'll need an ambulance.' Gavin pushed her arm away.

Emma rotated on her heels to look for help. 'Don't do this to me.'

'You've got to find Donna. She's in danger. She knows too much.'

Gavin's face twisted with pain, and his eyes rolled as if no longer under his control. Sweat caused strands of his hair to clump together.

'Gavin, hold on, please.'

He held onto Emma, and couldn't prevent himself shifting his dead weight onto her. They slipped down to the ground. 'I'll be fine. Donna needs you. Go.'

'I can't leave you.'

Gavin rushed his hand to his mouth and fought against an urge to vomit. 'Don't let Donna down *again*. Save her. Go.'

Emma's lips quivered, and she squeezed his hands. 'I love you.'

Tears raced down her cheeks.

'Go and get Donna.'

Their hands slipped apart, and Gavin's arm dropped, lifeless onto his thigh.

Emma stood straight and wiped water from her face. Slowly, she walked away. Her eyes fixed on Gavin's body until the last moment.

Then, she ran down the road while her mind raged with intense emotions. She wanted to stay with him. She kept hold of her sanity by filling her mind with pictures of Donna.

The Scotcost Ltd supermarket dominated the bottom of the street and a substantial amount of the surrounding area. As she ran to it, a stream of shoppers pushed food-laden trolleys to the car park.

Emma sprinted across the main road, narrowly avoiding a car turning out of the car park. Her eyes latched onto a public phone sign on the glass panel of an automatic entrance door. The noise of people in and around the supermarket gave her a welcome feeling of safety.

To the right of the automatic doors, she saw a row of eight checkouts, and behind them, aisles of shelf-stacked food products.

Ahead of her, lay the first aisle of fresh fruit and vegetables, and to her left, the trolley park. Beside the trolleys, a public telephone. Emma dashed to the phone and called the police.

She wiped sweat from her nose and forehead. 'My name is Emma Patersun. I need help. I'm calling from Scotcost in Eaglesham. I need an ambulance as fast as possible. No! It's for Gavin Shawlens. He's been poisoned. YES, it bloody well is life-threatening.'

Emma stared at the wall while her wounded hand trembled. Weakness spread down her legs. She lunged against the wall for support and dropped the handset, which swung on its cord. Her ears felt disconnected and the disturbing sensation brought panic.

The hustle-and-bustle noise of the supermarket stopped, and Emma heard only a loud whooshing sound in her head. *The damn enzyme*, she thought, as she rested her head against the wall. She wanted to burst into tears.

She stumbled into the middle of the aisle. A man apologised when she bumped into her with his trolley. Her eyes followed him and she peered down the aisle, past the shoppers.

It seemed to her they all moved in slow motion as they pushed their trolleys and picked up their groceries.

To see past them, Emma bobbed her head from side-to-side. Shoppers moved around her. A space cleared in front of her and her eyes snapped onto a display at the end of the aisle.

301

'I see it, ' she murmured.

Then, excited and with arms flailing, she sprinted out the door. With the determination of an Olympic runner, she ran back to Gavin.

An old couple had helped Gavin onto his feet, and helped him down the road. Gavin saw Emma running to him but couldn't make out her words.

Breathless, eyes glaring, exhilarated, Emma blurted out words in between gasps for air, 'Ugh. Fresh ... ugh, pineapple, ugh ... *inhibitors*!'

'Pineapple?' Gavin croaked as he struggled to speak.

'Come on!'

With help from the old couple, they shuffled across the road. Then, clinging together, Gavin and Emma stumbled toward the entrance. To support his body, Gavin grabbed a shopping trolley.

The automatic doors swished open. Emma guided Gavin's trolley as he pushed past a group of shoppers. They'd moved less than ten paces into the supermarket when his legs buckled and he fell to the floor.

*

Peter Bromlee's large black SUV and Julie Blackhest's Range Rover turned off the main road and swept up to the offices.

Henry Smythe had called Peter and warned him that police had set up a systematic search of all BARSCO buildings. Peter called Julie and they returned to Eaglesham to move the bodies.

At the building, Hugo rushed out to tell them that Patersun and Shawlens had gone. Peter sent Hugo back inside to collect Deakin and clear up the mess. Then, he said to Julie while they walked away from the office entrance. 'They can't be far.'

Peter gazed over to the fields beyond the office building.

Julie glanced down the road. 'The shop at the bottom of the street. That's where I'd go.'

Peter agreed.

At the Range Rover, Julie hesitated for a second at the driver's door, then shook her head. She stepped around to the passenger side of the car.

Donna grabbed her brightly coloured sports backpack, opened the passenger door. 'I'll come.'

Julie put her arm on Donna's shoulder, eased her back into the seat. 'I must do this alone. You have to stay here.'

Julie opened the glove compartment, withdrew a Walther P99, and then checked the ammunition. She locked eyes with Donna. 'I'll be fine, don't you worry.' Then, she hurried down the road to the supermarket.

*

A mouthful of Gavin's blood spilled on his clothes and hands. Streams of sweat dripped from his face. He appeared to be at death's door, and his condition frightened many of the onlookers.

Emma helped Gavin to sit up against a shopping display at the end of the aisle. Then, she pushed past a small crowd of onlookers, and rushed down the aisle to the fruit section.

After a frantic search, she picked up a carton of fresh pineapple juice. Next, she grabbed a box of kitchen knives and a single pineapple, then ran back to Gavin. The small crowd had gathered around him.

People screamed and scattered when Emma ran up with a knife in her hand. She crouched down beside Gavin and poured the juice into his mouth.

He spluttered and coughed some of it back. With the knife, Emma hacked into the pineapple and pushed chunks into his mouth to swallow with more juice.

Soon, his face became a mess with pieces of yellow pineapple flesh attached to his face and spread down his front.

A security guard appeared and grabbed the knife from Emma. The guard shouted down at Gavin, 'On your feet.'

The store manager weaved his way past the trolleys and addressed the shoppers gathered around Gavin and Emma. With arms open, he ushered the people away from the scene. 'Disturbance is over now, folks. Move along. Come on, please. Just some tramps, trying to steal food.'

Emma yelled, 'Wait. He needs this juice. Can't you see he's dying?'

The manager turned and gave the security man a stern look. 'Get them outside.'

303

Emma leapt to her feet and pleaded with the manager. 'He needs this juice. His stomach is bleeding.'

He turned to Emma, his face uncompromising. 'If you want a pineapple, you buy it. Same as everybody else.'

The weight of all the onlookers made the manager anxious.

'I've no money on me but—look—take my wedding ring, please. It's worth hundreds.'

Emma wrestled hard to pull off her wedding ring but her fingers had swollen.

The manager peered over the heads of the audience, and called in the direction of the office. 'Pamela! Call the police.'

The security guard stood over Gavin and prepared to haul him out of the store but the sight of blood made him hesitate. Emma stood in front of the manager. 'Please, listen. On my life. He needs this pineapple.'

'Move them,' the manager shouted to the security man.

Emma turned to the onlookers. 'Someone, please, help him.'

An old pensioner stood in the front line of the crowd. She counted coins from her purse and gave them to the manager. 'Give him a pineapple.'

Everyone had their back to the automatic doors but those nearest heard—swoosh—swoosh—when the doors opened.

Julie stepped inside the automatic doors with her Walther pistol clenched in her hands. Legs apart, she steadied her feet. She fired a warning shot above their heads.

People screamed, and the crowd recoiled. Most scattered, but some just stood and stared at Julie. The sound of people shouting and screaming became deafening.

Julie aimed her pistol at Emma. The store manager moved away from her side. Julie searched the sea of faces then settled on Gavin who lay slumped on the floor.

The security guard lunged at Julie with his hands outstretched. Calmly, she fired a slug into his leg. He fell to the ground and writhed in pain.

More onlookers screamed and ran away. The old pensioner stood in front of Gavin and obscured Julie's view. Seconds seemed like minutes.

Indecision rampaged over Julie's face, and her fingers grasped the pistol grip more tightly. She switched her head from side to side, searching for her target. Uncertain what to do next.

The automatic doors continued to close then jolt back open, and the noise made Julie more anxious. She stared at the startled people in front of her and their attitude confused her.

The wail of a distant police siren raised her anxiety. Then, the sound of an approaching helicopter forced her hand.

Emma took two steps toward Julie. 'It's over. Leave while you can.'

Julie aimed her pistol at Emma's forehead.

From the corner of her eye, Julie saw someone moving fast toward her. She turned to look, just as a two-pronged meat-carving fork pushed into the side of her neck. An explosion of screams and squeals drowned her thoughts.

Instinctively, Julie grabbed and pulled the fork out. The pain seared through her head but she still had the presence of mind to fire a shot at her attacker.

A woman with shoulder length hair, wearing jeans, a green t-shirt and white trainers.

Donna stood with her hand outstretched, having thrown the fork from less than three paces. She took the full force of the bullet and catapulted backward to land on her back where she lay motionless.

The fork had sliced Julie's carotid artery. Rapid heartbeats forced her blood out at speed, and she lost consciousness seconds after the attack.

Emma darted past Julie, her eyes fixed on Donna's prone body.

'*Donna,*' Emma cried at the top of her vocal range.

Emma shouted to the gathered people. 'It's my little sister. My baby sister.'

Donna lay motionless but conscious. Emma scraped her knees on the floor as she threw herself down beside Donna. She didn't feel the pain. Instead, she felt overjoyed when their eyes met. She kissed Donna on the forehead.

Carefully, she cradled her palm behind Donna's neck. With her other hand, she moved Donna's hair away from her face.

A kind man placed a rolled-up jacket under Donna's head. Oblivious to all the commotion, shouting, and scurrying around, their eyes locked together, welcoming, knowing and loving.

'Daddy left me all alone.' Donna spoke in a soft, child-like, voice.

Emma burst into tears. 'I didn't know. Daddy didn't tell me where you were. I love you. I'm going to look after you.' Emma closed her eyes and kissed Donna's head.

When Emma opened her eyes, Donna's head fell to the side. 'No, Donna. Please—No.'

Emma felt wetness behind Donna. When she raised her hand, she saw blood had turned it bright red. Emma collapsed in a heap beside her sister.

Fifty-five
Southern Hospital, Glasgow

The following morning, Emma Patersun woke in an isolation room, and for a minute, the room shuddered in and out of focus. Nausea, and a throbbing headache frightened her. She became conscious of wires and tubes attached to her body.

A wave of panic made her heart jump when she thought she lay on a rehab trolley. With an agonising scream, she sat up.

Woman Police Officer Jones rushed to Emma's side with a reassuring smile and pressed a buzzer at the bed to alert the medical staff.

The door swung open and Nurse Caldwell held it open for Doctor Ahmed to walk in without breaking his stride.

'I'm Doctor Ahmed. How do you feel, Mrs Patersun?' he asked and scanned the monitor readouts.

'Donna, where is Donna?'

'Donna is fine. The bullet passed through without hitting anything major. She needed a few stitches but she'll be fine,' Doctor Ahmed said.

'Where is she?'

WPO Jones stepped closer to the bed. 'She's with my colleagues. She keeps telling them you're her big sister.'

Emma squealed, 'I am. I really am. Oh, thank God.'

Her eyes welled up with tears of joy.

'If it's all right, I can have someone bring her over.' Jones looked over to Ahmed for approval.

'Please,' Emma pleaded as she wiped her tears.

Ahmed nodded positively to Jones. 'Okay, but only for a short time.'

Jones walked away and spoke into her personal radio.

Ahmed examined Emma's face. 'Well, you do look much better.'

Emma half-smiled. 'I'm tired. I have a sharp headache.'

She leant forward and scanned the room.

Ahmed droned on. '—and thankfully no harm has come to—'

Gavin where are you? Screeched into Emma's mind.

'Is he all right?' Emma asked.

'Yes, he's fine,' Ahmed replied as he lifted her wrist to take her pulse.

'Oh, thanks, Doctor. You've no idea how much it means to hear you say that. How is he doing?' she asked, and waited impatiently for his next word.

'As I said. He's going to be fine. Nothing to worry about.' Ahmed counted as he examined his watch.

An enormous sense of relief flowed through her body. She closed her eyes to see Gavin's face in her mind's eye. Ahmed finished taking her pulse, and moved to the end of her bed to mark her chart.

'When can I see him?'

Ahmed gave her an odd glance. 'Well … I suppose. When did you have your last scan?'

'What scan?'

'Ultrasound.'

Emma shook her head. 'I've never had an ultrasound scan.'

Ahmed threw a confused expression. 'How do you know it's a boy?'

'What are you talking about?'

'Your baby.'

Emma swallowed hard. 'Are you insane? I'm not having a baby. I have hormone issues.'

'You are. We're monitoring his heart carefully. Look.' Ahmed pointed to the second monitor at the side of the bed.

Emma grasped the blankets tightly. Stunned beyond belief. She felt unable to speak while powerful feelings and visions blasted back and forward in her head.

The nausea and sickness, she'd put down to stress from her ordeals. And the weight gain to comfort eating.

Ahmed continued, 'We've deactivated the enzyme in your body but we'll continue with inhibitors for another twelve hours.'

'Gavin Shawlens. Is he all right?' Emma asked with apprehension in her voice.

Ahmed turned away. 'Rest for now and—'

'Doctor. I need to know.'

'His stomach was nearly destroyed. It had to be removed. I'm so sorry.' He spoke in soft tones he used for conveying bad news.

Emma hid her face in her hands. 'Gavin? This can't be happening.'

'Mrs Patersun, you must rest. Anxiety will stress your baby.'

Tears filled her eyes, and she leant back to rest her head on the pillow. Liquid ran down through her nose and she wiped it with the back of her hand.

She composed herself, and turned to face Ahmed. 'Take me to him. I want to be with him.'

He shook his head. 'No. I'm sorry, I can't do that.'

He didn't know of the bond between them. Emma sat up erect in the bed.

Ahmed raised his voice a notch. 'Your sister will be here soon.'

'Doctor, I have things I need to tell him.'

Emma pulled her covers back and fumbled with the monitor leads and drip tubes. More tears slipped down her cheeks while she tried to coordinate her fingers and remove the wires.

In frustration, she raised her head to look at the ceiling and utter a forceful grunt.

Ahmed took a firm hold of her covers to prevent her from moving. 'Mrs Patersun. Think about your baby.'

'I am. My baby will know his father—if only for a moment.'

'Listen, please. It's not possible.'

'*Doctor.*'

The Nurse gave Emma a handful of tissues to mop her tears.

Ahmed said, 'Mrs Patersun. You must wait until he comes down from surgery.'

Emma's wide, watery red eyes focused on Ahmed's face. 'What?'

'He's undergoing transplant surgery.'

'Now?'

'Yes. The woman who died in the supermarket and Mr Shawlens; they both carried donor cards. By enormous luck, he is a fair match with the dead woman.'

He rested a hand on Emma's shoulder. 'It is a major operation. You must not take on the additional worry.'

Emma smiled. 'You're wrong. I have nothing to worry about. He'll come back to me. I know he will.'

Ahmed smiled when she relaxed back into the mattress. 'You saved his life with the pineapple. Another thirty minutes would have breached the main gastric artery, and he would have suffered a fatal haemorrhage.'

'How long will I be in the hospital?' Emma asked.

'Two or three more days, why?'

'I need to find an old lady with a black beret and grey overcoat. She lives in Eaglesham. She doesn't know it yet, but I owe her a pot of money.'

'Now rest, please. Think of your new baby.'

Emma laughed loudly. 'Which one, Doctor Ahmed, which *one*?'

Ahmed and the nurse gave each other puzzled looks. Emma's heart soared with thoughts of her three babies. The lights in her life shone brilliantly with a physical love for Gavin, a tender sisterly love for Donna, and a special mother's love for her son to be.

The nurse adjusted her pillows. Emma slipped her body down further into the bed and underneath the covers.

She pulled the sheet up past her eyes and turned onto her right side. She closed her eyes and summoned her most favourite pre-sleep dream, when she and Gavin were teenage lovers.

Fifty-six
Saffron Walden

In the warm late afternoon sun, Penny Orcherd relaxed on her sumptuous reclining sun lounger and sipped a glass of cool French Chardonnay. The soothing noise of a marble two-tier water fountain, added to the tranquil ambience. A couple of attractive goldfinches flitted around the fountain, taking sips of water and catching insects.

With the bottle of wine a good bit more than half empty, the world and everything felt fine and dandy. Through her Miu Miu cat's eyes sunglasses, she watched her daughters play happily in the large gazebo at the bottom of the garden.

Nick Orcherd arrived home and strolled through his house to the garden. He dropped his briefcase on a garden chair, paused and waved to his daughters. He seemed more preoccupied than usual.

Penny switched on a seductive voice. 'Hello, my handsome darling.'

She pushed her sunglasses onto her head and greeted him with a warm kiss as they hugged. He held onto her longer, and squeezed a little tighter, than usual.

Penny smiled smugly when she thought how her short white tennis skirt and close-fitting white polo shirt had produced the desired reaction.

The children shouted over their 'Hi Dads' and continued their play.

'Sweetheart, did you sell the awful Renoir?' she asked.

'No. They're holding out for me to drop my price.'

'Heavens, well, two can play that silly old game.'

He sat down on his oversized comfy lounger then flicked off his shoes and swung his legs around. With a sigh, he stretched out his body.

Dutifully, the sun had warmed the soft cushions, and Nick relaxed when they gave way under his weight.

Penny lifted the Chardonnay from the black marble wine cooler, wrapped a thick white napkin around the neck, and poured a glass of wine for him while he adjusted his lounger to sit upright. From his briefcase, he extracted a large brown envelope.

'A new Lot has arrived.'

Her eyes lit up. 'Oh, that's jolly decent of them. The school fees are due at the end of the month. What delightful timing. Cheers.' She raised her glass to the blue sky.

'Well, I'm—'

'Where are we off to this time?' Penny took a sip of wine.

'It's more complicated … this Lot has three artefacts.'

Penny turned to face him but needed to drop her sunglasses to her nose to block the sunshine. 'Yikes. Times three is rather jolly indeed.'

'Sixty grand in advance.' Nick drew a wad of banknotes from the envelope to show her then dropped them back inside.

When she saw the money, she gasped. Excited, Penny waved her hand in front of her mouth as if she'd swallowed something hot. 'Oh golly, golly. That's awesome. Please— please—please. Can we take out my option on BabyBlue Gilt?' She clasped her hands in prayer.

Delirious with joy, Penny reached to pour more wine, not bothering this time with the napkin. She removed her sunglasses and left them beside the wine cooler.

She spoke with urgency. 'My beauty is going to win at Royal Ascot next year. I can feel it in my bones.'

'That would be wonderful.'

Her face lit up, and her voice rang with excitement. 'Just think, darling, owner's enclosure. The St James's Palace Stakes. BabyBlue Gilt romps home by a head. Woohoo. Of course, I'll have to chat with the Royal Family after the race. I can't wait. I'm so excited.'

She sat beside Nick but couldn't stay still. She rose up again and went behind his chair to massage his shoulders.

Her mind raced ahead. 'I'll need a superb outfit and a spectacular hat. Plenty of time to get something designed especially for me. We can spend a few grand on that, pumpkin. It will be a truly fabulous day.'

In a subdued voice, Nick replied, 'Of course.'

Penny kissed the top of his ear and whispered, 'Sixty grand is just perfect.'

'Yes.' Nick tilted his head around to look up at her.

Penny smiled her gorgeous naughty-girl smile, cupped his ear in her hand and whispered, 'Don't look now, darling, but I've got no pants on.'

Subdued and thoughtful, Nick sighed.

Finally, Penny discovered his mood wasn't what it should be with such great news. She came back around the lounger and sat down.

'Oh, what's the matter, sweetheart? A frightful day in the shop with those idiots and the Renoir.' She took his hand, squeezed it and kissed it.

Nick stared longingly at the envelope. 'I'll have to think quite carefully about this Lot.'

Penny let go of his hand. 'Three will be just oodles of work but I'll help you, darling. Of course, I will.'

'I know you will.' Her offer didn't perk him up.

Penny tried to overcome the alcohol fog and appear professionally interested. 'Are there special logistical thingies or whatevers to be sorted out?'

He faced her with a look of concern. 'One of them is a doctor. A university chap.'

Penny gave Nick a supportive pat on the arm. 'Oh, I see now, pumpkin. It's not the normal garbage we usually sweep up. But, you know very well, darling, there are baddy bad apples in the middle classes. Don't let that worry your pert little bottom. It's just a few rotten ones that need to be recycled. We can do that.'

Nick pulled photographs of the women from the envelope. 'The other two are women.'

Shock and disbelief washed over Penny's face as she put down her glass of wine and cupped her jaw.

'Women. Are you serious?'

'Afraid so.'

'We make widows, darling. They know we don't do women. Never have done. What are they thinking?'

Nick thought back to the woman he saw in the laboratory. 'I don't want to extend this work to include women.'

'Widower makers. Ugh! Too clumsy. Doesn't sound right to me.'

Nick sat up and rubbed his eyes. 'Actually, the whole Lot doesn't feel right to me.'

'What else is bothering you, my sweet hunk?'

'No crime sheets. Just a couple of lines saying they abused dozens of children. No press clippings, police files, court reports and none of the usual detail.'

'They've always been top notch in the past. Surely, they must know what they're doing.'

'I expect so. As you say, the cash for a treble is most welcome.' Nick took a large swallow of wine.

'It'll be all right, darling. I promise. This time, I'll go with you on the delivery.'

With renewed concern, Nick, said, 'The targets live near Glasgow.'

'Well, that's fine. We can have a short break and visit the Burrell Collection. A large suite with a four-poster near Loch Lomond. We'll make the mountains rattle again. Do you remember? How does that sound?' Penny put cheer into her voice.

'We've never had to go there to collect a Lot. The factory is in Glasgow, for heaven's sake. They have people there.'

She didn't like the look of concern on Nick's face. They thought more deeply, drank more wine and he held her hand.

'Darling. They know we're the very best and just think about all the jolly lolly.'

She flicked through a wad of banknotes, closed her eyes, and thought of BabyBlue Gilt leading a race.

'I know, and it says they've abused children, so we need to stop that.'

Penny spoke positively. 'Let's just be thankful the delivery will only take five minutes.'

'Factory delivery isn't required,' Nick replied.

'No delivery, darling. What then, for heaven's sake?'

'These three are earmarked for elimination only.'

Penny forced herself to whisper when the idea crashed in her mind. 'Oh, my Gawd, Nick! Do you mean they want us to what—kill these people?'

'Apparently so.' Nick raised his eyebrows.

'In actual ... cold blood. Seriously. We haven't ever done that before.' Penny's voice squeaked but she kept it quiet so that her girls didn't hear.

Nick glanced over at the children.

Penny sat back in her lounger and took a deep swallow of wine. 'This is appalling. What about the rehab chappy? Does he not want the thingy bits, you know, parts for the spare people?'

Penny felt distraught, and didn't see herself as a cold-blooded killer. Now, they both felt this Lot had departed from their routine collection and delivery of waste.

'Seems not. Something in here about overstocked or something. It just doesn't feel right, does it?' Nick glanced at her.

Penny examined the photographs of Emma Patersun, her sister Donna, and Gavin Shawlens. 'This man is an academic, and these women are obviously not a bad sort, looking at their home. These two look like sisters.'

'I think they're trying to push us into a different business. I'm not happy.'

Nick put the photographs in the envelope and checked his wife for a decision.

Deep in thought, she flicked the cash against her fingers. 'Nick. We are widow makers, for battered and abused poor women. Not cold-blooded killers, for Gawd's sake.'

Nick grimaced. 'We could draw a line here, but I would be the happiest chap in the world with you on my arm at Ascot, rooting for our horse to win. Sixty grand might just be the right time for our swan song.'

He stroked the back of her hand with his thumb, and his expression remained undecided.

Penny stood, pulled on his arm. 'Given the obvious complexities of this Lot, we must have a full negotiation. Put everything on the table, examine all the angles and force a solution into the open.'

Penny called over to the children, pointed her finger at them, and said in her no-nonsense voice, 'Girls! Daddy and I

315

have business to negotiate. No fighting, or I'll be very, very, cross.'

With the brown envelope clasped tightly under her arm, Penny led Nick up the stairs. They stood together on the landing at the top. He put his arm around her waist and kissed her gently on the neck.

Penny peered into his eyes. 'Darling, will this be a firm negotiation?'

'It might be quite firm, this time.'

'Well, that's rather good because, you know, we didn't come to a joint agreement last time. Your silly little premature bid went through far too quickly. I need longer to dwell on these things.'

'I know. I'm sorry about that. I'll do better.'

'I must insist on a satisfactory agreement.' She squeezed Nick's arm. 'Get it right this time my boy, or you'll receive a thoroughly well smacked bottom.'

He followed her into their bedroom and tried hard to keep a straight face.

Fifty-seven
London

In Sir Christopher Aden-Brown's Lambeth Group office, the silence vanished when his PA knocked on the door and entered the room. He raised his eyes up from his papers and Irene told him Alan Cairn had arrived for his two o'clock appointment.

Aden-Brown rose when Cairn opened the office door inward. Irene followed, carrying a tray, and set it on a leather-covered coffee table, positioned between the Queen Anne high-back wing chairs. The two men sat, Irene served tea for them, and then closed the door behind her.

Aden-Brown extend his arm and opened his hand. 'What have you got for me?'

Cairn consulted his file. 'My office has discovered a series of events, originating from a university department. We believe a research project has backfired. I want to begin an investigation.'

Cairn handed over police and medical reports then gave a verbal summary.

Aden-Brown listened with care, then said, 'The research area falls neatly within the expertise of Gavin Shawlens.'

'I agree. Is he back on the grid?'

'Not yet. He's fit enough but needs time to get over the shock.'

'What does he know about the Patersun women?' Cairn asked.

'Nothing.'

'Good. I want to keep things simple.'

Aden-Brown reflected for a moment. 'Did you ever find out why the Americans got into a flap when they discovered that Zavarok had kidnapped Shawlens?'

Cairn stared at the coffee table for the best part of a minute. 'I do know they dispatched two F16s out of Ramstein. We had to give them emergency straight arrow air space. Our Chinook defences detected missile lock on.

'The Americans were about to fire on the Russian ship when the SBS video feed showed Zavarok killed, and

Shawlens retrieved. Had they fired, they would have taken out the Chinook as well the Russians. Very nearly a complete bloody mess.'

Aden-Brown showed his concern. 'I didn't know about this.'

Cairn seemed surprised. 'You didn't order extreme measures?'

'Certainly not.'

Cairn rubbed his nose. 'Well then, it seems our American cousins have an issue with Shawlens.'

'For what possible reason would they need to silence Shawlens? Surely, it's nothing to do with his Lambeth Group work?'

Cairn frowned. 'All I got from their station chief was "the Shawlens business is way above my pay-grade." I do know she's monstrously pissed off about it.'

'Most peculiar. I do think we should take steps to find out what this is about.'

'Yes, I couldn't agree more.'

'What news of James Barscadden?'

'He's on the run. SAS teams are on standby. We will get him.'

Aden-Brown said, 'If I put Shawlens into this new investigation, he'll need backup in case Barscadden tries to execute him. Someone from your top drawer.'

Cairn picked out a file and handed it over. 'I have someone in mind. She has exceptional initiative, savvy and courage. I can't say enough about how impressive she is at thinking on her feet. I would trust her to guide my family through a war zone. She's that good.'

'Who is she?'

'Captain Zoe Tampsin. Seconded from Special Forces.'

Aden-Brown rose from his seat. 'Very well. I'll put Shawlens back on the grid. Keep me fully informed.'

'Of course.'

End

Author

I hope you enjoyed this story from the Lambeth Group Thrillers.

If you did enjoy it, I'd be thrilled if you could post a review. Reviews help indie writers and feedback is always welcome. It needn't be more than a few lines but it does make a difference.

My website can be found here:
http://gordonbickerstaff.blogspot.co.uk/
You can find me on Twitter: @ADPase
#LambethGroupThriller and on Facebook.

If you would like to know more about my stories then please visit my website above.
Sample PDF chapters (1-8) of each book are available FREE to download.
No sign-up required.

Thank you for reading my story.

Gordon Bickerstaff

Story Notes

SEM (secure encrypted module), connects to a secure satellite for secure communications.

CASTER (Committee for Accountable Science and Technology Ethical Research), a covert group that scan UK research institutes for fraud, corruption and unethical research.

Official Secrets Act, used in the UK to protect state secrets and official information.

COBRA, Cabinet Office Briefing Room A.

CDS, Chief of Defence Staff.

CPNI, Centre for Protection of National Infrastructure.

MI5, Security Service.

MI6, Secret Intelligence Service.

ACPO, Association of Chief Police Officers.

JIC, Joint Intelligence Committee.

HMG, Her Majesty's Government.

GCHQ, Government Communications Headquarters.

CIA, Central Intelligence Agency.

NCS, National Clandestine Service.

Lambeth Group Thrillers
Deadly Secrets
The truth will out ...

Gavin's life will be turned upside down when he joins a company to work on a product that will revolutionise the food industry. His initial gut instinct is to walk away until he discovers one of the company directors is the former love of his teenage life.

The financial implications are global and incredible. Powerful individuals and countries are prepared to kill as they compete to seize control of the company. Corruption at high levels, a deadly flaw in the product and the stakes jump higher and higher.

Against overwhelming odds, Gavin must rescue his former love from the hands of an evil cult as they prepare her for a living nightmare.

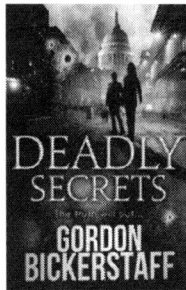

Everything To Lose
The chase is on …

A research team claim their new product will boost the performance of every athlete in the world. The claims cause alarm, and the Lambeth Group send Gavin Shawlens to investigate.

The product is stolen, top athletes disappear, and the research team are unaware that their product arose from the ashes of evil Second World War research. Gavin must stop the product launch before more people die horribly. When Gavin disappears, Zoe Tampsin, his associate from the Lambeth Group, must find him before he becomes the next victim to die.

As if Zoe doesn't have enough on her plate. Past events in Gavin's life catch up with him. A powerful US general has decided that Gavin Shawlens must die to prevent exposure of a 60-year-old secret capable of world-changing and power-shifting events.

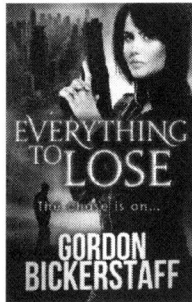

The Black Fox
Run for your life ...

Zoe Tampsin is resourceful, smart and Special Forces-trained but she has been given an impossible mission. She has to protect scientist, Gavin Shawlens, from assassination by the CIA, and discover a secret trapped in Gavin's mind that the CIA want destroyed.

As the pressure to find Shawlens escalates, the CIA send Zoe's former mentor to track her down and her fate seems sealed when he surrounds Zoe and Gavin with a ring of steel.

With each hour that passes, the ring is tightened, and the window for discovering Gavin's secret will shut. Zoe is faced with a decision that goes against all of her survival instincts.

If she's wrong, they both die. If she's right, she will discover the secret, and somehow avoid becoming the next target for assassination.

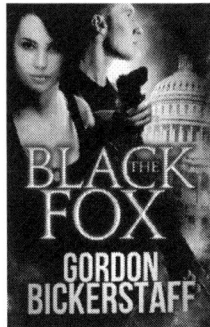

Toxic Minds
The damage is done ...

'There's a special place in hell for women who don't help each other'
Madeleine Albright

Alexa Sommer had it all - stellar career, beautiful home, successful children, and a devoted husband. Then came meltdown and divorce. Her children's love turned to hate. She is forced out of the job she loved.

Desperately, she tries to rebuild her life around a new job but her work is controversial. Her enemies want her work stopped, and a few of them prepare to take their protest to the ultimate level.

A handful of Alexa's new colleagues have a compelling reason to want her sacked. Only one colleague can help her. Gavin Shawlens has nothing to lose - his train has already crashed, and his career is finished. He is all Alexa has on her side as a perfect storm of dreadful nightmares bear down on her. 'Come on Alexa, don't give in - fight back.'

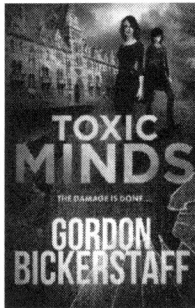

Tabula Rasa
The end is nigh ...

A hundred years ago, a wealthy family of visionaries prophesied the devastation that global warming would bring to world food supplies in the 21st century. They decided to prepare for the worst, and embark on an ambitious plan of revolution.

Lambeth Group agents, Zoe Tampsin and Gavin Shawlens, prepare to investigate the unusual death of a government defence scientist. Someone is determined to stop their investigation before they get started. Zoe uncovers two unfamiliar words, Tabula Rasa. The only other clue is the curious behaviour of the dead scientist's son, Ramsey.

Posing as a couple, Gavin and Zoe enter the secret and dangerous world of Ramsey's aristocratic guardians, headed by philanthropist billionaire, Lord Zacchary Silsden.

What Gavin uncovers, shocks him to the bottom of his soul. Does he have the courage and the conviction to interfere in the greatest revolution the world has ever faced?

What Zoe discovers about Gavin—words can't describe. Zoe is faced with an impossible choice but one thing is certain, she will not hesitate to do her duty, no matter the cost.

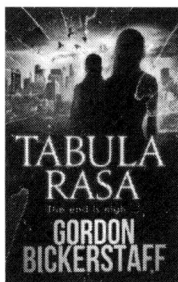

Tears of Fire
The clock is ticking ...

Two serial killers have been getting away with murder for years. For them, it's a well-paid hobby while they bide their time. It's about to stop when everything slots into place for them to leap to the next level. Payback for the people who made them orphans.

Lambeth Group investigator, Gavin Shawlens, has started on their trail. But all is not as it seems and he is pushed way out of his depth when the killers turn on his family. Gavin's Lambeth Group partner, Zoe Tampsin, is cut off from him and fighting her own battle to stay alive.

They need to connect but Zoe will face an impossible choice. Stop the killers before they pull off the most audacious murder that will shock the world and change it forever. Or, rescue Gavin's family from the jaws of evil.

39119911R00180

Printed in Great Britain
by Amazon